JACK CARSON had always been a man of few words. Like many men of his generation who'd been taught to speak through action, he also had a deeply-embedded respect for language, for the power of words and what they could do.

But Jack's words fail him when he witnesses the murder of Stanley Tedros, a local soft-drink mogul. In the late stages of Alzheimer's, Jack can't give more than scattershot details to the police. He wanders hopelessly with a voice recorder in his shirt pocket—a gift from the dead man's nephew, a grasp at the hope of memory and words. Stanley's death was arranged by his nephew's wife, an ambitious, unsatisfied woman named Corrine. She sees a future in the family business, but only if they sell, which Staley refuses to do. His murder, for her, becomes less a means to an end than a twisted justification for her whole life. For her husband Buddy, it was the crushing loss of his father figure.

Ben Decovic, a recent transplant to Magnolia Beach, South Carolina working Patrol, takes an interest in the case. Coming from his own devastating loss, it's vital to Ben that he understand the motives behind this lurid crime.

Dark and beautiful, Late Rain explores the fear that drives how far people are willing to go to find what they want, and the irreversible steps they'll take to get it.

Also by Lynn Kostoff

A Choice of Nightmares

The Long Fall

LATE RAIN

LATE RAIN

A NOVEL

LYNN KOSTOFF

TYRUS BOOKS
MADISON, WISCONSIN

Published by
TYRUS BOOKS
1213 N. Sherman Ave., #306
Madison, WI 53704
www.tyrusbooks.com

This is a work of fiction.
Any similarities to people or places,
living or dead, is purely coincidental.

15   14   13   12   11   10   1   2   3   4   5   6   7   8   9   10

978-1-935562-13-9 (hardcover)
978-1-935562-12-2 (paperback)

This One's For Melanie, With Love.

IN MEMORIAM:
Randall Kostoff; Scott Gagel; Tony Huggins. Good Men All.

PART ONE

ONE

PATIENCE WAS ALWAYS A SUCKER'S GAME.

The way Corrine Tedros saw it, the meek could take their places, dutifully line up, and patiently stand there until eternity tapped them on the shoulder and Judgment Day rolled around, but the only portion of the earth that they would ever lay claim to or ever call their own was the portion that had been, and forever would be, embedded beneath their fingernails.

Corrine understood the difference between patience and waiting.

Sunday afternoons, however, were a different story. Corrine felt as if she were trapped within a single moment, the same one opening and unfolding over and over again, fourteen months of Sunday afternoons in Magnolia Beach, South Carolina, and having to sit across the dining room table from her husband's uncle, Stanley Tedros, Stanley wearing the same brown suit and starched white shirt buttoned all the way to the neck each week as he held court, shoveling food and talking at the same time.

It wasn't a pretty sight, and for that matter, neither was Stanley. A gnome, that's what he reminded Corrine of. One of those ceramic lawn ornaments. You could stick him in somebody's front yard, and nobody would know the difference.

By all rights, Stanley should have been in the ground years ago. He was old, his odometer clocking eighty-five, and when Corrine had married Buddy fourteen months before, she had assumed, erroneously as it turned out, that Stanley wouldn't be around for long.

Stanley liked to tell everyone he was too busy to die.

Today, Stanley was riding one of his favorite topics—the current shabby state of American culture. "My parents weren't born here," he said. "They were immigrants and saw the country for what it was, and they made themselves Americans. They didn't have a lifestyle. They had a life. Nobody understands the difference anymore."

Corrine looked down at her plate. Nothing different there either. The same meal Stanley made a show of preparing each Sunday—pot roast and a pile of vegetables that had been boiled so long that the color had leached from them.

And to drink, a can of Julep, of course.

Julep was Stanley's cash cow. Before it hit the market, Stanley had been nothing more than a third-tier bottler and distributor of a line of generic soft drinks, the anonymous six-for-a-dollar variety cluttering the lower shelves in a Piggly Wiggly or Winn Dixie. Julep changed all that, starting out with a strong regional following and then unexpectedly catching national attention when Jack Brandt, star of the hit TV series *Firing Pin*, closed the season with on-site filming in South Carolina and shipped thirty cases of Julep to L.A. and served it at a heavily media-covered bash he threw to celebrate the six month anniversary of his graduation from detox to sobriety.

After that, Julep caught on big.

Corrine looked up from her plate. Stanley was still talking and chewing. "At bottom," Stanley said, "everything's a question of character. Always has been." She watched him wave a fork at Buddy.

No, Corrine thought, keeping her expression neutral. At bottom, it was an older story. Luck and timing. That's what mattered. You kept your eyes open and your hands free. When you saw what you wanted, you grabbed. She had learned that lesson by the time she turned eight.

Stanley set down his fork and got up from the table. "Time for Side B," he said, before disappearing into the living room.

That was another element in the Sunday afternoon ritual that Corrine had to endure—Stanley's taste in music. He alternated every other week with his favorite albums.

This afternoon it was the Broadway version of *Zorba The Greek.*

Last Christmas, in an admittedly transparent conciliatory gesture that she hoped would cut some of the tension that existed between Stanley and her, Corrine had bought a state-of-the-art sound system and the CDs of *Zorba* and Savina Yannatou, Haris Alexiou, Angela Dimitriou, Stella Konitopoulou; a hit parade of names she had no idea how to pronounce. Stanley, however, characteristically went on and undercut the gesture, making a show of thanking Corrine, but then saying he would stick with the ancient turntable and albums, maintaining they best captured the "authentic" qualities of the music.

From the living room came the opening strains of "Only Love."

Corrine looked over at her husband. Buddy shifted slightly in his seat and still wore the all-purpose smile, easygoing and deferential, that substituted for sustained thought and a backbone when he was around his uncle.

"When?" Corrine asked.

"I haven't forgotten," he said. "I'm just waiting for the right opportunity."

"Now, Buddy," Corrine said.

He nodded, his gaze grazing hers, and when Stanley returned from the living room, Buddy cleared his throat and finally got around to the subjects of the buy-outs, asking Stanley if he didn't think it might be a good idea to meet with the reps again and reconsider what they were offering.

"You know," Buddy said, "just listen, that's all. Keep an open mind. It can't hurt."

"Hyenas," Stanley said around a mouthful of pot roast. "Nothing else but. All of them."

Stanley chewed and looked over at Corrine. He had the mien of a prosecuting attorney who'd just finished his closing statement to a jury he knew he had in his pocket. Despite herself, Corrine felt the hairs on her arms rise.

Buddy cleared his throat again and gamely went on. "I mean, James Restan, just as an example. He's put together a very attractive package. You sell, you'll be doing all right."

"How about Anita Duford?" Stanley asked.

"Who?" Buddy quickly glanced over at Corrine and then back to his uncle.

"Anita Duford," Stanley said. "You think she'll be doing all right if we take Restan's offer? Restan's or either of the other two nosing around?"

"I don't know any Anita Duford," Buddy said.

"That's because you don't pay attention. I introduced you." Stanley leaned forward in his seat. "Anita's forty-two, five kids, and a grandmother three times over. Quit school in the eighth grade. A couple of husbands along the way, never stuck around. Sings in the choir at Ironwood Baptist. Makes a nice pecan pie. Has worked on the line, first shift, for sixteen years. Missed three days of work in the last five years."

Stanley speared two stalks of asparagus, folded them around his fork, and jammed them into his mouth and continued. "What do you think is going to happen to Anita when Restan takes over and starts restructuring?"

"He said there would be minimal cuts," Buddy said quickly. "He stressed that."

"You want to be the one to explain that to Anita, Buddy? Or to Lora Hilburne, Hank Owen, or Brenda White? Or any of the others you forgot the name of that'll be shown the door if we sign over Stanco Beverages to James Restan?"

Stanley picked up his knife, carved another slab of pot roast, and dropped it on his plate. "Stanco's mine," he said. "And it will stay that way. I've got my own plans for distribution."

Corrine imagined Stanley choking on a piece of food.

A chunk of boiled potato, say, or a nice rare wad of pot roast, Stanley's face going as red as her nails, Corrine sitting back and enjoying the show. Her husband Buddy would be of no help, as clueless as ever when it came to acting decisively, and Stanley Tedros would gasp and thrash his way to a slow and painful death.

Corrine snapped back to the afternoon as Stanley said, "God gave man two heads, Buddy, but just enough blood to make one of them work." He pointed his fork and, around a mouthful of food, delivered a follow-up that Corrine almost missed.

The air left the room. Corrine dropped her silverware and pushed back her plate.

"Are you going to let him get away with that?" she asked.

She brushed Buddy's hand off her arm. "Are you?" she repeated.

Buddy adjusted the tiny collar on his dark blue polo shirt. "Just calm down, ok?"

"He called me a hooker."

Buddy frowned. "He did? You sure?"

"You're going to just sit there?"

Buddy lifted, then dropped his hand.

Stanley tapped the side of his glass with a fork. "Ok, there. Enough." He paused and probed his upper plate, using his index finger to adjust the fit of his dentures. His eyes never left Corrine's.

"I was explaining a basic truth to Buddy," he said finally. "About God giving man two heads."

"I heard that," Corrine interrupted. "And I heard what you said afterwards. You said, 'And that's what you get for marrying a hooker, Buddy.'"

"*Looker.* I said that's what you got, Buddy, a *looker.*"

"You're lying, Stanley. I heard what I heard."

"Corrine," Buddy began, but she told him to shut up. Her hands had begun to tremble, and Corrine dropped them into her lap, balled them into fists. Something lurched in her stomach.

Stanley went back to cutting his meat.

Corrine knew she should drop the whole thing, but she couldn't shake Stanley's mocking smile or the way his eyes had zeroed in on hers when she challenged him. Her anger pushed her on, and she leaned forward and said, "You couldn't pay a hooker enough to fuck you, Stanley."

He barked out a short laugh, then winked. "You might be surprised, Corrine. And then again, maybe not."

Corrine turned to Buddy. "I want to go home. Now."

Stanley waved off her words. "A little misunderstanding," he said. "That's all it was. You need to be more forgiving, Corrine. You're too high-strung."

"I don't think so."

"Hey, what are we talking about here? Words. That's all. Sticks and stones and all that." He paused and ran a napkin across his mouth. "Just words, Corrine. Besides, if you think about it, can't a looker be a hooker or a hooker a looker? It's like the song says, 'You say Poe-tay-toe, I say, Poe-tat-toe.' Any way you slice it, in the end, you're still looking at French fries."

"I'm leaving, Buddy. I'll wait for you in the living room."

"Hey, what about dessert?" Stanley said, not bothering to get up when Corrine walked past.

The living room bore the stamp of Stanley's origins. It was dreary and oppressive and cluttered, and despite Stanley's net worth, relentlessly blue-collar in its furnishings and décor. He was living in the same North Shore neighborhood and the same house he'd bought when he moved to Magnolia Beach. Nobody upon entering it would find any sign of what Stanley was actually worth.

Buddy's voice carried from the dining room as he tried to placate Stanley.

Corrine walked over to the turntable as Side B of *Zorba The Greek* finished. She watched the arm lift and return to rest. Then she opened her purse.

It took her a while to find her nail file.

TWO

MID-SHIFT WAS THE USUAL PLATTER. Ben Decovic worked his patrol sector, North Shore to the border of the downtown district and west to I-17. He responded to calls involving a stolen ATV, a lost German Shepard named Brigadier, two fender benders, a noise complaint involving a cadre of college students pilot-testing a couple twelve-packs and attempting to break the sound barrier with a new entertainment system. He took his dinner break at a Denny's, pushing an undercooked omelet around on his plate and drinking two cups of watery coffee. The rest of the time, he ran the routine, driving in repeated loops through his sector, as swallows darted and the light drained from the sky.

He stayed on the move, fell into a rhythm that ran like an alternating current. He anticipated. He reacted. He drove and he watched. He monitored the radio.

After he'd resigned from the Ryland Ohio Homicide Division,

Ben had drifted south and eventually taken the first available opening on the Magnolia Beach Police Force and had seen it as a sign of sorts that it had been in Patrol. That had been fine with him. He told himself he could live with the step down in salary and status. He'd been on the job for ten months since then. Working Patrol carried its own kind of sense.

Homicide required a different set of eyes, and Ben Decovic had come to distrust his.

So he returned to Patrol, a part of him welcoming the reassurance of its rhythm and routines, and another part, one that was tied to his past and everything he once believed he was and knew, saw each shift as an unruly hybrid of penance and test.

He was waiting for a day that did not hold a reminder of the need for each.

At a little after nine, he swung down Pine Street and parked curb-side opposite a small white house with green shutters. The front porch light was on, a high-watt bulb throwing a wide semicircle of light almost halfway down the slope of the lawn.

Ben radioed in his location, and Juanita, the dispatcher, laughed and said, "Right on schedule, as usual, Decovic. Tell your honey hello for me."

Ben took out his flashlight and walked up a blacktopped driveway, pausing a moment to check the lock on the garage door and then moving into the backyard and the long tangle of shadows that the mercury light perched on the lip of the garage roof could not unknot and scatter.

He walked the perimeter of the yard. Then he returned to the front of the house and knocked on the door. Ben reattached the flashlight to his belt and listened to the click of the deadbolt.

"All clear, Miriam," he said.

"Thank you." She stepped away from the door. "I've already poured us a cup."

All the lights in the house were on. Ben followed her into the living room, Miriam Holmes taking a seat on the couch, Ben dropping into a green plaid easy chair angled so it faced an ancient color television on low and tuned to CNN.

"Thank you, once again, for checking," Miriam said. "You must think it silly, but the news these days, it's just full of such stories that an old woman like me can't help but worry some."

Ben smiled. "You're not old, Miriam. And a little worrying about the state of the world is ok, too."

She nodded slowly. "Better safe. That was what Fredrick always said, and it's still true." She pointed at the cup on the table next to Ben. "It's going to get cold."

The house was small and cluttered with memorabilia and possessions from the forty-seven years of marriage Miriam and Fredrick Holmes had shared, everything anchored in place by Miriam's memories. The fireplace mantel was thickly clustered in photographs. Ben sat in Fredrick's favorite chair. He drank his coffee from a cup belonging to the set of china Fredrick had bought her on their thirtieth anniversary. He knew the story behind the print of Charleston's Rainbow Row hanging above the couch, the one behind the braided oval rug on the pine floor, and the two small sweet grass baskets on the end table.

Just as he knew the story of Fredrick Holmes's last day on earth, all the details of the Thursday morning in an Indian summer October three years ago: Miriam having started the coffee, Fredrick, though retired, up early and already dressed for the day and standing at the front window, waiting for the delivery of the paper, which turned out to be twenty minutes later than usual, Miriam bringing two cups of coffee into the living room just as it finally arrived, Fredrick opening the door and Miriam taking his place at the window, watching him start down the lawn surrounded by that early autumn light and brilliant color, a calendar day she remembered calling it, the lawn still bright green though the trees had turned, Fredrick moving with his characteristic purposeful stride, a moment and a morning like so many others in their lives, until she noticed a sudden hitch in Fredrick's step, and a second later his heart exploded and Fredrick collapsed, and forty-seven years of marriage ended as abruptly as fingers hitting a light switch, no time for 9-1-1 or EMS calls, for defibrillators or nitro or for even setting down the two cups of coffee Miriam was still holding.

"I hate to be a bother," Miriam said. She remained perched on the lip of the couch.

"You're not," Ben said.

"What you hear," she said. "The world and all. What goes on. So many disturbing things."

Ben nodded.

"If only …," Miriam began. She looked away for a moment, her gaze lingering on the fireplace mantel and the photographs crowding it.

Ben felt his smile tighten. He drowned it in the coffee cup.

"Hostages," Miriam said, "to Fortune. That's what Fredrick used to call them. I never fully understood what that meant until he was gone, and they moved away."

Ben worked on a nod. The mantel held a crowded chronology

of a boy and girl moving toward early adulthood, but even though he was sure Miriam had told him their names, he drew a blank on them. A small blossom of panic opened in his chest.

"An old woman going on and on." Miriam pulled and straightened the sleeves of her housedress. "I don't know where my mind is tonight. I just remembered I forgot to bring out the pound cake. Everything is turned around. Even the weather. It's too warm and dry for the first week of March. I can't remember one like it."

Ben got up from the chair. "That's ok, Miriam. The coffee was fine."

"I've already cut you a slice," she said. "I'll wrap it up. Won't take a minute."

"That's ok," Ben said. "I really should get back to the car."

"Won't take a minute," Miriam said.

She turned and hurried into the kitchen. Ben glanced at the photographs. He spidered the front of his uniform, touching the buttons, his fingers abruptly falling away when he reached the center of his chest.

Then Miriam was back, smiling and pressing a square of pound cake wrapped in wax paper on him, thanking him again and wishing him godspeed, and Ben was out the front door and moving across the lawn, the wind running through the trees and threaded with the faint cries of gulls, Miriam at the window watching, as he retraced Fredrick's last steps on the way to the cruiser parked curb-side.

THREE

THE BATHROOM DOOR off the master bedroom was open and leaking thin clouds of steam. Buddy was in the shower, singing an off-key rendition of some Beach Boys song that had been on an oldies station on their drive back from Uncle Stanley's earlier.

Corrine had yet to undress or completely calm down. She paced the length of the bedroom, still feeling the weight of Sunday, the peculiar way that time gathered itself, swelled, and pressed against her insides.

She held her hands out before her. They would not quite stop shaking. She was not sure if she felt angry or apprehensive. The warm, queasy feeling still nested in her stomach.

Corrine told herself she would not think of Phoenix.

She would not think of Betsy Jo Horvath or Wayne LaVell.

She was Mrs. Corrine Tedros now.

She had never been in Stanley's plans for Buddy. Stanley was big on plans, especially if they originated with him. He'd always intended for Buddy to settle down with one of the eligible Greek women in the community, and when Buddy ended up marrying

Corrine, Stanley had gone Old Testament and pronounced, *I don't give it eighteen months. You'll see.*

And kept saying it. Publicly and privately.

At times, he made it sound like a statement of fact. At others, it came across as a prediction, a warning, a command, threat, or promise.

But never as a question.

From the shower, Buddy sang about California Girls.

Corrine stopped pacing and kicked off her shoes. They were low-heeled sensible shoes that along with hose and the navy blue dress were standard fare for Sunday dinner with Stanley. Something conservative and wifey.

Once again, she'd made the mistake of expecting more out of Buddy than he could deliver. Corrine had coached and prodded, counted on his making a strong case for the Restan buyout of Stanco Beverages, but Buddy had characteristically rolled over at the first sign of disagreement from Stanley.

The buyout would have changed everything.

She'd be stuck in Magnolia Beach until Stanley died. Or until he tried to make good on his pronouncement on the marriage.

When Buddy finally inherited Stanco Beverages, there was no guarantee that the current buyout offers would resurface or if they did, that they would be as lucrative as the present ones.

Right now, the Restan offer was the kind of money that changed things forever.

Julep was the beverage of choice at the moment. No one, let alone Stanley Tedros, could have predicted its meteoric rise and reign among men and women from thirty to fifty, particularly white-collar workers. Julep was embraced as the first genuine adult soft drink. Its relative scarcity, Stanco Beverages being the sole manufacturer and distributor, only added to its allure. It was a marketer's wet dream. The public was already sold on Julep; they simply wanted more of it.

Restan and the other two reps for the soft drink conglomerates were talking figures attached to a dizzying number of zeroes for the right to give that public what it wanted.

Corrine had hoped Buddy could get Stanley to come around. Buddy's parents had died in a car accident when he was six, and Stanley, who'd never married, had taken in his brother's son and raised him as his own. Stanley Tedros might have wanted to bill himself as a hard-working, self-made entrepreneur, but at bottom, he was a Greek and big on family and blood ties. Buddy, if anyone, should have been able to convince Stanley to take Restan up on his offer.

The problem, though, Corrine knew, was and would always be Buddy himself. He had no backbone. Stanley might have mentored him in preparation for taking over the business, forcing Buddy, after he'd graduated from college, to learn it from the ground up by making him work on the line and then methodically moving him through each of the company's divisions, and Buddy might have dutifully done everything his uncle asked, but in the end it was a lost cause, the equivalent of a Doberman trying to train a Chihuahua to be an attack dog.

It turned out to be patently simple for Corrine to lead Buddy through the steps of eventually proposing to her. Corrine had read him correctly from their first encounter when she'd been waitressing at Sonny Gramm's supper club in Myrtle Beach and been tapped one Friday night to cover a bachelor's party in the banquet room. Buddy and a bunch of his former frat brothers meeting in Myrtle Beach, acting like bad little boys, spilling their drinks and oogling the two by-the-numbers strippers performing to bad Areosmith, Corrine making sure Buddy was included in her station after another waitress pointed out who Buddy was, Corrine knowing just how to move and how far to lean over and how to flash a smile that promised more than the two strippers could ever hope to deliver, and by the end of the night making sure she delivered on that promise, giving Buddy the fuck of his life, and then the next morning retracting that promise with a nicely timed bout of tears, a carefully constructed heart to heart full of orchestrated remorse and guilt and fear that Buddy would get the wrong idea about her, Corrine going on to bookend the session by blindsiding Buddy's vanity, quietly telling him with averted eyes that Buddy had unlocked something in her that she didn't know was there, a level of sexual ecstasy that she had never experienced before that left her feeling vulnerable, happy, and afraid at the same time because she didn't know what all this meant or where it left them.

They were married three weeks later.

Corrine had been Buddy's first and only real rebellion against his Uncle Stanley's influence and plans for him, and she'd worked hard to make sure Buddy's loyalties were divided, but though Corrine might have gotten Buddy, in the end it had not been on her terms. Stanley Tedros had monkey-wrenched her plans. She'd gotten worried that Buddy had been on the verge of caving in to Stanley's plans that he marry a nice Greek girl. Corrine had done everything she could think of, but Stanley was immune to her charms and continued to stonewall her, and Corrine eventually had to jettison the MGM-scale wedding she'd envisioned and push Buddy into an on-the-run elopement and honeymoon in Hilton Head.

Stanley had countered by giving them a house as a belated wedding present, forcing Corrine to once again downsize her desires and trash the blueprints for the place Buddy had promised to build for them and then manufacture some enthusiasm and appreciation for the two and a half story that mimicked one of three possible floor-plans in a subdivision named White Pine Manor, full of young professionals in west Magnolia Beach.

Corrine swallowed her resentment and went into full wifey-mode whenever Buddy and she were around Stanley, but it didn't seem to do any good. She couldn't get Stanley to buy into the package. He might pretend to for a short time, but inevitably he would begin to torment her, taking small potshots, tossing out insinuations that always threatened to become the Judgment Day accusation or revelation that Stanley, biding his time, was happily waiting to deliver.

The drumming of the shower stopped. A couple moments later, Buddy stepped into the bedroom with a towel knotted at the waist. He moved to the bureau and mirror and picked up a comb. Corrine asked him if he'd left her any hot water.

"Plenty to go around," he said.

"Good. I want to take a long, hot bath."

Corrine finished undressing. She caught Buddy looking at her in the mirror. He raised his eyebrows and smiled.

"You could talk to him again," Corrine said. "And try a little harder this time. Maybe if I wasn't there, he'd listen."

"He's right, you know," Buddy said, running the comb through his hair. "You're too high-strung."

"That's not the problem here, Buddy."

"Ok, ok," he said. "I'll talk to Stanley first thing in the morning. Give it another try."

"Don't forget what James Restan said about the stock options."

"I know, I know," Buddy said.

Corrine dropped the clothes she had bundled in her arms. She wasn't in the mood, but Buddy was the only thing she had to work with right now.

She turned and pulled down the covers on the bed. Buddy unknotted the towel at his waist and followed his bobbing erection to her.

He'd put on weight in the last five months, a good fifteen pounds thickening his waist, and it was just starting to show up in his face too, blunting his features so that Buddy appeared to be exactly what he was: a thirty-two-year-old boy who was edging his way into early middle-age, one of those men whose eyes and smile were always at odds with the rest of his flesh.

Buddy climbed into bed and over her. "Oh Corrine," he said. "You're the last word on lovely."

Corrine closed her eyes and a moment later felt Buddy's lips on hers, gentle at first, then increasingly insistent, Buddy, like all the men she'd known, impatient to move those lips down her neck to her breasts where need eventually betrayed them. Long ago, Corrine had discovered a simple truth: all men want the tit. And she had come to understand the power that truth bestowed.

Corrine arched her back. Buddy mouthed and sucked and dropped a hand between her legs.

"Oh honey," Buddy said. He worked two fingers inside her.

Corrine let herself slip into the sequence of practiced responses that would result in a believable orgasm on her part, Buddy moving inside her now, Corrine murmuring encouragement, lifting her hips and letting them fall with each thrust, Buddy's weight pressing on her.

Corrine kept her eyes closed.

Along the way, she began thinking of Stanley Tedros.

She could see him on the back of her eyelids, an image that slowly sharpened and came into full focus with the clarity of a Polaroid photo developing.

A funeral home. Stanley in his casket. Arms crossed on his chest. A carnation in the lapel of his omnipresent brown suit.

Stanley dead. She could see it. Absolutely and once and for all.

Corrine felt Buddy's breath coming in shorter and shorter bursts on the side of her neck and then something else, a tremor from deep inside her that followed its own demands, and she was suddenly wet, Corrine squeezing her eyes tighter, carrying the image of Stanley in his casket with her as Buddy moved in and out and said her name over and over again, her body suddenly taking over, running ahead of her and crashing in an orgasm that was every bit as histrionic as the one she'd been preparing to fake for her lawfully-wedded husband.

FOUR

THE AFTERNOON LIGHT WAS CLEAR and unsparing and reminded Ben Decovic of the lighting at a line-up. It set its own
terms, requiring you to look closely, and then waited for the rest
of you to catch up and recognize who or what was suspect.

Decovic U-turned the cruiser at the county line and approached the city limits and a sign reading

WELCOME TO MAGNOLIA BEACH, SC

"The *Other* Myrtle Beach."

More boomtown boosterism.

The sign was new, the brainchild of the Magnolia Beach Tourist
Bureau and City Council. The same one was planted at each of the
city's compass points, the slogan duplicated on the home page of the
city's website as well as on the borders of the brochures and flyers funneled through hundreds of travel agencies across the country.

He'd heard someone say the bureau and council were working
to fund a series of commercials to be run on the major networks.

He'd been living and working in Magnolia Beach for ten

months.

At the time, it seemed as good a place as any to start over.

Decovic followed Ocean Drive into North Shore, one of the city's oldest neighborhoods. North Shore had yet to be trammeled by the development mania. It was hit and miss middle class, most of the houses built in the forties and fifties with generous lots by current standards and filled with magnolia, pine, and live oaks. The neighborhood reminded Ben of a radio station whose signal wavered in and out of focus. He drove past blocks of homes maintained in a time-warp Norman Rockwell respectability, bordered by others sliding toward a low-rent destiny straight out of Erskine Caldwell.

The light followed him.

His fingers twitched on the steering wheel. He reached up and adjusted the visor.

What's there and what's not, he said to himself. Keep the line between each clear. That's all for now. Enough for now.

He glanced down at his left hand and the pale blue ink smudge on the inside of his wrist.

Decovic passed a scattering of home-based small businesses. A welding shop. Florist. Lawnmower repair. Sewing and alterations. Second-hand clothes and used appliances. A corner grocery. A bait and tackle shop.

He was the first to respond to the call from the Bull's Eye.

Edwin, the owner, was waiting for him outside in the oyster-shell parking lot. Flanked by a couple of muddy pickups and pampered muscle cars, he waved at Ben and then glanced back at the bar's entrance. True to its name, the entire front of the building was haphazardly papered in fading shooting-range targets, most of which were trembling or flapping in a steady ocean-laced

March wind.

"The problem here, Edwin?" Ben said.

"See for yourself." Edwin ran his hand over his head and stepped away from the door.

The inside of the Bull's Eye was steeped in a murky light. Next to the cash register a cheap plastic boombox cranked out early Metallica. Ben nodded at the regulars lining the bar. Most returned the greeting, but a couple made a point of turning their backs.

"Down there," Edwin said, then ducked behind the bar to serve up new orders.

A man circled one of the small tables fronting the long pool table and the cues racked on the north wall. He was wearing a gray sweatshirt and brand new blue jeans, the square cardboard tag still attached to the right rear pocket. His off-white athletic shoes were untied.

Ben cleared his throat. The man paused in his circling. Ben put him in his early forties, the eyes a decade ahead of him. They were dark brown and blurred by an afternoon of boilermakers, their corners a stack of weather-worn wrinkles.

Amidst the empties on the table were a black disposable lighter, a box of wooden kitchen matches, and five complimentary matchbooks from a local pancake house. Hanging on the top rung of one of the chairs was a black baseball cap with the front brim awkwardly scissored off.

"For all intents and purposes," the man said and then sat down. He set his hands on the table. His fingertips were blistered and bright red.

Ben waited for him to continue, and when he didn't, Ben

asked his name.

"Ronald." He lowered his head and pulled over the kitchen matches. He lifted the box to his ear and shook it as if he were about to roll a set of dice.

"Ronald what?"

"Fill in the blank," he said. He looked up at Ben. "Come on. Nothing to it. Think hamburgers and then tell me what kind of parents would do that to their own offspring."

Ben, caught off-guard, smiled despite himself.

"There you go," Ronald said, nodding at Ben. "I saw that."

"Take it easy," Ben said.

After three tries, Ronald got one of the wooden matches lit. Its tip sputtered, then flared. Ronald touched it to his left cuff.

"What exactly is going on here, Ronald?"

"What's going on," he said, looking up at Ben, "is I'm trying to set myself on fire, but I can't get this sweatshirt to catch." He shook his head. "I mean, go figure. All the synthetics they use in these, you'd think they'd go right up."

Ben let his hand drop near the baton on his belt. He wondered where Poston was. He'd confirmed he was running back-up.

Ronald twisted in his chair and shouted in the direction of the bar, "Edwin, there was no need to call the cops. If I'd got the sweatshirt going good, I'd have taken it outside."

Ben moved quickly with the cuffs. Ronald lowered his head and tried to palm one of the matchbooks. Ben leaned over and pushed them all into the center of the table.

"Protect and Serve," Ronald said. "What's that mean exactly by the end of the day?"

"What's that have to do with the matches, Ronald?"

He shook his head and smiled. "Some things can't be helped. You ever think about what it means to say that?"

"Not sure I'm following, Ronald," Ben said.

Ronald tilted his head, making a show of furrowing his brow and studying Ben. He seemed disturbed by what he saw. "You're right," he said. "You're not following me. You're already ahead of me. I see that now. You better watch your step."

"That sounds like it might be a threat."

"Maybe it was meant as a warning, maybe a sign of concern." Ronald paused and looked at the ceiling. "You know, the easiest person in the world to fool is always yourself."

Edwin called over that Poston had just pulled into the lot.

"What rhymes with ambulance?" Ronald said.

"That's enough," Ben said.

Ronald looked at the matches Ben had pushed to the center of the table. He nodded once, then said, "If I was a Buddhist monk, a couple gallons of high-test, and we'd be talking *Holy*."

Poston cleared the door, quickly looked around, and then hustled in Ben's direction. "I'm sorry, man," he said. "I radioed in, but all the closest available units were tied up. A tractor-trailer overturned on 17."

Poston's face was flushed as if he'd been exercising or out in the sun too long. That and the buzz cut and the clear, untroubled blue eyes made him look even younger than he was. Poston was less than a year out of the academy. He hadn't lived or worked long enough to cast a shadow yet.

Or to have to live in one, Ben thought.

"I got here as soon as I could," Poston said.

"It's ok. Everything's under control, right, Ronald?" Ben leaned over and pulled him to his feet.

"It'd be nice to think so," Ronald said.

"You want me to take him in and run the paper?" Poston said.

"He's all yours," Ben said.

"His name's really McDonald?" Poston said.

Ben nodded, then filled him in on the charges.

"He tried to set himself on fire?" Poston said. "Jesus. Why would anyone want to do that?"

Ronald smiled at Ben.

A moment later, he lifted his cuffed hands and pointed at Ben's chest.

"You're missing a button, Officer," he said. "Third one down from the neck. Center of your chest. There's nothing there."

FIVE

FURNITURE WAS Corrine Tedros's revenge.

For now, it was the best she could do to get back at Stanley and his unwavering ideas of home and character.

She couldn't push it further than that. Stanley Tedros kept maintaining her marriage to Buddy wouldn't last a year and a half, and even though Corrine had soldiered through fourteen months with Buddy and he was as pliable and clueless as ever, Stanley's pronouncement was still quietly unnerving. It was like thinking you were alone in a dark room and then suddenly getting tapped on the shoulder.

Corrine checked the living room clock against her watch. King Street Furniture had promised to deliver by noon. They were close to an hour late.

She had ordered a new loveseat and two matching wing chairs and three new lamps. Corrine wanted them in place before Stanley swung by this evening.

She was determined to never let the house even come close to a home.

Corrine could already anticipate Stanley's disorientation and disdain when she led him to a seat in the living room, Stanley who had not redecorated his home in over forty-five years and who prided himself on never throwing anything away because he could never be sure he wouldn't find some use for it. Stanley, all immigrant thrift, sacrifice, and no-nonsense, exquisitely uncomfortable in his nephew's and wife's house because with the furnishings constantly changing he was never able to get his full bearings or give anything even close to his blessing to the lives within its walls.

Stanley's obvious discomfort and bewilderment over the new and ever-changing furnishings was the closest Corrine could come to outright revenge.

At least for now.

The next door neighbor's dog started barking, a signal that the mail had arrived.

There was a reassuring weight to seeing her name on the mail she took from the box next to the front door. She rifled through the envelopes, watching her name appear over and over. She was *Mrs. Corrine Tedros*. The name erased everything else. She was clean and clear of Phoenix and the names she'd lived in there.

Corrine left the front steps and walked into the middle of the front lawn, then stopped. She kicked off her shoes. She looked up and down the street. At this time of the afternoon, everything was empty and quiet. The houses up and down the block shadowed each other, all of them in White Pine Manor having three basic layouts. Corrine had memorized each, just as she knew each of the houses tipped the scales at 3100 square feet and the lots clocked in at one-third acre.

She turned and faced her house. A two-and-a-half-story Mock Tudor, with the emphasis on the *Mock*, it had been a wedding present from Stanley Tedros, his way of literally and figuratively putting Corrine in her place. She and Buddy had talked about building their own home, Corrine conjuring up the layout to its rooms, savoring each detail, Buddy and she even scouting out lots, but as their wedding approached, Stanley had gone to work on Buddy's resolve and Corrine's character, Stanley constantly pointing out to Buddy all the eligible Greek women in the area and praising their virtues, evoking family, tradition, and the importance of the blood flowing through each, until Corrine, worried about how things were beginning to play out, had convinced Buddy to elope. Stanley had the last word though, giving them the house in White Pine Manor as a belated wedding present and making sure Corrine understood its point: White Pine was peopled by those who had yet to fully arrive, the development occupying a nebulous position just north of the mid-point on the slope of the area's social register.

Still holding the mail, Corrine stood in the middle of her front yard and lifted her arms and closed her eyes and felt the warmth of a spring sun on her face and imagined the whole of White Pine Manor on fire, every home ablaze, every shrub and flower and lawn burning beneath a sky empty of clouds, any rain coming too late.

SIX

THE OFFICER DRIVING the blue and white reminded Jack Carson of a minor league saint, some obscure foreign holy man whose gaunt Byzantine profile belonged in a dusty corner panel of stained glass or stamped on a small coppery-green religious medal.

"Did I hurt him?" Jack asked. He waited. The name eventually bumped into view. "Don Meade."

The cop glanced over at Jack, then went back to his driving. Outside, the afternoon light was pale and thin.

Jack Carson thought it was probably April. Maybe March.

The officer hesitated, then said, "Meade's ok."

It might have been afternoon, but the inside of the cruiser smelled like a late Saturday night, the point where promise collided with disappointment but had yet to curdle into regret or resignation.

"I've got references." Jack cupped the back of his neck with his left hand. "I do good work."

He shook his head and then looked out the window. "Don

Meade doesn't. He doesn't have to."

Jack closed and opened his fists. The skin around the knuckles was tight. The cuts he expected to see weren't there.

"The bids, they were supposed to be sealed," he said.

"I wouldn't know about that," the officer said.

"You know the apartment complex over on Warley? Barely five years old and you see what shape it's in. That's Meade's work."

The officer reached up and adjusted the rearview mirror.

"You have kids?" Jack asked.

The officer waited a long moment before answering, "No."

"If you did," Jack said, "you'd understand why I needed the bid on renovating the recreation center."

Just as he would have understood what tore loose in Jack Carson when Don Meade walked into the High Tide and started buying everyone drinks, a little early celebration, Don Meade everybody's pal, brother-in-law to the president of the city council and star of his own television and radio commercials, *Meade Construction, let us build your dreams*, and Jack Carson for his part wondering if he could make this month's payroll, his own construction company once again losing out to the bigger outfits, Jack angry and afraid in equal measures because his word and his work had always been good, and then Don Meade stepping up and setting a beer in front of him and dropping his hand on Jack's shoulder.

Jack was not sure how many times he'd hit Meade.

He looked out the passenger window. A street sign, white on green, popped up and disappeared in a blur of consonants. Two vowels, *a* and *e*, followed like a comet tail.

"Almost there, Jack," the officer said.

Jack leaned forward and tried to read the left pocket on the cop's chest. *D-E-C*-O-something. The light kept getting in the way of the rest.

Jack hoped it wasn't something about the bus. They hadn't pressed charges yet, but there'd been some ugly undercurrents.

The officer hit the signal and turned down a street lined with magnolias. The leaves were a dark waxy green and shaped like a hand with its fingers extended and tightly pressed together.

Jack kept bracing himself for a smudge of yellow among the green and then the appearance of the bus, squat as a loaf of bread.

Over the next block, he counted his breaths.

Something was not right, he told himself.

Like a magician who didn't know anymore what his hand would pull from the hat.

That's what it felt like sometimes.

The bus thing, it had just gotten away from him. He hadn't meant anything. He needed the paycheck.

The officer took another left. Jack craned his head and barely managed to catch the street sign: *DeHaviland*.

The movie star or the airplane. That's what he was thinking. They sounded the same, but he was pretty sure one of them had two *l*'s.

The officer turned his head in Jack's direction. "You know where we are, Jack?"

Jack didn't remember saying the name out loud.

The radio crackled and buzzed. It sounded like some movie extraterrestrial clearing its throat.

The obvious tapped Jack on the shoulder. He wondered why he hadn't thought of it earlier.

He was sitting up front in the cruiser.

That meant no crime or charges. It was something else then.

A slow panic began filling his chest. Jack glanced over at the cop.

"Is it Carol?" he asked finally. He thought of murky ultra-sounds, Henderson the OB/GYN man clearing his throat, Carol soldiering it for seven and a half months, the baby, their first, riding low and ticking in her womb.

"No," the officer said and smiled. "Carol's ok."

The smile didn't match the eyes though. They saw more than they were giving back.

Jack's panic slowed but didn't subside. He needed to ask the cop something about Carol, or maybe it was that he needed to tell the cop something about her, but everything inside was running away from him.

The officer cleared his throat. "Hey Jack, you still with me here?"

Jack nodded and looked toward the street. The long slant of afternoon light. The parallel lines of magnolias. Older middle-class homes, most of them white and vinyl-sided, their lawns shedding winter and working their way to green.

He tried to insert a life into the scene.

The cop followed DeHaviland to Farrow and took a right. He drove three blocks north. Along this stretch, the houses had a frayed respectability, their former middle-class seams showing.

The cop slowed and then glanced over at Jack. He hit the turn signal and pulled into a T-square driveway full of crushed oyster shells. The afternoon light threw itself against the windshield.

The house was a weathered one-story with a wrap-around porch and sat on a wide lot dotted with white pines, live oaks, and crepe myrtles. It was a good twelve feet off the ground, supported by six telephone-sized poles. The space beneath the house to the left of the front stairs was used in lieu of a garage. This afternoon it was empty.

"Shit." The cop peered over the steering wheel and rubbed his jaw. "Any idea where she is, Jack? Aren't Tuesdays her day off?"

Jack frowned. "You told me Carol was all right."

"I'm talking about Anne, not Carol," the cop said. "Anne, your daughter. It's Tuesday."

Jack pointed through the space between the rearview mirror and the passenger-side visor. "Isn't that her?"

A girl, somewhere between eleven and thirteen, stepped onto the landing and peered over the railing. She was wearing jeans and a pink knit top. An expression that Jack couldn't read scuttled across her features.

The cop was already opening his door. "No," he said. "That's not Anne. Sit tight, Jack, until I find out where she is."

The radio crackled and buzzed, the voices a call and response that was buried in static. Jack watched a gull break over the roofline of the house and disappear into the afternoon. He closed his eyes for a moment and repeated the name of his wife to himself, a makeshift chant, keeping its syllables alive on his lips.

SEVEN

"WE'LL TRY THE RESTAURANT," Ben Decovic said, backing the car around.

The Salt Box was a little over a half-mile away, one of the dozens of family-owned restaurants clustering the northern shoreline of Magnolia Beach. Ben had gotten into the habit of eating there on a regular basis.

He called in his location. Once out of the car, he tied Jack's shoe and then led him inside. The greeter was in her early twenties, left eyebrow pierced, a T-shirt designed to mimic a painter's palette, and dark red shorts. She tapped a clipboard against an overly thickening thigh. "Forty minutes, minimum, for a table. We're really swamped today."

Ben looked over her head into the crowded interior. "I can see that. But we're not here to eat. I need to talk to the assistant manager."

The greeter sighed. "Ok. You can wait over there."

Ben led Jack to a small alcove. There were seats built into the walls and a large hibiscus with salmon-colored blooms sitting beneath the front window.

A few minutes later, a short, dark-haired woman appeared. She wore a green Salt Box apron tied around the waist of a new pair of jeans, a white oxford shirt, and white athletic shoes. She was pretty in a way that surprised you, possessing a quiet under-stated beauty that only came into focus after a second or third look. Her eyes were a very light brown, large and startlingly clear, but today the flesh beneath them was smudged with exhaustion.

"Oh no," she said. "Not again. That's the second time in less than three weeks."

"I found him on Crescent."

"Oh Dad, what am I going to do with you?" She stepped to-ward him, then stopped.

"Ms. Carson —," Ben began.

"Anne." She held up her hand. "Remember? I told you to call me Anne?"

Ben remembered too late and inwardly winced. He liked the woman and had been stopping by the restaurant on breaks and the end of shifts for a while now. The beer was always cold, the hush-puppies homemade, and the seafood gumbo top-notch. The Car-son woman had a nice smile and a way of making you feel at home.

"I need to get to work," Jack said, abruptly standing up.

Anne Carson lifted her arms, putting her hands on her father's shoulders, and slowly pushed him back down to the seat. Then she sat next to him and began gently to rub his arm.

"He kept mentioning something about a bus," Ben said.

Anne Carson sighed. "After dad lost the construction com-pany in Myrtle Beach, we moved here. He hung in as an inde-pendent contractor but still picked up odd jobs." She reached up and touched her father's cheek. "One of them was driving an el-ementary school bus."

Ben waited.

"When he started to get confused …," she said and paused, looking over Ben's head toward the door.

"I'm sorry, but we're talking a little bit more than confusion here."

It was her turn to wait before speaking.

"All of us who know him missed the signs at first," she said. "Ok? Or we didn't want to see them."

Ben saw where she was headed. "Then your father lost a busload of kids."

Anne Carson nodded. "Nobody was hurt." She went back to slowly rubbing her father's arm. "But that was the beginning of where we are now."

She looked up at Ben. "Look, I'm really sorry. I had to come in because another manager took a half-day. Mrs. Wood was supposed to be watching him this afternoon, but she had to leave early. Then my daughter Paige missed her ride home from school." She paused and raised her hands. "I get off in an hour. I thought he'd be all right til then."

"You mentioned something about new medication last time," Ben said. "It's not working?"

"The doctors were optimistic. They'd seen some encouraging signs in some of their other patients." She paused and squeezed the bridge of her nose. "It doesn't seem to be making much of a difference with my father though. At least none that I can see."

Ben glanced down at his watch. "What are you going to do with him until you're done?"

She bit the lower corner of her lip. "The banquet room's not being used. I'll put him in there."

"Ok, but I have to point out—," Ben started.

Anne held up her hand. "I know where you're headed. I've talked to Social Services. And I've checked out nursing homes. I can't afford to put him in a good one." She paused and looked away. "And I'm not sure I would even if I could. My daughter and I are all he has left."

She turned and took her father by his arm, and he got unsteadily to his feet.

She nodded and smiled at Ben, and once again, he was struck by her eyes, how pretty they were, and he wondered too as she led her father away, how long it had been since they'd seen a full night's sleep.

It was a familiar question. One that he'd asked himself on more than a few occasions.

EIGHT

OFF SHIFT AND LEAKING insomnia like a slow wound, Ben Decovic prowled his apartment at the White Palms.

It was 3:07 AM.

He'd tried reading. Television. The radio. The internet.

Nothing sufficed.

Three AM set its own terms.

The Poes, that's what he'd come to call these interludes. It felt like Edgar Allen himself was calling the shots. Time slipped from its mooring, and neither *late night* or *early morning* fit the clock. For Ben Decovic, three AM was a nameless zone overcrowded with interlocking regrets and a bottomless yearning, all fueled by a waking nightmare logic.

Three AM was a place where you lost and found yourself whether you wanted to or not.

He checked the underside of his left wrist, counting the inked hash-marks.

He was still within limits.

He prowled his apartment.

He eventually started thinking about his wife's kisses.

The Math: he'd been married for a third of his life.

Ben told himself he had passed beyond the standard-issue responses to her death. He's had his ticket punched by grief. What he was left with was something more nebulous and frightening.

All the old certainties had evaporated.

He'd been a natural, a virtual artist of the eye, when it came to reading a crime scene or homicide, but all that changed after Diane's death.

He eventually resigned from the Homicide Division of the Ryeland, Ohio Police Department, jettisoning a promising fast-track rise through the ranks and moving South to Magnolia Beach in what he told himself was a clean break.

But nothing was clean, and everything broken, at three AM.

For example, the names.

Nicholas. Meredith. Emily. Laura. Andrew.

Then a few moments later, the others eventually crowding in.

Karl Metz. Suzanne Raschella. George Gearhart. Thomas Linneti. Diane Decovic.

What was there and not.

He was left finally with the memory of his wife's kisses.

The way her hair curtained when she inclined her head, the taste of lipstick, the soft press of flesh upon flesh, the warmth of her breath disappearing into his, fifteen years of kisses, Ben replaying them in his head, closing his eyes and trying to hold on to something as fundamental and deep as marrow.

Without those kisses and the weight of their memory, he was left in a perpetual three AM freefall through crime-scene images of his wife bleeding out late one afternoon in the parking lot of Central Dry Cleaners in Ryland, Ohio and a hit parade of post-mortem shots of the subsequent autopsy.

NINE

THE VERBS WERE THE FIRST TO GO.

Jack Carson had always been a man of few words. Like many men of his generation who'd been taught to speak through action, he also had a deeply-embedded respect for language, for the power of words and what they could do. His silence was simply a way of acknowledging that power. He'd learned early on to choose his words carefully.

Like many men of his time, Jack Carson also married a woman whom he came to believe could speak for the both of them, a woman with music in her voice, who could read his silences and flesh out what he was feeling or thinking whenever they were together.

He still had every love letter she wrote him.

There were days when he heard a voice he didn't entirely recognize recite passages from those letters verbatim, and he would then belatedly come to realize that it was him speaking.

There were days he remembered his wife had been dead for over thirty years. Days he recognized the attractive young woman moving around the house as his daughter, Anne, and days when he could summon up his granddaughter's name, Paige, which sounded like something you opened a book to.

Most days, though, he fought against a different type of silence from the one he'd been taught spoke louder and truer than words, a silence that did not shadow what he felt and thought but rather stole them from him, an immense silence into which things disappeared.

It had been that way with the verbs.

Jack Carson had been standing in the kitchen of the house he shared with his daughter and granddaughter, and his daughter had been turning the faucet over the sink on and off and pointing out a persistent leak, and he had nodded to her and said, "I can...," and that's when it had started, the verb suddenly deserting him, the main verb breaking off from its helper and spinning and falling away into that new silence, and Jack Carson had stood there and started the sentence, "I can...," over and over again, but had not been able to summon up "fix."

Like many men of his generation, Jack Carson had had an English teacher who had forever marked him. In his case, a Mrs. Allen in the seventh grade who'd taught him the parts of speech, and Jack Carson had learned how to build a sentence and appreciate the fit and function of its parts just as, years later working as a contractor, he could see a quiet and pervasive beauty in the precise lines and proportion in a set of blueprints.

He knew, for example, that verbs expressed an action, occurrence, or state of being.

Verbs told time.

And time, like the verb *fix,* which had deserted his tongue and gone spinning off into an immense silence when he'd faced the leaky faucet and asked for his tools, was something that Jack Carson had come to suspect he'd lost the blueprint for.

TEN

JAMES RESTAN had the kind of mustache you saw on aging gun-fighters in old black and white Westerns, a Palm Springs tan, and clear, hawk-like eyes that never seemed to blink. His hair was carefully cut and was a half shade lighter than his charcoal-gray polo shirt. Corrine judged him to be in his mid to late fifties.

They were sitting in a quiet section of the restaurant in the Marriott near the regional airport. Most of the east wall was a bank of windows softly refracting the pale rays of a noon sun. Restan had a scotch and soda in front of him. Corrine ordered an iced tea.

"I appreciate you agreeing to meet," she said.

"Unexpected, but still a pleasure. I have a late connecting flight and nothing pressing. I figured to get in a round of golf. Try out that new course the mayor and tourist bureau's so proud of."

"In that case, I appreciate it even more." Corrine tore open a packet of artificial sweetener and sifted it into her tea. "I wanted to talk to you about the buy-out offer."

James Restan cocked his head and smiled. Corrine saw that the mustache was a decoy, a front for a thin-lipped smile that held no warmth. She could easily imagine Restan in bed, knew the type, a lover who prided himself on technique, confident that he knew just what to do with his hands, mouth, and cock. He would be a lover whose self-regard masqueraded as generosity, sexual passion always something he negotiated, a transaction that would leave him secure in his belief that he'd earned his orgasm.

"I'm not sure how much we have to talk about," Restan said. "Stanley Tedros did not strike me as being open to any further discussions. And frankly, right now, I feel the same way." Restan paused and squared his scotch and soda in the center of his napkin. "So why exactly are you here, Ms. Tedros?"

"I want you to consider an extension on the buy-out offer."

Restan cupped his chin with his left hand and waited, watching Corrine, before he responded. "The American public has a short memory and insatiable appetite. Right now, it's convinced itself it wants Julep. That's a plus, Ms. Tedros, but in itself means nothing. What counts is the American public still desiring Julep three, five, or ten years from now. What's imperative is breaking down that infamous short memory and lodging Julep in the psyche of the American consumer. And that requires time, commitment, and not a small amount of money."

Restan picked up his scotch, sipped, and replaced it in the center of the napkin. Corrine reined in her impatience, told herself to let him talk. They would get to where they were headed soon enough.

"Long before I ever met with Stanley," Restan went on, "I had my marketing and research and development people working on how Julep fit with our anchor sodas and doing detailed projections about its future place in the line. I knew what a major soft drink company, like mine, could and could not realistically do with a product like Julep, Ms. Tedros, and I knew what my competitors could and could not do with it, but what I did not know, and should have, was just how stubborn and foolish Stanley Tedros would be when we brought the offer to the table."

Restan signaled the waiter for more drinks and then turned back to Corrine. "You know, Stanley will end up running Stanco Beverages into the ground if he tries to market and distribute Julep on a nation-wide basis himself. It can't be done, not given his present resources."

"I know," Corrine said.

"Which brings me back to my original question," Restan said. "Why this meeting and a request for an extension? My offer's not going to change. It's fair, more than fair, and the total package is better than what my competitors offered."

The waiter brought the drinks. Restan waved away the offer of a lunch menu.

He sat back and made a show of taking Corrine in. "One thing I'm curious about," he said. "Who sent you? Buddy or Stanley? I'm betting Stanley. Another is, am I first on the list? Or have you already slept with the other two reps?"

Restan picked up his drink and saluted her. "Not that you're not quite a piece, Ms. Tedros, and very likely more than adept in the bedroom, and certainly more appealing than another round of golf, but a little between the sheets action is not going to change my offer. Tell Stanley he's overreaching on this one."

"Is that what you think? Stanley sent me here to fuck you?"

"Not exactly an original idea," Restan said, "though I'm sure it's worked admirably well on other occasions."

Corrine shelved her anger and shook her head no. "You have it all wrong."

"I do?"

"Yes."

"Then why?" Restan asked, smiling. "Why are you here, and why are we having this conversation?"

It was the question Corrine had been waiting for, and she thought she was prepared to answer it.

She was conscious of Restan watching her and of a slow change taking place, as if his pupils were adjusting to a different light than the one streaming through the bank of windows.

Corrine felt something lurch inside her.

She slid back her chair and got up. "Would you excuse me for a moment?" she asked, then turned and walked quickly across the room.

In the restroom, a woman on the long side of forty stood before the mirror adjusting the lines of her lipstick. Corrine found the first available stall and just managed to lift the lid of the toilet before she threw up. She'd barely finished before she dropped to her knees and started all over again. It felt as if her insides were being ripped out. She went through one more cycle before she was completely empty.

She heard the woman ask if she were all right, then move toward the door and leave. Corrine lifted her head and wiped her mouth with the back of her hand and got up.

Her throat burned, and she blinked back tears.

For a moment, she'd forgotten where she was.

She leaned against the inside of the stall. Her forehead and underarms were damp, and her heartbeat raced and stuttered. She lowered her head. The inside of her mouth tasted like a burnt match.

Corrine understood *empty*. How *empty* fed an unruly mix of fear and anger that inevitably led to a moment like this one, a moment as small and tightly confined as the bathroom stall itself.

She could just leave. Go back home, play wifey, and wait for Stanley to die. Hope to win the tug of war she and Stanley were waging over Buddy and that Stanley didn't make good on his pronouncement that the marriage wouldn't last eighteen months.

Corrine cradled her stomach and closed her eyes.

She thought about Julep, the string of zeroes in the buy-out offer.

She thought about *empty*.

About how a zero was a circle and a circle the symbol of perfection and completion.

James Restan's question still hung in the air.

Corrine left the stall and moved to the sink. She rinsed out her mouth and lifted handful after handful of water to her face, not caring what it did to her make-up. By the time she'd dried her face, she'd replaced making a decision with a bet, throwing everything to chance, and keeping its terms simple.

She would step outside the bathroom and look across the restaurant. If James Restan was still sitting at the table, she would join him and go on to answer his question. If Restan had already left, she would drop the whole thing.

Yes or No.

As simple as that.

No middle ground.

ELEVEN

BEN DECOVIC dropped into the quiet. The air around him was layered with the smell of old incense, like the aftermath of fireworks on a damp summer evening.

He had just signed off first shift and was still in his uniform.

He sat in the nave of St. Katherine's, the Greek Orthodox Church off Medloe Avenue.

He wanted the quiet and dark.

God was optional.

Ben Decovic figured the feeling was mutual.

Directly above him was an oval dome set in the ceiling, a painting of Christ occupying its center like the sun and banked with concentric rings of angels.

All around Ben were more frescoes and icons and mosaics: the serpent and Eve and the apple; Abraham and Isaac and the ram in the thicket; Jonah and the whale; Mary with Child; the Last Supper; Christ kneeling at Gethsemane; the crucifixion at Golgotha; the empty tomb and Christ's Ascension, all buttressed by an army of saints and martyrs whom Ben didn't recognize and couldn't name.

Behind him, the door to the narthex opened, and in his peripheral vision, Ben saw Father Amarantos enter. He paused in passing and nodded, briefly reaching over to rest his hand on Ben's shoulder before continuing through the nave to the paneled wall fronting the sanctuary. Ben thought he remembered Father Amarantos calling it the iconostasis.

Father Amarantos opened the central panel and stepped through, closing it behind him, leaving Ben looking at an icon of a thin, flattened-faced Christ flanked left and right by Mary and John the Baptist and north and south by the archangels Gabriel and Michael.

Father Amarantos was old-school, a patient and practical and stoic man who believed Ben would one day again return to the church and sign on this time for the whole package deal, the liturgy and all the accessories, despite the fact, as Ben pointed out, that he was not Greek nor confirmed in the Orthodox Church. Ben had grown up buttoned-down Midwestern Methodist, all Original Sin and Bake Sale theology. His closest contact to a liturgical church had been his wife, Diane, who'd been a sporadic Catholic.

"You need the Holy Mysteries," Father Amarantos had said. "You just don't see that, or them, yet."

Then he gave Ben a key to the church and left him alone.

Ben stopped by St. Katherine's two or three times a week but never during mass.

He didn't pray. He didn't confess. He didn't look for Revelations or Holy Mysteries or take Communion. He sat in the quiet and dark and tried to hide from his life.

Ben Decovic had come to understand the curse of early promise.

How, if you were not careful, early promise could turn on you and begin to promise too much, and you started to think you and your life and plans were inviolate and unassailable.

At thirty-seven, Ben Decovic discovered the fine print to that promise.

Until that point, possibility followed him like his own shadow.

A gangly teenager, he'd spent the summer of his sophomore year in high school on a blacktopped city basketball court, drilling himself on the fundamentals and playing in an endless stream of pickup games until his top-of-the-key jumper was as automatic as striking a match and his passing could thread the eye of any needle the defense put up.

Before that, music lessons, the piano, junior high, the same deal. Ben had large hands and a good ear. Ran the scales until they were chasing him. Worked through a song three times and could play it from memory.

An honors student in high school. Named three years in a row to the All-City basketball team.

A Merit Scholar who caught a full-ride to Kent State. A succession of majors—geology, psychology, philosophy and religion, secondary education, history—his interest snagged by each new semester's schedule. Pocket money garnered by delivering pizzas four nights a week and spent on Diane Walsh, a pre-vet major with pale green eyes and a quick laugh and slow kisses.

A top-end LSAT score and acceptance to Ohio State Law School. Second in his class at the end of his first year before he got restless and dropped out.

A little bit of time off to figure out exactly what he wanted to do with his life. He'd learned it wasn't practicing law.

An impulsive application to the police academy. A holding-action decision that eventually took hold of him.

A return to Ryland, Ohio. Ben's home-ground. Patrol, Crimes Against Property, Vice, and then Homicide.

Ben doing the job and doing it well. Natural aptitude. Discipline and concentration. Talk among the higher-ups. Ben a quick-study. An impressive closure on his case loads. Administrative potential. The hometown boy with promise.

In the meantime, Diane Walsh and her slow kisses.

In the meantime, marriage, her finishing vet school, then setting up a practice.

In the meantime, love and work and the life they built from each, the old words made new again.

In the meantime, talk of starting a family.

Plans and a future as cleanly calibrated as a blueprint or map.

All they had to do was follow it.

And then the fine print.

And where that led and what it took away.

Ben had come to fall asleep with and wake to one overriding fear: that despite all the bonhomie and Hallmark moments the culture could muster, all the self-help and esteem manifestoes and reconstituted Cinderella stories, all the come-from-behind sports mythos and metaphors and sanguine third-act movie logic, despite the natural mother-lode of raw optimism and the it's-always-darkest-before-the-etc., Ben Decovic was afraid that at the heart of it all, there was only one chance, one *real* chance, and Diane Decovic nee Walsh had been his — a chance and a love that left no room for anything else, that was as necessary as breath and reduced everything else to an anemic approximation of what he knew as true and binding; a love and a chance, like early promise, that came to mark him and his days.

So he sat, off shift, in his uniform in the dark and quiet of St. Katherine's a couple times a week, having stopped in the narthex on his way in, stepped past the icon stand with Katherine's visage and moved to the bank of candelabras where he struck matches and watched the flames appear at his fingertips, Ben saying the names as he lit each candle, starting with *Nicholas* and moving through to *Emily* and then repeating the process, *Karl Metz* to *Diane Decovic*.

He always left two candles unlit.

One for Greg Hollinger.

The other for himself.

TWELVE

WHEN CORRINE had laid out her proposal to James Restan at the restaurant in the Marriott, he had waited a full minute before responding, and then after he was sure Corrine was serious, he had taken a felt-tip pen and a bar napkin and written down a telephone number, swiveling the napkin in her direction and telling her to memorize the number, and when Corrine had, Restan took his near empty scotch glass and set it back on the napkin, turning the numbers into a damp smudge, and he'd gone on to tell Corrine the phone number would work once, just once, and would connect her to a service that he referred to as a "resource clearinghouse," and the next day, when Corrine put in the call, an anonymously pleasant male voice simply asked her name and city and state of the party in question, and after putting her on hold for five minutes, no confectionary muzak icing the wait, just five minutes of faintly humming silence, he came back and gave Corrine another telephone number, asked her to repeat it for him, and then thanked her and hung up.

That second telephone call had led her to Conway, South Carolina and the office of one Raychard Balen, Attorney at Law.

The red brick building was a one-story square with tall narrow windows set equidistantly across its face. The flowerbeds on either side of the front door were empty except for churned dirt.

Raychard Balen was expecting her. Corrine guessed he was somewhere in his midforties. Balen was slight in build but had a disproportionately aggressive waistline, the swell and girth of his stomach throwing everything else about him out of balance. He wore a pair of wire-frame glasses and had pale, watery blue eyes. His suit was out of season and wrinkled, and his tie, banded in orange and black, lay on his chest like a sluggish coral snake.

The mustache, though, was what kept drawing her eye. Unevenly trimmed, perched like two sides of a triangle beneath Balen's nose, the mustache was a seedy anachronism, pencil-thin.

He ushered Corrine to a chair, poured her a cup of coffee, and moved behind his desk and went to work on the remains of a fast-food breakfast.

"Eleven hundred dollars for a retainer," he said. "Check's fine. Everything else is cash."

When Corrine hesitated, Balen said, "You want to jaw about the weather some, fine, we can do that, but nothing else is on the agenda here, Mrs. Tedros, until you officially retain me as your lawyer."

Corrine pulled out her checkbook.

She waited until Raychard Balen had finished his breakfast and dumped the jumble of grease-stained bags, plastic forks, and Styrofoam cups into the trashcan before sliding over the check. Balen folded and slipped it into his breast pocket without glancing at it, then got up to pour himself another coffee.

The east and west walls of the office were covered in photographs, one side given over to black and whites of local landmarks over the years, the other wall to Raychard Balen and an assortment of prominent clients leaving court after their arraignments, all of them attempting to duck the cameras and hide their faces with varying degrees of success, Balen standing next to them in each one and smiling broadly.

Balen produced the same smile for her and set down his coffee. "I guess it's time we got to know each other, Mrs. Tedros." He patted his breast pocket, then leaned back in his chair, summoning the smile again.

Corrine had barely gotten beyond her name and address when Balen closed his eyes and raised his hand. "Point of clarification, Mrs. Tedros. I meant you getting to know me. I checked up, already know everything I need about you. If I didn't, you would have never gotten through the door."

Corrine listened while Balen made his point, self-importantly running through the particulars of her life, the warm queasy feeling moving from her stomach to her throat the further back he went, but in the end, Charlotte, North Carolina held. She waited, but Balen made no reference to Phoenix or Bradford, Indiana and didn't appear about to.

"And now," he said, with a sweep of his arm, "yours truly, Raychard Balen. I'm forty-four years old, an exceedingly undistinguished graduate of the University of South Carolina law school, and a rather unprepossessing and unattractive specimen of manhood if you are prone to judge solely on appearances. I have never been arrested. I have more money and expensive possessions than a universe governed on the principles of fairness and justice would ever permit. I've been told I have absolutely no taste in clothes, music, landscaping, or women. I'm prone to corns, cold sores, and hemorrhoids. I've never missed my church tithe, not once. I do not like swimming in the ocean. I have a pair of lucky socks that I only wear when closing cases. I have no real friends to speak of and more enemies than I can count. And I do not like the color blue in any of its various and manifold shades."

Balen paused, took a sip of coffee, then resumed. "My mother was a whore, the Madam of a first-class Pussy Farm outside North Myrtle Beach. I grew up on the premises. She never made mention of the father from whose loins I sprang, and I never pressed the issue. Growing up, I never lacked for attention, in fact, was excessively doted on by the succession of males passing through the house, most of whom unimaginatively and predictably appended 'Uncle' to their surnames on their visits.

"It wasn't until much later that my mother informed me of the true identities of all these Uncles, and it wasn't much later after that, when she been diagnosed with breast cancer, that my mother bequeathed to me the trove of materials, including photographs, she'd collected on the house's patrons over the years and explained to me the various uses it could be put to and how an enterprising young man, such as myself, could benefit from that."

Raychard Balen spoke in a soft sonorous voice and with a practiced delivery that told Corrine both that Balen was enjoying himself and that he probably inflicted this same story on each new client, and so Corrine prepared herself to wait him out, listening to Balen summarize the lowlights of his college years, his inglorious stint as a law student, a disastrous first and only marriage, and of his return home to set up practice and be a permanent thorn in the side of all those, and the friends and relations of all those, for whom his mother had ever opened her legs.

Balen paused, then leaned further back in his chair, steepling his fingers and resting them atop his head. The armpits of his sports jacket held faint overlapping stains resembling old coffee spills.

"To this day, Mrs. Tedros," he said, "I remain my mother's son. I am completely indifferent to the guilt or innocence of my clients and have no qualms whatsoever about representing some of the lowest members on the food chain. I do not have to worry about compromising my ethics or principles because I never had any to begin with. I am the human equivalent of a toilet. An absolutely necessary but underappreciated component of everything we pride ourselves on and value as a civilized culture. Without people like me, everybody would be up to their necks in shit."

"Ok," Corrine said and waited, half expecting Balen to continue.

"That's what your retainer has bought," he said. "Now, why don't you tell me what you've done."

Corrine set her coffee cup on the edge of the desk and crossed her legs. "Nothing yet," she said.

"The problem, then?"

"Somebody's standing in the way of what I want," Corrine said.

Balen scratched his cheek and nodded. "An impediment. Ok, I may be able to help you out there, Mrs. Tedros. I'll make a couple calls and get back to you."

Raychard Balen stood up, resting his fingers on the desk, and asked, "This impediment, what will be necessary to remove it? In short, how badly do you want this person hurt and for how long?"

"Six feet and forever," Corrine said.

THIRTEEN

BEN DECOVIC stood on his third-story patio at the White Palms Apartments, or what approximated a patio: thirty-two square feet of pre-cast, freestanding cement that jutted from the outside wall like a lower lip in an exaggerated pout. Besides Ben, the patio held enough room for two small deck chairs and a Hibachi grill.

The railing gave slightly when he leaned into it. Ben looked over the parking lot at a halogen light that had begun to flicker and strobe, an earthbound cousin to the moon throbbing in the southeast corner of a night sky cut by streams of low-lying and fast-moving cloud masses.

The wind carried the scent of the ocean and the overripe contents of the dumpsters in the northeastern corner of the lot. Ben glanced once more at the flickering moon and then turned and went back inside, closing the sliding glass doors behind him and crossing to the kitchen where he opened the refrigerator and took out a cold beer. After opening it, he inked a blue hash-mark on the inside of his left wrist. The mark joined the four already there.

The television was on, more for the noise than anything else. On the shelf above it, the digital clock read 12:21, time sandwiched, mirrored, and folded on itself like a slice of bread or piece of paper.

The phone started in, and Ben picked up on the second ring. It was an old habit, pure reflex. He knew who was on the other end of the line before a word was spoken just as he knew what the first words would be. The routine never varied.

"Figured you'd probably be up," Andy Calucci said.

Calucci, his former Homicide partner in Ryland, Ohio. When they'd worked together, Andy had gotten in the habit of calling Ben shortly after midnight when something was bothering him and wouldn't let him sleep.

"This morning, we got another three inches of snow," Andy said, "and that's on top of the two we got Monday. It's the last week in March, ok, and not that unusual, but still." He paused, and there was a glassy clink followed by an abrupt cough. A moment later, he continued. "Tonight, I'm watching the Weather Channel, you know, what we're looking at the next few days, and the anchorwoman, she says South Carolina, you're unseasonal, no rain and the temperatures running high for the middle of March — short-sleeve weather she called it, an exact quote there — and I get to thinking it's been a while, you and me talked."

Ben set down his beer, picked up the remote, and killed the sound on the television.

"That what they call it?" Andy asked.

"What?"

"Short-sleeve weather," Andy said. "That how they talk down there?"

"No," Ben said. "At least not what I've heard."

"I didn't think so," Andy said. "Short-sleeve weather. I'm betting that's just some Weather Channel lingo."

Calucci paused. On the other end of the line, there was a soft, irregular clinking. It was followed by two sharp clicks.

Ben recognized the soundtrack. It too was part of the late-night call routines. Ice cubes bumping against glass, a Seagrams-and-Seven kickback. Followed shortly by Andy firing up his Zippo and burning a Kool.

"Phil Varner," Andy said after a while. "He's got the pancreatic." More ice cube and glass action. "Even with the chemo and all the other stuff, we're talking months here. Basically, the Big Countdown."

"Jesus. I'm sorry to hear that," Ben said, and he was. Varner showed up each day and did the job, and there was something to be said for that. He may not have cleared as many cases as some of the others in Homicide, but Phil Varner was steady.

Andy Calucci worked on clearing his throat. "So the thing is, Ben, what with Phil V. and the pancreatic, we're going to be looking at a slot soon."

Ben went back into the kitchen and got another beer, then hunted down a pen and pushed back his left shirt cuff.

"You still there?" Andy said.

"Look, I appreciate the thought," Ben said.

"Something to consider is all," Andy said. "I mean, the opening, it'll be there, and it'd be good, you back here again."

"I don't think," Ben said slowly, "that's in the cards right now."

"Jesus Christ," Andy said. "No offense, Ben, but Patrol? What exactly you think you're doing down there?"

When Ben didn't reply, Andy started ticking off some of the major homicides they'd closed when they'd worked together. "No reason that has to stop," he added.

"I can think of a couple," Ben said. "Father Sarko not pressing charges being one."

"Water under the bridge," Andy said and fired up the Zippo again.

"A little more than that," Ben said. "Thanks to you."

"Yeah, well," Andy said. "Ok." He paused, then asked, "You getting out at all down there?"

"What?" Ben said.

Andy sighed. "Look, you know you got the tendency since Diane and all to shut everyone out, go to ground, and not even mean to or notice that's what you're doing, and then if you're not careful, you get jammed up."

"You're calling," Ben said, "because you're worried I'm going to try to shoot myself or someone else, is that it?"

Ben waited to see if Andy would add an *again*.

"All I'm saying, you're alone, it's easy to get jammed."

"I'm doing ok," Ben said.

Andy went quiet.

There were bets you made with the world, Ben thought, and those you made with yourself. If you were lucky, they turned out to be the same ones.

If you weren't, you ended up with your days having dwindled to the half-life of a prayer and a chambered .22 semi-automatic.

"The thing is," Andy said finally, "you can't watch your own back. Nobody can. I know you miss her. You can't help but. Hell, we all do."

"I'm doing ok," Ben said again. He crossed the living room and paused before the sliding glass doors leading to the patio, his reflection appearing, then disappearing in the lightning-like stutter of the faulty halogen parking lot light.

"Ok then," Andy Calucci said. "I hear you. I was just getting worried we might be looking at some serious déjà vu action here."

"No déjà vu," Ben said. "I'm doing ok."

FOURTEEN

JACK CARSON was at the kitchen window, the early morning sun slow and just starting to snake through the tree lines and over the neighboring rooflines. He was in a brown terrycloth bathrobe and a pair of old slippers. He held a plastic glass covered in cartoon figures. Jack Carson was trying to remember if he'd already drunk what the glass held or if he needed to go on and fill it.

At eye-level to his right, between the sink and refrigerator, was a calendar topped by a glossy colored photograph of a dramatic series of rapids, all dark jutting rocks and white veils of spume, and a heavy salmon suspended like an apostrophe mid-leap above them.

Jack Carson looked at the month and ran his fingers over the days.

"Look, we've already covered this ground," a woman said. "You need to come straight home from school and watch your grandfather."

On the other side of the kitchen was a brown-haired woman in a starched white shirt and dark blue jeans. She held a compact in her palm and tilted its cover so that the mirror let her follow the path of the make-up she was applying.

Below her, at the kitchen table, was a girl sitting in front of a bowl of cereal. Her hair was ponytailed tight against her scalp. Hanging from the back of her chair was a red and blue bookbag.

"Jennifer's," she said, pointing her spoon at the woman. "I was supposed to go over to her place after school. It's important."

The brown-haired woman said something about a Mrs. Wood and her having to leave early so that Paige needed to come home right after school.

"It's not like Jennifer asks just *anyone* over to her house," the girl said. "Her dad's a surgeon, and her mother's beautiful enough to be a model."

The brown-haired woman said she was sorry and then turned to Jack. "Dad, it's what, the second, third, time I've told you to get dressed, and you're still in your bathrobe? I laid out clothes."

"What does it matter?" the girl said. "It's not like…" Her voice broke off, and she shrugged.

"It matters," the woman said. "It matters that your grandfather gets dressed every day. It matters that you don't talk in front of him as if he isn't here."

The girl shook her head. "He ruins everything. You know he does, and you're just pretending not."

"That's enough, Paige." The woman angled the tube of lipstick and went back to work on her mouth. She paused and looked over at Jack. "Dad, *please*, get dressed."

"If my father were here, he'd just leave all over again," the girl said.

The woman snapped the compact closed. She was pretty, but had sad eyes. Jack suddenly remembered her name and who she was.

There was a short blast of a horn. "The bus, Paige," Anne said. The girl grabbed her bookbag and slammed out of the house without a goodbye.

"I'll find him," Jack said.

"Who?"

"The one the girl was talking about." Jack waited, and the name bumped into view. "Raymond."

"Oh Dad," Anne said. "We've been over this. It's been over three years. He's not coming back."

"He needs to do the right thing," Jack said. *In Trouble.* That's how Jack thought of it and then immediately felt ashamed because there was something fundamentally dishonest about the phrase. It was the equivalent of saying *passed* instead of *died.*

In Trouble. That's what they called it when Jack was younger. You got a girl in trouble.

Anne walked over and took Jack by the arm and led him through the living room and down a hall. They stopped and turned into a bedroom.

"Claude Rains," Jack said, pointing at the clothes on the bed.

Anne looked over, puzzled.

A set of clothes was laid out on top of the covers. Jack said it looked as if the Invisible Man were taking a nap.

"Please," Anne said, handing Jack the pants. Then she left, closing the door behind her. After a while, he heard the doorbell and then Anne talking to someone named Mrs. Wood.

Jack unbelted the bathrobe and started to get dressed.

It struck Jack that he lived in a house full of women's voices.

He got his pants on and his shirt buttoned halfway and then

sat on the edge of the bed and hunted down his shoes. He looked out the bedroom window. It overflowed with pale morning light. He picked up his left shoe. He looked at the closed door and listened to the faint voices of the women drifting down the hall.

At that moment, Jack Carson understood what was happening to him. Even if, right then, he could not name the condition, he recognized what it felt like.

It felt like each moment of what he'd once been able to call his life were being reshuffled over and over like a deck of cards.

It was like standing in front of a door, then bending over the lock with a fat wad of keys and trying one by one to fit them and having to start over again and again because all the keys were the same size and shape and color.

It was like a magician who'd lost control of his magic, who knew the moves for each trick but had lost the ability to manipulate the outcome anymore, the tricks tricking him now.

It was like standing behind the wheel of a boat, far out at sea and waiting, against the immensity of the horizon, for the anchor you'd dropped to catch, but knowing through your fingertips on the wheel that it hadn't, that in the depths below the hull, the anchor drifted and dragged, unable to find purchase.

And it was like standing in the kitchen before an open cabinet, and the item he needed was on the uppermost shelf, and as he stretched for it, his fingertips brushed against but could not grasp what he needed, and he ended up pushing it further back each time he tried, until finally it was out of reach, his fingers grabbing air.

Jack got up from the bed and started looking for his other shoe.

FIFTEEN

THIS MONTH it was *Initiative*.

Last month it had been *Concern*.

Ben Decovic could chart his ten months with the Magnolia Beach Police Department with the appearance of each bumper sticker the state of South Carolina issued for the blue and whites. He'd started out with *Honesty*, rode for thirty days with *Sharing*, and moved on to *Responsibility* and *Duty* and then continued with *Compassion, Integrity, Faith,* and *Sacrifice.*

The black and white bumper stickers bothered him in a way he could not quite put his finger on, the stickers evoking the same type of ambivalence he felt whenever he encountered another of South Carolina's favorite practices, that of putting *Jesus* on the plates of seemingly every other car or truck on the road. The point of it all seemed either too obvious or opaque to make any real sense.

Ben had been working the three-to-eleven and had an hour to go on his shift. He worked his way through the lots of the strip malls and businesses off Atlantic Avenue, most of them closed or about to.

On his way out of the Walgreens lot, he spotted Carl Adkin climbing out of his patrol car at the 7-11 across the street. Ben waved. Adkin looked over at him for a moment, then nodded, pausing near the front doors and flipping open his cell phone.

The Passion Palace was three blocks farther down the street and Ben's last stop before returning to headquarters. There was nothing particularly palatial about the Palace. It was flat-roofed with no front windows and constructed of cement blocks spruced up with a paint job that vacillated between lavender and pink under the two hooded mercury lights out front. There was a portable billboard street-side that simply read LIVE GIRLS and MEMBERS ONLY, the latter, Ben knew, taken care of by a twenty dollar bill at the door.

There were two Passion Palaces, the other in North Myrtle Beach, a small but lucrative skin kingdom overseen by Sonny Gramm, who also had controlling interests in a half-dozen adult video stores as well as ownership of a supper club and three restaurants popular with tourists who equated gargantuan buffets of all-you-could-eat deep-fried food with a meal.

One of the bouncers at the Palace, Terry, was standing outside the front door smoking a cigarette. Ben stopped and rolled down his window and asked how things were going.

"Other than the fact that my girlfriend has a major-league yeast infection and Sonny pink-slipped me tonight, the world is a fine and wonderful place, Officer."

"Gramm cut you loose?"

Terry nodded. "Five years, I've been working for him. Then bam, he does this." Terry lifted his head and blew a stream of smoke over the roof of the blue and white. "He's doing the same thing at the other places. Cutting back to one bouncer and thinning out the ranks of the waitresses. Then kicking up the hours and duties of the ones who are still around."

Terry looked over and down at Ben. "Money problems. That's all he talks about now." He shook his head. "Used to be a nice guy, Sonny. You did your job, you got a decent paycheck, a comp on drinks, he had you out for parties at his place, but the last few months, he's Scrooged-out large-scale. The whole thing sucks, man."

"What's that?" Ben asked, leaning his head out the window.

"I didn't hear anything," Terry said.

"That," Ben said. From the rear of the Palace came a mix of sounds, metal on glass, metal on metal, loud voices.

"I told you, I don't hear anything," Terry said. "I think something happened to my ears after I got pink-slipped. They're not working right tonight."

Ben called in the disturbance and requested backup. On more than one occasion, some of the patrons of the Palace got a little out of hand near closing. Whatever was going on didn't sound good. Adkin radioed that he was on the way and to wait for him before proceeding.

The sounds continued, the volume rising and spiking.

Ben took the blue and white toward the rear parking lot.

When he made the corner of the building, he saw Frank, the other bouncer, fly out the back door of the Palace and run toward a knot of people in the southeast corner of the lot, most of them yelling and hooting and scattering at Frank's approach and the sight of the cruiser.

Then suddenly, Frank wasn't anywhere to be seen.

Ben wasn't sure if he'd been knocked down or had gotten lost running after some of the hecklers. The source of the noise, however, was now very apparent.

A thin man in a black sleeveless t-shirt was methodically working over Sonny Gramm's vintage '68 Mustang with a crowbar. He was wearing a cheap plastic mask, a Halloween Lucifer. The hood of the car looked like a rumpled sheet of aluminum foil. The front windshield, as well as the headlights, was already a memory.

Ben looked around for his backup, hit the siren, and climbed out of the front seat, cutting across the lot at a diagonal and yelling at the guy to put the crowbar down.

It seemed to be a night for hearing problems. The guy ignored Ben and continued pounding the Mustang.

Ben again yelled for the guy to stop. Same results.

He drew his Glock, carefully moving among the parked cars. The guy in the black T-shirt and devil mask was Meth-scrawny and looked to have unlimited reserves of energy. He brought the crowbar down again and again in an unvarying rhythm. The Mustang was well on its way to scrap.

Then three things happened in quick succession.

Ben moved around a blue Taurus and stepped on Frank's, the bouncer's, hand. The guy in the black T-shirt suddenly quit with the crowbar action and looked over what was left of the car's roof and waved. Then Kermit the Frog popped up and punched Ben in the throat.

Ben rolled over and was halfway to his feet when the guy in the Kermit mask hit him again.

As he went down, Ben caught the lower edge of the mask, momentarily pulling it away before it snapped back in place.

Ben lifted his head and then his right arm. The short man in the Kermit mask, however, was already in the middle of his swing, this time bringing a dark object up and over his shoulder and catching Ben's wrist, knocking the semi-automatic from his hand.

The guy swung again, hard, the object whistling through its trajectory and rattling like a pocketful of loose change when it made contact with Ben's forearm.

Ben heard himself yell, and then he was on the ground, lightning running the length of his arm and his nerve endings short-circuiting, his fingers instantly going numb.

The guy leaned over and snatched Ben's Glock. He turned and hollered something to the guy in the black t-shirt and devil mask.

A couple moments later, the two of them took off running.

Ben tried to move his fingers. His arm twitched and jumped.

He had just managed to get to his knees when the backup arrived. He tried to catch their attention, point out the direction the two had taken off in, but there was too much going on.

Lee—Ben couldn't remember if it was his first or last name—made it over first. Ben gave him the gist, and Lee sprinted back to his patrol car to put in the call to alert other officers about the two men on foot.

Adkin checked on Frank. The EMS people arrived.

Ben put his left arm along the fender of the Taurus and slowly worked to a standing position. Residual pain still ghosted the length of his arm, but nothing seemed to be broken.

At his feet was a large gray athletic sock with a mound of heavy gauge washers spilling from its mouth.

A paramedic examined Ben and said he needed to go back for X-rays, but Ben said it could wait. He asked about the bouncer and was told Frank had a probable concussion and a definite broken jaw. Three patrolmen were working follow-up with witnesses from the crowd who'd been in the lot earlier. Another bagged the sock and washers. Others radioed in, passing on the news that there was no news. The two guys who'd taken off on foot were still on the loose.

Carl Adkin walked over. "You ok, Decovic?"

"What the fuck took you so long?"

"What do you mean?"

"You heard me."

"I got here as soon as I could." Adkin fired up a cigarette.

"You're lying. You should have been primary backup. You couldn't have been more than three or four blocks away. I saw you at the 7-ll off Atlantic."

Adkin jetted a stream of smoke. "You called. I told you I was on the way. You should have waited."

Ben tried to remember what he'd overheard about Adkin around the department. Nothing came to mind except a few stray references. Adkin, an all-state cornerback in high school who couldn't cut it in college. A stint in the Marines. A sour marriage to a high school sweetheart. A couple of kids. Superior ratings on the pistol range. Adkin, raising and selling pitbulls on the side.

"I went in expecting backup," Ben said. He winced and cradled his throbbing forearm. "You left me hanging. I'm writing this one up."

Adkin dropped the cigarette and stepped on it. "I told you to wait. There was a reason. I need to spell it out for you?" He made a show of incredulously shaking his head.

"Maybe you should."

"It looks," Adkin said after a moment, "that you're a guy bears watching."

"That works both ways," Ben said.

"That's how we're going to play this?"

Ben nodded.

Adkin smiled.

"Ask anyone. I'm a regular guy." Adkin walked over to his cruiser and squatted near the right front fender. "Primary back-up's late on the scene," he said, "all sorts of things could happen to the officer already there. I'd never leave a fellow officer hanging. He's counting on me, right?"

Adkin took out a pocketknife and slid it into the front tire, then worked it around before folding the blade and standing up.

"Still going to write me up, Decovic?" he asked, walking over. "I told you, the call came in and I'm here as soon as I could. My fault, a tire's going flat on me? Thing like that, it could happen to anybody."

"You son of a bitch." Ben gingerly moved his arm. His nerve endings felt like an overturned anthill.

"A flat, something like that, it happens," Adkin said. "Couldn't be helped."

Behind them in the parking lot, Sonny Gramm, the owner of the Passion Palace, circled his ruined Mustang and bellowed, bringing down God's curse on them all.

SIXTEEN

CORRINE TEDROS kept catching red lights. She was on Queensland Avenue, the main east-west artery connecting Route 17 to downtown Magnolia Beach, and no matter how much she adjusted her speed or took the Lexus through lane changes, she ended up beneath a traffic signal stuck on red, her knuckles steadily whitening on the wheel.

Both sides of Queensland were stacked and packed with standard-issue commercial-strip clutter, a free-zone sprawl of fast food chains, car dealerships, mini-malls, grocery stores, and outsized department and hardware stores, the clutter steadily thinning the closer you got to downtown where, like so much else in Magnolia Beach, development was still boom or bust.

Magnolia Beach was like something half-birthed. When Corrine had moved there with Buddy, she had liked that quality. *Half-birthed* was protective coloration. She lived in a place that was simultaneously disappearing and emerging, a place where she was known and not known. A place where the future lunched on its own history.

Outside, the ambient light on Queensland pushed back dusk. Corrine cut to the left and passed a blue and white pickup belching exhaust and whose bed was filled with a half-dozen Mexican day laborers in white T-shirts and black caps. The radio held the local news, most of which was underwritten by the sis-boom-bah boosterism of the city's tourist bureau.

A green Camry with out-of-state plates suddenly pulled into her lane. Corrine hit the brakes. A block later, she caught another red. She listened to a news story about the string of fires that had been appearing around and just inside the city limits. So far they had all been quickly contained, but the Fire Marshall had issued a county-wide burn alert due to the unseasonably high temperatures and critically dry spring. The announcer said there was an ongoing investigation as to the origin of the fires.

Corrine hit the Off button. In the right lane, a man in a dark blue Mercedes convertible pointedly smiled at her. It was seven-thirty.

Buddy and his pals would just be looking at menus, getting ready to order supper.

Supper at the Oyster Emporium followed by a private bachelor party in one of the back rooms at Sonny Gramm's Passion Palace. The groom-to-be, Danny Demiotos; Buddy his best man.

The bride-to-be, Angie Trankopolous, had not asked Corrine to be part of the wedding party.

Corrine got the point. Stanley Tedros was a pal of Angie's father and had tugged on a few strings to make sure Corrine was excluded and to make sure she got the subtext, which was Corrine was not Greek and forever would be on the outside.

Permanently, if Stanley Tedros had his way.

The Demiotos-Trankopolous wedding with all its attendant

preparations and pre- and post-parties would give Stanley added reinforcements for his assault on Corrine's place in Buddy's life and the family.

Buddy was weak. Stanley as much as Corrine understood that. And how to use it.

Over the last few months, Stanley had intensified his habit of cataloging the number of eligible Greek women that Buddy had overlooked in the Magnolia Beach and surrounding areas—*Real women*, he'd said, *with real beauty.* Whenever the opportunity presented itself, Stanley had also launched into a running commentary on any number of local marriages steeped and simmering in long-standing unhappiness or ending like monumental train wrecks, all of which he attributed to the singular folly of a Greek marrying a non-Greek.

So far, Corrine had been able to hold her own, but it hadn't been easy. She knew nothing was foolproof. Stanley might yet still find a way back to Phoenix, Arizona. That prospect had begun nightly to infect Corrine's dreams.

She wished Stanley would die. That would solve everything.

But that was a wish that would forever be a wish. A response to Stanley Tedros' presence in her life that was as puny and ineffectual as her practice of trying to get back at Stanley and his sacrosanct idea of home by buying and changing out furniture that clashed and ruined the atmosphere of the house Stanley had bought Buddy and her in White Pine Manor.

A puny wish that went no further than itself.

Stanley Tedros was eighty-five and looked one-hundred but had the blood pressure, sugar, and cholesterol numbers of a man twenty-five years his junior.

There was a small bottleneck in traffic near the intersection of Danbury and Queensland. Across the street from Corrine a Cinema Fifteen was letting out. Corrine briefly debated pulling in but knew a movie would be nothing more than an avoidance mechanism, a holding action against where she knew she eventually had to go.

She continued down Queensland toward downtown.

Dusk disappeared.

Corrine glanced into the rearview mirror and ran into her mother's eyes.

Her hands tightened on the wheel.

The urge to run, to simply keep driving, overtook her. She would forget Stanley Tedros and Magnolia Beach and just take off. She'd empty her bank account and leave and then offer to divorce Buddy long-distance and no-fault, Stanley only too happy to pay her off, and then like so many other times in her life, Corrine would start over.

A new name and a clean bankrolled break.

Except.

And it was a big *except,* one which wouldn't let go of her or, finally, her of it.

In its center was James Restan and his buy-out offer for rights to Julep.

All Corrine had to do was shelve her second thoughts and drive east on Queensland to downtown Magnolia Beach and the ATM at the Maritime Bank and Trust and withdraw the last installment for the front money that would set everything in motion for Stanley's death.

All she had to do was not be her mother.

Her mother had the looks but never knew what to do with them except try to live in them, and that she had done badly.

Episodes, that's what Corrine's mother had called those times when she simply dropped out of sight and out of their life. She might disappear for an afternoon or a day or weekend. Maybe a week, sometimes a month and change. One day Corrine's mother was there. Then she wasn't. When she eventually returned, she always brought Corrine presents—lots of them. And usually had in tow a new boyfriend or husband. It was often difficult to tell the two apart.

There was no pattern to her mother's episodes. No early warning signs.

Her mother had episodes, and she collected husbands and boyfriends, and then as a makeshift family, they moved around the country. Like the episodes, there was no clear pattern to the moves. Instead, an emotional vertigo and a vague whim that broke down or disappeared before it could become a real promise or plan.

Corrine remembered standing in the bedroom of an apartment in Biloxi, Mississippi. It was July, and she was eleven. Her mother was sitting and facing her vanity mirror and brushing her hair. Corrine was behind her, looking over her mother's shoulder, and she could still remember the crackle of the static electricity and how it lifted her mother's hair with each stroke. Corrine remembered too looking into the mirror and meeting her mother's gaze. Their eyes were interchangeable, exactly the same shape and shade of gray.

I'm scared sometimes, her mother had said when Corrine had asked about her disappearances. Corrine had waited for her mother explain why or of what, but her mother went no further than that. Later, she took Corrine to the mall and bought her a thin gold bracelet with her initials engraved inside, and then they'd stopped at the food court and each had a chocolate sundae.

A year later, her mother and new husband named Kelly had dropped Corrine off at Corrine's grandparents' house in Bradford, Indiana, a small town north of Gary.

Her mother and Kelly drove off in a blue Thunderbird. It was the last time Corrine saw her.

Corrine sat through one last red light and then took Queensland through old downtown Magnolia Beach past the town square that doubled as a small park with its gravel pathways, gazebo, granite war memorial, and central fountain surrounded by thick-trunked trees whose leaves appeared painted on the evening sky.

Corrine drove through five blocks of cheek-to-jowl red and brown brick buildings, mostly two or three stories, caught in a stalemate between gentrification and neglect, boarded-up or empty storefronts alternating with trendy coffee shops and law offices and specialty boutiques.

Queensland eventually T-boned with Atlantic Avenue, the north-south commercial strip that roughly paralleled the beach. Corrine took a right and drove three blocks. She pulled into the lot of the Maritime Bank and Trust.

I get scared sometimes, Corrine's mother had said.

Corrine couldn't afford that luxury.

At the ATM, she withdrew the last installment of the front money she would pass on to Raychard Balen. Corrine had taken pains not to draw attention with her transactions, carefully spacing each out, everything a matter of time.

She'd call Raychard Balen tomorrow morning and give him the final go-ahead.

Then she could literally begin to number Stanley Tedros's days, the phone call making it real again, Stanley Tedros's death now clearly on the horizon, positioned and in place like the morning star, something not so much to wish upon anymore but to navigate by.

SEVENTEEN

BEN DECOVIC responded to a domestic disturbance in northeast Magnolia Beach, a couple who'd taken their late-night argument from the kitchen out into their front yard where in addition to an operatic display of obscenities, they had begun flinging pieces of the Colonel's extra-crispy at each other, each with a full bucket tucked under his or her arm and a seemingly inexhaustible set of grievances, Ben finally able to calm them down, surrounded the whole time by neighborhood dogs combing the front yard for stray drumsticks and wings.

He swung by Miriam Holmes' and reassured her with an all's-right-in-the-world check-in and left with his obligatory piece of pound cake.

He broke up the knot of teenage boys loitering and working on their best impersonation of disaffected gangbangers in the parking lot of a Taco Bell after the manager called in the complaint that the crescendo of competing bass lines from their car stereos was drowning out customer orders at the drive-thru window.

A half hour later, he raced to the residence of a panicked single mother with a break and enter in progress only to discover that it was one of the wannabes from Taco Bell attempting to sneak in after curfew.

He handed out two DUIs. He shut down an impromptu electronics shop run out of the trunk of a rust-eaten Buick. He assisted a Statie at the scene of an accident, directing traffic until the ambulance and wrecker arrived.

He ran paper on three missing or stolen property stops.

He drove through an hour and forty-five minutes of nothing, his patrol sector gone eerily quiet, the world on hold.

Throughout the shift, Ben kept his eyes open, hoping to spot either of the two guys from the Passion Palace. It was going on four days since he'd been attacked, and it wouldn't be unusual for them to still be in the area. Most criminals, outside the pros, were stupid or vain or arrogant enough to trip themselves up, given half a chance.

The vanity, though, cut both ways, and Ben didn't like to admit it, but he'd been more embarrassed than angry that the guy who'd ambushed him had gotten away with his service pistol. The post-shift session with La'Shawn Samuels, his supervisor, had done nothing to improve his mood either. Ben had decided not to mention the incident with Carl Adkin. He didn't want to push things just yet. La'Shawn Samuels had let Ben off with a verbal reprimand about going in solo and too soon.

For a while, Ben worked on reconstructing the image of the man who'd assaulted him in the parking lot, but hard as he tried, the results were unruly. He could not bring an impression into focus. In the moment he'd pulled the Kermit the Frog mask loose, Ben thought he'd seen gray hair and a blue or green eye and square chin. The flesh tones of the face, however, had seemed to belong to someone much younger. He was sure the man had been short, but his arms had seemed out of proportion to his height. The problem was the whole thing happened too quickly in light that was bad to begin with, and the longer Ben attempted to coax out the image, the more the man began to resemble others that Ben had rousted or arrested in the past, the car slowly filling with jailhouse ghosts. When Greg Hollinger threatened to appear, bringing with him everything that had led to Ben's resignation from the Homicide squad and the move to Magnolia Beach, Ben dropped the whole thing and concentrated on the job. He ran the routine and tried to keep things simple.

Near dawn, he pulled into a twenty-four hour convenience mart and parked at the far end of the lot and went in for a soda, nodding to the clerk and heading to the rear of the store. Near the cooler was a large placard of Stanley Tedros holding up a can of Julep with the slogan *You Know It!* emblazoned across its top.

Leon Douglas was sitting in the front seat of the cruiser when he got back.

"You late," he said. "And you forgot to lock the door."

Ben handed him the soda and a palm-sized bag of Skittles. "These ok," Leon said, tearing into the bag with his teeth, "but Shock Tarts, they the one I like best."

"I'll keep that in mind," Ben said.

Leon Douglas had started working on his credentials as a renaissance man of misdemeanors in his early teens, and even with the juvie records eventually being sealed, he managed to add a couple pages to his resume before he turned sixteen. Last November, Ben had busted Leon boosting a late-model Explorer destined for a chop shop in Charleston, and facing an entry-level look at some serious time, Leon had offered a deal and said he'd work for Ben.

Ben was under no illusions that Leon wasn't still working his own action, but Leon's news was almost always solid. Unlike a lot of other informants Ben had worked with, Leon did not pad out the inconsequential to look good or attempt to deliver last week's weather as tomorrow's forecast.

"I've been expecting a phone call," Ben said.

"No sign of your Glock," Leon said. "Someone either be sitting on it or already move it out the state."

"Anything you turn up," Ben said, "you call me. No waiting until the usual meet. I want that pistol."

Leon nodded and thumbed a yellow Skittle into his mouth.

"Ok." Ben drummed his fingertips on top of the steering wheel. "Say I'm in the market for a few copies of *The Annihilator*."

"*Annihilator One* or *Two*?" Leon asked.

"*Annihilator Two*. And let's also say I might be interested in *Death Squad Three, Hotel Torture, End of Sleep,* and *Sing Me A Nightmare*."

"How many you looking at?"

"Roughly four hundred or five hundred of each."

"You might be wanting to talk to Robbie then," Leon said. "The flea market, Section D, Row Five. Robbie's the one got himself one of those Fu Manchu mustaches."

"He's not trying to move that kind of volume through the flea market, is he? He can't be that stupid." Ben looked over at Leon. "Or lucky. Somebody would have busted him by now for sure."

Leon shook out another Skittle and held it up between thumb and index finger before popping it in his mouth. He went on to explain that Robbie with the Fu Manchu was the go-to guy and that if anyone wanted bootleg video games, CDs, or DVDs, Robbie would put him in touch with Tommy, his brother, who rented any number of empty buildings around town and kept the inventory moving among them.

"Ok, then," Ben said. "The fires that have been springing up. Anything?" At last count there'd been nine, all contained with minimal damage, but no pattern in the intervals between occurrence or location.

Leon took a hit of soda, then shook his head. "Figured you be asking about that and I check around, but I'm not hearing anything about any Match Artists in town."

Ben gave in to a long yawn. To the east, the skyline was edged in a pale yellow line. A warm wind rose and sent a Styrofoam cup bouncing across the lot.

"What about Sonny Gramm's Mustang?" Ben asked finally. "You hear anything about why someone went after it in the first place? Gramm wasn't exactly helpful when we interviewed him."

Leon crumbled the candy bag and stuck it in his shirt pocket. "What I hear is Mr. Sonny Gramm been talking to some of the brothers." Leon paused and shook his head. "And everyone know Mr. Sonny never be a big fan of Dr. King."

"Why then?"

"He looking for a new bodyguard," Leon said, "but no brother want to work for no crazy white man." Leon finished off the soda and set it on the dash. "Mr. Sonny get scared, he have himself a few drinks. Or Mr. Sonny decide to have a few drinks, and then he get scared. Either way he end up crazy and mean."

"What's Gramm scared of?"

Leon shrugged.

"Ok," Ben said. He took a folded bill from his breast pocket and handed it to Leon. "I appreciate the news. You take care of yourself."

Leon hesitated, folding the bill another time before slipping it into his pocket. He glanced over at Ben. "You don't mind me saying, you need to do that too. It showing, man."

"It?" Ben said. "What?"

"Whatever you chasing or whatever chasing you." Leon opened the door, got out, and then poked his head back inside. "It showing, man."

Leon stepped back, waved, and disappeared around the back of the convenience store. Ben cranked the blue and white and pulled out of the lot and headed back to the City-County Complex.

Against the dawn, the downtown skyline of Magnolia Beach looked as if it had just caught fire.

As Ben drove past, he noticed a side door at the Passion Palace was open and flapping back and forth in the wind.

An old red pickup listing on the driver's side from worn shocks was parked alongside the Palace's north wall.

Ben got out of the cruiser and checked the door, poking his head inside the frame, calling out Sonny Gramm's name and identifying himself.

The chairs were up on the tables and the lighting minimal. The place shared in the same forlorn quality of any bar after closing. The floor was damp, and the smell of disinfectant hovered like a layer of ground fog.

Ben thought he heard a noise coming from the other side of the room. He called out Sonny Gramm's name again.

He unsnapped his holster and started to draw his pistol, but someone had already placed the barrel of a gun against his spine.

"Face forward," he said. "Hands where I can see them."

Ben recognized the voice as Sonny Gramm's and identified himself.

Gramm prodded him across the floor and through the office door. "Take off your badge and set it on the desk and then do the same with the pistol."

Ben did what he asked about the badge but refused to surrender the Glock. He said he'd already lost one semi-automatic at the Palace and wasn't about to let that happen again.

"Fuck it," Gramm said. "Lower yourself, and I mean slowly, into that chair and sit on your hands."

Gramm was slurring his words and seemed none too steady on his feet. He waited for Ben to sit and then moved behind the desk, whose top held an open newspaper, an ashtray, a bottle of Beam, and a smudged glass tumbler.

Sonny Gramm picked up Ben's badge.

"Give me your number."

Ben did.

"Ok, but that doesn't necessarily prove anything. Anyone can memorize a number." Gramm dropped the badge, sat down, and a moment later, poured himself a drink. His hands were slow-dancing, and the bottle rattled against the lip of the glass.

The office was small and windowless, its walls covered in cheap imitation pine paneling and holding black and white publicity shots of some of the Palace's strippers, one of Sonny Gramm's boat, another of the vintage Mustang that had been vandalized, and one that must have been taken at a family reunion, a group shot under a large live oak, many of the men sharing Sonny's squint and high-rise pompadour. Directly behind and above Sonny was a faded Confederate flag thumbtacked to the wall.

"How'd you get in here?" Gramm asked.

"I'm on the job. I was checking up. The side door on the north side of the building was open. I identified myself before I came in."

"That door was locked. I checked it myself, not more than a half hour ago."

Ben spoke quietly, reiterating the sequence of events, wary of the level of Beam in Sonny's mood, the early morning hour, and the gun he kept, more or less, trained on him.

When Gramm squinted, his face broke into competing networks of wrinkles. "I checked it," he said. "I'm sure I did. It was right after I had to fire that bastard Melvin for showing up late." He looked over at Ben. "What good's a bodyguard who doesn't show up on time? Tell me that." Gramm closed his eyes for a moment and rubbed at his forehead as if he'd forgotten Ben was there.

Ben cleared his throat. "I work Patrol, Mr. Gramm. The Palace is in my sector. I was one of the officers responding the night your Mustang was vandalized."

Gramm coughed into his fist.

"It won't stop with the Mustang," he said. "But you already know that, don't you?"

"No," Ben said, "I don't."

"I can take care of myself," Gramm said. "You tell Wayne LaVell that. Or that shyster, Balen, who's fronting for him. Whichever one of them sent you."

"I don't know a LaVell or Balen," Ben said. "And I'm an officer of the law, Mr. Gramm. You have my badge in front of you."

"You shake hands with either LaVell or Balen," Gramm said, "you better count your fingers afterwards."

Gramm tipped back the glass and then wiped his hand across his mouth. "LaVell will have all of you in his pocket soon enough. He's already working on the mayor."

Gramm suddenly slammed the top of the desk. "Maybe you don't think much of me. I'm just a guy owns two titty bars, a few restaurants, a little land. I've made some money over the years, maybe not so much as some, but I've always paid my own way."

Gramm paused, eyed the bottle of Beam, poured another drink, but left it sitting at his elbow. "Let me ask you something. Is it wrong for a man to want to hold on to what is his? Or you one of those who believe everything has a price tag?"

"No," Ben said. He started trying to work his right hand out from under his leg and flex some life back into his fingers.

"A man can't call himself anything unless he's got some claims on him," Gramm said. "No different for a woman either. Or for that matter, a country. You got to answer to something bigger than you or you're nothing."

He picked up Ben's badge, looked at it, then tossed it in Ben's lap.

"Get out of here," he said. "I don't need your kind of help."

Ben slowly got up from the chair.

Gramm lifted the tumbler and rested it for a moment against his forehead.

"Make sure you lock that door on the way out," he said.

EIGHTEEN

IF THE UNITED STATES COAST GUARD had not dropped the Beretta M9 Semi-automatic as its standard-issue firearm and gone on to adopt the Sig Sauer P229 .40 Caliber, Ben Decovic's wife might yet still be alive and not forever bleeding out in the parking lot of Central Dry Cleaners in Ryland, Ohio, and he would not be sitting in St. Katherine's in Magnolia Beach, South Carolina on an empty Saturday night, afraid to go back to his apartment and five rooms of blunt-edged insomnia.

But the layered quiet that, if he was lucky, approximated a temporary respite, had gotten away from him a few moments after he sat down in the nave.

Ben had not expected the perfume.

At first he thought he was imagining it, and then got caught up in wondering if it was actually possible to imagine a smell, but it lingered, persistent, refusing to go away.

Ben recognized the smell. In their bedroom, it had ghosted his wife's pillow, and he had found it most times he'd leaned in and kissed her neck. It had been his wife's favorite perfume, the one she'd worn most frequently, and someone sitting in the nave earlier in the evening had been wearing it too.

He closed his eyes for a moment.

Ben tried to summon the name of the perfume but failed.

That wasn't the case with the other names that followed him around. Ben would never forget who they belonged to or their addresses or what their owners had done for a living or, finally, the order in which they'd died.

The black-market Baretta that Greg Hollinger eventually ended up with had been traced back to Orlando, one of a dozen pieces missing and unaccounted for at the Coast Guard Amory after inventory when the new Sig Sauers were issued.

Fourteen months ago, on one of those clear, achingly cold January afternoons that only the Midwest can produce, Greg Hollinger finished his shift at Assurance Plus, a health insurance company where he worked as a claims processor, and made five stops, shooting someone at each, before driving home, parking in his driveway, and then putting one carefully placed bullet in his own head.

Greg Hollinger did not leave a note. He did not maintain a blog or personal website. He did not leave an angry explanatory videotape or DVD. He did not have a Facebook account. His parents were dead. He had no siblings or close relatives. He had never been arrested. He had not served in the military. He had never been married nor had anyone in his life who could even remotely be seen as a girlfriend or significant other. He was a good student, but one who never generated an impression beyond well-mannered, studious, and quiet. He did not belong to a church or any professional organizations. He had no known ties to extremist or hate groups. He had no one inside or outside of work who qualified as a friend. His neighbors gave the customary scripted answers when interviewed by the media: *Greg Hollinger kept to himself. He wasn't exactly unfriendly, just quiet. A nice young man. Who would have thought.*

On the first stop, Greg Hollinger shot Karl Metz, a line supervisor at the county recycling plant.

On the second, he shot Suzanne Raschella, an elementary school teacher.

On the third, George Gearhart, a bartender.

The fourth, Thomas Linnet, a CPA.

And the fifth, Diane Decovic, a veterinarian.

A Beretta M9 held fifteen to a clip. Karl Metz was a large man and had taken two to finish off. Everyone else took one. That left eight in the clip after Hollinger took himself out and no clear reason why those eight were left unfired.

There was no clear reason to anything connected to Greg Hollinger. His life was a null set, Greg Hollinger himself a rock that when overturned revealed another rock. He was an absolute cipher. The snake swallowing its own tail.

Ben Decovic wanted clear reasons. His career and reputation had been built on them. He had the eye and instinct at a crime scene or witness interview. He believed in motive. A motive was ultimately something as basic and fundamental as a pulse. Ben knew if he looked long enough he'd find one.

He'd believed that until Greg Hollinger had shown him otherwise.

In the nave pew, Ben lifted his hand.

Jesus.

His face was wet.

Five more names crowded in.

They were names as ephemeral as the lingering scent of the woman's perfume and as holy in their own way as any of the icons or frescoes crowding Ben in St. Katherine's.

Nicholas. Meredith. Andrew. Laura. Emily.

Diane and he had done the math, looked at both sides of their families and calculated the odds of them having a girl or boy and had come up with three to two. The names had quickly followed, possibilities waiting for Diane and Ben to breathe life into them.

All that was before Greg Hollinger.

The names had become envelopes, stamped and addressed, but forever empty of the letters they were supposed to hold.

And Ben was left with what Greg Hollinger and his black-market Beretta M9 had shown and not shown him.

Nothing more. Nothing less.

NINETEEN

MID-MARCH and Corrine Tedros had her killer.

Three days ago, she'd driven to Raychard Balen's office in Conway and sat across the table in the conference room with a man named Croy Wendall.

Even if Raychard Balen had not insisted that Corrine, Croy, and he meet face-to-face, emphasizing his one-sin-fits-all policy by keeping each of them equally implicated and making sure Corrine understood her money had bought a killing but not full immunity, Corrine Tedros would have shown up anyway.

She wanted the opportunity to meet the last person Stanley Tedros would ever see on earth.

At first, she had not been able to fully hide her disappointment. Perhaps it was too many movies, she thought, too many stylized renditions of hit men, all dark tailored suits and icy souls and practiced ease with weapons, or the other side of the killing coin, the garden-variety psychos, all devil tattoos and stringy hair and rock-and-roll mayhem.

Corrine had been expecting something other than a Croy Wendall.

There was a blank quality about him, the suggestion that something fundamental was missing or irretrievable. He was short and thick-shouldered with a boyish face whose features were slightly flattened, and his hair was prematurely gray. He had a child's small, tightly-spaced teeth and milky green eyes. He'd sat impassively, hands folded in his lap, while Corrine had gone over the details for Stanley's murder. At Balen's, then her, request, Croy had repeated Corrine's instructions about the murder, but he spoke slowly and gave back what she'd said without any inflection whatsoever. It was as if language had nothing to do with where he lived.

At the end of the meeting, Croy had pocketed the envelope with half his fee up front and then asked Corrine if she wanted Stanley killed with a knife or gun.

Once she'd set Croy Wendall loose on Stanley, Corrine had started building her alibi, which was how she'd come to be sitting next to Terri Iles at the mall cineplex in Magnolia Beach watching *Any Day Now* during the heart of a Saturday afternoon.

Corrine knew Stanley was a man of ingrained habits and routines. He worked a half-day each Saturday, returning home to fix and eat lunch, head upstairs for a short nap, and then take his boat out for a little fishing before returning home to watch a couple pre-dinner segments of the History Channel. Afterward, one of Stanley's Greek cronies came over for an evening of drinking ouzo, listening to music, and playing gin rummy.

Croy Wendall was going to drop into the middle of Stanley's Saturday routine. He'd make it look like a home invasion, a simple burglary gone awry when Stanley, awakening from his nap, supposedly surprised and panicked the intruder.

Corrine's husband, Buddy, would be occupied by having to dutifully squire a foursome through eighteen holes at the country club. They were some suits from Wachovia Bank that Stanley was courting to help finance his plans to expand the distribution lines for Julep.

Corrine, for her part, settled on Terri Iles. Terri was the wife of one of the regional sales managers at Stanco Beverages, and Corrine had always found her company insufferable, but Terri could be counted on to make her presence known, and thus remembered, wherever she went. She wore too many tanning bed sessions and her hair short and dyed a citrus-yellow, had outsized ambitions for her husband and was forever talking about the "richness" of life and "bonding" opportunities, and tried to dress like someone twenty years her junior. She never stopped talking and was sure that everyone in the vicinity was interested in her observations, most of which were fourth-rate truths culled from fifth-rate self-esteem gurus on obscure cable channels.

An afternoon of clothes-shopping, some woman-to-woman bonding over yogurt and decaf, and a matinee at the mall cineplex. A long trail of witnesses and time accounted for.

Any Day Now was one of those earnestly heartfelt dramas about the joys and tribulations of being a single parent, the blonde female lead in her late twenties, perky and resolute and engagingly quirky, forced to work at a job for which she was overqualified in order to make sure her standardly winsome and precocious little girl had everything she needed to stay winsome and precocious. There was lots of coping as well as tender mother-daughter moments while the lead fended off advances from a variety of ill-suited men until she inevitably found one who appreciated her for who she was and who just happened to want to spend the rest of his life helping raise a standardly winsome and precocious six-year-old step-daughter.

Needless to say, Terri Iles loved it.

The film, though, unearthed a core of resentment in Corrine that she had worked hard to keep buried. On more than one occasion, after Terri had leaned over to whisper her appreciation of a scene, Corrine had wanted to slap her and then tell her what a place like Bradford, Indiana did to the childhoods of winsome and precocious little girls who'd been dumped on their grandparents by a part-time mother and her approximate husband as they put one of those precocious and winsome little girls in their rearview mirror once and for all. And then slap her once again and tell her what those winsome and precocious little girls had to do later to get out of places like Bradford so that they could eventually end up sitting in a theatre on a Saturday afternoon with a pampered, self-absorbed bitch watching a movie that celebrated the richness of life and family.

Instead, Corrine surreptitiously lifted her arm to check her watch.

Stanley would be just settling in for his nap around now.

Corrine sat in the dark next to Terri and thought about what she was going to wear to Stanley's funeral.

TWENTY

JACK CARSON looked into the next room where a girl in a green T-shirt did her homework at the kitchen table, and then he got up from his recliner and turned off the television and in the ensuing silence began to move through the rooms of his house. Something tugged at him, but it was as if he were caught in a tedious game of hide-n-seek, and Jack moved haltingly, slower and more deliberately than whatever was tugging at him demanded, and he'd find himself standing in front of the refrigerator, and he would suddenly pause as if he'd heard a sound he couldn't identify, and he would try to chase it down, only to find himself in his daughter's bedroom standing over a stack of library books piled on her nightstand, and when he picked up the top one and opened its back cover, the due date made no sense, the year off, some kind of mistake, and then he realized he hadn't put on his shoes and he needed them for what he had to do, and he started down the hallway and moved to the bathroom and brushed his teeth, and the sound of the water pouring from the faucet was like an urgent whisper telling him he needed to hurry, and he moved back into the living room and turned on the television, and he listened to a man in a blue suit gravely explain that two new fires had started in west Magnolia Beach, and then Jack saw the note taped to the front door. He looked over toward the girl at the kitchen table. She looked back at him.

The note was from someone named Anne who'd written she'd be back in two hours, and underneath in all caps was: STAY IN THE HOUSE. GO BACK AND SIT IN YOUR CHAIR, DAD. PAIGE WILL FIX YOU A SNACK.

Jack turned the knob. The door was locked.

He walked back into the kitchen. He looked for the girl, but she was gone and so was the homework. Behind him he heard the man's voice talking about the fires and saying there were no suspects and that three fire units were trying to get the fires under control and reminding everyone of the burn alert.

Jack started down the hall, and then he found his shoes and put them on, and the house suddenly went quiet, and when he walked into the kitchen there was a sandwich on a white plate sitting in the middle of the table, and then Jack heard a noise, one small and compact, like loose change in a pocket, and he crossed into the living room where the television was on but with the volume turned low as a pulse, and on the screen, a car raced across a flat summer landscape at dawn, and then Jack stepped over to the front door and turned the knob, and the door opened and the screened one after it, and he walked out onto the porch and then down the stairs and across the front lawn.

After Jack made the street, he turned left.

The sky was pale, the wind dry. Jack walked past a woman planting flowers. Next to her were two flats of orange marigolds.

Small puffs of dust appeared each time she jabbed the hand trowel into the earth.

Jack's shoes were rubbing on his heels, and he stopped to retie the laces. He heard a dog barking in the distance.

The kitchen calendar had said March, but nothing around him resembled it.

He started walking again. The wind in the trees sounded like teeth chattering.

He walked some more, and then he stopped. He hadn't been paying attention and must have gotten turned around. He was standing across from a Burger King, and he could smell meat frying.

Jack took out a bandana and wiped his forehead and wished he'd remembered to put on his cap.

He wondered why he'd decided to walk to Burger King. He didn't even like Burger King. He wasn't hungry either.

He started walking again. After a while, he ran into a large green and white sign that read: *Thank you for visiting Magnolia Beach. Come back soon.*

The sign made no sense. He lived in Myrtle Beach, not Magnolia Beach, with his wife Carol. They were expecting their first child in two months.

She was a good woman, Carol was.

He loved her more than breath.

He didn't want her to worry, but he knew they were in trouble.

A tight spot, for sure. A child on the way and the Myrtle Beach he'd grown up in disappearing right in front of him. It was no longer the small sleepy tourist town full of family-owned and run businesses, a place where someone like Jack Carson could start his own construction company and count on his reputation for doing quality work to bring in the jobs. It had been like that when he first started Carson Construction, but there was a new ethos at work now, housing developments springing up all over, national hotel, restaurant, and shopping chains moving in, the promise of money everywhere, and Jack was finding it harder and harder to compete with the big construction outfits. They used cheaper materials, bought them in larger quantities and for bigger discounts from wholesalers, paid more and had better benefit packages for the crews, and met deadlines more quickly than Carson Construction. The owners and managers of the large outfits had also quickly figured out whom they needed to buy off to expedite processing and approving permits and inspections.

The air smelled like car exhaust, and the feeling arose again that something was tugging at him. Jack looked at the sign once more and then turned around and started walking.

He was a little dizzy. The joints in his knees felt like they were packed with sand.

The sky was white, as if it had been bleached.

He heard a dog barking and then a lawnmower start up.

He walked by a large wooden house in need of paint. There were mold streaks along the eaves and around the windows.

A while later, when he walked past the house again, he pushed down the panic opening like a hand inside him and tried to walk faster.

He'd just remembered his wife Carol had died giving birth to their daughter Anne.

He wiped his face with a bandana. He had trouble getting the bandana back in his pocket.

The air felt baked.

Then suddenly he was surrounded by four boys on bicycles. Jack wasn't sure where they'd come from. They circled him like lazy bees.

The boys looked to be around eight or nine, and they all had buzz cuts, and they were all wearing green T-shirts with X-Men on the fronts, and Jack wasn't sure which one of them said, "You got any change, Mister? We're really thirsty."

Jack was thirsty too. He'd just realized that.

One of the boys said, "Forget it, Brian. That's Paige's grandpa. She said he's a head case."

Another said, "Paige Carson is a bitch."

"He walks funny," another one said.

"My dad says he's the one who got lost driving a bus with all the kids still in it."

"Ask him what day it is," one said. "I'll bet you a quarter he can't tell you."

The boys kept circling on their bikes and firing questions, and a lot of the questions were simple, and when Jack answered them, he couldn't understand why the boys laughed, and then he was getting angry and was going to tell them to stop, but before he could, they were gone as suddenly as they'd appeared.

And then Jack was very tired and a little afraid because he'd begun to suspect that a lot of what he'd set out to do this afternoon had already happened.

He suddenly knew, for example, that he didn't live in Myrtle Beach anymore and hadn't for over ten years.

He wanted to get home, but he was afraid of getting confused again, so he told himself to watch the telephone wires and follow them. The telephone wires were like lines on a blueprint, and he'd always been good at reading blueprints.

He told himself to hurry.

He tried to remember if his shadow had been falling in front of or behind him.

He was very thirsty.

He needed to get home.

The light looked different. There was less of it than he remembered.

He decided to take a shortcut and left the street and started following the shoreline of the inlet in North Shore.

Off to his right, three gray and white pelicans skimmed, circled, and dropped straight down into the inlet, breaking the water like divers. Farther out, five small boats trolled, running in wide figure-eights. Beyond them was the east shore of the inlet, and beyond that the Atlantic.

Just ahead, atop a long sloping backyard was a large two-and-a-half-story house planked in weathered pine.

Jack recognized it. It was Stanley Tedros's place. Jack had done work on the house. They were neighbors. Jack lived less than a half-mile away.

Stanley would give him a glass of water, and then Jack would walk home. Everything was all right.

The ground rose at a steep angle from where it met the water, and the lot next to Stanley's backyard was wild and overgrown. Jack slowly picked his way up the slope. He was conscious of the light leaving the afternoon.

There was the sound of a boat approaching, its outboard throttling back to a low rumble.

There was wisteria growing everywhere, matting the ground, grabbing his shoes, wrapping around the trunks of the live oaks and magnolias and pines. It was like a huge spiderweb.

The motor on the outboard trailed off and died.

He cut left, then right, then left again, slowly working his way through the overgrowth across the lot toward Stanley's house. His calves and lungs burned.

Below and to his right were a small dock and boathouse. Stanley Tedros tied up his boat and began unloading his fishing gear.

Jack ran into a wall of holly. When he tried to push through, the leaves sliced at his hands and forearms. The pain was sharp and surprising, like paper cuts. Jack backed off and moved to his right.

He stumbled, then stopped next to some crepe myrtles to catch his breath.

There were long shadows on Stanley's lawn.

Stanley Tedros began walking up from the dock.

Jack told himself to move, but he couldn't. His legs were trembling.

Someone called out Stanley's name, and Jack was pretty sure it wasn't him.

Stanley stopped in the middle of the yard and lifted his hand to shield his eyes. He looked toward the back of the house.

A glass of water.

Jack would feel better after that.

His breath was still high and fast in his chest, so he stood very still at the edge of the overgrown lot and waited for his legs to return, and he watched a short man with short gray hair walk down the lawn toward Stanley.

TWENTY-ONE

CROY WENDALL WAS LATE, and it seemed like everything in the universe was trying to remind him of that. The dashboard clock in the car. The sign flashing the time and temperature at Nation's Bank. His wristwatch. His pulse. The afternoon sun, itself, in the slant of its light.

Nothing in his day so far though had gone right. First off, at breakfast, Missy had finished the box of Lucky Charms, and Croy had to settle for Shredded Wheat. Then Jamie had wanted to go talk to Mr. Balen about doing some more crimes to Mr. Sonny Gramm. Jamie had already spent his share of the money they got for smashing up the Mustang, and he needed some more. Croy had to put Jamie off on account of he was already doing a job for Mr. Balen and Miss Corrine by killing the old man, but Croy couldn't tell Jamie that because he promised Mr. Balen he wouldn't. Mr. Balen didn't want Jamie helping on the killing because Jamie had never killed anyone. Mr. Balen said in matters like this, experience counted.

When Croy had said he couldn't go with Jamie to see Mr. Balen, Jamie had wanted to know what Croy was going to do instead, and Croy wouldn't tell him, and that made Jamie even more insistent about finding out about Croy's plans, and Croy had to keep coming up with things to change the subject. After a while, Jamie drank some beer for lunch and went and watched some HBO in the living room.

Throughout it all, Croy hadn't been paying attention to the time. He'd gone back to his own room, and as periodically happened, he wondered if it had been such a good idea to move in with Jamie and Missy in the first place. He paid his share of the rent, which Jamie had worked out one time based on the square feet in Croy's room and of the number of square feet Croy generally took up in the other rooms of the house when he was in them.

Croy had met Jamie when they were both working temporary and off-the-books for a landscaping service, and he hadn't minded getting to be friends and doing some crimes together, but he'd never been fully comfortable with the living arrangements. The house was small, and Missy, who was Jamie's common-law wife, was always around and wore these little nighties instead of normal clothes, and she would often come into Croy's room without knocking until he finally had to put in a new lock.

After Croy had gotten away from Jamie and all his questions, he sat in his room and went over in his head what Miss Corrine had told him about killing Stanley Tedros. He did that five times. Then he checked his watch. It had been almost noon. Croy wasn't hungry, so he took a chair and moved it to the window and looked at the sky and imagined it looking back at him. Then he looked at the backyard and watched one of the neighborhood cats stalk a robin.

The problem was, when Croy got around to checking his watch again, he discovered it had stopped and that it was still almost noon.

So Croy got in his car and drove as fast as he dared. Whenever he was in situations that left him uneasy or agitated, he'd do the numbers or a rhyme in his head. Sometimes he'd find a way to do both.

This afternoon he tried thinking about how *time* rhymed with *crime,* which was what he was driving to do, and then he thought about *ides,* which was what the calendar said the day was, and then Croy thought about *four,* which was the number of the letters in *ides. Four* also had four letters, which made them like the skin of the number, and *skin* had four letters, and so did *Croy,* and then he started thinking about *ides* again and the word *dies* that lived inside it.

He got to North Shore and parked the car in the spot Miss Corrine told him to, and then he walked around to the back of Stanley Tedros's house and broke in.

The place was dark and high-ceilinged and had an old people's smell to it. Croy circled the living room a couple times, then veered off to the kitchen where he discovered the remnants of Stanley's lunch on the counter, and remembering what Miss Corrine had said about Stanley's routine, Croy climbed the stairs and hunted down the master bedroom. The digital alarm clock flashed the message that he was over two hours late for killing Stanley during his nap.

He went back downstairs again and looked for something to steal. That's what he was supposed to do, make the whole thing look like a burglary that got messed up, but Croy didn't see anything. Everything in the place had the feel of being handled past the point of any fence's or pawnshop's interest.

Croy had seen the billboards for Julep and the cut-out placards of Stanley at convenience stores, and he'd figured a man like Stanley Tedros would be living like a king and had even come to think of him that way, as King Stanley, and Croy didn't know what to think about the old house and its dark, worn furniture. He thought there would be swords and tapestries on the walls and a banquet hall and dungeon.

Every time he came across a clock, Croy changed it to a number he was thinking of.

He spent a while looking for hidden panels that led to secret rooms full of untold treasure.

Then he went out to the kitchen and made a sandwich.

Eating with latex gloves on gave the bread a funny taste even though Croy was careful to keep his fingers away from his lips. He poured a glass of milk and finished it in two swallows. Then he washed everything up in the sink.

He sat in an old chair next to a record player on a table.

Croy suddenly remembered he'd left his gun in the glove compartment. He looked at his dead watch. He wondered if he could run back and get the gun in time to shoot Stanley Tedros.

He heard the sound of an outboard motor.

Croy moved to the back door.

An old man in a boat edged up to the dock.

Croy stood at the door and went over in his head what Miss Corrine had told him to do until he could see it happening, except he'd forgotten the gun in the car, and that changed some things, and then Croy was getting jumpy because what he could see happening in his head couldn't happen now because it was supposed to be happening when Miss Corrine had told him to do it, and Croy's hands got very wet inside the gloves while he tried to make the two times fit what he was seeing in his head, but everything was mixed together now, and finally Croy quit trying to unmix them and just opened the back door and started down the lawn.

As he walked, Croy called out Stanley's name and pulled out a gray tube sock he'd tied to one of the belt loops on his pants.

Croy called the name again, and Stanley stopped and lifted his hand to his eyes.

Then Croy stepped up and hit him with the sockful of heavy-gauge washers. Stanley turned at the last moment though, and Croy hit him in the shoulder instead of the head.

Then Stanley swung back and hit Croy with the stringer of fish Croy hadn't noticed he was carrying.

Croy could smell the fish on his cheeks, and the skin underneath his left eyes was stinging from where one of the fins had cut him.

Stanley swung the fish again. It felt like Croy was getting slapped by three pairs of hands at the same time.

He dropped the sock and took out his knife.

Stanley had a bunch of brightly colored lures attached to his vest, and after Croy knocked him to the ground, he was careful not to catch his gloves on them when he tore open the vest and started stabbing Stanley in the stomach.

He wasn't sure exactly how much noise Stanley made because Croy was doing a rhyme in his head while he stabbed him.

After a while, his arm got tired, so he stopped.

Croy rocked back on his heels.

Some of the washers had spilled out of the tube sock where he'd dropped it, and Croy started gathering them up, but then he remembered his knife was still inside Stanley. His arm had been so tired he'd let go of it without thinking.

Croy leaned back over and started rummaging around Stanley's insides. His fingers were slippery and made a lot of sounds like rubber boots stuck in mud.

It took a long time to find the knife.

Just as he was about to straighten up, Croy noticed the thin, shiny chain spilling from Stanley's pocket, and he wrapped it around his index finger and pulled, and a gold pocketwatch followed.

Some blood had gotten on it. Croy wiped it off and put the pocketwatch in his pocket. He liked the idea that its name matched where you were supposed to put it.

Two egrets landed on the dock and moved in little circles on the planking. There were shadows on the lawn now.

For a moment, Croy thought he saw someone standing among some bushes down in the corner of the yard.

It looked like another old man.

A car door slammed shut on the other side of the house.

Croy hesitated, looked toward the bushes again, then picked up his knife and took off running for his car.

He made sure he kept the blade pointed down when he ran.

TWENTY-TWO

BEN DECOVIC WAS WORKING the North Shore sector and ended up the first one on the scene at the Tedros place. An old man in a green cardigan and baggy pants was standing at the end of the drive and frantically waved him in. He identified himself as Leonard Renisopolos, a friend of Stanley's, and told Ben he'd found the body, and then he pointed to the rear of the house and said, "From the bushes. He walk right up I am making the call to the police."

Renisopolos suddenly stopped and gestured for Ben to pull his gun. "Maybe he still there."

"What do you mean? Who?"

"The man I'm thinking is the one did it to Stanley. He just stand there. I hurry to wait out front for you."

Ben sprinted back to his car and called in the full platter. Two other patrol cars pulled in, and Ben waved one officer to the front of the house and motioned the other to follow him.

Stanley Tedros was lying in the middle of the backyard. Jack Carson stood a few feet away from the body.

Ben and the other officer walked down the lawn, guns still drawn. "You ok, Jack?" Ben asked. "What are you doing here?" Ben stepped over and quickly patted Jack down. No weapons.

The other units arrived.

"I'm thirsty," Jack Carson said.

"Oh man, look at this," the other officer said.

Ben had spent enough time in bars with off-duty cops who, over drinks, talked up the number of corpses they'd seen and then tried to top each other with stories of the ones who'd been in the worst shape, the cops—at least publicly—all subscribing to the conventional wisdom that seeing enough corpses eventually toughened you to the reality of death, but Ben, like most cops, knew that conventional wisdom worked fine when you were perched on a bar stool but was not much help anywhere else.

Stanley Tedros looked like someone had run over his abdomen with a lawn mower.

"Jack," Ben said, "did you do this? You can tell me."

"Something's wrong with this man," Jack said, then went silent and studied the stringer of fish lying next to Stanley's right leg.

"Did you see what happened here, Jack?"

"Yes."

The EMS people arrived.

Another patrolman appeared at the back door of the house and shouted down that the place was clear.

A moment later, Leonard Renisopolos, gesturing and talking excitedly, walked down the lawn flanked by two Homicide detectives, Hatch and Gramble. Both had on anonymous brown suits. Above his, Hatch's face was lean and sharp-featured, topped with a military-sized buzz cut. Gramble's face wore a fast food diet and a pair of unfashionably long sideburns.

Hatch stepped over. "You're the one caught the call, right?"

Ben gave him what little he had and was explaining who Jack Carson was and how he more than likely had ended up in Stanley Tedros's yard when Hatch interrupted him and said, "You're telling me we got either a suspect or eyewitness here, and the guy's got Alzheimer's? Wait'll Gramble hears this." Hatch shook his head.

Three officers finished the initial sweep of the adjoining lot. Someone yelled that the tech people were here. Another patrolman appeared at the top of the lawn and shouted down that they had a woman out front claiming to be the old man's daughter.

"Which one?" Hatch said. "We got three old men here. One dead. One who can barely speak English. And one with Alzheimer's. Probably a couple more too we haven't met yet."

"Carson," the patrolman said. "She said her name's Anne Carson."

Hatch waved to let her through, then told Ben to move the old man out of the way so the crime techs could work. "Babysit the daughter and old man until I see what Gramble's got from the Greek."

Somebody called out that the coroner was on her way.

Anne Carson ran down the lawn and up to her father. "You're all right," she said, grabbing him by the arms. "I've been looking for you. I heard the sirens and saw all the lights and thought that—" She stepped back and started crying.

Despite himself, Ben felt it, that tug, faint but unmistakable, of old ambition, the desire to be at the center of things, working a homicide again, the pull of everything he'd told himself he'd left behind when he resigned from the Ryland police force.

Hatch walked back over, introduced himself to Anne Carson, and then said, "See if you can get your father to tell you what happened here."

Anne wiped at her eyes and over the next twenty-five minutes did her best to elicit a response from Jack, but got nowhere. Jack just became more agitated and disoriented.

The crime tech people had set up arc lights and were sweeping the lawn. Another group was working the house.

"I'm sorry," Anne said finally. Hatch said she'd have to accompany Jack to the station when they were done here and see if they could try again to work up something resembling a statement.

Jack kept swiveling his head, taking in the action around him, opening and closing his left hand. He kept the other in a tight fist and pressed against his leg.

"Is something wrong with his hand?" Ben said. "Look, the right one."

Anne lifted his arm and gently worked on unlocking her father's fingers, asking him if he could tell her what he'd seen as she did so, and Jack said nothing but slowly unclenched his fist. In the center of his palm were a half dozen heavy gauge washers.

"You find these here?" Hatch asked Jack.

Jack furrowed his brow.

Hatch asked Anne to check her father's front shirt pocket. She pulled out a small fistful of tangled paper clips, a bottle cap, some string and rubber bands, a pen, some salt and pepper packets, and three lint-covered Life Savers.

"A little bit of a pack rat, huh?" Hatch said.

"The guy who bushwhacked me at the Passion Palace," Ben said, "we found some washers on the scene afterwards. He put them in a sock."

Hatch juggled the washers in his hand. "This the one where you lost your Glock, right?" He looked over at Anne and smiled.

Ben involuntarily clenched his fist and then chastised himself, embarrassed. Ego, the pecking order, were nothing new in a Homicide squad.

Hatch pushed it a little more. "Decovic, you go back out front and help with crowd control and traffic. Once the coroner's done, we'll be moving the body."

He paused for effect.. "And don't worry, I'll have the crime tech boys and girls look for any others like these that might be around."

Ben nodded and just managed to avoid eye contact with Anne Carson before turning and starting up the lawn.

He slowed, then paused, when off to his right, a patrolman and a man and woman appeared. The man looked to be in his early to midthirties, heavyset, with thick black hair. He was wearing a brightly colored golfing outfit. The woman had dark blond hair spilling to the middle of her back. She carried herself with the self-conscious posture of a model and wore a pair of tight black jeans and a pale blue short-sleeved sweater.

The heavyset man suddenly broke free and ran down the lawn, the patrolman hurrying to keep up.

The woman stopped and looked over her shoulder toward the back door of the house.

It was a small thing, easily lost in everything else going on in the yard, the rigid posture and backward glance held a couple beats longer than you'd expect, and Ben might have summarily dismissed it if he hadn't seen the expression on her face when she brought her head back around. The initial puzzlement had hardened into what looked like a mask of pure rage. It suddenly disappeared when she noticed Ben standing off to her left.

She lowered her head and walked down to the middle of the backyard.

Ben waited a moment, curious.

There.

Another quick glance back. He caught it.

Then the heavyset man turned and pulled her to his chest. He was crying.

Ben moved to the front of the house and joined a young patrolman behind the yellow crime scene tape stretched across Stanley Tedros's drive. The street was full of neighbors, onlookers, and local media people clamoring for details.

The young patrolman stepped closer to Ben and winked. "Hope my mama's watching the Eleven tonight," he said, nodding toward the cameras. "They've been taking my picture."

Ben asked, "Who were the two you just let by?"

"Buddy Tedros," the patrolman said. "He's the nephew. The other was his wife." He paused and leaned closer. "Did you get a look at her? That sweater? Those jeans? She's really something."

"Yes, she is," Ben said.

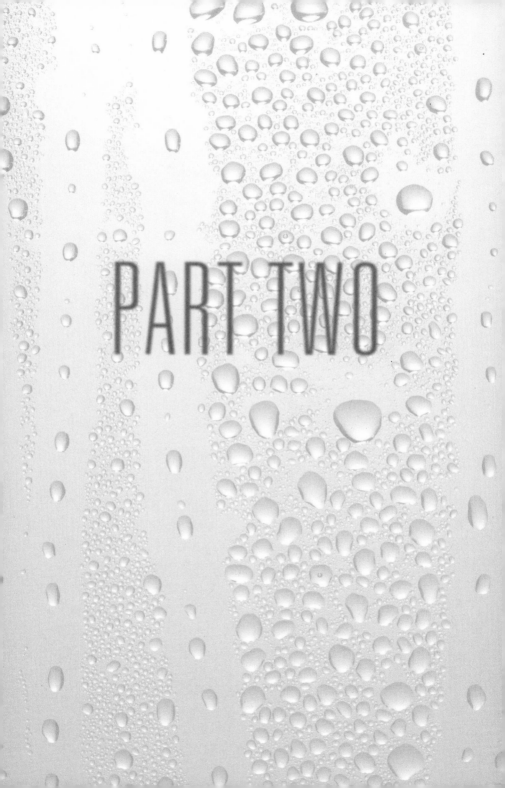

PART TWO

TWENTY-THREE

BUDDY HAD GONE to meet with the probate lawyers early, and Corrine Tedros had slept in, and now as she dressed for her hair appointment, she practiced the postures of grief, running them through her mind like a set of calisthenics, visualizing the appropriate reactions to the seemingly endless succession of social functions and obligations that a death dragged after it.

There were times you were expected to be strong. Times when you were supposed to give in to grief and break down. Times when you were supposed to be upbeat. Times when solemn. Times that called for a combination of reactions, a shading of grief and loss.

Reminding herself that Stanley was dead helped. It was difficult though to reconcile the Stanley Tedros everyone else evoked and mourned with her memories of those pot-roast-laced Sunday afternoons soundtracked with *Zorba* and Stanley's verbal jabs, all the insinuations he tossed Corrine's way about her character.

The calling hours at the funeral home had to be extended for two days to accommodate the crowds. The service at the Greek

Orthodox Church had been SRO, with the mayor, the entire city council, and the governor present, and the graveside ceremony had pulled in a huge crowd, Buddy having shut down Stanco Beverages for all three shifts. A wake, held at Stanley's buddy, Nick Renisopolos's, house had lasted all night, and the kitchen and dining room of Corrine's and Buddy's house were overflowing with Greek casseroles and desserts from well-wishers and friends.

The CBS evening news had given over one of its closing segments, forty-five seconds, to Stanley's funeral and Julep's current popularity.

Wherever Corrine turned, Stanley's name was on somebody's lips, his presence everywhere, his personal qualities continuously paraded in impromptu and official testimonials, and Corrine had to remind herself to stay focused and not let her guard down, and in order to do that, she found herself thinking more and more often not of Stanley Tedros but of her life in Bradford, Indiana and the anger and fear embedded in those memories.

Anger and fear, she'd discovered, could produce a very workable facsimile of grief.

Corrine finished dressing, got in her car, and drove to Le Nouvelle Femme Salon. Richard, her stylist, had the third chair waiting for her.

After she was seated, he started moving his hands through her hair, stopping at various lengths to provide commentary on the effect of the cuts.

"For most women," he said, "my goal is the creation of beauty. I take whatever Nature has bestowed and find the cut that will enhance or reveal what is beautiful in the woman. For that, I need the eyes of a sculptor."

He paused, gathering Corrine's hair at shoulder length and studying her image in the mirror before them. "With you," he went on, "it is something different entirely. I do not create. I discover. The beauty is there always. It's rare and uncanny. No matter what the cut, you are beautiful. With you, I am like a painter who must understand light."

Richard knew how to earn his tips. Corrine would give him that. She watched him set out his line of scissors, then drape the black vinyl apron over her and tie it at the neck. She dropped her head back over the wash basin and closed her eyes, enjoying the feel of the weight of the water in her hair and the smell of the shampoo and conditioner.

Richard began combing out her hair. Even wet, it still held the three strains of blond that had been there since she was a child, thick competing layers of honey, pale wheat, and sun-bleached silver.

Corrine was comfortable and drowsy. There'd always been something about salons that encouraged a soft-focus reverie in her, a feeling that she was safe and untouchable, and she listened to the methodical click of the scissors backdropped by Richard's soft voice, expecting to hear his customary monologue on the lives of the other customers and their army of affairs, illnesses, money and child problems, but today his voice pulled Corrine back into her own life, breaking the spell she had slipped into.

"Everybody's been talking about it," Richard said. "Our thoughts and prayers are with you and your husband."

"Thank you," Corrine said with effort.

"It's scandalous that your husband had to put up the reward," Richard said. "The police should be doing their job."

Corrine closed her eyes, waiting for Richard to change the

subject, but she knew it was too late to recapture her earlier mood. Buddy's announcement of the reward at the close of the Chamber of Commerce testimonial dinner for Stanley had caught her completely off guard. Buddy had made no previous mention of it whatsoever. She was waiting for him to wear out his grief and revert to the man she'd married. The new, resolute Buddy, like the reward itself, Corrine hadn't seen coming.

She had called Raychard Balen who told her not to worry, that the odds were very long that a tip for the reward would produce a lead of any substance. Balen, himself, had been in contact with Croy Wendall and told him to low-profile it for a while. Balen had also checked up on the witness to the murder and confirmed he was in the late stages of Alzheimer's.

Even if by some chance Jack Carson managed a description, Balen said, he would make sure nothing would hold up in court.

When Corrine pointed out that it could still lead the police to Croy, Raychard Balen had paused, then reminded her that Croy Wendall's status as a sentient being could always be renegotiated if necessary.

"Hold still now," Richard said. "Yes. Lovely. I'll be finished soon. You sit tight."

Despite Balen's assurances, Corrine felt as if something were about to be taken from her. She'd known that feeling all her life. It was part of the immense emptiness that had opened up around her as a child when her mother would disappear for days at a time without warning.

It was an emptiness that would swallow you and everything in the world unless you swallowed it first.

At twelve, Corrine had learned how to do just that. She was living in Bradford with her grandparents by then.

She'd been changing out of her school clothes when she noticed Mr. Pawls, their next-door neighbor, standing outside her bedroom window.

Corrine took a step toward him, but something in his expression made her stop. Mr. Pawls worked at the post office. He was round-faced and balding and unfailingly polite and pleasant, and in Corrine's eyes, interchangeable with most of the older adults in the community.

He was not a tall man either. His head and the top part of his shoulders were framed in the lower portion of the window.

Corrine stood in the middle of her bedroom, facing him. She'd taken her shoes off and her good jeans for school.

She bent over and took off her socks.

When she straightened again, Corrine came to a decision without quite knowing she had. She did not look at Mr. Pawls again, at least not directly, Corrine only dimly aware of him on the periphery of her vision as she began to move around her room, doing exactly what she would have done on any other day after coming home from school, but as she did, Corrine noticed a change in herself, her movements and gestures slowly becoming more deliberate and stylized, Corrine more aware of the body that had begun to outrun her, the shift and heft of breasts under the T-shirt she'd pulled over her head, the blond explosion that followed removing the band from her ponytail and shaking her head, the flex of calf and thigh as a leg slid into her old jeans, the shiny red of her nails as she zipped and buttoned them.

When she was done dressing, Corrine glanced over at the window. Mr. Pawls was gone.

Impaled on one of the lower branches of the hemlock that had shielded him from the eyes of anyone passing by was a five dollar bill.

It was two days later before Mr. Pawls appeared again, and Corrine repeated the after-school ritual of a girl changing her clothes and lounging about her room.

Over the next six months, Mr. Pawls showed up on the average of three times per week, standing outside Corrine's bedroom window while she changed from her school to home clothes and leaving a five dollar bill stuck on a hemlock branch and pale trails of semen on the side of the house.

Fingers and lips. The spill of hair over a shoulder. The sock that momentarily caught on your instep when you bent to take it off. A languid hand straying through thick blond hair. Corrine came to inhabit each gesture.

She kept the five dollar bills in an empty coffee can she'd secreted away in the basement.

The emptiness didn't seem so bad anymore.

Corrine eventually discovered something else though.

Mr. Pawls had been at his usual station at her bedroom window, and Corrine had just changed out of her school clothes. She stood in the center of the room in her bra and panties and slowly lifted her head and made eye contact with Mr. Pawls.

Corrine held his gaze while she went on to do something she had never done before. She reached back and unhooked her bra, then slid her panties down her legs and off.

The air in the bedroom was cold. Corrine felt her nipples grow hard.

She cupped her breasts and slowly moved her fingertips to her nipples.

She dropped her right hand between her legs. It was warm there.

She looked at Mr. Pawls. His face was red and his lips tight, and then he made a strangled sound and slowly came to rest his forehead against the window.

Afterwards, he left two five dollar bills on the hemlock branch.

He never showed up at her bedroom window again though, and it was years later, Corrine already having run away from her grandparents and Bradford, before she fully understood what had happened that afternoon. By that time she was living in Arizona and already in the jam that she had yet to find a way out of, and it was a lesson she would learn many times after that, one she took with her to Myrtle Beach and Sonny Gramm's supper club and then to the altar with her husband, Buddy Tedros.

The truth, like the emptiness, served nothing but itself.

It got you nowhere.

There was another kind of truth though, one that Corrine had seen in Mr. Pawls's face that afternoon and in the faces of the men who'd followed him over the years, a truth that lay behind the lies that men told to protect themselves and their needs. They all carried that bedroom window inside them and were willing to pay any price to look through it as long as it held what they wanted to see.

And as long, too, as you were willing never to look them directly in the eye.

"Beautiful," Richard said from behind her. He'd finished combing out her hair. "Absolutely beautiful."

TWENTY-FOUR

BEN DECOVIC HAD NOT BEEN SURPRISED to see the direction the Tedros murder investigation was taking, but he had not expected in the aftermath of Stanley Tedros's death to find himself in the Publix at the intersection of Hawthorne and Queensland buying groceries for four.

Ben could not exactly say for sure how that had come about. But it had.

He was sleeping with Anne Carson.

Proximity and Frequency. When Ben had started in the Ryland Police Department, the phrase had doubled as a motive for most home invasions and burglaries, the phrase a convenient shorthand for why most break-ins occurred, and Ben figured it worked equally well as an explanation for how he'd ended up in Anne Carson's bed.

Their lives kept unexpectedly crossing and recrossing each other.

Since joining the force and beginning Patrol, he had gotten into the habit of dropping by the Salt Box for lunch or dinner, and more often than not, Anne was there in her role as assistant manager, and their customary small talk had over time grown large and gained a weight neither of them had anticipated or fully understood.

At one point, Anne Carson had stopped and put her hands on her hips. Something that was a cross between a smile and frown passed across her face.

"Are you flirting with me?" she had asked.

"I think so," Ben said after a moment.

She'd given him a long look, then walked off.

Nothing else had happened between them until Jack Carson inadvertently witnessed Stanley Tedros's murder.

Off shift and on impulse, Ben had stopped by a few times on his way home to check on Jack and to see if he'd remembered anything.

The evenings had the quality of a tableau. Paige at the kitchen table doing homework. Jack in his green plaid recliner watching television. Anne cooking the evening meal.

Ben found his spot in the tableau, and suddenly there was an extra place set at the table.

Then, with Paige and Jack in their rooms for the night, the house quiet, Ben and Anne on the couch, a couple of deep glasses of wine and Merlot-tinged kisses, and Ben and Anne followed the one thing that always led to another, but what that *another* was, Ben could not say for sure because Anne and he never quite got around to talking about it. For now, things felt right and good between them, and that was enough, more than enough in fact.

Ben left before Jack or Paige woke up. Anne wanted them to have a little more time to get used to his presence in their lives.

At the Publix, Ben worked his way department by department through the grocery list. He supplemented almost everything Anne had put down. It hadn't been hard to read between the items to the least-common-denominator lifestyle of a single mother with limited resources taking care of a daughter and father. No more than it would be for anyone to spot the none too quiet desperation behind the contents of Ben's kitchen cabinets at the White Palms apartment. Each time Ben dropped something into the cart, it felt as if he were throwing out a lifeline. He wasn't sure if it was to Anne or himself or if that mattered at all right then.

In the checkout line, Ben scanned the front pages in a rack of newspapers. While Stanley Tedros's murder might have temporarily fallen off page one of the national papers, on the regional, state, and local levels, it was still receiving saturation coverage. The story continued to rampage through the tabloids too.

Ben had seen it happen before, a homicide investigation side-tracked and then finally run by local politics and the media.

He was seeing it again with the Stanley Tedros case.

Despite all the promotion by the Greater Magnolia Beach Tourist Bureau and the mayor, the city was basically a small town at its core, defensive and overly protective of its ethos and image in the way all small towns were. Magnolia Beach tenaciously clung to and celebrated its down-home, family-friendly idea of it-self, a place that offered middle-class Americans leisure unclut-tered by culture. You came to there to golf, shop, eat, have a few drinks, and lie in the sun and didn't have to apologize or feel guilty for doing so. To the rest of the country, Magnolia Beach promised a safe, PG version of hedonism. It did not have room for the murder of old men who'd been stabbed thirty-nine times

in the stomach, especially if the old man in question was the orig-
inator of a soft drink that the rest of America seemingly could
not get enough of.

A special task force had been set up devoted solely to working
Stanley Tedros's murder, and Ben was afraid any real progress
would be lost in bureaucratic in-fighting and duplication of efforts chasing down leads that went nowhere but produced
enough activity to make good copy in press conferences and news
releases.

The department had Buddy Tedros to thank for that.

His announcement at the close of a memorial supper hosted
by the chamber of commerce virtually guaranteed that the case
would only go one direction. Buddy, while praising the force and
its work, wanted to assist in the swift apprehension of his uncle's
murderer and put up a reward of ten thousand dollars for any information leading to an arrest and conviction.

By the end of the next day, over one hundred and twenty tips
had been logged in.

Under the media's eye, the mayor had immediately author-
ized overtime funding.

Stanley had been dead for a week, and Ben and the rest working Patrol had been assigned split shifts, half spent on maintaining regular patrol routes and half given over to following up on
tips from citizens. Today Ben had dutifully checked up on eight
of them, among them, a man in the Willows Trailer Park who
claimed that his seventy-eight-year-old wife was responsible for
the killing. As evidence, he had Ben watch him count the steak
knives in the silverware drawer, triumphantly stopping at nine in
a set that originally came with ten. Ben had then talked to a

woman who maintained the Vatican and its minions were behind Stanley's murder and another who believed Stanley had been murdered by the CIA.

The few leads that had possessed any degree of credibility had quickly bottomed out, each potential suspect having a solid alibi for the time in question.

What the reward assured was more tips and somebody who would eventually take the fall for Stanley Tedros's murder. You started turning over rocks, and sooner or later, you'd come across a loser who was mean or stupid enough to give you something to hang him with, whether he had anything to do with Tedros's death or not.

After paying, Ben put the groceries in the trunk of his car, then stopped for gas and headed back to Anne's. He automatically slowed when he passed Stanley's house, though there was nothing to see. The driveway was empty, the windows dark, and the front door still crisscrossed with yellow crime scene tape.

Ben was bothered by how quickly the Homicide people had cleared Buddy Tedros and his wife. He knew it wouldn't be the first time that a murderer or someone who'd hired a murderer offered up a reward to deflect attention elsewhere.

He kept returning to Corrine Tedros at the crime scene, her backward glance and the expression that followed it. However small, the detail nagged.

In fact, most everything about Stanley's murder bothered him. Once Jack Carson had been cleared of any part in the murder except the witnessing of it, they were looking at a home invasion that wasn't, the house broken into but nothing taken. Nobody could explain why all the clocks in the house were set at different times either. Stanley's wallet had still been on his corpse and had held over three hundred dollars in cash. He'd been killed in the back-yard and not the house. If the killer had been coming through the back door and spotted Stanley, why hadn't he simply turned and run back through the house and out the front door? Stanley had been stabbed thirty-nine times when once or twice would have been more than sufficient. The killer had taken Stanley's pocketwatch, of no real value except as a family keepsake. None of the neighbors noticed anything unusual until the police cruisers started showing up. The whole thing was one anomaly and dead-end after another.

Ben pulled into the driveway and parked behind Anne's car. It took four trips to unload the groceries.

After the last one, he joined Anne in putting everything away. Jack was in the living room listening to the radio. The station was playing Big Band tunes. Ben recognized Glenn Miller's "Moon-light Serenade." He remembered his parents listening to it.

The house itself as much as the music conspired to evoke those memories. Ben liked the feel of its rooms. There was some-thing solid to the house, a fullness that invited you in, welcom-ing you without pretense to the lives that inhabited it. It was a house very much like the one Ben had grown up in.

Anne abruptly stopped unpacking groceries. She had her back to Ben and looked down at the kitchen floor where the empty bags rustled and trembled under the movement of the ceiling fan.

"Ben, this is overkill," she said in a quiet and even voice.

"It's ok, really," he said and rested his hand on her shoulder. He'd not been able to convince her that there were no strings to his fi-nancial help. He had the money, and he wanted to help. It was that simple. Anne continued to resist, not accepting his stepping in so much as finally resigning herself to a half-hearted stalemate.

Ben felt Paige's eyes on him and dropped his hand from Anne's shoulder. Her eyes spooked him. Her gaze overrode her age, and her eyes managed to take everything in and give nothing back. Like her often overly precise speech, the eyes remained perpetually at odds with the rest of an otherwise skinny eleven-year-old girl.

Ben asked her how school was going. It seemed a safe enough topic.

"The extra-credit work is often very challenging and instructive," Paige said. "My teachers do not assign extra-credit to the rest of the class. I'm smarter than they are."

Anne again paused in putting up the groceries. "We've talked about this, Paige. People can be smart in a lot of different ways."

"They can also be dumb in a lot of different ways," Paige said, "and I know the difference."

"I'm glad you're doing so well in all your subjects," Ben said. He immediately felt like a fool. How much more lame of a statement could he possibly have come up with? He picked up the water filter he'd bought and moved over to the sink and began working on installing it.

"Of course," Paige said after a moment. "I'd be doing even better if I had a laptop. Our computer keeps freezing up. It's ancient."

Anne slowly let out her breath. "I told you, Paige. Four months. It's in layaway."

"In four months, school will be over. I need it now." Paige sat back in the kitchen chair and ran through, once again, all the problems with the current family computer and then launched into an equally detailed account of all the new worlds she could conquer with a laptop.

Ben finished tightening the filter. "How about," he started, but Anne stepped over and said he'd already done more than enough.

"Call it a loan instead," Ben said.

Anne shook her head no and began gathering the plastic grocery bags.

Paige watched them from the kitchen table. "The tape recorder then," she said. "Perhaps Grandfather will remember who murdered Mr. Tedros, and we can use the reward money for the laptop *and* everything else we need."

"Tape recorder?" Ben said

"A voice-activated one, small enough to fit in Dad's shirt pocket," Anne said. "Buddy Tedros brought it by this afternoon."

"I see," Ben said.

Anne walked into the living room, and Ben glanced over at Paige and then joined Anne.

Jack Carson sat in his recliner. Anne gave him a quick kiss on the cheek, then extracted the tape recorder from his pocket and showed it to Ben.

"Buddy thought it was worth a try," she said. "There are still times when I feel like I'm getting through to Dad."

"How well do you know Buddy?"

"We were in high school together when I moved here with Dad from Myrtle Beach," Anne said. "Buddy was a couple years older than me and, well, moved in different circles, but he was always friendly."

Ben nodded and handed back the tape recorder.

"I feel so bad for him," Anne said. "Buddy, I mean. He's taking his uncle's death hard. They were very close. Mr. Tedros raised

Buddy after his parents died."

Jack started to get up from the chair and then sat back down.

Anne jerked her head, frowning and looking over Ben's shoulder toward the kitchen and Paige.

"I heard that," Anne said. "Don't talk about your grandfather like he's a walking lottery ticket, young lady."

Paige opened her math book. "But that's what he is now," she said. "You can't pretend otherwise, Mother." She paused, then added, "I heard you tell Mr. Decovic grandfather doesn't even have life insurance."

Ben started to touch Anne's shoulder and then dropped his hand. He couldn't say for sure, but he thought that conversation had taken place two nights earlier behind a locked bedroom door after Anne and he had finished making love.

TWENTY-FIVE

JAMIE DIDN'T LIKE THINGS WITH FUR, so it was Croy Wendall's job to get the rats. Croy had found all he needed at the landfill south of town, and he'd put the rats in two large cardboard boxes and taped the lids shut after punching holes in the top.

The two boxes were in the back seat of Jamie's car, and Jamie kept adjusting the volume on the radio as he drove because of the noise the rats made. Jamie told Croy all that scrabbling of claws on cardboard and the overlapping high-pitched squeals sounded like a windstorm from Hell. Croy just thought it sounded what it was, like two crowded boxes of rats.

Other than that, Jamie was in a good mood, and Croy didn't mind doing some crimes with him. It was a sunny March afternoon, and the world felt like a letter with your name on it.

"Man, I'm already counting the cash," Jamie said, drumming his fingers on the steering wheel. "This job's a walk."

Jamie liked money, but he was always running out of it. He'd already spent what Mr. Balen had paid him for smashing up Mr. Gramm's Mustang, and the same thing had happened to Missy's disability check for the month.

Croy had heard them, Jamie and Missy, talking about where the money went and what they'd do with more, but it always ended up sounding as if the money spent itself while Jamie and Missy were out doing something else.

Croy still had all the money for smashing up the Mustang as well as for killing Stanley Tedros, except for thirty-five dollars he spent when he went to Myrtle Beach's Ripley's Aquarium for a ticket to get inside and then for a souvenir T-shirt. The T-shirt was green and had *Amphibians Rule!* silkscreened on the front.

The man on the radio had been talking about no rain and the watertable and all the fires popping up that had to be put out, and then a song came on, and Jamie reached for the dial. "Hey, good omen," he said. "Hear that?

The man on the radio said it was Dylan's "Maggie's Farm" from *Bringing It All Back Home*, and Jamie said that's exactly what they were going to do to Mr. Sonny Gramm today. It was their job to bring it all back home.

Dylan rhymed with *killin'*. *Home* rhymed with *comb*. *Home* didn't rhyme with *some*, even though it looked like it should. Croy had to take things like that into consideration when he was building a rhyme to say in his head.

Croy took out the pocketwatch he'd taken from Stanley Tedros and checked the time. He'd begun doing that a lot lately. The pocketwatch was confusing, just like trying to rhyme *home* with *some,* because there were black capital letters on its face instead of numbers.

"Hey, where'd you get that?" Jamie asked, glancing over. "That's a nice one."

"I found it," Croy said and then immediately wished he hadn't because it was not the kind of answer that made the right kind of fit in Jamie's mind.

"Found it, huh?" Jamie said and smiled. "Sure, Croy, I hear you."

Croy was glad that Jamie had taken some of the prescriptions the doctors gave Missy after her car wreck. Jamie liked the prescriptions almost as much as he liked money, and he didn't ask as many questions or remember the answers after he swallowed some.

Croy had to be careful because that's what Mr. Balen told him. Mr. Balen would be very upset if he knew Croy was out doing crimes with Jamie because he wasn't supposed to do anything that might draw the attention of the police, and Croy understood that, but Jamie had needed the rats and wouldn't quit asking Croy to get them, and after he did, Jamie wanted him to come along for the job because he didn't want to handle them then either, and Croy had said ok.

But he was still going to be very careful. He just wished he'd asked Jamie what time it was instead of looking at the pocketwatch.

Jamie drove them to Mr. Gramm's house. It was almost twenty miles outside the city limits and had a long driveway lined with oyster shells and a lot of old pecan trees. The house was big and white with a wide front porch that had wicker rocking chairs on it.

He and Jamie put on some gloves, and then Jamie broke in through the front door. He took a small piece of paper from his shirt pocket and stepped over and punched in some numbers, deactivating the alarm system. Mr. Balen had given him the numbers as well as the times the house would be empty.

Croy carried in the two boxes of rats. He set them down in the middle of the living room.

Jamie handed Croy a crowbar. He had one too.

"Let's do it," Jamie said. He hopped up on a coffee table and swung at a big chandelier dangling above him.

Croy started in too. After a while, he moved from the living room to the den.

He worked fast, so fast that he watched things breaking in his head before he hit them.

Wood, metal, glass. Glass, wood, metal. Everything made a sound when it broke.

In the kitchen, Croy watched Jamie lever the door off the refrigerator and then carry an armload of frozen roasts out to the backyard and fling them into the swimming pool.

Croy put a loaf of white bread in the microwave and turned it on High and peered through the little window in front until the outer wrapping puckered and melted.

Jamie came back in and broke some pipes under the kitchen sink.

Then they moved upstairs.

They saved the rats for last. Croy opened one box in the bathroom and then shut the door behind him on the way out. The other box he opened in the kitchen. The small and medium rats followed the biggest one to the open face of the refrigerator and scrambled inside, nesting among the shelves. Croy watched one of them chew through the side of a milk carton, and then he walked back to the living room where Jamie was waiting.

Jamie winked and reactivated the alarm system, and then they left.

Croy took a nap on the ride back. Doing crimes always left him feeling sleepy afterwards. He dreamed about tadpoles and race cars. Jamie woke him up when they got home.

Missy was wearing her neck brace and one of those little nightie things that she called a teddy. She handed Jamie a Schlitz, and Jamie went to call Mr. Balen. She gave Croy a soda, and then she tried to give him a hug, but Croy sat down on the couch. He could hear the pocketwatch ticking against his leg.

Jamie came back and sat in his recliner and tipped his beer at Croy and said he was going to pick up the money for the job from Mr. Balen tomorrow morning.

Missy brought some snacks in from the kitchen. There were little dots of mustard down the front of her teddy. Jamie turned on the television, and they ate the snacks and watched some shows.

TWENTY-SIX

BEN DECOVIC'S SUPERVISOR, La'Shawn Samuels, tapped him for desk duty on the Task Force when the wife of one of the regulars working full time on the Task Force went into early labor. Ben spent the shift evaluating and ranking the tips still coming in about the Tedros murder, as well as coding those tips that had proved dead-ends and those that warranted some follow-up, and then typing them into the computer system.

In order to process the tips, Ben needed access to the murder book on the Tedros case, and Homicide had provided copies for the various support units of the Task Force. The murder book was a compendium of everything that had been gathered on the Tedros case so far, and Ben cross-referenced the tips against it.

The case was going nowhere. The media people were growing restless, and their slant on the case was becoming more critical concerning how it was being handled. The mayor was not happy. The city council was not happy. Neither was the tourist bureau. High-profile unsolved murder cases did not encourage moms and dads to book hotel reservations and spend money and frolic on the beach with the family.

For many of the citizens, the reward Buddy Tedros had put up for information on the murder had come to be seen as another form of playing the state lottery. The tips proliferated, the citizens vetting long- and short-term grudges against family, friends, neighbors, lovers, coworkers, bosses, clergymen, and teachers. Conspiracies, terrestrial and otherwise, abounded. People smelled money and pointed their fingers. By the end of the shift, Ben figured the ratio of unreliable to reliable tips was running at six to one.

On his way home, Ben decided to swing by North Shore and see if Anne Carson wanted him to pick up anything for supper.

Conventional wisdom might dictate that you shouldn't expect more from sex than pleasure or procreation, but Ben believed if you were lucky, you also found an earthborne grace. Flesh yielded more than flesh. Ben had found that unexpected grace with his wife, Diane, their passion and desire underwriting a future together, a life that carried its own sweet weight.

Ben saw the outline of that passion and grace with Anne. They'd found each other and took off their clothes. They took off their clothes and found each other. In the dark, in Anne's bedroom, they took and found, and in doing so, for a while, they gave each other what the world couldn't and wouldn't. Grace. If you found it, you didn't question why. You lived it.

On the way to Anne's, he passed Stanley Tedros's place and saw a large moving van parked outside the front door.

He slowed, then found a spot to turn around, and pulled into the driveway.

Corrine Tedros stepped out of the house, holding a clipboard.

Ben sat for a moment behind the wheel, waiting for his better judgment to null and void the decision he was already following by lifting the door handle and stepping out of the car.

He reached back inside for the small notebook lying on the dash that he used for things-to-do and grocery lists.

He'd read the field notes on the interview with Corrine Tedros in the murder book and had noticed something. The time line in her statement was fuzzy. There was a clear sequence early in the afternoon but a gap during the period the coroner had established for the murder.

It was small and probably meant nothing.

But it had caught his attention and nagged, just as her reaction, the backward glance and then puzzlement and rage that had flashed across her features, had at the crime scene.

Corrine Tedros watched him approach. She wore a scooped-neck summer dress and a pair of thin-soled sandals, and her hair was loose, falling free and just past her shoulders. She was almost as tall as he was.

Two men came out the front door with a metal steamer trunk and loaded it in the truck.

Ben introduced himself to Corrine and asked if he could trouble her for a few minutes of her time. Her eyes were a light brown, instead of the blue a first impression would lead you to expect. When she shook back her hair, he saw clusters of interlocking opals studding her earlobes. Her mouth was a little wide for her face despite the definition from a set of high cheekbones. Ben thought she was more striking than beautiful.

"You'll have to excuse the mess," she said, after Ben had followed her into the kitchen. "We're trying to sort through Stanley's things and separate keepsakes from Salvation Army donations." She drew them each a glass of ice water and suggested they sit out back where they'd be away from the movers.

They sat on a diagonal to each other in a pair of striped canvas sling chairs, Ben getting a view of Corrine's long left thigh when she crossed her legs, a view that she made no effort to change by adjusting a hemline.

She took a sip of ice water, then cradled the glass in her lap. "What exactly is this about?" she asked. "I already talked to one of the other detectives from Homicide. I think his name was Hatch. Did something new turn up in the investigation?"

"I wish I could tell you yes," Ben said, "but we're still hitting walls wherever we turn. I'm going back and dotting a few *i*'s in the field notes for the report, that's all. Routine stuff."

He could ask a few innocuous questions and back off and forget the whole idea. Or he could nudge things a little and see where they went. Ben figured this was probably the only chance he'd get.

"On the day Mr. Tedros was killed," he said, "you spent the early afternoon with a friend shopping and then catching a movie, right?"

"Yes. Terri Iles. We also stopped for some decaf and yogurt at the mall."

"Before or after the movie?"

"Before," Corrine said slowly.

"And afterwards?"

"I'm not following you, Officer Decovic."

"After the movie, did you drop Ms. Iles off at home?"

"No. We went in separate cars. Terri had to pick up her daughter at a friend's."

"And you? What did you do after the movie?"

"I already told all this to Detective Hatch. Why are we going over it again?"

Ben assured her once more that it was all a matter of back-tracking and fleshing out the initial notes for the official draft of the report. A routine job, tedious but necessary, that he implied had been dumped on him.

"Detective Hatch knows his stuff," Ben said, "but you wouldn't believe his handwriting. It's pure scratch. On top of that, his notes are a slash-and-burn shorthand."

Ben turned to an empty page in his notebook and went through the motions of pretending to decipher it. "Right here, for example," he said. "Your husband's name is written down, and there's a couple check marks next to it and then something that looks like 'bankers' and that followed by what looks like 'Clear'."

Corrine Tedros told him her husband had been playing golf in a foursome with some representatives from Wachovia Bank.

Ben nodded and made some random marks in the notebook.

"Couple more things here," he said, squinting at the page. "Did you go straight home after the movie?"

"No, I had some shopping to do."

Ben glanced up from the page. "But you'd already been shopping with Ms. Iles, correct?"

"Not that kind of shopping, Officer Decovic," she said. "I went to Walgreens on Harper Street."

"Did you take Queensland or Armstrong?"

"Why does that matter?"

"Helps clarify the time sequence, that's all," Ben said. "If you'd been on Queensland, you must have gotten held up, what with the traffic jammed because of the wreck. Two cars and a tractor trailer. Right where Queensland intersects with Old Market. A real mess. Tied everything up for close to an hour."

"Oh, that's what it was," Corrine said, tilting her head and shaking back her hair. "I never got close enough to see what caused the hold-up. First chance, I got off Queensland and on Armstrong and then took Everest to Harper."

"And then you went straight home?"

Corrine nodded. "I took a short nap and a long bath. My husband and I had dinner plans that evening."

"You wouldn't by any chance still have the receipt? From Walgreens, I mean." Ben busied himself with turning a page and flipping it back, then looked up and said, "The receipt would have the date and time and store number on it.

"It seems to me we've gone beyond dotting an *i* here, Officer," Corrine said, setting the glass next to the chair and standing up. "Where are you trying to take this?"

He looked past Corrine and down the yard toward the boat-house. He took his time answering. The grass was still trampled where they'd found Stanley's body.

"I'm trying to clarify your whereabouts during the time of the murder so that we'll have a clean timeline for all the principals. It goes in the report," he said. "A bureaucratic formality."

A patch of red had risen at the base of Corrine's throat. "You made it sound as if I was a suspect."

Ben propped the notebook on his knee and built a tic-tac-toe game at the bottom of the page, letting her statement ride.

He closed the notebook just as Corrine Tedros stepped over and stood in front of him, blocking his way out of the chair and forcing him to lean back and crane his neck to make eye contact.

"For your information, Officer," she began, "I did not save

the receipt from Walgreens. I stopped to buy some tampons. Since they are items I am not likely to return, I did not see any reason to save the receipt for the purchase."

The patch of red at the base of Corrine Tedros's neck deepened. "I came home with the tampons," she continued, "and I inserted one in my vagina. I was cramping and had a headache. I took a nap and a long bath. To my knowledge, no one saw me do either."

Ben slowly lowered his head. Just as she'd intended, he was left looking at Corrine Tedros's pelvis.

"After my bath, I got ready for dinner. My husband came home from his golf game. While he was changing for dinner, he got the call from Nick Renisopolos, Stanley's friend, who told us what happened. My husband and I drove directly to the house."

Corrine folded her arms across her chest. "Is that enough for your timeline, Officer? Or does having a menstrual period and getting ready to go out to dinner with my husband still qualify me as a suspect?" She stepped back and away, waiting while Ben unfolded himself from the sling chair and got to his feet.

He slipped the notebook and pen in his shirt pocket. "I never said that, Ms. Tedros. You did."

She picked up the clipboard that had been lying next to her chair. "Are we done, then?"

Ben nodded, taking his glass of ice water and following her into the kitchen, noticing the small differences in her posture and swing of her hips, nothing languid or sexy there now, everything tightened down by her indignation and, Ben hoped, a little bit of doubt and concern that she might have overplayed things.

A couple nudges, that's all it had been. Ben taking the temperature of a longshot hunch.

In the living room, one of the movers was in the process of boxing an old turntable and stereo system, but Corrine stepped in front of him and said, "Not that."

"Sorry," he said. "Your husband put it on the list of Keepers." He turned and carried it to the corner of the living room and dropped it with the Salvation Army items.

"You might want to reconsider," Ben said. "That turntable and system, they're probably a collector's item now. Or will be soon. Like manual typewriters."

"I don't like old things," Corrine Tedros said. She walked Ben to the door.

"Thank you again for your time," Ben said, "and I apologize for upsetting you. That wasn't my intention."

Corrine Tedros hesitated a moment before nodding. "I apologize too. My husband took his uncle's death very hard. It's left everything a little tense. We both want some closure."

"That's understandable," Ben said.

Corrine stepped back and rested her free hand on the door-knob. "If you'll excuse me," she said, "I really do have to finish up here."

Ben walked back to his car. He was feeling the old jolt he'd gotten when working Homicide, and he liked it, that express-line adrenaline rush accompanying a hunch that had kicked something loose.

It wasn't much, but it was there.

First off, Corrine Tedros had given a perfectly plausible version of her afternoon on the day in question. Even her reaction near the end of the interview was perfectly understandable, easily chalked up to the explanation Corrine herself had provided. Ben had investigated enough homicides to know that a person's reaction to death and being questioned about it were often one of the least reliable roads to a suspect. In the face of grief or guilt, anything was possible.

No, what interested Ben was why in the midst of explaining what she'd done when she left the theatre and Terri Illes, Corrine Tedros had felt the need to lie, and to lie very convincingly, about the detour she'd had to take to avoid the tie-up in traffic, especially since Ben had made up the incident, and there'd never been an accident or traffic jam in the first place.

TWENTY-SEVEN

IT WAS LIKE SOME CRUEL, ludicrous joke, some *last* last laugh, Corrine Tedros having left the meat counter with two heavy sirloins and moved on to the produce department—where she ran into a simulated cloudburst on the store's sound system that warned her and any nearby shoppers that the fresh fruits and vegetables were about to be sprayed, the nozzles opening in a fine steady mist—a facsimile of the rain that April and the sky outside the store withheld, and Corrine Tedros had yet to stop and select a wine to go with the steaks and had yet to turn the corner at the end of the aisle for the gourmet coffee where she would run into the punchline still some five minutes away, Corrine at that point still caught up in the moment, the power that came from the knowledge she could put anything in her cart—and as much of anything in the cart that she wanted and no one could stop her because she had the means to pay for it; the flashpoint between desire and the object of that desire the blink of a nerve ending, and it was because of those moments and for those moments that

Corrine Tedros always made it a point to shop for groceries when she was hungry.

She trusted to one truth, one that others went to any lengths to avoid, and that was, at bottom, everyone thought with his stomach, because when you stripped everything else away, there was only hunger, and that's all there ever had been and all that would ever be, an immense hunger, and you lived your life by and in the truth of teeth and digestive juices, and you never made the mistake of forgetting or trying to ignore the hunger because the hunger never forgot you, so Corrine had picked up a good bottle of red wine to go with the steaks and a loaf of French bread, and then she moved down the aisle holding the gourmet coffee and turned left.

And ran into Stanley Tedros.

Stanley was wearing his trademark brown suit and pork pie hat cocked at a jaunty angle. He stood with a wide smile and his arms outstretched, a can of Julep in his right hand.

Corrine wasn't superstitious.

As a child, yes.

Corrine had worked hard to board up that door, to seal off any access to the false comfort of magic or prayer when she was afraid.

Cardboard, she told herself, that's all she was looking at, a cardboard placard of Stanley Tedros, a promotional gimmick for pedaling soft drinks, nothing more than that: an image, not Stanley himself.

She told herself to move on because if she didn't, she'd start thinking about Betsy Jo Horvath. Betsy was someone she wanted to forget. Corrine couldn't move though and stood there with her hands clenching the handle of the grocery cart, and it was as if Stanley were blocking her way, and then suddenly she was crying, and she couldn't stop, and people had begun to notice, but she couldn't stop crying or make herself move, not even when the store manager appeared and launched into a long, profuse apology, an oversight he kept calling it, a simple mistake, and he was sorry because he had fully intended to have the placard removed after Stanley's funeral, but then he'd gotten sidetracked by having to oversee the in-store inventory, and it had slipped his mind, and he was genuinely sorry.

Corrine heard the words, but they didn't register.

For a brief moment, she thought she saw Ben Decovic out of uniform and standing at the back of the crowd watching her. When she wiped her eyes and checked a second time, he was gone.

The manager wouldn't stop apologizing, and Corrine couldn't stop crying, and the crowd of onlookers kept growing.

A stockboy appeared and picked up Stanley.

Stanley's head peered over the stockboy's shoulder as he headed toward two doors at the rear of the store, but it was not Stanley's eyes that spooked her, not his eyes that left her insides feeling as if they'd suddenly been torn loose and caused her to involuntarily raise one hand and touch the hair on the back of her head twice, a gesture from her childhood, like the practice of putting a pebble on her bedroom windowsill, all the childish attempts to conjure up a magic potent enough to meet what the dark or an empty house held.

It was not the eyes.

No.

It was the smile.

A cardboard smile with its own truth.

The manager and the others were looking at her, not the smile, so they missed what it held.

Corrine didn't.

The smile told her she'd been wrong about one thing:

Maybe even more than the living, the dead were forever hungry too.

TWENTY-EIGHT

AFTERNOON BUMPED INTO EVENING, and the sky began to leak its light into the cloudbanks that had amassed to the east over the Atlantic. The pine trees and live oaks in Anne Carson's backyard were coated in half shadows, and the wind carried its unseasonable warmth like a low-grade fever.

Ben Decovic stood at the counter below the kitchen windows and made a tuna fish sandwich. He cut the toast on a diagonal and set the finished sandwich on a white plate and bracketed it with two dill pickles. Then he poured a tall glass of ginger ale and dropped in ice cubes. He put everything on a tray and then shook out Jack Carson's evening meds. He carried the tray into the living room where Jack sat and watched television with the volume off.

Ben set the tray next to Jack. The screen was filled with a black and white shot of a sky swollen with hundreds of descending paratroopers. Ben wasn't sure if it was footage from a historical documentary or an early-fifties war movie.

"It was the right thing," Jack said, looking over at Ben.

"What was?"

"Coming back home, Raymond," Jack said. "You should never have left like you did. You have a wife and child, and they need you. I can't carry all the weight myself. It's not right."

Ben quietly explained that he wasn't Raymond.

"Thank you for the sandwich," Jack said. "You remembered to fix it exactly the way I like it." He went back to watching the television screen and the descending paratroopers. "They look like uprooted mushrooms," he said between bites.

Ben's cell phone rang. He walked back into the kitchen to answer it.

"We're going to be later than expected," Anne said. "They're running behind schedule with the conferences." She paused, then added, "Things ok with Dad?"

"Everything's under control," Ben said. "You take care of things there."

"This is not going to be pleasant," Anne said. "There are a lot of hurt feelings."

Ben assured her that things were ok and said they'd order a couple pizzas when Paige and she got home.

From what Ben gathered, Paige had managed to add a couple bonus features to the standard parent-teacher conference package.

Not surprisingly, there were no problems with academics. Paige was consistently working far beyond grade level in all her classes, Math and Language Arts in particular, but everywhere else, she'd garnered Public Enemy status for her behavior and attitude. Students, teachers, and parents alike had complained about her. She verbally bullied and mocked her peers and worked guerilla warfare on her teachers, alternately playing to and undermining their classroom authority. The principal had insisted the guidance counselor, a Mr. Deane, be present and a part of this evening's conference with the aggrieved teachers.

Anne wanted to blame all the behavioral problems on the hormonal turmoil stemming from the fact that Paige had just had her first period a month ago. It was a plausible explanation, but Ben still had his doubts. Anne was convinced that Paige had no inkling of Ben's late-night arrivals and early-morning departures from Anne's bed, but he'd felt on more than one occasion the weight of Paige's assessing gaze and thought Anne was overoptimistic about how much Paige actually missed.

Time, Ben thought. That's what they all needed.

Last night, in the fading arc of their orgasms, Anne and he had finally talked about the long shadows thrown by Anne's ex, Ray, and Ben's wife, Diane, over their days. Her head on Ben's chest, his arm cradling her spine and his hand resting on the rise of her buttocks, Anne told him about Ray and a marriage that imploded after nine years. In the beginning, Anne planning her freshman year at the University of South Carolina, Ray her high school sweetheart, their relationship run on the reckless intoxication of opposites, one that eventually ran aground when a condom slipped, Paige becoming a dot on a nine-month horizon, Anne dropping the college plans and marrying Ray because that's what you did, and they stayed married because that's what you did, and Anne overlooked Ray's all-night drinking sessions with his buddies and the sleeping around because that's what you did for the sake of family, and three years ago when your father's Alzheimer's was diagnosed you took him in because that's what you did, and then you awoke one morning a month later and found that your husband had left you, so you kept on working at the Salt Box and budgeted and watched your money and raised your daughter and cared for a father who didn't recognize you most of the time because that's what you did.

Ben's turn, when it came, was troublesome. Though Anne was quietly encouraging, Ben stumbled on his words and choked on his life. He could not explain their love. He started, backed up, and started again, managing only to turn her and their life into grist for a made-to-order sentimental romance with a tear-jerker ending.

Ben kept starting and stopping. Anne rested her hand against his cheek and, a moment later, she reached over and turned off the bedside lamp.

In the dark, Ben found his voice. He told Anne everything. Life before and after Greg Hollinger and his Beretta semi-automatic. Everything between Ben and Diane's meeting and first kiss to Diane bleeding out in the parking lot of Central Cleaners on a cold and clear January afternoon, and the ghosts of the children they never had following him around his apartment at three AM.

When he finished, Ben let out a long breath and then kissed the top of Anne's head. She said something he didn't catch. He leaned across her to turn on the lamp, but Anne put her hand on his arm, stopping him, and in the dark, they'd made love again.

Time, Ben thought.

That's all anyone needed. Anne and he had found each other. It didn't matter how quickly or gradually it had happened. That was the point. It happened. That's what mattered. Your life started on the other side of that.

Ben checked missed calls before repocketing his cell phone. Three from his old partner in Homicide, Andy Calucci, all after midnight over the last three nights when Ben had been at the house with Anne. He made a mental note to call Calucci back later.

Ben took the voice-activated recorder out of Jack's pocket, then replayed and erased the afternoon's non-sequiturs and white noise. He gathered up the dish and glass and made sure Jack had taken all his meds. The local news started. Ben stood next to Jack and watched a dumb show sequence of images. The mayor. Buddy Tedros. Stanley Tedros. Stanley Tedros's house and back-yard. Ross Tines, the Magnolia Beach Chief of Police. The main gates at Stanco Beverages. The mayor again. The shot of the beach that was used on the city's website as the home page.

Jack looked over and up at Ben. "You're that policeman," he said.

"Yes I am." Ben waited for Jack to add something, but he returned his attention to the television screen and a commercial for half-pound hamburgers.

Ben checked his watch, figured Anne and Paige would be at least another half-hour minimum. He checked the to-do list taped to the front of the refrigerator and decided to start a load of laundry. Anne had gone in to work early to compensate for the time she'd taken off for the parent-teacher conference, and he knew she'd be tired, more than tired, by the time she and Paige got home.

He walked down the hallway off the living room into Anne's bedroom and began stripping the sheets. They held a faint tidal flats smell and a series of pale Rorschach Blot stains from their lovemaking.

He bundled the bedclothes in his arms and hesitated for a moment next to the bedside nightstand. Then he started for the wash room. He dropped the clothes in the toploader and emptied the hamper. He set the water level and temperature and cycle. When the washer filled and began agitating, he added bleach.

Ben went back to the kitchen for a beer. He cracked it, not bothering to ink his wrist with a hash mark, and walked into the living room and stood next to Jack, who must have changed channels because the news was over and in its place was a horror film featuring a stocky man in the process of being transformed into a werewolf. The special effects were low-budget and the color watery. The volume was still muted.

Ben looked down the hall.

He walked back to Anne's bedroom and went to the nightstand. Anne and he kept the condoms in the top drawer. Ben opened the one below it.

The journal was bound in imitation leather. Anne's initials were embossed on its cover. Along its spine was a small sleeve for holding a pen. There was no clasp or lock.

Ben sat on the edge of the bare bed and opened the journal.

On the first page, Anne had written "My Time, My Life" and below that, the date, a September ninth three years ago.

The next page was blank.

As was every other page Ben flipped to.

He looked around the room. He closed the journal and put it back in the drawer. He went to the kitchen for another beer. He hesitated, then inked his left wrist with a single hash-mark.

He pulled over a chair and joined Jack in the living room. They watched the stocky man, now a full-blown werewolf, run through a park, then stop to tilt back his head and silently howl at a moon full and burning and wreathed in clouds.

TWENTY-NINE

SHE DIDN'T KNOW WHY she'd done it. Ben Decovic had asked her about the traffic jam, and Corrine Tedros should have just told him she didn't remember any problems, but Croy Wendall having killed Stanley off schedule and under different circumstances from the ones they'd originally set up had left Corrine uneasy, a little too vulnerable, and Ben Decovic had had the same effect on her, Decovic tall and gaunt and God-haunted, looking like he belonged in one of the stained glass windows Corrine had seen in the Greek Orthodox Church during Stanley's funeral, and when Decovic had pushed the questions about the timeline and her whereabouts, Corrine had lied, and the lie had been easy and automatic, but it had returned with a new set of teeth, and it kept returning, and though Corrine wanted to believe that everything was still all right, that she was simply overreacting, the phone call from Terri Illes had left her in a simmering panic.

Decovic had been around to talk to her too. Corrine had no doubt Terri Illes had used the interview to slander her. Terri was a permanent fixture at the Magnolia Beach Country Club, all social position and tanning beds and book groups. She was married to one of those mid-level managerial types at Stanco Beverages who always stood closer than necessary when talking to Corrine and tried to hide the fact he wanted to get in her pants by giving her boyish grins and telling self-deprecating stories about his golf game.

During the course of the twenty minute phone call, Terri had tormented Corrine with her sympathy and concern, continually evoking Stanley's death and her shock at its violence, repeatedly offering a sisterly shoulder for Corrine's grief while subtly taunting Corrine by withholding the particulars of Ben Decovic's line of questioning.

Afterwards, Corrine kept replaying her own interview with Decovic. She hadn't expected to have to account for her whereabouts more than once. She thought she'd had that covered, but then Croy Wendall had thrown everything off by killing Stanley almost five hours later than he was supposed to. Still, she told herself, everything in her statement came down to her word against Decovic's.

Except her reply to his offhanded question about traffic problems. That and her follow-up lie about having to stop at Walgreens for tampons.

Her period had started this morning.

Corrine wondered if Decovic was planning on getting around to talking to Buddy.

Two periods in one month. It'd be a little hard to explain that one away.

Buddy, though, was still too broken up by grief to ask for sex. Corrine could play the same card if she had to and put Buddy off until her period ended.

That left Decovic's question about the traffic problem.

It probably meant nothing.

It nagged though. She had a feeling about Decovic. Corrine had dealt with cops before and recognized the type.

She debated with herself over the next fifteen minutes and then put in a call to the Magnolia Beach Police Department and asked to speak with the dispatcher in the Traffic division. When the call was transferred, she put as much honey and helplessness as she could in her voice, telling the dispatcher she worked for a local insurance agency and needed to double-check the date and time for a claim involving an accident on Queensland and Old Market Boulevard.

The dispatcher ran it for her and then told Corrine there'd been no accident report filed for the date and time she'd given him.

It had taken four tries before she got through to Raychard Balen. By the time he was on the line, Corrine's nerves were shredded.

Balen kept telling her to calm down.

Corrine couldn't. She was lost to the same confusing mix of helplessness and rage that she'd felt when she stepped up to the placard of Stanley Tedros at the grocery store.

Balen said he'd look into the matter, and if the police showed up again, not to talk to them unless he was there.

Corrine had not liked the sound of that.

She told Balen she wanted him to do more than look into it. She wanted him to shut the thing down completely.

Balen had again told her to calm down and said he'd get back to her.

That left the rest of the afternoon.

Corrine had learned to watch her liquor intake, and except for a couple of bad stretches in Phoenix, she stuck to social drinking and usually confined it to nothing stronger than wine, but after talking to Raychard Balen, she'd spent the rest of the afternoon fighting the urge to sandblast her anxiety with the bottle of Beam in Buddy's liquor cabinet, going so far on two occasions as to pour the drinks, Corrine smelling the malt whiskey's sweet promises of escape, however temporary, before she dumped them down the sink.

It felt as if Stanley Tedros had followed her around the house all afternoon.

Buddy was putting in long hours at the Stanco plant since Stanley's death, and when he finally got home, he drove them to a barbecue place outside town. The Pig's Skin that was touted for its mustard-based sauce and Low Country hospitality, all of which translated, as Corrine had correctly assumed, into an unpainted building with all the charm of a shack, rows of rough-hewn picnic tables, plastic silverware and paper plates overflowing with greasy shredded meat, rice, cole slaw, and slabs of white bread, gallons of over-sweetened iced tea, and a clientele comprised of locals who rubbernecked and stage-whispered when she and Buddy entered and took their seats. Buddy, between bantering with the waitress, had run through his plate and most of Corrine's.

He'd waited until the drive back before he mentioned that James Restan had called and reinstated his offer to buy out Stanco Beverages and the rights to Julep.

"And you're just getting around to telling me about it *now*?"

He downshifted for a sharp curve and added, "I wish I'd never mentioned it at all."

"You mean keep it a secret?" Corrine said. "That's what you want our marriage to run on?"

Buddy took the curve and shifted up, the engine missing a little on the acceleration. "No, that's not what I meant," he said. "I wish I'd waited to bring it up, that's all. You're upset now. It's been a nice evening."

"What did you tell Restan exactly?" Corrine could feel the missing beat in the car's engine through the floorboards. It was like a mangled bar of music in a favorite song.

"I told him I wasn't ready to make a decision right now. I owe that much to the employees, but mostly to Uncle Stanley."

"But we talked about this, Buddy. The offer, it's good and might not be around for long."

Buddy nodded. "I know. I've been thinking about some things though, and I told Restan it didn't feel right to decide anything one way or another until Uncle Stanley's murderer has been brought to justice."

Corrine momentarily closed her eyes. "What did Restan say to that?"

"He wished me luck."

They followed the lines of the coast, and Corrine watched the ocean break in and out of view, the waters dark and wrinkled by lines of waves, a pale moon riding the horizon. The air coming through the vents was warm and swampy. A sharp pain moved high into Corrine's chest.

"I'll admit James Restan's offer is attractive," Buddy said carefully, "but you know, I've been looking over Stanley's plans to keep Julep within Stanco and to expand operations and distribution, and they have some merit too. He may have been on to something."

Corrine pounded her fist on the dash. "You're serious? You mean you're going to run Stanco yourself? You never said anything about this to me."

"Calm down," Buddy said. "I said I was considering keeping Stanco and Julep in the family. I was going to talk to you about it."

The sharp pain in Corrine's chest blunted and then broke down and reappeared in her stomach. She rested her head against the passenger window.

"What about our plans?" she asked after a moment. "Everything we talked about?"

No strings. That was the whole point of the buyout. No strings. They were going to travel. Go wherever and do whatever they wanted. The money would be there. Stanley wouldn't. They'd return to Magnolia Beach a couple times a year. There'd be nothing to hold them to one place.

Corrine wanted Paris first.

That's what they'd talked about after Buddy had formally announced their engagement.

"It's not like we're going to give them up," Buddy said. "We have our whole lives. There'll be time."

Buddy shifted and then reached over and rested his hand on her shoulder. It took all of Corrine's willpower not to flinch.

"He raised me," Buddy said and let his hand fall. "Whatever you might have thought of him, Stanley took me in and gave me a good life. It doesn't feel right to move on the buy-out right now."

The queasiness Corrine felt was warm and thick, and the motion of the car and the spill of its headlights intensified it. She fought back the urge to take off her seatbelt.

The reward Buddy had posted.

The tape recorder he'd bought and left at Jack Carson's.

And now this.

She glanced over at her husband.

Must be nice, Corrine thought, to be able to afford a conscience, to have a past and a life you'd want to call your own. Her husband would never understand that there were lives that left no room for anything but themselves, just as he would never understand how far someone would be willing to go to leave them behind.

THIRTY

BEN DECOVIC PARKED THE CRUISER in the lot adjacent to the tennis courts at the south entrance of the city park, then got out, taking a path along the treeline to a small clearing that held a cast-iron barbecue grill, a dark green metal trash container, and three pre-cast concrete picnic tables.

Leon Douglas showed up ten minutes later. He was wearing a bright orange Clemson T-shirt, a large white tiger paw imprinted on each shoulder, and he had shaved his head. He also wore a pair of wire frame glasses Ben didn't remember seeing on him before. He figured Leon was practicing passing himself off as a college student since the first wave of spring break was officially starting, and there would be untold opportunities for separating the students from their cash and credit cards and sundry vacation possessions.

Leon plopped down across from Ben at one of the concrete tables and opened the paper bag Ben had set in its center.

Leon immediately began shaking his head. He held up a long tube of Sweet Tarts. "How many time I be telling you it Shock Tart I like? Make me wonder what you hearing when I tell you anything." Leon cracked the top on the soda.

"Ok, Shock Tarts," Ben said. "Check." He leaned back and waited.

"An old pocketwatch," Leon said, unwrapping one end of the candy, "a gold one. That's what I've been hearing around." ·

Ben shrugged. He was surprised it had taken this long for the word to get out. The Department had withheld the detail of the killer taking Stanley's pocketwatch after Buddy Tedros had verified that Stanley always wore it.

"You get cops popping up at every pawn and fence in town," Leon said, "all of them asking did anyone try to lay off a watch, and after a while, the word, it get out. Lot of people wouldn't mind tapping that reward."

"Anyone or anything credible concerning that?" Ben asked.

"Man, if there was," Leon said, "I'm on my own way straight to Mr. Buddy Tedros."

Ben asked if Leon had dug up anything on his missing Glock. He'd expected, by now, that Leon would have turned up something or that the semi-automatic would have been confiscated after some standard-brand Saturday night mayhem.

"Nothing yet," Leon said. He took a lime Sweet Tart and threw it at a blue jay perched on the lip of the trash container.

"Sonny Gramm then," Ben said.

"Heard Mr. Sonny got a rodent problem and got a new alarm system install at his home."

"Old news," Ben said. "Unless you know who did it."

Leon shook his head no, then thumbed a pink Sweet Tart into his mouth. "There was some action two night ago, the Passion Palace though."

"What kind?"

"Mr. Sonny out of town few days on business," Leon said, "and this guy Wayne LaVell stop by the Palace and spread the green around, buying all the dancer drinks and tipping large. LaVell stay til closing. He be everybody's friend. Mr. Sonny, he lose it when he hear about LaVell."

"You know this for a fact?"

Leon nodded. "One of the dancer told me."

"Why would she do something like that, Leon?"

He sighed and shook his head. "'Cause dancing be high-stress, long hours, and this girl maybe she need get behind a little recreational weed to unwind the end of the day. That straight enough for you?"

A gust of wind burst around them. It smelled of salt. Ben waited a moment before nodding. He asked if there were anything else.

"Only if you want to talk about no rain," Leon said. "That's mostly what I keep hearing, people all the time talking about the weather, how hot and where the rain be. There a preacher over by Old Marketplace set up a tent and calling it End Times."

Leon slipped the envelope Ben handed over in his back pocket and adjusted the fit of his wire frames, then stood up. He tossed the empty soda can in the direction of the trash. "See you," he said.

"Be careful, Leon," Ben said, "in case you decide to help some of the students on break unwind like your dancer friend. A lot of cops know you."

"Hold that tiger," Leon said, slapping the front of his Clemson shirt, and walked off in the direction he'd come in earlier.

Ben finished his shift, signed out, and headed for the lot at the rear of the county complex building. Ed Hatch, from Homicide, was leaning against the trunk of Ben's car, stork-like, one foot raised and resting on the rear bumper. He sipped from a white Styrofoam cup as he watched Ben approach.

"Here we go," Hatch said. His partner, Bill Gramble, was sitting on the passenger side of the unmarked parked across from Hatch. Gramble nodded at Ben and went back to the fast food supper, soft drink, fries, and lopsided burger, that he'd set out on the dash.

"A word," Hatch said when Ben stepped up. He set the cup on the trunk and dusted off his hands. "You seem a little confused, Patrolman Decovic," he began, "about your job description. That or maybe you got a promotion to Homicide I haven't heard about yet."

"I left a message on your voice mail," Ben said. "I wasn't trying to hide anything."

"Oh, I got your message all right," Hatch said, "along with another from the esteemed barrister Raychard Balen."

Didn't take Corrine Tedros or her husband long to get in touch with Balen, Ben thought.

He explained that he'd been on patrol and spotted Corrine Tedros out in the front yard with the movers. He'd taken advantage of the opportunity to do some follow-up, fully intending to hunt down Hatch afterwards and pass on anything he'd found. He brought up the voice mail message again.

"And Corrine Tedros just happened to get the impression you were working the homicide with me all by herself?" Hatch said.

Ben slowly let out his breath. "I never directly said I was."

"But you didn't disabuse her of the notion either," Hatch said.

Gramble laughed and then swiveled the passenger side mirror and picked at a piece of burger caught in his teeth.

"I got something though," Ben said. "That's why I called you."

Hatch raised his eyebrows. "Really? Something to support your Washer Theory? Maybe Corrine Tedros jiggling a fistful of heavy-gauge washers while she tried to resist confessing to the murder of Stanley Tedros under your expert interrogation techniques?"

"A lie," Ben said. "I caught her in a lie when there was no reason or need for one." For now, Ben decided not to mention to Hatch that he'd also talked to Terri Illes.

"Hell," Hatch said, uncrossing his arms and picking up the cup from the trunk. "I'd lie to you too, Decovic, just on principle, if you showed up and tried to pass yourself off as part of a homicide investigation."

"The tips are going nowhere," Ben said. "I think you need to take a closer look at Corrine Tedros and her husband."

"And I think you need to reread your job description," Hatch said, "and start following it."

"That's it, then?" Ben asked.

"Not quite," Hatch said, crumbling the Styrofoam cup. "I don't appreciate getting phone calls at home from shitbags like Raychard Balen. I have a family, Decovic. I make it a rule to keep work and my home life separate."

"What did Balen threaten you with?"

Hatch bounced the crumpled Styrofoam cup off Ben's chest. "I'm getting mightily pissed here, Decovic. Let me clear up any misconceptions on your part. For one, Balen did not threaten me. He knew I was running lead on the Tedros case. Balen could have gone to the media or the chief or the damn mayor. You, not Corrine Tedros, would have been in deep shit then, Decovic." Hatch paused and pointed. "I'm no fan of Raychard Balen by any stretch, but he gave me the chance to settle this quietly and off the books. You want, I'll go to my division head right now and write up the incident. Make it official. It doesn't matter to me."

Ben didn't say anything.

"Ok," Hatch said. "And before I go, there's another misconception needs clarified. Anything that you or anyone else gets from the reward tips or anything I turn up on my own that points to Corrine Tedros, I will go after her. Have no doubts whatsoever about that. I will go after her."

Hatch looked down, crushed the Styrofoam cup with his shoe, and then looked back at Ben. "Understand this too. I will not go after Corrine Tedros based on evidence or hunches tied to irregularities in procedure," he said. "I will not walk there."

Hatch brushed by Ben and crossed to the unmarked. Before he pulled away, Bill Gramble stuck his head out the passenger window and said, "Hey Decovic, what did the blind man tell his wife after he shaved her cat?"

THIRTY-ONE

BEN DECOVIC HAPPILY WATCHED the life he'd made—or tried to make—at the White Palms Apartments disappear little by little. He'd quit stocking the kitchen cabinets and refrigerator with anything but the barest of basics. The drawers in the bedroom dresser were steadily emptying, ebbing like a waterline each time he packed. The center of the dining room table held piles of unsorted mail. The air, itself, in the apartment had come to feel thin and underused.

Ben's name remained on the lease, but another life was taking shape at 809 Farrow Lane with Anne, Paige, and Jack Carson.

Earlier in the evening, he'd felt as if he'd begun to fully inhabit that life.

Ben had found himself in the kitchen with Anne, and the radio was on some oldies station and the Everly Brothers were saying all they had to do was dream, while Ben stood at the sink peeling shrimp, the thin translucent shells gathering like some variety of seaborne cicadas.

Ben dropped the shrimp into a white bowl with a blue rim, the shells into a yellow plastic wastebasket. His fingertips smelled like the floor of the Atlantic.

Anne had been at the stove, sautéing a skilletful of diced onions, mushrooms, and red bell peppers, and she had glanced over her shoulder and smiled, and right then, all the habitual stress and exhaustion, all the worries about household finances and her father's health and Paige's problems with her classmates fell away, and Ben had seen what Anne must have looked like at nineteen or twenty.

At that moment, Anne's smile held the promise that March made to April and May collected on, an old promise that unexpectedly opened onto an earthbound grace that arose simply from the business of living.

Paige remained a major sticking point though.

Anne was still adamant about maintaining the façade that Ben was not staying over. He went along with it for Anne's sake, showing up after Paige and Jack were asleep and leaving before they awoke in the morning, but whenever Ben tried to convince Anne that Paige was not fooled and knew exactly what was going on, Anne stonewalled him. Anne needed the fiction, so he didn't push things.

To and for himself, Ben counseled patience. Paige undercut all other strategies. He would wait her out. He'd practice the mechanics of fatherhood until one day he looked up and discovered Paige smiling at him. Ben was banking on that.

Just as he was banking on leaving behind in the apartment all the attendant three AM despair and disorder and a kind of lonely deep and powerful enough to bend bones.

With Anne, he was not superfluous.

He was needed, and being needed was both an aphrodisiac and sacrament, Ben and Anne finding each other in the dark each night, an urgency of hands and mouths and breath and flesh, and on the other side of the bedroom door, three lives and now a fourth that were joined in an equally fundamental way.

Flesh and family.

He'd found a place in both.

THIRTY-TWO

CROY WENDALL WAS PLANTING VERBENAS. He pretended his hands were machines.

Jamie carried over the flats of flowers from the trucks. He was supposed to help Croy plant them too, but Jamie liked to pretend he was doing work and only really did any if Mr. Sharpe or one of the supervisors came over to see how things were going.

They were working for Mr. Sharpe planting flowers at a new subdivision because Mr. Balen didn't have any crimes for them to do right then.

Jamie had already spent all the money Mr. Balen gave him though, so Croy and he got up early and waited on the corner across from the Food Lion for the green truck to stop and pick them up to plant flowers for Mr. Sharpe. Jamie was not in a good mood because of the beer he drank last night, and he almost got in a fight over his seat with a man named Hector when they were riding on the truck.

Croy looked up from his planting and saw a yellow cat at the house across the street in the grass next to a crimson maple. Croy didn't like cats too much. They gave him a nervous feeling. He thought it had something to do with the size of their tongues.

He added the cat to the number he was thinking in his head and then subtracted one because that was how many syllables the word had, and then he multiplied it by three because cat started with the third letter in the alphabet, and when he got that number, Croy divided it by the number of houses he'd been planting verbenas at so far, which was four.

That made the number he was thinking about in his head *eight*.

Eight also matched *ate*. It was like they were shadows of each other, and Croy was the light that fell on either one and made the shadow when he said the word.

Croy got the nervous feeling again at lunchtime when Jamie and another man named Tommy started talking about what they'd do if they had the reward money for telling who killed Stanley Tedros, and Croy had made himself quiet inside and like he wasn't even there to hear Jamie and Tommy talking, but after a while, Tommy started talking about his car and something called a torque, so Croy unwrapped a sandwich and ate it.

After lunch, Jamie went to look for a place to hide and take a nap, and Croy went back to planting verbenas. The sun was like a mean dog that wouldn't leave him alone.

Croy counted the number of verbenas left in the flats, and there were thirty-nine of them, and Croy thought the number but did not say it because thirty-nine was the same as the times he'd stabbed Stanley Tedros, but then the number started moving around in his head and mixed with the words Croy had heard Jamie say at lunch about the reward money, and that was when Croy started pretending his hands were machines.

THIRTY-THREE

BEN DECOVIC HAD ARRANGED to switch and sub on the third shift so he could help Anne Carson get ready for Paige's birthday party. Ten kids had shown up, though there were easily enough food and treat bags and game prizes for more than twice that many. The living room and kitchen were filled with streamers and banners and clusters of helium balloons, most of whose faces held cartoon characters Ben didn't recognize. In the middle of a large sheet cake *Paige* was written in a rainbow of M&M's and circled with twelve thin candles, the rest of the cake thick with whorls of white icing and bordered by alternating red and blue roses.

Anne slipped into the kitchen and gave him a quick kiss and whispered thanks. Ben nodded and smiled. Two nights ago, after they'd made love, Ben woke and found Anne sitting in her nightgown at the kitchen table. She'd been crying. In front of her were the monthly bills she'd sorted and resorted in an attempt to leave enough to cover Paige's party. Ben had insisted on helping, and Anne had not tried to talk him out of it. She'd simply taken his hand, and they'd gone back to bed.

In the living room, Anne organized a game of Charades. Ben set out more chips and popcorn and refilled a line of paper cups with soda. Outside the kitchen window was the brightly colored piñata Ben had hung from the lower limb of the magnolia tree earlier. In the afternoon light, it resembled a psychedelic hornet's nest.

He sensed movement on the landing, and opening the door, Ben found one of the kids from the party standing by herself at the railing. Her fists were clenched and her arms tight at her side, and she was doing a poor job of fighting back tears. Ben stepped over and asked her name.

"Lucy," she said.

Ben squatted next to her and asked what was wrong.

The girl glanced at him, then away. "Are you Miss Anne's boyfriend, the policeman?"

"Yes."

"Will you arrest somebody?"

"I can if they've done something wrong," Ben said.

The girl turned and directly faced him. "Well, you need to arrest Paige Carson then," she said.

Ben started to smile, stopped himself, and asked why.

"Because she told me my gift was retarded. Because she's very mean and not just today."

"What did you get her?"

"A board game: Life. I picked it out myself."

"That's a good one," Ben said. In fact, he'd considered something along the lines of that for Paige himself, but finally he'd been undone by the logistics of wandering the aisles of Toys Plus, a mammoth franchise that lived up to its name, trying to find something he thought Paige would like, and settled in the end for sticking two twenty dollar bills in a card with *It's Your Day!* emblazoned across its face.

"Why don't we go back inside?" Ben asked. "I think they're playing Charades."

"Nobody likes Paige at school," Lucy said. "That's why so many kids didn't come to the party. I didn't want to either, but my mother made me even though she doesn't like Paige very much herself."

Ben glanced through the window into the living room and tried to come up with something diplomatic, but his words sounded like dialogue from a bad after-school television special. "Growing up is never easy. It's hard to know how to act sometimes."

"Paige needs to grow down, not up," Lucy said. "She thinks she's the boss of the world."

Ben eventually cajoled her back into the living room, and once there, she threw herself into the game. Ben stayed and watched and thought about how good a cold beer was going to taste later on. Anne and he had given up trying to hide the fact from Paige that Ben was spending the night, and for her part, Paige had not exactly welcomed him to the fold. Ben felt the weight of Paige's eyes on him, the unflinching dark brown watchfulness, and at best there was a stiff acceptance of his presence and a lot of terse monosyllabic responses to his attempts at conversation.

In the living room, a little boy with a spiked haircut pretended to be a grizzly bear. Another kid, a ferris wheel. One kid mimicked a mailman. Another a tree in a strong wind. When Paige's turn came, she was a spider spinning a web.

When the game broke up, Paige walked down the hall to her bedroom. Ben, curious, followed and stopped in the doorway. Paige had pulled back the curtain and was looking out toward the driveway and street. He asked if something was wrong.

"I'm expecting someone," Paige said. "It appears he's late."

"He?" Ben said. He tried to imagine what brand of boy would develop a crush on Paige.

"Mr. Deane," she said. "He said he was going to come by."

It took a moment for Ben to place the name. Gerald Deane. The guidance counselor who'd begun working with Paige at school. According to Anne, Paige was evidently taken with him, but from what Ben gathered, that had yet to translate into any improvement in Paige's behavior and attitude.

Paige let the curtain fall back into place and turned to Ben and said, "May I ask you a question?"

Ben nodded.

"Are you using a condom when you have sexual intercourse with my mother?" She dropped her hands to her blue-jeaned hips. "I hope so," she added.

Ben didn't know what to say.

Someone began knocking on the front door.

"Maybe that's him," Paige said, brushing by Ben to answer it.

It turned out to be Buddy Tedros. He wished Paige a happy birthday and handed her a present with wrapping paper covered in row upon row of leaping dolphins. Paige added it to the pile on the living room couch and then headed for the kitchen where Anne had just announced she was cutting the birthday girl's cake.

Buddy Tedros shook Ben's hand and introduced himself. He looked around the living room and asked, "Where's Jack?"

Ben told Buddy that Anne thought the party might agitate him and so Jack and Mrs. Wood were at Ben's apartment for the afternoon.

Buddy and he crossed the room and stood just inside the doorway to the kitchen and watched Anne move among the kids, handing out napkins and teasing them about eating like wolves.

"I'm glad you two hooked up with each other," Buddy said. "Anne's good people. I've known Jack and her since high school. She deserved someone better than Ray."

"You knew him?"

Buddy nodded. "From high school. After graduation, Ray drove trucks for Stanco Beverages for a while, but got let go or quit. I forget which. That was pretty much the story with Ray."

Anne waved hello to Buddy and brought them over a piece of cake. She thanked Buddy for remembering Paige's birthday, then smiled and squeezed Ben's arm and went back to the party.

"Nothing like a roomful of kids, huh?" Buddy asked. "All that energy."

"There's that," Ben said.

"Wouldn't mind a couple of them around the house myself," Buddy said.

Ben overheard Paige tell another girl that the Harry Potter books sucked.

"I meant that, about hoping things work out for you and Anne," Buddy said, "and that you're as lucky as Corrine and me. I knew she was the one the first time I met her."

Ben asked where that was.

"Corrine was waitressing at one of Sonny Gramm's supper clubs in Myrtle Beach, and I was there for a bachelor party. Wasn't long after that, I was walking down the aisle."

"Funny how things turn out sometimes," Ben said.

Buddy forked a piece of cake, then asked if any of the reward tips looked promising.

"We're following them up," Ben said, "but I won't lie: All those tips, they take up a lot of extra hours, and I'm not sure it's worth it. Most of them are worthless or end up going nowhere."

"Stanley's pocketwatch hasn't shown up yet?"

Ben shook his head no.

"Oh man," Buddy said. He went silent for a moment.

"Maybe Corrine is right," he said finally. "She thinks I need to move on. The reward and the tape recorder with Jack, she didn't like the idea of either." He looked at Ben. "I couldn't do *nothing*, though. Stanley was the only family I had."

From the living room came a loud welter of voices and then Paige's overriding them. "It's my birthday," she said. "You have to do what I say."

"You know, Jack might still remember something," Buddy said. "It's not impossible. I know it wouldn't hold up in court, but maybe a lead. Anne says she can tell he's trying." Buddy paused and went back to his cake.

"Have you talked to Raychard Balen lately?" Ben was tired of Buddy's routine. He was overplaying the family friend number. Ben had decided to give him a push. See what happened.

Buddy frowned. "Why would I do that?"

"Balen doesn't represent you?"

Buddy shook his head. "Will Patterson's been our family lawyer for years. I've never had any dealings with Raychard Balen, except to nod and say hello at a social function now and then."

"What about your wife?"

"I'm not sure she's ever met him," Buddy said. "Why do you ask?"

Ben was starting to wonder if Buddy Tedros was exactly what he appeared to be. His puzzlement seemed genuine.

"Balen's name came up in passing the other day," Ben said. "That's all. I thought he represented you. Otherwise I'd have never brought it up."

Anne stepped over from the kitchen. Her face was flushed, and she brushed back a dark lock of hair from her forehead. "Hey, you two, the natives are restless. They want the piñata."

Buddy and Ben set down their plates, and the three of them herded the kids outside and into a rough semblance of a line near the magnolia. Ben expected Paige, as the birthday girl, to once again assert her right to be first, but she let her classmates go before her, less from manners or affection Ben soon discovered than a belief the others would fail, Paige standing next to Anne with her arms crossed and a bemused expression as Buddy blindfolded and turned each kid in circles and then stepped back as the kid began swinging.

The kid with the spiked hair managed to dent the side of the piñata. The others missed it completely.

"My turn," Paige said.

Buddy blindfolded her, but Paige complained it was too tight. She handed Buddy the bat and said, "I'll fix it."

Ben noticed Paige left the lower left portion of the bandana a little higher than necessary.

"That's better," she said, taking back the bat.

Buddy Tedros spun her around.

Paige connected on her first swing, and the piñata exploded, a blur of rainbow-colored fragments and treasure flying everywhere.

THIRTY-FOUR

THE PALMER WAS IN DOWNTOWN Magnolia Beach across from the old courthouse and overlooked the square. The building was unprepossessing, two-story and brown-bricked, wedged between two storefronts, one an antique store and the other a realtor's office.

The East Room on the second floor of the Palmer was the unofficial watering hole for select segments of the city's politicians and businesspeople, a place to hatch deals, cut deals, and break deals and the ideal site for long private lunches or quiet assignations. By unspoken agreement, Mondays and Wednesdays from eleven to three were reserved for Republicans, Tuesdays and Thursdays for Democrats, and Friday and Saturdays were free zones. The Palmer was closed on Sundays.

Corrine was meeting her husband there for lunch on a Thursday. She'd always suspected that the menu was more elaborate and the service better on a Monday or Wednesday, but she couldn't deny the small jolt of pleasure that came from being recognized when she stepped through the front doors and being politely escorted by a maître d' upstairs and handed over to another who exclusively worked the East Room. She liked dressing for the Palmer—today a dark blue dress and black heels—and liked the idea of stepping through the door and being lead to a table among those who truly counted because they had money and power and understood what could be done with each.

The East Room had a richly textured dark patterned carpet, dark mahogany paneling, and soft amber lighting. Scattered about the room in marble-based planters were thickly foliaged hibiscus with large dark red blooms. There were no mirrors, and the narrow windows running nearly from floor to ceiling were shuttered. There were thirty tables in the room, all of them filled, and Corrine spotted Buddy at a corner table talking to Will Patterson, the lawyer handling probate on Stanley's estate.

She was halfway across the room when someone called out, "April. April Rayne."

Corrine recognized the voice but wished to her marrow she didn't. She kept walking.

The voice followed her. "Hey, hold it a sec. April. Come on over here."

Corrine hesitated, then slowly turned, facing Wayne LaVell. He'd put on even more weight since she'd seen him last. He was sitting at a table with Raychard Balen.

Corrine worked up an expression suggesting mild puzzlement and said, "Pardon?"

"Can't believe it. Ms. April Rayne. Imagine that," Lavell said, struggling to get out of his chair. He wore a yellow shirt and red tie dotted with dozens of tiny mermaids.

"I think you have me confused with someone else," Corrine said.

Wayne LaVell let out a wet laugh. "Come on, baby, something like you, that's not likely."

Corrine thought Raychard Balen might help her, but he sat back, his tiny mustache and the corners of his eyes crimped, and waited to see where things were going.

"I'm afraid you made a mistake," Corrine said. "Please excuse me." She started to turn away and almost ran into a busboy clearing the next table.

"That's something I try not to do," Wayne LaVell said. "Make mistakes. At least not more than once. They end up costing you, mistakes do." LaVell smoothed his tie over the great curve of his stomach. "Come on, April, sit down and have a drink with my friend Mr. Balen, and me. We can catch up on things."

LaVell's voice was louder than necessary and carried around the room. Corrine was aware of the other diners taking note while studiously appearing not to and felt a warm flush building at the base of her throat.

Buddy was suddenly standing next to her, asking her if there was a problem.

"Corrine?" Wayne LaVell said. "Hey, that's a classy name."

"I'm not sure I'm following," Buddy said.

Corrine hooked her arm through Buddy's and said, "This gentleman's mistaken me for someone else."

Raychard Balen finally spoke up. "Wayne, we have a few more things to discuss here. Why don't we let Mr. and Mrs. Tedros get back to their lunch?"

"OK," LaVell said, stretching out the word. He shook Buddy's hand and nodded one time too many and then sat back down. "You got yourself a real looker for a wife there, Mr. Tedros," he said, smiling, before pulling his plate closer.

Corrine kept her arm linked through Buddy's, and even after they were seated she was reluctant to let it go. Will Patterson, the probate lawyer, stood up and said he had to rejoin his party, then added, "Are you ok, Corrine? Your color's not too good."

She gave him a weak smile. "I'm just hungry, that's all. I didn't get around to eating breakfast this morning."

When the waiter arrived, Corrine ordered more than she could possibly eat, as if trying to convince herself that what she'd said to Will Patterson was true and sufficient to explain away what she felt.

She half listened to Buddy saying something about a birthday party. She kept her head lowered and her gaze away from Raychard Balen's table and told herself she'd start to calm down once the food was set before her. At home, she kept the kitchen shelves and refrigerator crammed and overflowing, immediately replacing whatever was used. In restaurants, she'd long established the practice of ordering at least one item that she knew she wouldn't get around to finishing. There was a blind pleasure and deep comfort in the presence of surplus, of the simple and real fact of *more*.

There was nothing though to buffer the memories that Wayne LaVell dragged along with him.

Corrine wanted to leave but knew walking out now would only buy her more questions and problems. She watched Raychard Balen wave his fork and say something to Wayne LaVell and then LaVell put up his hand like a crossing guard and slowly shake his head.

Buddy was still talking and along the way mentioned a name that caused Corrine to ask him to back up.

"At Paige Carson's birthday party," Buddy said.

"You said something about Decovic." Corrine paused and forced herself to take a sip of ice water. "Who's that?"

"You sure you're feeling all right?" Buddy dropped his hand on hers and leaned closer. "That's what I've been talking about. The birthday party, the one you couldn't make."

He went on and told her again about meeting Ben Decovic and how Anne Carson and Decovic were seeing each other and how happy he was for Anne because she'd been having a tough time of it with her father and the Alzheimer's. Buddy said Decovic seemed like a nice guy, a little distant maybe, but he obviously cared for Anne and was trying to be the father Paige had never really had.

Corrine took another sip of ice water.

Across the room, Wayne LaVell broke into a deep, wet laugh at something Raychard Balen said. LaVell then leaned over and knife-and-forked his way into a thick steak.

"Hey," Buddy said, "you're trembling."

She watched LaVell jab a piece of steak. Its insides were pink.

Buddy rubbed the back of her hand.

THIRTY-FIVE

IT WAS JUST BREAKING ON MIDNIGHT when Ben Decovic called his old Homicide partner, Andy Calucci. Ben had talked to Anne Carson earlier, and she'd said there'd have to be a raincheck for his coming over tonight. She was tired, and she hadn't waited or wanted to elaborate. Ben didn't push things. Even over the phone, he could hear the layers of exhaustion in Anne's voice, and he knew that Paige and she had had another long round of after-school meetings about Paige's continuing classroom behavioral problems.

"Figured you'd probably be up," Ben said.

"Lemme turn down the television," Calucci said. "Shit, I can't find the remote." A moment later, he was back. "It's been a while, you and me talked."

"I know," Ben said. "I kept planning to call you back, but things have been a little crazy and unhinged here." He immediately regretted the word choice.

Andy let it go. "Yeah, well, it sounds like you got a real titwringer down there. I watched the Eleven tonight, and there was another segment about that old guy that bottles pop down there getting murdered." Andy paused. "He got stabbed, what, like thirty-five times?"

"Thirty-nine," Ben said.

"That'd do it too," Andy said. "They still probably got you running all those tips, right? That was on the Eleven too, the old guy's kid putting up the reward. I know what that means. A lot of Blue out there, humping down worthless leads, all the media people shoving microphones at you the end of the day."

"Absolute zero, so far," Ben said.

"Yeah, well, no surprise there," Andy said. "I saw your chief on the news too. Sounds like the higher-ups want to push the drifter angle. Hit and run. No forwarding address."

"They don't want to scare the tourists," Ben said.

"Well, it's a titwringer, any way you look at it."

Ben walked into the kitchen of his apartment for a beer. The sink was full of dishes from a meal he couldn't remember eating. He asked Andy how his wife Judy was doing.

Calucci laughed. "She hasn't left me yet, though, I figure, you talk to her, she'd say it's not like that hasn't crossed her mind on more than one occasion." Andy paused and then hesitated before going on. "She drove by the house the other day and noticed there was a sign out front."

"It was time," Ben said.

"Why'd you decide to sell all of a sudden?" Andy said. "Judy and me, we figured you'd keep renting it for a while, and then it's still there, you come back home."

"Things have changed a little," Ben said. "I met someone."

"No shit? That's good, man. Judy will be happy to hear that too." Andy went on to ask Ben her name and how they'd met.

Ben didn't get any further than the name before Andy interrupted him.

"Oh man," he said. "*Carson*. Did I hear that right? I'm thinking, that's the same last name as the guy saw the murder. Please tell me I don't already know where this is going."

"It just happened," Ben said.

"You don't get involved with witnesses," Andy said. "Rule One of the Job."

"I'm not working Homicide anymore," Ben said.

"Oh man," Andy said. "Listen to yourself. How many times did you have to split that hair?"

"I know what I'm doing, Andy."

He let that one go too, and when he did, their conversation started trailing off and then ended, a little strained on Ben's part, a little dubious and solicitous on Andy's.

Ben finished his beer and went into the kitchen for another and discovered he was out. He also realized he was hungry, very hungry in fact, but had no more luck there than he'd had with the beer supply. He'd gotten used to eating most of his meals out or at Anne's, and any groceries he bought tended to end up on her shelves or in her refrigerator.

Ben stood in the middle of his kitchen. The apartment was suspended in the same uneasy silence that arose in the interval between someone clearing his throat and speaking. Ben grabbed his keys and wallet and left.

The parking lot of the White Palms was coated in the lunar frost of the halogen lights. There was no wind. Ben felt a small pinprick of panic.

He got on Cantrell and took it to Bowman and then to Heritage, fully intending to end up in the aisles of the twenty-four hour Winn Dixie and restocking his refrigerator, but instead Ben found himself on Farrow and then parked with his lights off in front of Anne Carson's place. He rolled down the driver's side window and watched the dark house for fifteen minutes.

Whatever he'd hoped to find there tonight eluded him. The palms of his hands were damp on the steering wheel. His thoughts were not his friends.

He got back on Farrow and then took Edgewater, and over the next seventy-five minutes, he simply drove, heading initially through the industrial sector of northwest Magnolia Beach with its rehabbed textile mills and small manufacturing plants and the new trucking hub and warehouse complexes, slowing as he passed the main gates of Stanco Beverages, and then turning south and west when he came to Route 17, moving through new housing developments anchored by expensive new schools and the new commercial boom, the mall and factory outlets and car dealerships and chain motels and restaurants lining Old Marketplace Boulevard. Ben cut as far south as the airport, then mainlined it straight east on White Stone, catching Atlantic Avenue and following the coastline north toward downtown Magnolia Beach through a thicket of condos and resorts and restaurants.

Over the last ten months, Ben had driven the city, but he'd driven it as a cop with cop eyes and the structure and rhythm of Patrol shifts. Tonight he was driving it as a civilian, and all that structure had collapsed, and what he saw on the other side of the windshield was unbearably strange and foreign, and his thoughts had taken on the same cast, as if they belonged to someone else, and once that happened, he was back to where he had lost everything.

Dead was dead. Ask any cop or mortician. A corpse was a corpse. One was no different from another. Death was always a tautology.

Except somehow against all logic, it wasn't. You knew it in your bones that some deaths *meant.* They refused to be reduced to a least common denominator and flared, however briefly, in and against the darkness.

Ben Decovic's wife's death should have *meant.* Their love and her life should have ensured that it did.

Diane Decovic went to the dry cleaners, and then she was dead.

Cause and effect fled. Nothing held or fit. A sequence of events, that's all, no sense, all underwritten by Accident. She was alive, and then she wasn't.

Diane's sister had been getting married that weekend, and Ben was supposed to pick up his suit from Central Cleaners on his way home. Paperwork had kept him working overtime, so Diane said she'd pick up the suit instead. Ben thanked her and said he'd see her soon.

Her last words to him had been to ask what he wanted for dinner.

Then Greg Hollinger happened.

And Diane Decovic bled out in the parking lot of Central Cleaners under a cloudless January sun.

When Ben tried afterwards to inhabit his days, Greg Hollinger happened there too. Ben listened to and read all the subsequent news and police reports, patiently waiting for a motive to reveal itself, sure that one had to be there to account for the death of his wife and the four others, a motive that, in turn, would be the first step for him to find a way to give shape to his grief.

Greg Hollinger and his life, however, turned out to be their own tautology, and the deaths over the course of an afternoon of a line supervisor, elementary school teacher, bartender, CPA, and veterinarian ceased to be newsworthy. Without a motive, there was no narrative, and without a narrative, the newspeople could not call and present it as a tragedy because a story that was not a story made viewers uncomfortable. A story that was not a story would sooner or later be replaced by one that was, and Ben Decovic watched his wife and the others drop off the radar of the national news. It was as if she had died a second time.

He went back to work.

He discovered he'd lost his eye. He couldn't read a crime scene or a suspect anymore. There were fault lines running through everything he'd once believed. He was living on a different earth.

He stayed on the job, keeping busy, working extra shifts, wanting to believe that the touch, his eye, would return.

In the meantime, he started drinking.

Days and months passed. Ben didn't worry about distinguishing between them anymore.

One day, he found himself entering St. Mark's. Father John Sarko had just concluded morning mass and was heading for the sacristy when Ben called out to him.

Ben looked down and discovered he was pointing a Bersa .22 at Sarko. Ben recognized the gun—a sub-compact he'd bought Diane for when he was working late shifts—but did not remember how it had ended up in his hand.

Ben liked Father Sarko. He was a good man. He had done the funeral mass for Diane, and he had done it with solemnity and reverence, and Ben would always be grateful to him for that.

But it wasn't enough. There was not enough of *enough* to contain Ben's grief. Nor enough grief to contain the unruly and stubborn love Ben had for his wife.

Ben had moved further into the nave. He kept the Bersa trained on the center of Sarko's chest.

Ben wasn't sure if he'd come to shoot Father Sarko or himself or both.

Please give me the gun, Ben, Father Sarko had said. *You've been drinking.*

I want you to do your job, Ben had said. He pointed the Bersa at Sarko's head. *It's not enough to bury her. I want to know why. Why I didn't go to pick up the suit. Why Diane opened the door of Central Cleaners and started across the parking lot at the same moment Greg Hollinger pulled into it. Why Greg Hollinger did what he did. Why Greg Hollinger was born in the first place. Why love and work can't save you. Why every prayer sticks in my throat.*

Why. Ben wanted nothing less.

He had not heard Andy Calucci come up behind him. Just as he had not seen the acolyte crack open the door of the sacristy when Ben had begun yelling or heard the call the acolyte made on his cell phone. Just as he had not noticed that the acolyte was Andy's nephew, Tommy.

Andy Calucci was a member of St. Mark's. He and the Father went way back. Andy talked to Father Sarko, and then he powwowed with the brass on the force, and the morning and the drinking and the gun-pointing went away, and Ben went on to take a medical leave and dried out. When the medical leave finished, he extended it by taking an unpaid leave of absence and signed on for six weeks at a time-share at Magnolia Beach, South

Carolina, a place that existed as a speck on the far horizon of his childhood, embedded in a dim boyhood memory of standing on the ocean's edge and surf-fishing with his father while his mother sat further up the beach under a striped umbrella and read a fat paperback.

The time-share ran out. Ben resigned from the Ryland Police Department. He put Diane's and his house up for rent. He found an opening in Patrol. He took it. He moved into the White Palms Apartments. It was a sequence of events that he'd tried to convince himself passed for a fresh start.

THIRTY-SIX

CORRINE TEDROS had not made an appointment. She drove to Raychard Balen's Conway office, ignored the protests of the receptionist in the ante-room, and went straight through the door to the inner office without knocking.

Balen was working on a phone conversation and simultaneously circling items with a felt tip pen from sections of the *Sun News*, the *State*, the *Post and Courier*, and the *Magnolia Beach Monitor* spread across his desk. He glanced up at Corrine and gestured toward a chair. Corrine remained standing.

Balen cut short the phone call. There were small white flecks of what appeared to be dried toothpaste on the lens of his wire frames, and the left half of the thin black mustache he sported did not quite match up with the right. A pair of brown cloth suspenders hung loosely over his rumpled white shirt, and Balen had yet to get around to knotting his tie.

"A surprise visit," he said. He motioned toward the chair again. "You could have saved yourself the drive though. I'm scheduled to be at the Magnolia Beach branch tomorrow."

"There was a luncheon with the mayor yesterday," Corrine said.

Balen nodded. "I am aware of that. In point of fact, I was invited to attend but regretfully had other matters to attend to."

"My husband attended the luncheon. So did Wayne LaVell. In point of fact," Corrine said, leaning on the words, "LaVell sat next to him."

Balen raised his eyebrows, then shrugged. "The mayor's social secretary does not confer with me about seating arrangements, Corrine."

"I want to know what's going on with Wayne LaVell," Corrine said, "and what he wants."

"The same things you and I do," Balen said. "To live a long, prosperous, and happy life."

"Tell him to stay away from me and my husband then," Corrine said.

Raychard Balen lightly brushed the right half of his mustache with his thumb. "If I were to do so," he said, "I'd have to make some tonal adjustments to that statement. Otherwise, Mr. LaVell might perceive it as a threat. I know I'm certainly in danger of doing so."

"I have a life here," Corrine said.

Balen steepled his fingers. "Mr. LaVell is aware of that."

"No goddamn way you can call his showing up here a coincidence." Corrine felt her face begin to flush.

"Perhaps you are overestimating your importance in this matter. It's a common enough occurrence in our culture today." Balen paused. "Have you considered that Mr. LaVell is perhaps here on other business?"

"You won't tell me what he wants?"

Balen sighed. "I'm not at liberty to say. To do so would break client-attorney confidentiality."

"Fine. Play it that way," Corrine said, unable to keep the anger from her voice. "But you'd better understand something. If things go to shit, I'll take you and Wayne LaVell down with me. I'll say we were all in it together. I'll say you approached me with the idea of killing Stanley Tedros and that you were fronting for Wayne LaVell and his business interests, and I'll make a judge and jury believe I had no choice, absolutely no fucking choice, but to go along with both of you."

Raychard Balen looked down at his desk. He picked up the black felt tip pen. He uncapped and recapped it. He set it back down.

"You need to be careful, Mrs. Tedros, with what you say in the heat of the moment," Balen said, looking directly at Corrine. "Because they may be words that you will later deeply regret having spoken."

THIRTY-SEVEN

CROY WENDALL had been in his room working on the model of a small dinosaur with a complicated name that Croy could not make rhyme with anything when Jamie came home from an early afternoon of drinking beer at Mac's Shack, his favorite bar, and stood outside Croy's door and knocked until Croy set down the glue-capped toothpick and followed him out to the living room where Missy was sitting on the couch, knees to chin, watching television. Croy pretended she was wearing underwear.

Jamie waved two plastic bags with store names on them. His eyes had that beer look to them, and he was smiling a lot.

Croy sat down on the couch next to Missy. Some of her hair was caught under the neck brace, and it made part of her head look flat.

"I went shopping," Jamie said, weaving from foot to foot. "Presents." He handed Missy one of the bags and Croy the other.

Jamie had money in his pockets because he and Croy had been working for Mr. Sharpe and his landscaping business the last three days.

Croy opened his bag. Inside was a white T-shirt with black letters that said *I Mean Business* and a small can of beef stew that was Croy's favorite brand.

In Missy's bag was a new teddy that looked like it was made of pink cellophane and a pair of blue flip flops with little seahorses at the top where the toes went.

Croy and Missy took turns thanking Jamie, and then Missy got up to change into her present. While Jamie got some beer from the kitchen, Croy took off his T-shirt and pulled the new one on. It was a size too small, and squeezed his chest and shoulders the same way drinking something cold too fast did to the inside of Croy's throat, but Croy didn't say anything to Jamie about it.

"Looks good," Jamie said. He dropped into the recliner and set a six-pack of beer on his chest, then clicked the remote until the television was on a music video station. A band was standing on the shore of an island and playing very loud.

"Did Mr. Balen call?" Jamie asked.

Croy told him no.

"Maybe he will yet," Jamie said. "What time is it, anyway?"

Croy started to reach for the pocketwatch and then made his hand stop because he knew Jamie was watching him in that way that seemed like he wasn't, so Croy got up and checked the kitchen clock instead.

Another music video came on, and it had a band in an airplane. Jamie knew the names of the people in the band, and he told them to Croy.

Croy nodded, then looked down at the bag with the store name on it. It was lying next to his feet like a small pet.

Jamie had been in a good mood lately. Yesterday he told Croy twelve times that Croy was his best friend. Croy knew how many times because he'd kept count.

Missy came back wearing the pink teddy. Like Croy's T-shirt, it looked a size too small. She had put on some lipstick too, but most of it came off when Jamie handed her his beer and she took a long swallow and then wiped her mouth.

"My Queen," Jamie said when Missy stepped back and turned for Jamie in a slow circle.

The tips of Croy's fingers had a hard shell on them from the glue. He was careful, but the tube was very soft, and it was hard to keep the glue on the toothpick. His fingertips made a click whenever Croy rubbed them together.

"Tell you what, Missy," Jamie said, "why don't you fire up Croy's beef stew for him?"

Croy wanted to go back to his room and work on the model, but Missy was already on the way to the kitchen before he could say anything.

The television screen kept filling up with music videos, and it was hard to tell them apart. There'd been one with a girl singer in an elevator and a lot of people getting in and out of it, and then there was a girl singer in a car, and Croy wasn't sure if it was the same singer or not, and it was even more confusing because she was always stopping to let people in or out of the car, and when Croy looked over at Jamie, he winked and toasted Croy with one of the beers from the six-pack, and then Missy was back with some snacks and a bowl of beef stew, and Croy tried to make things slow down and separate into the right order by picking up his spoon and eating the beef stew, but Missy had microwaved it too high and Croy burned his tongue, so he just held the bowl in his lap for a while.

A commercial came on, and Jamie spilled some beer down his chin.

Croy tried to remember if he'd put the cap back on the glue before he followed Jamie into the living room.

Missy started dancing to the videos. She told Croy she thought his gray hair was cute even though it did not match how old he really was and that it was too bad that Croy didn't sex because she had a friend she could fix him up with.

Croy tried the beef stew again.

Missy mixed up the dancing, sometimes going fast, sometimes slow, and after a while she climbed up on the chair with Jamie and was sitting on his lap and licking at his ear, and Jamie set the beer cans on the floor and pulled Missy even closer, and they made noises and moved their hands around. Croy finished his beef stew and set the bowl on the floor next to the plastic bag and went back to his room, even though Jamie had told him it was ok to stay and watch television.

Croy locked the door and worked on his model. He glued the jawline to the head. Next were the hands and feet, which were claws, and Croy was very careful and did not mix them up with each other.

He did some numbers in his head while he worked.

Later, when he stepped out into the hallway because he had to go to the bathroom, the television was down very low. Croy poked his head around the corner and saw Jamie and Missy lying together in the chair. He thought they were asleep until he saw Jamie's hand slowly rise and stroke Missy's back, and then Missy started whispering.

"Are you sure?" she said.

"Look, I was sitting right next to the guy at the bar. He said it was a pocketwatch, a gold one. That's what the police kept out of the papers after the guy was killed."

"That's a lot of money," Missy said.

Jamie's hand moved back and forth. "One phone call, honey."

Croy went back to his room. He looked at his model for a while. Then he got down on the floor and reached under the box springs for the plastic bag with the gun he'd taken off the policeman in the parking lot of the Passion Palace.

Croy walked down the hall and into the living room and shot Jamie and Missy.

He went back to his room and put some underwear, sodas, and T-shirts in a tan canvas bag. He thought about the model but decided it wouldn't fit right, and that left a sad place in him, but he told himself he had to hurry, and so he got some snacks from the kitchen to put in the bag and some things from the medicine cabinet, and then all that was left to put in was the money he'd saved from doing crimes and planting flowers.

When he looked for it though, the money wasn't there. The box was, but not the money that was supposed to be in the box.

Croy wished he could make Jamie alive again. Then he could ask Jamie what he did with the money before Croy shot him another time.

You needed money when you ran away, Croy thought, and now he didn't have any except for what he had in his pockets.

There was a noise in the kitchen.

Croy found Missy crawling across the linoleum toward the back door.

He squatted next to her and asked about the money, but all
Missy would say over and over was "please" which was not helpful, and so Croy put his knee on her neck and counted in his
head, and then he stood up and went to the shed in the back that
had the broken lawn mower and two five gallon plastic containers of gas and carried them into the house because he was thinking of where his fingers had been and how many times, and Croy
threw some gasoline on the television and the rug and then on
Jamie and Missy and went around the house pouring until both
containers were empty.

Croy started up the matches and tossed them and grabbed his
bag and ran very fast to his car, and then he drove away.

THIRTY-EIGHT

CORRINE TEDROS went through the house room by room and turned on every light in each. Then, barefoot, she went downstairs and through the living room to the two large sliding glass doors, opened and closed them behind her, and walked into her backyard.

Dusk was leaving the sky, the stars beginning to break out. The grass was brittle beneath her feet. Like everyone else, she could not remember the last time it had rained. Spring had dried up from the inside out.

She turned and studied her house blazing with light. It looked like a doomed cruise ship.

Up the street, a dog barked. Someone, with a window open, began listening to music. A car started. A door slammed. Corrine Tedros wanted to hold on to each as if it were a life preserver. End of the day sounds. Simple and unassuming and emptied of menace.

She moved to the middle of the lawn and the wooden picnic table there, using the seat as a step and sitting on its top. Buddy had put it together from a kit he'd bought at one of the area home improvement stores, laboriously and patiently assembling it so that he could eventually present it to Corrine and Stanley like a bone, some proof of his prowess and happiness as a homeowner and husband.

Buddy had just applied the first coat of white paint when Stanley was killed. The paint had already thinned out against the wood. It looked like patchy frost on a dirt road.

Nobody got what he deserved. Corrine had never been sure if that were an indiscriminate curse or an equally indiscriminate blessing.

Or if, in fact, there was any difference at all between the two.

She was on Wayne LaVell's clock. Corrine wondered if it had ever been otherwise, if she had not somehow heard its tick even as she was riding in her mother's womb, if she had not, in fact, mistaken that tick for her mother's heartbeat.

The new, resolute Buddy, the Buddy with a backbone and iron-clad principles, the man now determined to honor his uncle's memory, was at the office working late on the presentation he would make to a group of investors in Charlotte. He still believed Stanley's plan was workable and he could run Stanco Beverages himself, but Buddy needed help funding the development and expansion of the present distribution lines for Julep. That would be his pitch to the Charlotte people.

It was a pitch, like the one Buddy had made to the Atlanta people, that would inevitably fail. Corrine already knew that because she had already put in the call to Raychard Balen who in turn had relayed the information to James Restan who'd have things fixed so that Buddy's plan would initially sound promising but would inevitably go nowhere.

Corrine wondered how many times they'd have to go through the routine before Buddy gave up once and for all.

She eased herself down on the top of the wooden picnic table and folded her arms beneath her head for a makeshift pillow. The night air was cool on her bare legs. She closed her eyes for a moment and ran through the names.

Betsy Jo Horvath. April Rayne. Corrine Keyes. Corrine Tedros.

At one time or another, she'd hidden in each of them.

She'd been Betsy Jo Horvath when her mother abandoned her at her grandparents' place in Bradford, Indiana. Beneath an immense Midwestern sky, Bradford huddled like a mouse under a hawk's wing. Everything about the town was small. She could walk from the eastern to western city limits in less than twenty minutes. Life in Bradford was sky and weather. For Betsy Jo Horvath, life there had been one endless impatience.

She tried to run away three times.

The first had been with her high school chemistry teacher, a tall pale man who'd told her over and over they belonged together, but when they ran off, they got not no further than Chicago and a Holiday Inn where after a long weekend of unimaginative and unspectacular sex, he suffered a predictable crisis of conscience and loss of nerve and decided to return to his family.

The second time, Corrine had taken off on her own, making it to the outskirts of Kansas City before a Statie picked her up and returned her to Bradford.

The third time, Corrine had taken off with Billy Watts, a local pot dealer with overinflated and movie-driven notions of the big score awaiting him in Phoenix. Once there, it had taken less than a month before Billy got burned on one of his sure deals, and when the buyers administered a fine-print beating as a coda to the business proceedings, Billy Watts had decided, like her chemistry teacher, that Bradford, Indiana wasn't such a bad place after all.

If you were a young attractive female on your own in Phoenix with no visible means of support, you sooner or later met Wayne LaVell. It was inevitable. You found him, or he found you.

Wayne LaVell stepped in and posted bail and paid for the attorney who represented Betsy Jo Horvath after she had been busted for solicitation at the Mid-Line Hotel and Restaurant downtown on North Catalina.

She had not been hooking, at least not technically. She made a casual circuit of some of the high-end lounges during lunch and happy hours. She was young, and she was pretty, and it never took too long for her to get noticed and invited for a drink. She never directly asked for money, but made sure during the conversation that she inserted a hard-luck anecdote that usually resulted in the man offering to "help out" after she'd slept with him. She'd steal, whenever possible, from those who didn't offer or in a few cases mention she'd noticed his wedding ring and pointedly ask about his family.

She was careful not to show up at the same place too often. She'd already been popped twice for shoplifting, pleading out each time with a fine.

It didn't take long for the Vice cop to make her at the Mid-Line and bust her, however. She didn't understand until much later, after she was already working for Wayne LaVell's escort service, that LaVell had sicced the Vice cop on her in the first place because the Mid-Line was one of his properties, and Wayne LaVell make sure he had a piece of whatever action took place there.

After the solicitation charges were fixed, she became April Rayne and had gone to work for LaVell's Valley of the Sun Escorts. Wayne LaVell had developed a system in which each part fed another. Corrine never saw any money from her escorts because they paid in advance. LaVell paid her a flat, base salary, plus bonuses if she went over her monthly quota of dates. The men took her out for dinner and drinks at one of LaVell's restaurants, and they later fucked her in one of his hotels. She had a small place of her own, as did the other girls working for LaVell, in an apartment complex in Tempe. The complex was one of LaVell's holdings, and he deducted her rent and utilities from her salary. He supplied recreational drugs for the girls, deducting their cost as well as monitoring their use. In the end, you were left with a comfortable life that went nowhere, a long-term limbo owned and maintained by Wayne LaVell.

The clientele for Valley of the Sun Escorts were screened and were comprised almost exclusively of businessmen and politicians from the region and the out-of-towners connected to Phoenix's year-round convention trade.

It had been the stories more than the semen that the men left in her that she resented most.

All that fear and loneliness and anger that their stories attempted to hide. Every one of them wanted to tell his story whether he understood that or not, and Wayne LaVell, for a price, offered a willing and beautiful and rapt audience for a night or two.

As April Rayne, Corrine could not remember a single face from her dates distinctly. They were men in suits who took her out to dinner and wanted to be seen in her company, and they talked about themselves, almost always in terms of their careers, their triumphs and trials in the marketplace or in office politics, and in the end, each story was the same story because they were all run on need.

Later, in the hotel room, in bed, the men wanted to be liked or feared or sometimes both, and they brought their need to her and put it in her, and her body and words gave them back the only thing they wanted, which was to have their stories and their places in their stories confirmed. They paid to fuck her so that for a little while they could be exactly what they said they were.

They were always undone by their orgasms though.

When she felt them getting ready to come, she made sure she kept her eyes open, and she watched their stories and their faces collapse as they spent their need, and no matter what the men had done or said earlier, she knew at that moment, with their eyes squeezed tightly shut and their expressions breaking under the weight of their orgasms, she saw all of them for what they were and what they spent their lives trying to cover up and hide from.

When they came, they looked like scared little boys fighting back tears in the dark.

Five years, and then by accident, April Rayne found her ticket out of Valley of the Sun Escorts.

A perk. That's what Wayne LaVell called her when he sent April Rayne out to meet Larry Delmae, a Zoning Commissioner with deep generational roots in Phoenix.

Larry Delmae, himself, filled in the rest of the story later in the evening back in the hotel room. During and after the meal, he'd had too much to drink and made two very unsuccessful attempts to undress her. April had covered for his ineptitude by guiding him to the edge of the bed and sitting him down and then doing an impromptu strip, taking her time and talking it out as if it were something that she was doing for him and only him, and by the time she was naked, Larry felt the need to return the favor and show April that he was a worthy recipient of her flesh and beauty and time, that he was, in fact, an important and powerful man, and he brought over the briefcase that he'd been carrying when April first met him that evening and then set it on the bed and opened it.

"Guess," he said, leaning in and cupping a breast.

She looked at the bound bills, the denominations, and ran the numbers through her mind.

"Thirty thousand," she said.

"Jesus, honey," Delmae said, stepping back. "You're good. There's thirty-five thousand there. Tax-free, courtesy of your friend and mine, Wayne LaVell. Ten grand an acre, a three-and-a-half acre package up soon for a new rezoning configuration, and all I got to do is talk to a couple people. And hell, they's people I've been knowing since we been kids. Easiest money I ever made."

Larry Delmae was snoring less than five minutes after his orgasm.

She grabbed the briefcase. She did not even consider going back to her apartment for any of her things.

She went to ground. She put in a call to Tim Farrell.

Tim Farrell was the brother of one of the girls at Valley of the Sun Escorts, and April had met him briefly when he visited his sister. She later told her what Tim did for a sideline, and April had filed that information away.

Tim Farrell could cleanse you of history.

Farrell so completely inhabited the stereotype of the computer geek that at first she had assumed it was a put-on, but Farrell, tall, gawky, pale-skinned, and slack-muscled, seemed oblivious and immune to irony. He presented his hacker credentials with an adolescent mix of diffidence and pride and told her he could give her a new identity that would stand up to some serious scrutiny for fifteen thousand dollars.

April lied and said she only had ten thousand. Tim Farrell said he'd settle for the ten since she was a friend of his sister, then paused, not meeting her eyes, and added if she would be willing to take the rest out in trade for one night.

She agreed.

He called her back four days later.

He introduced April Rayne to Corrine Keyes from Charlotte, North Carolina. Tim Farrell produced a birth certificate, social security card, high school diploma, driver's license, employment record complete with references, and two street addresses for former residences.

Farrell had done freelance work for various state and federal agencies and stole or pirated whatever forms he needed for reconstruction. Her social security number came from his practice of combing the archives of various city halls for those who had died far enough in the past to escape digital upgrades, and the street addresses fit homes that eventually were sold and torn down in Charlotte's development frenzy. A third grader, he told her, could hack into the school system's files. The references for the companies Corrine Keyes had supposedly worked at were friends of Tim's who would vouch for Corrine's work record if they were ever contacted.

She paid him the ten thousand dollars.

Her mistake had been in agreeing to sleep with him. Given the persona he projected, she'd figured him for a squirter, a premie, who could be dispatched in short order, and so she hadn't paid the attention she should have when they were back at his apartment and he offered her a drink. By the time the fourth cut from Pink Floyd's *Dark Side of the Moon* came on, she knew he'd put something in the drink when she tried to move her legs and couldn't.

She woke the next morning in a slow-motion panic. Little by little and in no particular order, pieces of memory of what Tim Farrell had done after he'd drugged her started crowding in, and with effort, Corrine waste-basketed the images and dressed and managed to leave before Farrell awoke, and by that afternoon, Corrine Keyes was on her way to Myrtle Beach, South Carolina. She wanted a place full of tourists for groundcover.

She eventually landed a job waitressing at one of Sonny Gramm's supper clubs.

Four months into the job, Corrine Keyes worked a bachelor party in the banquet room and met Buddy Tedros. She married him three and a half weeks later.

That should have been it, a close-enough to a happily ever.

Except Stanley Tedros wouldn't accept her as part of the family, and he wouldn't accept James Restan's buy-out offer.

And now Wayne LaVell could with one phone call hold Corrine hostage to her history by threatening to resurrect April Rayne and turn her loose in Corrine's life.

Corrine had no intention of letting that happen.

The evening air had grown cooler, but Corrine remained

where she was, lying on her back on top of the picnic table and looking up at a cloudless night sky and wide swathes of stars, and she almost prayed; but if that's what it was, the words had dissolved on her lips before she had the chance to speak them, and she was left with what Betsy Jo Horvath, April Rayne, and Corrine Keyes had always known too, whether they liked it or not.

If you looked at anything long enough, you'd end up seeing right through it.

THIRTY-NINE

THE REMOTE WASN'T ONE. Jack Carson thought that's what he'd been holding and pointing at the television, but instead it was something else entirely, a tape recorder, one that was compact and thin and expensive.

He wondered how it had ended up in his shirt pocket.

The television was off, and it was strange to be in the living room because the television was always on when he was there.

In the afternoon quiet, he listened to the house, its shifts and creaks, the rush of water through pipes, the occasional squeak of a ceiling fan in its rotations.

Jack smiled.

He liked the feel of the house and the afternoon. Jack had always thought working construction was like having a conversation with whatever he was building.

You couldn't make something without leaving a little bit of yourself behind.

Jack looked at the tape recorder in his hand. He cleared his throat.

The windows were open and the screens gridded in soft light, and Jack caught the smell of the tide rising, and he started building the sentences in his head that answered what his daughter and Buddy Tedros had kept asking him. The question was like a job he'd been hired to do, Jack painstakingly taking the words and lining them up and then moving them to where they belonged and then building another sentence that followed the last one—Jack seeing them in his head, each word in each sentence like a line of cement blocks for a foundation of a house someone had contracted him to build—and Jack ignored the sound of an old man's voice haltingly speaking in fits and starts and concentrated instead on what he was doing because, finally, that was how any job got done, and along the way Jack Carson found the clarity and grace he'd known as a young man when he'd backed his words with good work.

FORTY

EARLY APRIL WAS A HUSK.

By late afternoon each day, the sky took on a jaundiced cast, and the wind carried a fine, constant sanding of pine pollen that coated everything it came in contact with a pale green. Weather reports were an exercise in redundancy, the temperatures spiking and breaking records, and there was no sign of rain. Competing winds moving in from the plains and the Gulf broke and scattered whatever storm cells developed.

Everything baked.

Tempers were short and grievances long.

The first wave of students for spring break receded, and the city braced itself for the second.

Reverend Redd Benton, taking the weather as a sign, had come into town for an End Times Revival.

Ben Decovic's shift had been a petri dish of petty complaints and grudges that kept feeding on each other, and his reserves of patience had been sorely taxed by the time the white boat of a Continental ran the light at the intersection of Gilchrist and Ashe and he pulled it over a half block later.

The driver powered down the window as Ben walked up. He was a small man in an ill-fitting summer-weight suit. His black hair appeared frozen, and there was a thin lopsided isosceles triangle of a mustache running to the corners of his upper lip. On the passenger side was a heavyset man with an unfortunate comb-over and a wide round face, his cheeks blotched and filigreed with broken capillaries.

"Problem, Officer?" the driver asked.

"The last light," Ben said, "you ran the red." He asked to see license and registration.

"It was yellow," the driver said.

"I'm afraid you're mistaken, sir," Ben said. "It was red before you reached the intersection. You're lucky to have avoided an accident."

"I know my primary colors, Officer. It was yellow."

Ben asked, once again, for license and registration.

"We're on the way to a meeting with the mayor," the driver said, "and I am a close acquaintance of a number of your fellow officers, including Chief Newell."

"It's nice to have friends, sir," Ben said.

The driver unlocked the seat belt and rummaged for his wallet. The heavyset man on the passenger side touched the knot in his tie and watched Ben with eyes that gradually emptied of all expression.

"You don't know who I am, do you?" the driver asked.

"I will as soon as you hand over the license and registration," Ben said.

The driver did.

Sandwiched between the license and registration card was a folded one-hundred dollar bill, a sharp crease bisecting Franklin's face.

The driver pointed at Ben's uniform shirt. "You take blue and add yellow," he said, "and I think you'll find you get green."

Ben handed back the bill, license, and registration and said, "Not always, Mr. Balen. I think you'll find it depends on the shade of blue."

Raychard Balen laughed. He turned to the heavyset man. "I think we have ourselves a Boy Scout here, Wayne."

"Appears so," the man said.

Ben started writing out the ticket.

"Your name, Officer," Balen asked. "I want to be sure to mention you specifically next time I get together with Chief Newell."

Ben handed him the traffic citation. "It's on the bottom line, Mr. Balen."

Balen glanced down and laughed again, harder this time. "Well, well, well," he said. "It appears, Wayne, not only do we have a Boy Scout here, we have an *ambitious* Boy Scout, one who likes to vacation outside his job description."

Balen paused and tilted his head, studying Ben. His smile was small and yellow. He began slowly waving the ticket back and forth between them.

"Maybe running that light wasn't such a bad idea after all," Balen said. "Now, Officer Decovic, I have a face to put with the name."

"Yes sir, you do," Ben said. "And now, so do I."

FORTY-ONE

THE CALL CAME THROUGH, but not the one Corrine Tedros had been expecting. Anne Carson, not Wayne LaVell, was on the other end of the line, and she was asking to speak to Buddy.

"I tried the office," she said, "and then thought he might be at home."

"He's out of town for the day," Corrine said. That was another sore spot. She'd not been able to steer Buddy and get both feet moving in the direction of James Restan's buy-out offer. Buddy was still going forward with idea of implementing Stanley's plans to oversee production, distribution, and marketing of Julep himself. In the meantime, people all over the country continued to drink Julep and clamor for more.

"It's important," Anne said. "Have him call me please as soon as he gets back."

Something in Anne Carson's voice put Corrine on alert, and she had the feeling she already knew the answer before she went on to ask, "Is this about your father?"

"Yes. He remembered. Can you believe it? He gave a description of the man he saw kill Mr. Tedros. It's all on the tape. I wanted Buddy to know right away."

Anne Carson sounded like a schoolgirl anxiously awaiting praise from her favorite teacher.

Corrine circled the dining room table and then sat down. She massaged her temples with her free hand. Her skin felt overly tight. She pictured the cop, Ben Decovic, standing over Anne Carson's shoulder and smiling.

"Have you told anyone else about this?" Corrine asked.

"No, I promised Buddy I would call him first. I know how important this is to him. I figured he would take everything to the police."

Ok, Corrine thought. She still had some room.

"Ms. Carson, I have a favor to ask you, but it would be better if I was there in person. Could we talk?"

"I suppose so, yes."

"One other thing," Corrine said. "Please don't tell anyone about the tape until we do."

"I'm not sure I understand."

"You will," Corrine said and hung up.

Corrine choked off her panic and went into the bedroom to change, dressing quickly, then drove to the main office of Maritime's bank and hit her safe-deposit box. She'd been quietly diverting cash to the box since the first month of her marriage. Corrine was careful to keep the sums large enough for her purposes but small enough to avoid Buddy noticing. It was her breakout money, a hedge against repeating the lessons that Phoenix had taught her.

Traffic was heavy, and the drive to the North Shore neighborhood took longer than she'd planned, leaving Corrine both impatient and grateful, bouncing between unbidden scenarios in which every conceivable thing went wrong and slow stretches that let her work on angles for emptying the weight of the consequences crowding her.

She glanced at the brown envelope on the seat next to her.

That was it. The last of the break-out money. She'd spent most of it hiring out Stanley's murder.

She had nowhere to go but where she was going.

The traffic crawled.

She thought of all the Sunday afternoons she'd been trapped across the dinner table from Stanley Tedros.

She thought about James Restan's buy-out offer.

She thought about what she had and what she didn't and the price tags on each.

And then she was in North Shore and climbing the stairs and standing before the screen door that Anne Carson opened for her and moving into the living room where Anne Carson had already set out glasses and a pitcher of sweetened iced tea, and Corrine felt something settle inside her.

She was ready.

One look at Anne Carson and the inside of the house had told her that.

Anne Carson, under the right circumstances, could have been beautiful, but everything about her suggested that she had settled long ago for pretty.

The house was not as bad as Corrine's grandparents' place in Bradford, Indiana, but despite all the attempts at camouflaging it, the Carson house, finally, was cluttered and claustrophobic, full of furnishings long past any real value and hiding behind a tired charm and the thin sentimentality of family history. It was a house that had never known money, and there was a quiet hunger at its core, which Corrine recognized.

The tape recorder lay on the coffee table to the right of the glasses and pitcher.

Corrine leaned over and pressed Play and listened to the old man stumble through a very accurate description of Croy Wendall and the murder of Stanley Tedros.

Corrine stopped the tape, then sat back and crossed her legs. Anne Carson poured them each a glass of tea.

"This is not going to be easy, Ms. Carson," Corrine said.

"Just Anne, ok?"

Corrine nodded. "I love my husband very much. He's a good man, but at bottom, I'm sorry to say, he's a weak man. You know Stanley Tedros raised him after his parents were killed in a car accident, right? Buddy developed a very strong attachment to his uncle, and that attachment has blinded him to some very difficult truths."

Corrine leaned forward, resting her hands on her knee. "Anne, for his own good, I would like to keep my husband ignorant of those truths."

"I'm not sure I'm following you," she said, frowning slightly.

"Buddy does not need to hear that tape," Corrine said.

"But the man who killed his uncle, my father described him. How else are they going to catch him?"

"I hope they never do," Corrine said. "For Buddy's sake."

Anne Carson shifted positions in the chair. "You don't want the killer caught? That doesn't make any sense."

"Stanley Tedros was not the man he appeared to be," Corrine said, pausing to let the words gather their full weight, and then working at a credible facsimile of someone blinking back tears.

"Women are stronger than men," she said after a while. "We have to be. You're a single mother. Surely you understand that."

Anne Carson took a sip of her tea, the small frown still in place, pulling at the corners of her dark eyes.

"Did you know Stanley?" Corrine asked.

"No. Or not very well. I remember my father did some work for him a couple times."

"Did you ever think about how unusual it was for a man like Stanley Tedros to hit upon something as successful as Julep?" Corrine asked. "He was an immigrant, Anne. Hard-working, sure, but nothing more than a bottler of generic sodas. Then all of a sudden, Julep."

From there, it was easy for Corrine to embellish, to tease out damning implications and build on them, because, despite herself, Anne Carson was like most people who'd never had much money. When faced with someone else's astounding success, she secretly wanted to believe it was undeserved and somehow achieved at her own expense, that people like Stanley Tedros had cornered the luck that should have been due her.

Corrine evoked the image of the public Stanley Tedros, the industrious immigrant and old-fashioned man of principle, the hard-line businessman who still knew all the names of his employees, the Stanley Tedros from the placards advertising Julep, the self-made man who favored out-of-date brown suits and starched white shirts, and then Corrine systematically went about dismantling that image, suggesting that something dark and corrupt festered deep within the man Stanley Tedros kept hidden from the public's eye.

"Stanley didn't come up with Julep himself," Corrine said. "He had plenty of help from men you and I would never want to meet. Stanley cut a deal with them. Stanley went to them for backing and cut a deal to get Julep up and running. Things were fine until Stanley arrogantly and foolishly decided he didn't need them anymore."

"The man my father described," Anne Carson side, then stopped, looking down at her lap and finally back at Corrine.

"He works for the men who bankrolled Stanley and Julep," Corrine said. "Even if he's caught and charged, there will be no real justice because the men ultimately responsible for Stanley's death will remain untouched." Corrine paused, taking in a deep breath. "Or if he's caught and charged and talks, something even worse could happen. Justice will be served, but in the process, the truth will completely destroy Buddy."

Anne Carson sat quietly. She bit her lower lip.

"Buddy doesn't know any of this?" she asked.

Corrine shook her head. "Stanley loved his nephew. He sheltered Buddy. Protected him his whole life. Buddy worshipped Stanley and only saw what Stanley wanted him to see."

"I'm still confused," Anne said. "You, I mean. How do you know all this?"

"Stanley told me," Corrine said softly, then looked away.

"I don't…," Anne said and faltered. "I mean why? Why would he do something like that?"

Corrine had been expecting the question, had seen it slowly gather in Anne Carson's features as she'd talked, and Corrine uncrossed her legs and lifted her hand, then let it fall, dragging out the gestures and the moment for maximum dramatic effect.

"Oh, Anne," she said. "Stanley liked to brag after—" Corrine broke off the sentence and lowered her head.

Anne Carson hesitated, then leaned over and squeezed Corrine's hand.

"You know Stanley never married," Corrine said. "While Buddy was growing up, the only woman in the house was the housekeeper who came in once a week. To all appearances, Stanley Tedros was a confirmed bachelor."

Corrine thought she saw movement on the periphery of her vision, but when she glanced at the doorway to the kitchen, it was empty.

"After I married Buddy," she said, straightening the hem of her dress, "we spent a lot of time with Stanley. Buddy joked about it being a Greek thing, all the emphasis on family, so I didn't think much about it when Stanley started dropping by when Buddy wasn't around."

Corrine paused, letting Anne fill in a few of the blanks herself, before she wiped her eyes and continued.

"I tried to ignore it at first," Corrine said, "but then one afternoon—Buddy and I had been married less than two months—Stanley put his hands on me, Anne, he put his hands on places where he shouldn't, and when I told him to stop, he wouldn't, and he kept putting his hands on me, and he described what he was going to do to me and what he wanted me to do to him; they were vile things, Anne, and when I threatened to tell Buddy, Stanley laughed at me, he laughed and asked if it came down to my word or his, who did I think Buddy would believe, and before I could answer, Stanley turned the threat around, saying he'd tell Buddy that it was me who'd seduced good old Uncle Stanley because it was Stanley's money, never Buddy, that I'd been in love with all along, and Buddy and I were still newlyweds, Anne, and I was scared that my husband wouldn't believe the truth; I was really scared, because I loved Buddy and couldn't imagine what it would be like to lose him, and so I did, Anne, I let Stanley touch me, and I did what he wanted." Corrine paused, then plunged into a coda. "Stanley, he came by two times a week after that. He wouldn't leave me alone, and poor Buddy never suspected a thing the whole time."

There'd been a point where the story itself took over and wrestled free of Corrine's control so that it sounded true even to her, and the tears that Corrine was afraid she wouldn't be able to summon at the opportune moment found her instead and burned on her cheeks, leaving Corrine shaken and a little panicked at their intensity, unable to fully appreciate just how successful she'd been at playing Anne Carson.

Once again, Corrine thought she detected movement in the kitchen doorway.

Anne Carson handed her a box of tissues and blinked back her own tears.

"I don't know what to say, Corrine."

"Buddy can't—," Corrine said, "he can't hear that tape. You understand now, right? The truth would destroy him. He needs his illusions. We're women. We know better. You and I, we can protect Buddy. I'm begging you, Anne."

Anne Carson rested her hand on her throat. "What do you want me to do?"

"Erase the tape. Never tell Buddy or anyone else I was here."

Anne stood up and walked to the window. She stood there with her back to Corrine and her hands at her sides.

"Buddy and I, we're talking about starting a family," Corrine said. "Please don't take that away from me."

A moment later, Anne picked up the tape recorder. Corrine stopped herself from saying anything more. She waited.

Anne Carson rewound and erased the tape.

Corrine crossed the room and stood next to her at the window. The yard burned with afternoon light.

Corrine handed Anne a manila envelope.

She flushed when she opened it. "I don't understand," she said.

"I want you to have that."

"I couldn't," Anne said. "All that money, it doesn't seem right."

"It's the equivalent of the reward Buddy posted. Your father earned it. *You* earned it, Anne." Corrine paused. "I'll always be grateful to you. I owe you my marriage."

Anne Carson held the envelope to her chest like a clutch of schoolbooks and nodded.

There was a small noise behind them, and Corrine and Anne turned from the window at the same time.

"Paige," Anne said. "We didn't hear you come in."

"I was trying to be quiet in case Grandfather was taking a nap. I got some orange juice and was going to start my homework." She held up a laminated notebook whose cover depicted the layout of the solar system.

Anne lowered the envelope and let it rest against her leg. "My manners," she said. "Paige, this is Mrs. Tedros."

"It's very nice to meet you," Paige said.

FORTY-TWO

BEN DECOVIC CHECKED, then double-checked, the duty roster on the bulletin board in the locker room. He couldn't believe it. He'd just had two double shifts during the last week, and now his day off had evaporated because he'd been temporarily assigned to foot patrol.

Behind him, someone laughed.

"Who'd you piss off, Decovic?" Carl Adkin said. "This heat, foot patrol, spring break, you must of got on someone's wrong side."

Ben turned around. "You see Samuel anywhere? I'm going to talk to her."

Car Adkin stepped back and spread his arms. "La'Shawn's with the big boys meeting with the mayor for the third time this week. I'd say something's in the air." Adkin laughed again. "Come on, Decovic, tell me. Why'd you think you ended up on the foot roster?"

"Why don't you tell me?"

"Ok," Adkin said. "Your biggest problem is your neck. It's too stiff, my man. The time comes, you can't turn your head." He moved over to the row of sinks and started washing his hands. Adkin watched Ben in the mirror fronting the sink.

"Sometimes all that's required is to look the other way," Adkin said. "Just turn your head and do it. Nothing more than that."

"Is that what you did at the Passion Palace when you were late on backup?"

Adkin's smile was slower this time. "Someone tries to tell you something for your own good, and you strike an attitude."

"You never answered my question," Ben said.

"Manny Harrison says you're still stopping by the Palace and trying to talk to Sonny Gramm." Adkin shook off his hands and hunted down some paper towels.

"Someone vandalized his car and house. Gramm's scared. He doesn't trust anybody, particularly the police, right now."

"He's an old man," Adkin said. "He boozes. He sees threats everywhere. There's a word for that." Adkin paused and shook his head. "Christ, it's got to the point where he's so far gone he's scared to hire anybody but family to work for him."

When Adkin noticed Ben frowning, he said, "You didn't know Manny Harrison is family? He's Gramm's sister's kid. Sonny hired Manny and his three brothers as bouncers. Before that, each of them were burger jockeys. Taco Bell. McDonald's. Burger King. Hardees."

Adkin balled up the paper towels and threw them in the direction of the trash can. "Sonny's still shopping for a bodyguard. I'll give him one thing though. At least he was smart enough not to hire any of those boys as one. You want someone asking if you want extra pickles watching your back?"

Ben finished changing into civilian clothes and closed his locker. Adkin crossed his arms and leaned back against the sink.

"I have to go," Ben said.

Adkin let him get almost to the locker room door before he said, "You heard, didn't you, that the ballistics were in?"

Ben paused. He remained facing the door.

Behind him, Adkin said, "The two Sentinel Avenue shootings? The one where the house got burned down too? Those ballistics."

Ben waited. He'd heard the self-satisfied smile shadowing Adkin's words.

"The word is, your Glock, Decovic. The one you let get taken off you at the Palace. Ballistics match."

"They recover the Glock?" Ben asked.

"Yep. Extra crispy and yours," Adkin said.

Ben closed his eyes for a moment, then pushed the locker room door open. He was on his way out when he heard Adkin say, "You think about it, Decovic, if you'd waited that evening like I told you, just waited and looked the other way for a while, you wouldn't have gotten your Glock taken away, and the two people on Sentinel, they'd be alive right now."

Ben started down the hall. He worked on his breathing. The hallway appeared foreshortened, stretching on and on and narrowing. Ben felt as if he were looking down a long chute.

FORTY-THREE

CORRINE TEDROS, caught in traffic, watched two men in dark suits leave the curb and begin moving among the line of cars backed up at the light on Williams. Across the intersection in an empty lot next to a Shell station was a large canvas tent housing Reverend Redd Benton's End Times Revival and street-side a sign reading: THERE ARE NO FIRE EXTINGUISHERS IN HELL.

When one of the men stepped up to her car, Corrine saw they were not men at all, but boys, tall and thin, their adolescence swallowed by the dark lines of the suits.

The face framed in her window was wide and flushed from the heat. He held up a flyer. Corrine waved it away.

He smiled and began tapping lightly on the window. Corrine shook her head.

Still smiling, he pointed across the street at the tent and a moment later, directed his index finger toward the stretch of sky above it. Despite herself, Corrine looked up. As she did, he then slipped a flyer under her windshield wiper and moved on to the next car.

The light changed. Corrine glanced at the dashboard clock and took out her cell phone. She punched in Raychard Balen's number.

The flyer under her wiper jumped and flapped, creating momentary stills of a crudely drawn brown snake and a scattering of red stars, the question below them appearing and disappearing word by word: ARE ...YOU ... READY ...?

Corrine left Williams for Old Market Boulevard. This time Balen's secretary didn't try to deflect her and put the call through. Balen asked what he could do for her.

"For starters, Raychard, you could return my goddamn phone calls."

"The world is a large and busy place," he said, "and full of sundry problems caused by and for the people I represent and to which I have been devoting considerable time and energy in hopes of arriving at a satisfactory solution to said problems for all concerned."

Balen paused and added, "You, yourself, are included in that number, Mrs. Tedros."

"What's that supposed to mean?" When she placed the call, Corrine had hoped to catch Balen off guard. She had not expected him to go on the offensive.

"It means thanks to you husband's misguided zeal in posting rewards for information concerning his beloved uncle's murder," Balen said, "I have been busting my ass trying to locate Croy Wendall. It seems an associate of Croy's was about to turn him in, so Croy dispatched the associate and his significant other posthaste to the Hereafter." Balen paused. "The upshot being, Croy Wendall is on the loose."

"Oh shit," Corrine said. "I thought you told me Croy did what you told him to."

Balen sighed. "Croy *does* do what he's told, but unfortunately I have to be in contact with him in order to relay those wishes. Our one conversation literally dissolved into thin air when the cell phone connection broke up. I have yet to hear from him again, though I fervently hope to do so in the very near future."

Corrine tightened her grip on the steering wheel. "What about that cop, Decovic? He's still shacking up with Anne Carson."

"While I can't say that I'm happy over Officer Decovic's choice of mattress-mates, rest assured I have gone on and made some calls."

"Meaning?"

"Decovic's got a Boy Scout complex. You push too hard, you create more problems. I've talked to some people in the department. Our friend Decovic has found himself temporarily reassigned from Patrol to Beat. A busy man is the next best thing to a dead man."

Outside her window, block after block of chain restaurants, car dealerships, and the clutter of small businesses. A car with out-of-state plates pulled up behind, then alongside her. It was filled with students. The driver hit the horn twice. The others yelled and blew her kisses, flicked their tongues, and toasted her with cans of beer and sodas.

"Buddy hasn't, by any chance, changed his plans, has he?" Balen said.

"No," Corrine said. "He's supposed to meet with the Charlotte investors Thursday and Friday morning and then fly back that afternoon."

"The arrangements are in place. I talked to James Restan yesterday. On Thursday, your husband will find the Charlotte investors interested and receptive to his proposal to run Stanco Beverages himself and oversee the new distribution lines. By Friday, he'll find the deal they broker to underwrite those plans completely untenable," Balen said. "Perhaps he will then be sufficiently discouraged and reconsider Restan's buy-out offer."

"He's grieving," Corrine said. "He can't get past it. Buddy's got it in his head that running the company is something he owes Stanley's memory."

Balen cleared his throat. "Corrine, if you'll excuse the bluntness, I think you'd find the present situation brightened by more than a few kilowatts if you'd spend your time and energy employing your not inconsiderable charms, physical and otherwise, on making your lawfully wedded husband forget that grief. Sexual athleticism has a way of short-circuiting grief and memory. I truly believe such activities will further your ends more expeditiously than the desperate and frankly stupid moves you've attempted to run on me of late."

Corrine glanced in the rearview mirror and waited a moment before saying she didn't know what he was talking about.

Raychard Balen laughed. Over the cell phone, it sounded like a fire quickly running through dry leaves.

"I'm referring to you trying to circumvent the very clear terms of our original arrangement, Corrine. During the course of the conversation concerning Buddy's upcoming Charlotte junket, James Restan informed me you had repeatedly tried to contact him, this despite the unambiguous agreement that any communication between Restan and you would be through yours truly."

Balen paused, waiting a moment, before quietly adding, "If I were inclined toward paranoia, Corrine, I might believe you were trying to enlist James Restan's aid in finding ways to squeeze me to protect what you perceive as your own best interests." Corrine started to protest, but Balen interrupted. "I want to emphatically assert such a maneuver would *not* be in your best interests, Corrine."

Corrine looked up and saw that she'd missed her exit. The frontage road and the mall blurred by. She didn't bother taking the next exit. She kept the car in the passing lane and moving south.

"Let me hazard a guess," Raychard Balen said, "as to the reason behind your attempts to contact Restan. Is it perhaps connected to my luncheon guest at the Palmer and the admittedly overenthusiastic reunion scene on his part?"

"You think this is some kind of goddamn joke, Raychard?" Corrine said. "Some kind of game? Why don't you just tell me what the hell's going on then?"

"Mr. LaVell is an old friend in town for a visit. He is thinking of buying a summer house, and I'm assisting him in looking into some development opportunities as well."

"Cut the bullshit," Corrine said.

"I think it necessary to point out," Balen said, "you're letting your emotions do your thinking for you and making unwarranted assumptions."

"Fuck you and unwarranted assumptions," Corrine said. "I know Wayne LaVell. What does he want from me?"

"I explained what Mr. LaVell wants," Balen said. "I also took the opportunity to explain at length to Mr. LaVell during the course of our lunch at the Palmer that mistaken identity, like déjà vu, is a very common and mundane phenomenon in the course of everyday life, and I strenuously counseled that one should take pains not to put too great a stock in such things." Balen paused for a moment, then continued. "I'm pleased to say that Mr. LaVell came to share my view, and we then went on to discuss other matters."

Corrine had almost reached the city limits and took the exit for the regional airport, intending to turn around and get back on Old Market Boulevard. Instead she ended up following the access road and pulling into short-term parking and killing the engine.

"You're saying Wayne LaVell is going to leave me alone, Raychard?" she asked. "And you really expect me to believe that?"

"Trust is the cornerstone of any relationship," Balen said. "I have matters under control. As I suggested earlier, Corrine, in order to bring our business to a happy conclusion, you can do yourself the most good by working to realign your husband's attitude concerning James Restan's buy-out offer. The rest will take care of itself."

"That's it, then?"

"Patience, Corrine. You'll see."

"Right." Corrine shut down the call.

She leaned back in the seat and closed her eyes. Her stomach hurt.

She opened her eyes a few moments later and watched a turboprop commuter pass the control tower and then bank and begin its descent through a bright, cloudless blue sky, the plane growing in size and definition at each stage of its approach, its landing gear dropping and locking, the plane coming right at her, the wings tilting and righting themselves, the buzz and whine of the engines slowly increasing in volume as it prepared to leave the sky and touch down.

FORTY-FOUR

SPRING BREAK ERUPTED AGAIN.

The massive PR campaign, buttressed by the slogan *Magnolia Beach: A Paradise Waiting To Be Discovered*, and approved by the mayor and underwritten by the city council and tourist bureau had done its job. There were students everywhere. The slick website, the mass mailing of flyers, and a couple of strategically placed commercials on MTV and ESPN had drawn wave after wave of students from the Eastern seaboard and the Midwest.

The anomalous mid-April weather brought them down too. There'd been a couple short segments on the national news about the record temperatures and lack of rain.

The town's hotels and motels were booked solid. The overflow were sleeping in their cars or on the beach.

Ben Decovic had pulled foot patrol again. The shifts were an exercise in bottled water and sorely taxed patience.

He was working Atlantic Avenue, which ran parallel to the beach and was basically two lanes sandwiched by hotels and condos and bars and restaurants and souvenir shops, a long cluttered stretch that was broken by narrow walking lanes between buildings and public access stations, small niches with gravel aprons for parking and a plank walkway to the Atlantic.

During spring break, the locals were pretty much staying off the Avenue. With all the foot traffic and the parade of muscle cars and customized pickups inching their way through the crowds spilling over the sidewalks, it could take as much as an hour to make five blocks.

Magnolia Beach, this spring, had discovered the classic double-standards of any popular beach town or resort. The locals resented the intrusion but wanted the students' money, and the amount of money changing hands depended on giving the students what they wanted. What the students wanted was to raise hell and get laid. The students called it having fun. Having fun meant anything goes. Anything goes meant property damage and racking up misdemeanors. However, getting charged with a misdemeanor meant a crimp in your fun and a tendency to keep the wallets closed. A closed wallet meant a significant dent in the locals' profit margin. The locals, therefore, expected the police to help them keep that cash crossing the counter by not putting too fine a print on the students' extracurricular activities except those, of course, resulting in property damage, and the students, for their part, expected the police to be absentee babysitters, only stepping in if the fun got out of hand and they needed rescued or excused. For a cop, spring break was like trying to dance to two different songs playing at the same time.

Ben cut across the Avenue between a cherry-red Camaro and a black pickup sitting atop a set of tires that looked like they belonged on an earthmover. Waves of music came at him from all directions, from the sound systems of the cars and trucks, from the balconies of motels, from storefronts and bars and restaurants. Country, rock, rap, R&B, hip-hop, grunge, heavy metal, all pounding the air, overlapping with each other.

The sun baked everything. Ben passed a Beach Body T-Shirt outlet and a deli, and moved slowly in the direction of Screaming Jay's Arcade, which lay at the heart of Atlantic Avenue. He worked his way through the crowds, the young women in thongs, bikinis, tight one-pieces, hip-huggers and halter tops, most of the men in baggy shorts and shirtless, or wearing T-shirts bearing the logos of trendy local clubs or silkscreened advertisements for the owners' sexual prowess and organ size.

The students either looked through him or away from him or smiled and nodded as they would to any authority figure who had the power to wet-blanket their fun. Others cracked wise, showing off. Some of the women flirted, putting a little extra sway in their hips or slowly lowering their sunglasses and sizing him up, one of the straps on their bathing suits slipping off a shoulder when they stepped up and made a pretense of coyly asking for directions.

His thoughts kept returning to Anne Carson. When she was the age of these students, her father Jack had lost his construction business and moved to Magnolia Beach, and she had already given birth to Paige.

Lately, things had become a little confusing between Anne and him. A change; small, but still there. It was as if she had decided to take a step not exactly away but back from him, and she was watching, waiting for something to happen. Anne seemed more tense than usual, but didn't want to talk whenever Ben brought up the subject, so he didn't push things.

Instead, things had a way of pushing them.

After an interval when things had seemed good and solid between Anne and him, there were nights when Ben was not sure where his words or touches would lead. Anne might unexpectedly abandon herself to her body, giving herself over to its demands, all hunger and urgency and tightly-wrapped limbs, nights when desire overran the boundaries of the dark and the bodies they moved in. At other times, their lovemaking was tentative and awkward, taking on the furtive groping and confusion of a high school romance, of clumsy and desperate backseat trysts. At others, it was as if Anne retreated completely but left her body behind, a corporeal ghost

Jack's periods of disorientation were also getting longer and more tangled.

Anne was still having to juggle her work schedule and long after-school meetings two or three times a week with Paige and the guidance counselor.

For his part, Ben was exhausted from having to deal with the hormonal chaos of Spring Break and chasing down the increasingly baroque tips from the Stanley Tedros case.

Ben worked his way down Atlantic. More bodies. The smell of sunscreen. Music that Ben felt a decade too old for.

He passed Fat Larry's Bar and Grill, then Mama Evelyn's Tattoo and Piercing, another Beach Body outlet. On each street corner were palmettos planted in pre-cast concrete containers. Ben paused and watched three students drunkenly try to work an ATM.

A half block away was the entrance to Screaming Jay's Arcade and just beyond that, the north end of the boardwalk running for four ocean-side blocks. The crowd of students was at its thickest here, spilling into and eddying in the street.

As Ben approached, a small break in the milling students opened, and in that instant, Ben spotted him.

He stood eating a vanilla cone in the middle of the sidewalk. A short man with oversized arms and shoulders. Hair the color of weathered tin. A white T-shirt with *I Mean Business* across his chest.

And then, in a blink, the crowd closed.

Ben started after him, taking his time, not wanting to spook the guy.

He couldn't say for sure the guy was the one who'd ambushed him in the parking lot of the Passion Palace, but the momentary glimpse in front of Screaming Jay's had mimicked the glimpse Ben had gotten when he'd pulled aside the Halloween mask of the man who'd appeared from behind the Taurus and hit him with the sockful of heavy-gauge washers.

Ben was thinking too of the Glock the man had taken from him and the ballistics report on the murders of Jamison Blake and Melissa Newton.

Below the boardwalk, both Ben and the gray-haired man were hemmed in by the crowd. The street was jammed with a line of customized pickups, sound systems blaring, students dancing in the truck beds. Along the railing of the boardwalk was a long wall of bodies shouting and jostling each other, a knot in the middle waving open containers and toasting the crowd and each other.

One of them tossed an empty over the railing into the street.

The gray-haired man looked up. Then over his shoulder.

Nothing in his face suggested he'd recognized Ben.

A couple seconds later, though, he bolted.

More yelling. Bodies dominoed.

The guy jumped onto the hood of one of the pickups and then off onto the opposite sidewalk.

More falling bodies.

Ben followed the best he could. He radioed the two other foot patrol working the south end of Atlantic. Talbert responded first. She was near Bluecrest Street, a block to the west of Ben. Brewer was two blocks away. Ben alerted them to the general direction the gray-haired man was taking and warned them he might be armed. He then called in to the cruisers in the vicinity.

The gray-haired man's size made him hard to track. Ben had to count on following the cursing and fallen bodies in his wake.

He thought he saw the man duck into the entrance of Fun City.

Once inside, though, Ben again lost him. Fun City was a sprawl of amusements. Tiered miniature golf courses. Serpentine go-cart tracks. Ranks of batting cages and basketball goals. A large carousel and Ferris wheel. Water slides. Bungee jumps. Fast food outlets and picnic areas. Another video arcade.

The place was jammed.

Someone called Ben's name. He spotted Brewer making his way toward him. Brewer shook his head and thumbed-down the question on Ben's face.

Ben scanned the crowd.

Nothing.

He and Brewer split up and began working their way toward the Bluecrest entrance to the park.

Talbert radioed in. She'd spotted the guy near the parking garage on Everest. Ben told her to keep him in sight but not to approach until he and Brewer or further backup got there.

Ben and Brewer moved as fast as the crowds would allow, pushing their way to and clearing the west entrance of Fun City and then sprinting up Bluecrest.

Near the parking garage, as they ducked around a shirtless group of young men all wearing crimson and black USC caps, Brewer yelled to Ben that he couldn't raise Talbert on the two-way.

Less than a block later, they heard the screams.

Talbert had been thrown through the window of the Gulf Stream restaurant. She lay between two vacated tables amidst a fan of broken glass and an overturned miniature ficus, her face cross-hatched with lacerations and an artery in her neck geysering.

Ben yelled to Brewer to call EMS and more backup and knelt beside Talbert and worked on pressure-pointing the artery.

Talbert looked up at him and choked out something that sounded like *hot* or *hat*.

Ben kept his index and middle fingers pressed against her neck and his voice soft, as reassuring as he could make it, but he floundered for a moment, drawing a blank on Talbert's first name.

"Ginger," Brewer said from the other side of the broken window. "It's Ginger."

"Ok, Ginger," Ben said, "slow now. Slow and easy. You'll be all right, a while longer, that's all, so slow, that's it, slow."

The artery jumped and throbbed. His fingers were red and slick. He could feel shards of glass cutting into his knees.

Ginger Talbert looked up at him. She tried to say something. Then her eyes rolled back in her head.

"Where are those people?" Ben shouted. "I don't even hear sirens yet."

Brewer leaned through the window and looked over Ben's shoulder. "Oh man," he said.

"This is bad," Ben said.

"Oh man," Brewer repeated. He leaned further through the window frame and pointed.

"Her holster's empty," he said.

FORTY-FIVE

WHEN THEY GOT BACK to the room in the Sandpiper Motel, Croy Wendall put his shirt on again and gave the one named Roy the crimson and black USC cap back, and then Croy pretended to drink the beer Jay handed him. There were seven other guys in the room besides Jay and Roy, but Croy couldn't remember their names. They were all wearing the same caps and no shirt.

One of them turned on the television to Sports Center very loud. Jay passed out some beers. Three of them were playing catch with a jumbo bag of Cheetos. A couple of others moved onto the balcony and were yelling things at girls.

"You can chill here a while if you want," Roy told him and then went to watch Sports Center.

Croy thought about the wallets in the room.

That's what he'd been doing ever since he killed Jamie and Missy, hanging out with the students on their break and then stealing their wallets. At night he slept in his car or on the beach. He counted the money he already had in his head and figured he'd have enough soon to get away.

The problem with that though was Croy wasn't sure where he was going to get away to. He'd bought a map of the United States and studied it, but every place seemed like every other place except for the weather, and the weather was just what it was, like a big piece of wallpaper that had been put up on the day.

Croy wouldn't have minded going to a place if someone told him that's where he was supposed to go, but the only person who would have done something like that was Jamie, who had taken all Croy's money and who was also dead.

Croy considered asking Jay and then changed his mind to no.

Jay and all the other ones wearing caps might start asking questions back at him.

Croy wondered if the policewoman he threw into the window was alive. He was very happy to have a gun again. The other one had burned up in the fire at Jamie and Missy's.

The policewoman had been very nervous, and even with the gun pointed at him, she'd stood too close. The policewoman didn't know Croy or how fast he could make his hands.

When she went through the window, it sounded like a big handful of quarters tossed into an empty sink.

Afterwards there were a lot of people shouting things and screaming, and Croy had looked around for the tall policeman who'd been following him. Croy kept remembering his eyes. They were dark and the kind that didn't miss things. He'd seen those eyes on some of the men in shelters, eyes that were somehow sad and scary-looking at the same time, and Croy had always made it a point to steer clear of them.

Croy had looked around and started to run again, north and west, away from the beach.

That's where he met Jay and the other students who weren't wearing shirts. They were on the sidewalk in front of a little grocery store and asked him to buy them some beer. Croy made a quick idea in his head and told them there were a lot of policemen around, so it would be better if they went somewhere else.

Jay high-fived him for that and put his cap on Croy's head, and then Croy got in the middle of the group and took his shirt off too. He made sure to tie the T-shirt so its front hung over the back of his jeans like the others. That way, it hid the gun he'd taken off the policewoman.

Croy and the students were clustered together, and they walked back towards Atlantic Avenue. The tall policeman with the dark eyes and another one had run right by them to get to the people screaming at the restaurant.

Jay and the others didn't even seem to notice the screaming. They were very happy about the beer in their futures.

Croy got the beer, and they invited him back to their motel room to drink some. Croy knew there would be more than the two policemen looking for him now, so he did.

Jay and the others were lying around and talking about what they were watching on Sports Center and about sexing girls. Croy nodded every so often but didn't say much because he didn't know sports and he didn't sex.

Croy got up from the chair and went into the bathroom and emptied his beer down the sink. When he walked back into the room, Jay handed him another before Croy could say anything about it.

Croy knew he had to do something. He couldn't sit in the motel room pretending to drink beer forever.

Croy said some rhymes in his head. Then he did some numbers.

He imagined the world filling up with policemen.

He ate some Cheetos.

Jay let him use his cell phone. The battery in Croy's cell phone had died right in the middle of their words when Croy and Mr. Balen had been talking before, and Croy had not called back because Mr. Balen had been very upset and mad because Croy shot Jamie and Missy, and when Mr. Balen got upset and mad, it made Croy very nervous and jumpy inside, so Croy didn't call Mr. Balen and took wallets from the students instead.

Right now though, Croy was thinking about the tall policeman and his eyes and all the other policemen looking for him, so he took Jay's cell phone into the bathroom and dialed the number Mr. Balen made him remember. Croy waited for Mr. Balen to be mad at him for shooting Jamie and Missy, but Mr. Balen didn't say anything about that. He just asked where Croy was and then told him not to move or do anything until he got there.

Croy didn't.

FORTY-SIX

DETECTIVE JACKSON TOWNE was uncharacteristically on time for work when Ben Decovic stopped by the Homicide division before starting his shift. Towne was turned toward his computer and surfing the net for discount plane fares. He kept Ben waiting while he clicked on a couple more links, then swiveled his chair away from the screen, stretching his arms above his head.

Ben told him who he was.

Jackson Towne held up an index finger and frowned slightly. "Give me a minute," he said, "it'll come to me." He snapped his fingers and said, "Blake and Newton, the ballistics report, your Glock."

Ben nodded. It looked like Towne spent more on his wardrobe than Ben did on rent. He was wearing a light tan suit meticulously cut to fit the frame of the athlete he'd been at NC State fourteen years ago when he'd played power forward and led them to a division championship. Towne had blown out his knee the next year.

"Got the file right here," Towne said. It looked pitifully thin.

"I was going to pull the other one, you getting jumped, later today, do some cross-checking, and then get in touch with you." Towne leaned back and laced his fingers behind his head. "Now you can save me a little time."

Ben waited a second, expecting Towne to take out a pen, and when he didn't, Ben went on and filled him in on the assault at the Passion Palace, one man vandalizing Sonny Gramm's Mustang, the other taking out the bouncer and then ambushing Ben with a sock full of heavy-gauge washers, Ben losing his gun, the two men getting away on foot.

Towne nodded in the right places, but as Ben finished, talking about the difficulties and dead-ends with the follow-up, Sonny Gramm's refusal to cooperate and entrenched belief that Wayne LaVell was behind the vandalism, Ben had the distinct impression that Towne had quit listening some time ago.

That impression reinforced everything Ben had heard around the department about Towne. He was the first African-American to get his gold shield under the new restructuring of the force, and there'd been no little amount of resentment from certain quarters about the promotion. At one time, Towne had been a good cop, but somewhere along the line, he'd become more interested in exploiting affirmative-action quotas than in field work. He cut corners everywhere except in paperwork; he knew that's what ultimately counted for the higher-ups, and Towne had become a master at paper-trailing and padding out reports. He gave no sign he cared what any of his fellow officers of equal or lesser rank thought of him. He dressed sharp and looked good in PR photo shoots. There were any number of division heads looking over their shoulders and worrying about the status of their jobs within the next couple years.

"The two at the Palace," Towne asked. "What'd they look like?"

"They were wearing masks, and some of the lights in the lot were out," Ben said. "They were Caucasian though. The one with the crowbar was about six feet and thin. The one that jumped me was short, his chest and arms out of proportion to the rest of him. He had short gray hair."

"I had people out canvassing right after the shootings," Towne said, "but you know how things go on Sentinel. You got to assume 99 percent of what you get is 100 percent bullshit." He paused and glanced down at the file. "A neighbor, one Marilyn Keane, said there was a guy hanging out all the time at Jamison Blake's. She said he was a white man. Nothing about short or gray hair though."

Towne turned a page. "Blake's house is pretty much a total loss. The fire department did what it could, but the place went up quick. We're not going to find a lot to help us there."

"No other leads on the shooter?" Ben asked.

"To repeat, we're talking Sentinel Avenue here and all that entails about cooperating with the police," Towne said. "Right now, the only thing we know for sure is it was your gun used in the shootings."

"What about Blake and Newton?" Ben asked. "Any priors that might point at something?"

Towne glanced down at the file. "Jamison Blake, a string of assaults and B&Es. Melissa Newton, shoplifting, disturbing the peace, one resisting arrest. We're not talking master criminals here."

"Are you going recanvas?" Ben asked.

Towne's tie was pale blue and the same color as his shirt. He carefully smoothed the front of both and said, "We did a solid sweep the first time. I'm not sure a second is warranted. A case like this, you know how it usually works."

Ben did. Down the road, someone gets picked up on something unrelated and ends up confessing to the Blake and Newton murders or cuts a deal and snitches out the one who did. Wait and see. The case closes itself.

"Still," Ben said, "another look might kick something loose about the gray-haired guy."

"There's that," Towne said and nodded. "Of course, the odds are equally good that the guy sold your Glock right after he took it from you and has nothing to do with who eventually used it on Blake and Newton." Towne sat back and smoothed his tie again.

"He threw Talbert through a window," Ben said.

"How do you even know it was the same guy?" Towne said. "What, there's only one short white man with gray hair who's committed a crime?" Towne paused and shook his head. "You're on patrol, a gray-haired guy spots you and starts running. Because he's guilty. But not necessarily of ambushing you at the Passion Palace. You said yourself, the guy and his partner were wearing Halloween masks. You can't be sure he's the same one."

Towne tapped his pen against the desk top in a miniature drumroll. "Like I said, someone more than likely unloaded the piece on the street and then somebody else used it on Blake and Newton. Remember, we're talking Sentinel. You don't need much of a reason, pull a trigger there." Towne got up from behind the desk and straightened the lines of his suit.

"I'll keep you posted," he said, "anything turns up."

A dress rehearsal, Ben thought. That's what this session with

Jackson Towne had been, a dress rehearsal, Ben giving him the opportunity to practice his lines, work out the scenario that would eventually end up in the paperwork. Sentinel Avenue, after all. Wait and see. The case will close itself.

Ben went back to Atlantic Avenue. Foot patrol, the weather continuing to confound the meteorologists, the hottest April in fifty-plus years, the driest on record, and the students on break going native under that sun, getting more than a little restless, and by the end of Ben's shift, the holding cells were full, and Ben was awash in paperwork, and Mommy and Daddy and their lawyers were calling in or showing up at the station.

Ben was in the late stages of the day's paperwork when a sergeant from Booking waylaid him.

"We got a real noise-maker in Holding," he said, "keeps asking for you. Name of Leon Douglas."

Ben checked his watch and walked quickly to the north wing of the complex and with enough badgering managed to get Leon released from the cell packed bar to bar with students and into an empty interrogation room.

Leon's nose was angled in a new direction and one eye nearly swollen shut, and there were freckles of dried blood across the front of his shirt.

Ben asked what he got popped for and by whom.

"Receiving Stolen," Leon said, "and Resisting. But neither one be the case. I'm in my car, couple guys ask can I give them a ride, I'm ok with that, then a blue and white pull up behind us at a light, the guys out of the car and running, leave all their shit in my back seat, and I'm the one get brace on account I give those two brother a ride."

Ben knew Leon was probably the wheelman and let his version by, asking once again who the arresting officer was.

"Carl Adkin. That man, he could take a patent on mean." Leon paused, looking around the room. "He come up my car, I put my hands on the top of the steering wheel so he can see both of them, and then he hollering to his backup and pulling his gun, saying I'm attempting to flee the scene. See, I got my hands where they suppose to be, but I forget to turn off the engine, and I'm trying tell Adkin 'whoa' and get out the car, but he's not listening, and when he go to cuff me, Adkin claim I start with the resisting, and next thing I know my face is making friends with the pavement and my nose is broke."

"Ok," Ben said. "I'll see what I can do."

"I be trying to tell Adkin over and over that I'm your Ear, and he need to talk to you," Leon said.

Ben repeated what he'd said and then told Leon he'd have to take him back to the holding cell.

"Those college boys, they whiners," Leon said. "Puke and whine all the day long."

Ben repeated, once again, he'd do what he could.

"You need some motivation keep me in your thoughts," Leon said, "I heard something from my second cousin about Wayne LaVell." He paused, looking over at Ben. "My cousin, he work at the Palmer as a busboy there, and he say Wayne LaVell eating lunch and in walk Corrine Tedros and LaVell get all agitated and call out her name, only he don't call her Corrine, he keep saying April Rayne instead."

"You sure about this?"

Leon nodded. "My cousin say Corrine Tedros say Wayne LaVell mistaking her for someone else, but LaVell don't stop calling her that name until the lawyer guy Raychard Balen that LaVell eating with call him down. Mean time, Corrine Tedros looking scared, like a big dog chasing after her."

"Ok," Ben said. "One other thing, Leon. You have any relatives out of town?"

"I got an auntie in Raleigh."

"Good. I think it might be time to pay her a visit."

After signing out, Ben stopped by the hospital to check on Ginger Talbert. Her condition was stable, but she wasn't seeing visitors. A nurse told him that it was too soon to tell about the extent of the damage on the facial lacerations.

The waiting room on Talbert's floor was empty. Ben ducked in. He put in a call to his old partner, Andy Calucci.

"A favor," Ben said. "Your buddy Joey Romatta is still working Phoenix PD, right?"

Andy Calucci said he was.

"A favor," Ben repeated.

"Who and why?" Calucci asked.

Ben explained what he needed.

"Oh man," Calucci said. "You got any idea where this is headed?"

"Just a hunch," Ben said. "Nothing more."

After leaving the hospital, Ben doubled back to Queensland Highway, following it west and skirting the edge of the old downtown district. The radio was full of old love songs and used car commercials. He cut south and passed the site for the new high school, stopping three blocks later for the light where two men in black suits were working the traffic, each proffering a wicker basket and asking for an End Times offering. On the other side of the intersection, Reverend Redd Benton had set up a large tan revival tent. A streetside sign proclaimed: EXPOSURE TO THE SON WILL PREVENT BURNING.

Ben took Old Market Boulevard and continued south toward the regional airport, moving through a long cluttered stretch of fast food restaurants, motels, and small businesses. He passed the exit for the new mall and cut east again and drove through a large residential area comprised primarily of clusters of small subdivisions until he found the entrance to Delmar Woods.

As far as subdivisions went, Delmar Woods was your basic lock-and-load ranch houses and its layout an exercise in repetition and variation. All the streets were named after trees. He parked in front of 1228 Chestnut Lane.

Carl Adkin's place was not out of range of a patrolman's salary, but there was a lot of conspicuous icing.

A generous lot, the lawn wide and at least three shades deeper than any of the surrounding ones, the grass thick and putting-green quality, the surrounding landscape a carefully choreographed sequence of mimosa and crepe myrtle and palmetto, beds of verbena and marigolds and petunias, and borders of rhododendron and azalea and gardenia, all of them lush and thriving as if they'd cut a deal with the drought conditions that were leaning on everyone else.

There was a new black Dodge pickup maxed out on detail work parked in front of the two-car garage, the rear end of a late-model SUV framed in the opposite bay. Next to the garage were a john-boat, two jet skis, and a Bayliner speedboat setting on a trailer.

Ben was almost to the front door when he heard voices out back.

Carl Adkin was on a pine deck that opened on two sliding glass doors at the rear of the house. He stood, wreathed in smoke, over a black barbecue grill. He glanced down at Ben.

"How's foot patrol? Heard Talbert kissed the glass," he said. "Tough break. She never was one you'd want as primary on the scene. She's nervous, and it shows."

Ben walked up three steps to the deck. In the middle of the backyard was a large pecan tree. Two women, one blonde, the other red-haired, sat in webbed lawn chairs at the edge of its shade. There was a white Styrofoam cooler between them. The red-haired woman held and tried to quiet a persistently crying infant. The blonde watched two boys chase each other on ATVs around the yard.

Carl Adkin looked at Ben and then went back to flipping burgers that were the size of flattened softballs. "Angus," he said. "Prime cut." He smiled and slapped a belly softening at the waist-line of his jeans.

"You could say that about a lot of the things around here." Ben nodded toward the buzzing ATVs, the kennel and enclosed runway along the property line, the wired workshop, and elabo-rate swing set and two-story wooden fort tucked into the south-east corner of the yard.

"I like nice things," Carl Adkin said.

"Last time I heard," Ben said, "nice things cost money." He paused and scanned the backyard again. The red-haired woman juggled the baby and lifted the lid of the cooler and pulled out a beer. The baby moved from crying to wailing.

"It stands to reason," Ben said, "a lot of nice things must cost a lot of money."

"I'm waiting to hear why any of that is your goddamn business." Adkin went from burger to burger, cutting into each with the edge of the spatula. The insides were pink and wet.

A moment later, a line of pit bulls appeared in the enclosed wire runway of the kennel and began barking and throwing themselves against the fence.

"Meat in the air," Carl Adkin said. "You're hungry, you can't help but smell it."

"I want you to lose the paper on Leon Douglas," Ben said.

"I don't think so," Adkin said. "We go back, Leon and me. A little history there. He's got an attitude."

"Eye and Ear," Ben said. "He's helping me."

"Your problem, right there," Adkin said. "Trusting that little coon to bring you anything that holds water."

There was movement behind the sliding glass doors. A small girl walked into the living room with a juice box and climbed up on the couch. From where he stood, Ben could hear faint strains of cartoon mayhem.

"I need you to lose the paper," he repeated.

Adkin put the face of the spatula on the burgers and pressed them against the grill top. The meat popped and sizzled. "Give me one good reason for why I should lose the paper on our friend Leon."

"Because I'll scare up a couple of Leon's friends and get them to testify they were on the scene and witnessed you using unnecessary force in the arrest." Ben paused and took a step closer to Adkin. "They'll perjure themselves from here to Sunday, and with the newspaper and television play, the chief and mayor will push for an investigation, and we'll see how that resisting charge you slapped on Leon holds up."

Adkin pointed the spatula at Ben. "You're making a mistake here."

"The paper," Ben said. "It's gone. You can go in or call it in. I don't care as long as it's today."

In the backyard, the red-haired woman handed the crying infant to the blonde and then rummaged in the cooler. The boys on the ATVs chased down a cat that had wandered in from next door. Adkin nodded, but didn't look at Ben. He kept his gaze on his property line and on the wide evening sky simmering in the remains of the day's heat.

FORTY-SEVEN

NEAR DUSK, and Croy Wendall crouched along the Two Bridge River and watched what was left of the sun sheet the surface of the water in a thin pale yellow. He waited for a wrinkle in the light that signaled movement or looked for the small knob of a head breaking the surface. The rain had gone missing for a long time, and the waterline was low, and Croy could smell mud slowly drying out in layers.

His hand shot out. He added the frog to the others in the burlap bag he'd set on the bank. Then he dipped the bag in the water, and when he pulled it out again, its bottom portion was all jump and squirm.

Croy thought about nerves firing along a spine. He'd seen a television show about that once. A cut-away of a human's insides with small fiery red dots pulsing where the nerves were.

Croy's hand shot out again. He kept adding frogs to the bag until the light had melted into the water, and then he took the bag and climbed the bank and walked back to the cabin.

The cabin was above the river on a small flat-topped rise, and it was ringed on three sides by live oaks. On the other side of the trees the ground ran into an immense swampy field bordered on the west by woods, which was where Croy had hidden his car.

Croy filled the portable generator with gas and started it up and watched the lights flicker on inside the windows. He put the sack of frogs in an old galvanized washtub that held the other bag of frogs he'd caught yesterday.

He stood at the door for a moment and looked at the tree directly behind the cabin. The tree had worked its way into his dreams. At some point it had been struck by lightning, and its trunk carried a long jagged break. The limbs on the north side were bare, but the other side was still green with new leaves the size of fingers.

Croy went into the cabin and made supper. He chewed on the right side of his mouth because the left side hurt from a missing filling in a back molar. The gumline around the tooth was swollen and tender, and a sweet taste leaked from the tooth and mixed with the taste of the food.

After supper, Croy put three aspirin directly on the molar and chewed them to paste.

Then he checked his belt to make sure the cell phone was clipped to it and charged. Mr. Balen had told Croy to carry the cell phone with him everywhere, and Croy did.

At first, Croy had been afraid Mr. Balen was going to be mad at him for shooting Jamie and Missy and for running away after burning down the house and then almost getting caught by that policewoman and having to throw her through the restaurant window, but Croy had explained about Jamie having stolen all of Croy's savings and about Jamie getting ready to turn Croy in for killing Stanley Tedros and getting the reward.

Mr. Balen didn't yell at Croy though. He was very nice. He talked to Croy in a voice that sounded like it was on a commercial for things that people would find handy to use around the house, and then he drove Croy to the cabin, and together they took apart the gun Croy had taken from the policewoman and threw the pieces in the river, and Mr. Balen gave him a new gun. Later he brought Croy all the supplies and snacks he needed to stay there.

Croy had promised to stay close to the cabin and not go anywhere else.

After he'd moved into the cabin, Croy had some bad dreams, but he didn't watch them long. Even asleep, he could stop one dream and start another. It was like changing channels on television. He'd been able to do that ever since he was five years old.

Sometimes at night, he listened to the frogs.

Sometimes, he said rhymes or numbers in his head.

He found a picture in one of the magazines left in the cabin that he liked, and he carefully tore it out and put it on the wall next to his cot. It was an advertisement for juice, and there was no writing on it at all, just a perfectly round orange set in the center of the page against a bright white background. Looking at it made him feel the same way as listening to the frogs did. Croy also liked the word itself. *Orange.* It was everyday and mysterious at the same time, the name of the thing indistinguishable from the color describing it, a perfect seamless fit.

Croy didn't exactly remember when he started dreaming about the tree.

He was pretty sure it was right after he tried to fix Stanley Tedros's pocketwatch.

No matter how many times Croy wound it, the watch kept losing time. Only a couple minutes at first, but then the hours started piling up, and Croy got very nervous in his stomach, and he finally pried the face of the watch off with a kitchen knife, but that made him even more nervous because the sight of the watch's insides, all those tiny gears and wheels and how they fit and worked somehow got mixed up in his head with the times Jamie and Missy had sexed each other while Croy was in the house and the walls would hold all the noises they made, and Croy couldn't make the nerves firing inside him slow down until he took the watch and buried it outside and then went down to the river to catch some frogs for a while.

After that, Croy felt fine.

Tonight, after finishing the dishes, Croy took a spool of nylon fishing line and his pocketknife, chewed two more aspirin, and went back outside. He crouched next to the galvanized washtub holding the two bags of frogs.

There was no wind.

When he looked up through the bare branches of the live oak, Croy saw a pale slice of moon directly above. The moon looked like a coin that had been inserted in a slot that had not been jammed home yet.

He began cutting the fishing line, varying the length, one piece approximately a foot and a half, the other slightly less than a foot, and put them in two piles.

Bats showed up. They skimmed the sky above the roof.

While Croy cut the line, he thought of words that rhymed with *bat*. There were a lot of them.

Bat spelled backwards was *tab*. *Bat* and *tab* didn't rhyme, but Croy liked them anyway because they reminded him of amphibians, one thing that was like two things because they could live on land or in the water, and it didn't matter to them which.

Croy kept cutting the fishing line. His molar ached. He tasted blood and something sour when he pressed his tongue against the gumline around it, so he quit doing that.

His eyes and skin felt hot.

Everything was very quiet except for the thin whine of mosquitoes that had come up from the river.

Croy went back and forth between the two piles of fishing line he'd cut, taking a long piece and tying it to a short one.

Then he got up and took out one of the screens from the cabin windows.

He returned to the washtub and emptied the two sacks of frogs. He grabbed a frog and then set the screen over the tub.

The frog felt like a handful of cold Jello wrapped in cellophane.

Croy tied the frog to one end of the fishing line by its leg, and then he caught another frog and tied it to the other end by the leg.

He draped the fishing line over the back of his neck and started over, repeating the process.

It took a long time, and it was very hard work, but after a while Croy fell into a rhythm of catching and tying the frogs that was like the rhythm of digging and planting flowers he found when Jamie and he had worked for Mr. Sharpe and his landscaping business.

Every time Croy tied frogs to each end of a line, he draped it over his neck. The frogs dangled and jumped against his chest like someone knocking on an old door.

After a while, the pieces of fishing line started to cut into the back of his neck, so Croy figured he had enough for now, and he stood up and walked to the base of the live oak and grabbed the lowest branch and pulled himself into the dead side of the tree.

He crawled out onto the branch, listening to it creak beneath his weight, and then lifted one of the strings of frogs from his neck and draped it over the limb. He moved back a few feet and put another one on the limb.

Croy moved up the tree, hanging the pieces of fishing line with the frogs on them, until there wasn't any more left on his neck.

Then he climbed down and went back to tying more frogs.

He could smell the river, and on the next trip up, he was high enough over the roof of the cabin that he could see it too and the pale streak of moonlight running down the middle of the dark water.

Two limbs broke under his weight, and each time Croy had to scramble back closer to the trunk. He strung one set of frogs on them anyway.

In the northeastern corner of the sky were some clouds that looked like torn pieces of cloth. The rest of the sky was just stars and the moon.

Every so often Croy thought about the picture of the orange he'd taken from the magazine and put up on the wall of the cabin next to his cot.

Croy made four more trips up the tree before he ran out of frogs.

He was sweating a lot, but it was a fever sweat, not the other kind. The molar smoldered in the back of his mouth.

Croy stepped back to take in his work. It was like he had invented wind. The frogs hanging from the limbs jumped and twisted, sometimes showing their green side, sometimes their white underside.

The other half of the tree was very still.

Against the night sky, the pieces of fishing line were invisible. Croy watched the frogs for a long time. He was standing on the spot where he'd buried Stanley Tedros's pocketwatch.

Above him, the frogs flopped and squirmed.

The cell phone chirped. At first, Croy thought the sound came from something live. He took the phone off his belt.

Mr. Balen asked how he was doing and then explained the crime he needed Croy to do.

Croy said ok to both.

FORTY-EIGHT

SUNSET HAD BROKEN the lower portions of the horizon and stacked it with color, thin slats of orange, pink, and purple that the wind left undisturbed, when Corrine Tedros pulled into short-term parking at the Magnolia Beach Regional Airport.

Inside the terminal, she checked the arrivals board. Southeast Air and Star Aviation were the only two commuter lines based at Magnolia Beach and were primarily used for regional travel or for connecting flights at larger airports in Atlanta, Jacksonville, Raleigh, Columbia, and Charlotte. Puddle Jumpers were what the local businesspeople called them. That, or the Grim Reaper Express, since neither airline was particularly noted for its safety or maintenance records. Two of the pilots Corrine saw standing at the check-in counter for Southeast and chatting up the attendant looked as if they were barely out of high school and would be more at home checking your oil than piloting turboprops.

Buddy's flight was already in, and Corrine found him at the baggage claim. He spotted her and waved. His smile, as well as his black suit, was badly rumpled. He found his bags, and they walked back to the car.

"You drive, ok?" he said. "I'm bushed."

Corrine took Old Market Boulevard north. It was a full ten minutes before Buddy spoke again.

"It was a wash," he said.

"I'm sorry." Corrine almost meant it. Right then, Buddy looked old and tired.

"I don't understand," Buddy said. "First Atlanta and now Charlotte. The same thing each time." He rubbed his forehead. "A day and a half of meetings. I was ready with the figures and projections. The Charlotte people kept picking them apart. I couldn't get them to see the restructuring for what it was." Buddy paused and shook his head. "Quick returns, that's all they were interested in. We never found common ground."

"Maybe," Corrine said and let it hang.

Buddy looked at her, then away. He took out his cell phone and punched a number.

"Hello, Anne? It's Buddy Tedros."

Corrine listened to the hope wilt in his voice after Buddy asked if Jack Carson had remembered anything about Stanley's murder and he got the answer that Corrine had paid for.

"Nothing at all?" Buddy said and lowered his head. "You never know, maybe Jack will come through yet." Buddy added a moment later, "You too, Anne. Tell Paige hello."

Buddy sat with the cell phone cradled in his palm and looked out the window. "There's still Birmingham," he said after a while. Corrine listened to him try to resuscitate his optimism and confidence in the distribution plans that James Restan, with a couple calls to Birmingham, would doom in advance.

Fifteen minutes later, Corrine pulled into the entrance of White Pine Manor. The sunset had softened, and the swallows were out, cutting and darting through the gathering dusk.

"I made a nice meal," Corrine said. "It was supposed to celebrate you closing in Charlotte. Let's call it a welcome home meal instead." She leaned over and kissed Buddy lightly on the cheek.

Buddy went upstairs to change and shower, and Corrine checked on supper, set the table, and hunted down a bottle of good red wine.

She told herself not to rush things.

Buddy was slowly on his way to again becoming the man she married. He was discovering what everyone did sooner or later. He could not sustain his grief, and his grief could not sustain him.

A little more time to forget, that's all he needed. In the act of forgetting, you found absolution. Memory and memories were overrated. Dead weight. You forgot, and you were clean again.

Tonight, they would have a nice meal. Corrine would not bring up James Restan's buy-out offer. After supper, they'd open another bottle of wine. Perhaps she'd steer the conversation toward starting a family. A kid would be a hedge, some insurance, against any trouble Wayne LaVell might make. Then she and Buddy would have sex.

Corrine was sure of one thing. The body had no use for memory or grief. It took care of itself.

FORTY-NINE

THE CENTER OF GRAVITY for the house was the kitchen, and Ben Decovic and Anne Carson sat across from each other at the kitchen table, glasses of wine at their elbows, the lights low and the radio even lower, the radio seemingly tuned perpetually to an oldies station, an easygoing synchronicity at work this evening as Wilson Pickett sang "In the Midnight Hour," and Ben glanced over at the wall clock and saw that its hands were about to overlap and eclipse the twelve.

"You're off tomorrow, right?" Ben said.

Anne nodded.

"Maybe you can sleep in a little then."

Anne shook her head. "Doctor's appointment at eight-thirty. Dad's always a little better in the mornings. I need to talk to the doctor about getting dad's medication adjusted. Things aren't right." She and Ben went on to talk about Jack's new tendency to break into tears at unexpected moments. Anything, it seemed, could set him off. Ben had noticed it too.

"Growing up, I never saw him cry once," Anne said. "Not once. I don't know what I'm going to do. Earlier this afternoon, he broke down and cried for twenty minutes over a commercial for aluminum foil."

Ben reached across the table and rubbed the back of Anne's right hand.

"I don't know what's next," she said.

Ben tried to locate a smile that might pass for reassuring. Anne slowly slipped her hand out from under his and picked up her glass of wine.

Over Ben's shoulder, the radio played doomed rock and rollers, starting with Buddy Holly, then segueing into Richie Valens.

"Well," he said, pointing to the end of the kitchen table, "Paige must be happy. I see she got her laptop. I thought it was still in layaway for a while."

Anne tucked her hair behind her ears and took a sip of wine before answering. "I had an extra good week in tips at the restaurant. I knew Paige needed it. Mr. Deane, the guidance counselor, thought so too."

Ben had interviewed enough suspects to know when one was lying, and Anne wasn't a good liar to begin with, but he let the whole thing go, chalking it up to pride, figuring that Anne had gone out and gotten a loan to finish up the payments on the laptop. He wasn't about to make her feel worse by pushing too hard. She wasn't a criminal or suspect, after all.

"Mr. Deane thinks Paige is making real progress," Anne said. "He says she has a lot of anger that she can't find ways to productively channel. He told me she's learned to use her intellect as a weapon."

Ben didn't say anything. He lifted the bottle of wine and held it against the light, checking its level, and then topped off his glass and reached across the table to do the same for Anne.

"I've been thinking," Anne said.

Ben's cell phone went off. He checked the number and slowly let out his breath. "I need to take this one, Anne. It's important."

She sat quietly for a moment, then nodded and picked up her glass of wine and moved to the kitchen sink and stood with her back to him and looked out the window. From where Ben sat, she was silhouetted by the ceiling light.

Ben checked missed calls and hit send.

"Figured you'd be up," Andy Calucci said. "I tried calling the apartment a couple times but kept getting your machine, so I figured you might be over at the other place." He paused. "I'm not interrupting something, am I?"

"No," Ben said. "It's ok." He listened to the inevitable click of Andy's lighter as he fired up a Kool.

"You probably figured why I'm calling," Andy said. "My friend Joey Rommata sent on the first batch of photos and bookings."

"And?" Ben said.

"I can't say I'm exactly fond of the smell here." Calucci paused, then asked, "What exactly are you planning to do with these?"

"Follow up on a hunch," Ben said. "Nothing more than that."

"There's never a *nothing more* with you," Andy said. "I know how you work. I partnered with you in case you forgot."

"Come on, Andy," Ben said. "How many did Rommata send to you?"

Calucci sighed. "Ok, sure, against my better judgment here. Four of Raine. Three of Rhain. Two of Rhayne. One of Rain. One of Rayne."

"Is she in the batch?" Ben glanced over at Anne, who still stood at the kitchen window with her back to him.

"I considered not telling you that Rommata sent them at all," Andy said. "They came in, I took a whiff, and I'm thinking, something smells like this, the best thing to do is bury it."

"Except you didn't," Ben said.

"There's still time."

"Listen, Andy, I told you, it's a hunch. Anything turns up, I take it straight to Homicide. The one running the case is a guy named Hatch."

Calucci went into another sigh. "I don't like the smell here," he said after a moment.

"I think your olfactory distress over the booking photos has been fully and clearly established, Andy."

"Ok, Ben, ok, she's in there, ok? The one spelled R-A-Y-N-E. She's younger, her hair a different shade of blond, but it looks like her."

"So you're sure it's Tedros?" Ben saw, out of the corner of his eye, Anne look over her shoulder, then turn back to the kitchen window.

"A one hundred percent?" Andy said. "No. I saw her picture on the TV and in the newspapers a couple times, and I'm saying it looks like a match to me."

"Sounds good enough." Ben asked Andy if he could fax all the photos and booking sheets to the main office at the White Palms Apartments first thing tomorrow morning.

"The apartment office?" Andy said. "Why not the Department?"

"It just might be better that way," Ben said slowly.

"I gotta ask," Andy said. "You drinking down there?"

"A beer. Occasional glass of wine," Ben said. "Not like before. Nothing like before."

"So you're telling me, things are under control?" Andy paused, and that was followed by the click of his lighter. "I fax this stuff to you, you're not drinking and going to do anything stupid, like cowboying it and trying to use it as leverage and somehow ending up shooting the Tedros woman or her husband or yourself because you let things and you get turned around?"

"Nothing like that, partner," Ben said.

"I'm not down there, so this time I can't bail you out." Andy paused. "Why you doing this at all? I thought you liked Patrol."

"It's just a hunch, Andy. Probably won't lead anywhere."

"Oh man," he said and hung up before Ben could say anything else.

It was at least two full minutes before Anne broke away from the kitchen window and returned to the table. The radio was playing Dusty Springfield. Anne poured what was left of the wine into her glass. Ben noticed her hand was shaking a little.

He waited.

Anne lifted her glass, then set it down. "I heard you say *Tedros*. Which one? Buddy? Corrine? Stanley?"

Ben said Corrine in a tone that he hoped would discourage further questions, but Anne nodded one too many times and then went on to ask why Ben needed his former partner in Homicide to check up on Corrine Tedros.

"Has Buddy ever mentioned someone named April Rayne?"

"No," Anne said.

"He ever talk about how he met Corrine? Her past?"

"Yes, sometimes Buddy talks about his wife," she said. "He talks about how much he loves her. He talks about how devoted they are to each other. He's there for her. She can count on him."

Ben waited a moment before asking, "Does it work the other way too? Can he count on her?"

"They're in *love*, Ben," she said. "That's the way it's supposed to work."

"Look," he said.

She finished off her wine, then sat back.

"Corrine Tedros is hiding something," Ben said. "I already caught her in one lie. I have the feeling it won't be the last."

"Maybe Corrine Tedros has her reasons," Anne said.

Ben looked at her in surprise. "I don't get you. It sounds like you're defending her."

"People have reasons," Anne said. "That's all I mean. Not all of them have to be criminal. Though you don't really seem happy unless they are."

Anne abruptly got up and crossed the kitchen and living room, heading for the hallway and bedroom. Ben sat at the table and finished his wine, then turned off the radio and the lights and sat back down. He listened to the night sounds the house made.

FIFTY

THE ITCH OF OLD AMBITION.

Ben Decovic, off shift and on his own clock.

A thin rind of a quarter-moon in the center of his windshield. A restlessness underwritten by a passel of questions that were bigger than the answers he had on hand tonight.

Sentinel Avenue. The heart of old south Magnolia Beach. The place where everyone's luck stalled or dead-ended. Block upon block of matchbox houses and shacks. Chaotic trailer courts. Failed tenement projects. Discount liquor stores. Bottom-end pawn shops and check-cashing services. Storefront beauty shops, tattoo parlors, and churches with hand-painted signs in their windows. Backyard barbecue joints. Clubs and bars like the Blue Zone, Skinny Lee's, and Smooth Rudy's, all of which generated their own private crime waves every Saturday night.

Ben parked across from the Milforde Hotel, five stories of crumbling bricks and foundation shifts and fire code violations, and started canvassing, and over the next hour, the residents of Sentinel Avenue lived up to their reputations among police cir-

cles, Ben running into the same locked doors, hostilities, eva-
sions, and outright lies that Jackson Towne in Homicide had predicted he would.

No one Ben talked to seemed particularly distressed or surprised or interested that Jamison Blake and Missy Newton had
been shot.

The itch of old ambition had been with Ben that morning
too when he checked the faxes that Andy Calucci had sent on.
Though the photo was smudged, there'd been no doubt whatsoever that April Rayne had been an earlier incarnation of Corrine
Tedros.

Ben had studied the accompanying booking sheet and played
a hunch, impatiently waiting out a three-hour time difference before putting in a call to Andy's friend Joey Rommata and asking
him about the lawyer named Vince Noldern who had represented
Rayne after the booking. Ben had stretched the truth a little with
Rommata by implying that Andy was busy and had suggested
Ben call Joey himself.

Joey Rommata was able to connect some basic dots. Ben's
hunch had paid off. Bill Manning in Phoenix Vice arrested young
runaways or homeless women for solicitation. Manning then contacted Vince Noldern, the lawyer who worked for Wayne LaVell.
Manning got a nice little kickback for doing so. Noldern got the
girls off. They then ended up working in one of Wayne LaVell's
massage parlor franchises or in his Valley of the Sun Escort Service.

According to Joey Rommata, there was no shortage of young
lost women in Phoenix.

Tonight, two blocks from the Milforde Hotel, he approached

the rubble and char of what had been Jamison Blake's house. He thought he'd already put all the ambition and desire for closure behind him. His sense of direction, however, had been off. It wasn't behind him. It was right in front of him and always had been, and he had fooled himself into believing otherwise. It had taken Stanley Tedros's murder and the shootings on Sentinel Avenue to show him that. Despite his wife's death and all the dead-end circumstances surrounding it, Ben still wanted to believe in motive.

At bottom, Jamison Blake and Melissa Newton were dead. They had been shot with his service Glock.

Ben moved curb-side and ducked under the yellow tape surrounding the remains of Jamison Blake's house. There wasn't much left beyond the all too easy bathos of a crime scene: a charred hairbrush, a pile of melded CDs, the blackened frame of a dining room chair. Ben stepped among the damp ashes and rubble and tried to summon up the layout of the rooms.

He put Blake and Newton in them.

Then he dropped in the short white guy.

Whether the short man had lived there or been a frequent visitor, the house was a tight fit. It was a place that would not hold secrets or charged emotional states well or for long.

The house to the east of Jamison Blake's was abandoned, its front porch roof collapsed and windows gone. Beyond it was a trash-strewn lot and more tightly packed houses, a bump up from a bungalow. Running among the houses was a labyrinth of backyard wooden privacy fences, all in various stages of disrepair.

The house next door to the west was still dark. Ben had tried earlier in his canvassing but had come up empty, and it was no different this time. He checked the notes he'd taken from his meeting with Detective Jackson Towne. The occupant's name was Marilyn Keane. Two kids. Unemployed. She'd mentioned a man who'd hung at Jamison Blake's place.

Ben shelved his frustration. He needed to talk to her. If not the man's name, she could at least tell him the guy's height and color of his hair. Ben was betting under five-six and prematurely gray.

Ben continued moving through the rubble. Fragments of clothing. A blackened alarm clock. Scorched kitchen utensils. The fried intestines of an entertainment system. A heat-twisted toothbrush.

He kept returning to the one thing he was sure of. Blake and Newton had been killed with his semi-automatic.

The gun he'd lost after he'd been ambushed in the parking lot of the Passion Palace when he'd come across a thin man in a cheap Halloween mask vandalizing the owner's Mustang.

The man who'd ambushed him had been short, white, and gray-haired.

Who may or may not have been the one hanging out at Blake's and Newton's house.

The Passion Palace was owned by Sonny Gramm, who refused to cooperate with the police after the vandalism of his car and the follow-up vandalizing of his home, but who still kept hiring and firing bodyguards.

Sonny Gramm who had made an absolute mess of his financial affairs and was now afraid he was about to lose everything.

Sonny Gramm who fueled on desperation and a steady diet of Jim Beam had become paranoid enough to cast around for any available scapegoat to lay off his troubles on.

Someone like Wayne LaVell, who would fit any paranoid's delusions.

Or the Wayne LaVell who could also give any sane person a reason to be more than a little paranoid.

Wayne LaVell who just happened to be in town looking at investment opportunities.

Wayne LaVell who'd been eating lunch at the Palmer with Raychard Balen when he spotted Corrine Tedros and called her April Rayne.

Wayne LaVell who counted among his Phoenix holdings the Valley of the Sun Escort Service.

Which April Rayne had more than likely worked at.

April Rayne who was eventually incarnated as Corrine Tedros.

Who had lied unnecessarily when Ben had interviewed her after Stanley Tedros's murder.

A small lie, unnecessary and unimportant, which had nevertheless resulted in a phone call to Ed Hatch in Homicide and some pressure from Raychard Balen.

Corrine Tedros who also knew Sonny Gramm, had in fact been waitressing at one of Sonny Gramm's supper clubs in Myrtle Beach when she met her future husband, Buddy Tedros.

Buddy, the nephew of Stanley Tedros, the generic soft-drink king, who'd hit it big with Julep and, if the rumors reported in the papers were accurate, had turned down some very large-scale buyout offers from the major soda companies.

Buddy Tedros who had gone to high school with Anne Carson.

Whom Ben was sleeping with.

And whose father, Jack, had been the sole witness to Stanley Tedros's murder and was unable to remember a single detail from it.

A collection of connections that never quite connected.

Nothing more than the improbable tangle of coincidences that daily life served up all too often to mock our hunger for order. The ground clutter from a group of people whose past and present lives crossed and recrossed each other's.

If you colored between the lines, everything became circumstantial and could be explained away.

Like the fresh start a marriage offered, and the past a woman wanted to keep from her future husband in order to have a chance at happiness.

Like the washers Jack Carson had been holding in his fist at Stanley Tedros's murder scene. Which belonged or didn't belong with the rest of the odds and ends his pants pockets had held.

Which may or may not have matched those from the sockful of washers the short white man had hit Ben with in the parking lot of the Passion Palace before taking his gun.

Or like the fact that Ben's gun had eventually been used on Jamison Blake and Missy Newton but not on Stanley Tedros, who'd been stabbed thirty-nine times instead.

Connections that weren't quite.

Except.

That *except* was at the heart of what had once made him a good cop. He took his time. He had the eye. He had believed the dots eventually connected.

Maybe they would this time too.

Ben ducked under the yellow tape and started back to his car. The night sky was empty of clouds, the air dry. Above the Milforde Hotel, the moon was a thin slice of light. From down the block came the sound of glass breaking, then laughter.

FIFTY-ONE

UNFINISHED BUSINESS.

That's what Wayne LaVell called it after Corrine had driven five miles west of the city limits to the DeSoto Motor Lodge. The DeSoto was a throwback to the early sixties, a single-story line of rooms facing the road and a cluster of adjoining bungalows, all flanked by small mushroom-gray satellite dishes and tired palmettos, the whole place painted an anemic white and trimmed in bright red and run by a family of Pakistanis, the clientele mostly transient construction workers who paid by the week or month.

Inside bungalow A-8, Corrine Tedros dabbed the corner of her mouth with a paper napkin and then redid her lipstick while Wayne LaVell crossed the room to a built-in desk where he had set out a bottle of gin, two plastic cups, some lime slices, ice, and tonic.

"Degradation becomes you, April," he said. "You're positively glowing."

"I told you. Corrine. My name's Corrine." She dropped the wadded napkin in the wastebasket.

LaVell handed her a drink. "Absolutely," he said. "Pardon my manners."

"Are you still trying to sell the idea that your showing up in Magnolia Beach is a coincidence?"

"In your case, that's true." LaVell toasted her with his cup.

"I find that hard to believe, Wayne."

"In many respects, that's always been your problem, *Corrine*." The smile was gone now.

"I'll get you your money," she said.

LaVell plucked the plastic cup from her hand and went to fix another round. "I don't think so," he said, his back to her. He grabbed a handful of ice cubes and dropped them into the drink.

"What do you mean? I told you, I need a little time, but you'll get it."

LaVell handed Corrine her drink and sat down and then nodded Corrine toward the chair opposite him. "Not interested in the money. I need something else." He paused. "Two things actually. Then we'll call it even between us."

Corrine quickly stood up, but before she could say anything, LaVell told her to sit back down.

"Raychard Balen told me about your little outburst in his office and that you included me in your threat."

"I was upset. That's all it was." Corrine felt the sides of the plastic cup start to buckle and eased her grip.

"I hope so," Wayne LaVell said. "I think it prudent that Balen, you, and I maintain some common ground among us. We each have some interests to protect, and there's no reason not to keep them mutually beneficial."

"I told you, I was upset." Corrine lifted the cup and took a long swallow.

"Then it's time to move on to new business," LaVell said. He sat farther back in the chair, crossing his legs at the ankles. "I understand you used to work for Sonny Gramm."

Corrine nodded, confused. She'd thought that LaVell was going to play some angle connected to Stanley Tedros's murder and had been going through a panicked inventory of possible responses to the extortion demands she'd been sure LaVell was about to drop on her.

"I was a waitress," Corrine said, "at one of his supper clubs in Myrtle Beach."

"Did you fuck Gramm?"

Corrine shook her head no.

"He try to?"

"Sonny never pushed it that far," Corrine said. "He hit on a lot of the waitresses. He liked the attention more than anything else."

"I'm interested in acquiring some property," LaVell said, "and I want you to broker the offer to Sonny Gramm." He paused for a moment. "A final offer, by the way. So you'll need to be particularly convincing."

"Why not Raychard Balen?" Corrine asked. "Wouldn't it make more sense if he took the offer to Sonny Gramm?"

"Balen has already tendered two offers as well as implemented some additional outside encouragement to take them," Wayne LaVell said, "but none of them have turned out as we'd hoped. We thought a new tack might be in order."

"And what happens if I agree to help you?" Wayne LaVell had never directly mentioned Stanley Tedros's name, Corrine thought, and then realized he didn't have to. It was the way Wayne LaVell had always wielded his power, the unpredictable combination of blunt coercion and nuanced manipulation he brought to bear on any issue. Wayne LaVell always said and did both more and less than you'd expect. He let Corrine know he knew about Stanley Tedros's murder by never bringing it up, and Corrine felt the weight of that knowledge loom even larger and more ominously for his having done so.

LaVell made them more gin and tonics. "Sonny Gramm is a very truculent man and an even bigger fool," he said. "Gramm's overextended, heavily in debt to a number of people who've lost faith in his financial prowess. I stepped in and bought off Gramm's debt to those same people. My name might not be officially on the paperwork, but Sonny Gramm owes me, and I intend to collect. Magnolia Beach affords some interesting development opportunities. I would prefer to pursue those opportunities in a discreet but energetic manner. Sonny Gramm is aware of this, but insists on casting the transaction as a reenactment of the Alamo."

"And what happens if I agree to help?" Corrine asked again.

LaVell gave a short dismissive wave with his free hand. "It'll even the bookkeeping between us."

"Ok, but you said you needed two things before. What else?"

The network of tiny broken capillaries spreading across the bridge of his nose and upper cheeks bunched and gathered under Wayne LaVell's smile. "I want you and your husband Buddy to give me a party," he said.

"I don't understand."

"After I assume ownership of Gramm's properties," LaVell

said, "I want to establish my presence here in Magnolia Beach as a respectable businessman and good neighbor. Your husband knows a lot of the right people here. A party in my honor would go a long way to opening doors that might otherwise remain closed to me." Wayne LaVell paused, smiling again. "You've done all right for yourself here. There's no reason any of that should have to change."

Corrine took a swallow of her drink. She tried to remember how many Wayne LaVell had handed her. She wasn't drunk, but it felt like the gin had burned away everything but this moment. She felt trapped in a terrible lucidity, her world reduced to a series of X-rays that Wayne LaVell held up to the light to read.

"What if I can't convince Sonny Gramm to sell the properties?" Corrine asked. "You said he'd already turned down your first two offers."

"I have faith in you, Corrine."

"But if I can't. What?"

Wayne LaVell glanced at his watch and stood up. "Well, Corrine," he said, "then you can help me set Gramm up to be killed. One way or another, those properties are going to be mine."

FIFTY-TWO

SUNRISE REALTY was on Atlantic Avenue, tucked between a Mercedes dealership and a day spa named Younger Than Yesterday. Ben Decovic parked two cars down from the entrance to the realty office. Along the roofline was a stylized logo of a pale yellow sun appearing to emerge from four thick blue parallel brushstrokes. Two V-shaped birds flew along the horizon line. The same logo was painted on the front door to the office.

Ben Decovic had finished first shift forty minutes earlier. He'd turned in the blue and white, logged his reports for the day, and managed to avoid what he was sure would be a less than pleasant encounter with Ed Hatch and his partner Gramble from Homicide in the parking lot at the rear of the City-County Complex. By the time they noticed Ben, he was already in his car and backing out. Ed Hatch had never quite given Ben a pass for his impromptu interview with Corrine Tedros shortly after Stanley's death. Hatch would be none too happy to hear that Ben had begun following up on some of his other hunches after the booking photos had been faxed in from Phoenix.

Though off shift, Ben was still wearing his uniform. He'd taken his civilian clothes from his locker and transferred them to a paper bag and had tossed them on the front seat of the car. He had a couple stops to make before swinging by the Salt Box to see Anne, and he needed the uniform as a prop for each.

Vicki—with an *i*—Grant was owner and manager of Sunrise Realty. She was in her early fifties, carefully made up and well-tailored, with thick highlighted hair and botoxed vestiges of the runner-up positions she'd been named to in a half-dozen or so regional beauty pageants twenty-five-plus years ago. She wore enough gold jewelry to qualify as a portable Fort Knox.

Before she had taken over the office, she had shared duties with her second husband until he widowed her by express-lining his cholesterol numbers into massive coronary territory. On her own over the next two years, Vicki Grant had more than doubled the office's revenue and profit margins.

Ben Decovic had done his homework. He knew, for example, that Grant and her office never bothered to list a house or property unless it was, at minimum, deep in the six-figure range.

Which was why it was more than an anomaly for Ben Decovic to have spotted the Sunrise Realty signs with the Sold announcement planted among the despair, abject poverty, and general chaos and mayhem of south Magnolia Beach.

Ben did some more homework. At the Title and Deeds office, he discovered the property had been bought by a holding company named Maricopa Enterprises. It had offices in Chicago, Houston, D.C., Atlanta, and L.A. Its home office was in Phoenix.

After the homework, Ben played a hunch. He was feeling good. He had his eye and the old ambition back. Motive and mirage weren't synonyms anymore. For a while, at least, the world held, and Ben was starting to believe that he might yet survive the after-effects of Greg Hollinger and the private apocalypse he'd visited upon Ben when he'd taken the life of Ben's wife as well as those of four other people.

The décor of Vicki Grant's office was tasteful and understated. A few plaques and awards with driftwood frames on the walls. Sand-colored carpeting. A large rectangular oak desk with a cut-crystal bowl of wrapped mints, a laptop, and two pots of African Violets. A few shots of Vicki with the last two mayors and presiding over a meeting of the Magnolia Beach Tourist Bureau, Vicki in a hardhat and holding a shovel at a groundbreaking ceremony, but no family photos anywhere.

Vicki Grant's smile never wavered, but the temperature in the room dropped more than a few degrees when Ben made his request.

"I'm afraid I can't help you there, Officer Decovic," she said. "I'm not at liberty to divulge that information."

Ben smiled. "You certainly have the inflections down, Ms. Grant."

"Pardon?"

"Your political ambitions. Vice President of the tourist bureau for now. Two terms on the city council. A possible mayoral candidate down the road. Then, who knows?" Ben smiled again.

"I don't appreciate the direction this conversation is taking." She started to get up from behind her desk.

"I'm betting you haven't spent any significant time in south Magnolia Beach, Ms. Grant. That is, beyond recently closing on a few properties and getting one of your flunkies to put a Sold sign out." Ben paused before going on. "We're talking tooth and claw, Ms. Grant. Long-term mean streaks. People with nothing to lose."

Vicki Grant sat back down and waited a long moment before asking, "And what exactly are you offering, Officer Decovic?"

Ben added a little of his own tooth and claw to the act. "The staff of life," he said. "Protection. Your client wants to buy and develop property in south Magnolia Beach, he'll need it. A lot of it. I'm offering a reasonable deal here." Ben went on to add that he would subcontract the help and set up security schedules and double as paymaster. "I'll handle all the details," he said. "It'll keep things nice and simple and your client's properties safe and secure."

Vicki Grant tapped a pen against the desktop. "I can see where an offer like that might appeal to my client." She pulled over a small notebook. "Give me a number where I can reach you, and I'll put in a call and get back to you."

"I'm afraid not," Ben said. "I deal directly with your client from here on in or not at all."

"I'm not at liberty—," Vicki Grant began again.

"Are you at liberty to nod your head?" Ben asked. "Let's say I correctly guess the name of your client. You nod once, and we'll leave it at that. Technically, you haven't directly divulged anything. Consider the nod an involuntary tic."

Vicki Grant sat back in her chair.

"Wayne LaVell," Ben said, "with the esteemed barrister Raychard Balen as front-man."

Vicki Grant looked at Ben, then through him. She kept her head perfectly still.

"Ok," Ben said, stretching out each syllable. He unbuttoned his right shirt pocket and took out a folded piece of paper. He handed it to Grant.

"That's the Police Blotter for last Saturday night," Ben said. "Take a good, close look at it and notice the number and type of crimes we typically field on that night. Then note the location of the arrests and compare that to the addresses of the properties you sold in south Magnolia Beach. I'll let you draw your own conclusions."

Ben took one of the mints from the bowl on Grant's desk. He made a show of taking in all the Chamber of Commerce and Rotary Club Achievement Awards and plaques on the office walls. "You're obviously an enterprising woman, Ms. Grant," he said. "I stopped by today out of respect for you and thought we could work together. I would hate to see Wayne LaVell take his business elsewhere because he had come to believe you weren't looking out for his best interests."

Ben paused and smiled. "But since you didn't nod when I mentioned his name, I guess that's not going to be a problem for you, is it?" Ben slipped the mint into his mouth and left.

He sat for a moment in his car before pulling out and taking a left on Atlantic. He was willing to bet that Vicki Grant was already on the phone to Wayne LaVell or Raychard Balen. At least he hoped so. Ben had long ago learned that sometimes you had to shake things up a little in order to shake something loose.

Four blocks later, Ben stopped by the Wine Cellar and bought a pricey Merlot for later that evening with Anne and then hunted down a DVD at Beachfront Films that he remembered her talking about wanting to see. He'd already done the grocery shopping yesterday afternoon and was planning to make Jack's favorite for supper tonight: Shrimp Po' Boys with homemade coleslaw. Maybe he'd sneak Jack a little cold beer to go with his.

The afternoon still held its light. Ben checked his watch. Anne would not be on break at the restaurant for at least another hour and change. He left all the cluttered affluence and new construction of Atlantic Avenue and headed toward south Magnolia Beach.

He drove to Sentinel Avenue and caught another break.

When he parked across from the ruins of Jamison Blake's house, Ben spotted a car parked in the drive of the house next door.

The east side of the lawn had been scorched black from the fire, the house itself a small box, its paint scabbing and the roof a checkerboard of missing shingles. The woman who answered the door was small and bone-thin. She wore a tight yellow knit top and black jeans. Her hair was permed and dyed the watery shade of greenhouse-ripened tomatoes wrapped in cellophane.

Ben asked if she were Marilyn Keane.

She nodded and then looked behind him. "I thought you were the babysitter. I have a date."

She held a compact in her small left hand and had only gotten around to applying half her eye make-up. From behind her, a baby suddenly began crying, its wails wave-like in intensity and duration.

Ben began questioning her about Blake and Newton, but she interrupted and said, "I already talked to the police."

"I know," Ben said. "Just a couple follow-up questions if you don't mind."

"I'm getting ready for a date." She didn't invite him in. She continued standing in the doorway and tilted the compact's mirrored lid and started working on the other eye. "My divorce was final this week," she said. "I'm celebrating tonight." The baby kicked up its crying a couple notches.

Ben looked over her head. The interior of the house was painted a dingy yellow and smelled of things boiled and over-fried. A little girl in pajamas that were too small for her sat on the couch holding a juice box and watching television.

Marilyn Keane squinted into the compact mirror and edged her right eye with charcoal-colored liner. "What's with the questions anyway? I might have mentioned I'm getting ready for a date, and I'm getting concerned you'll scare the babysitter off." She adjusted the angle of the mirror. "The babysitter, she's a little nervous around the police."

"It's important," Ben said.

"Hey, so's my date. I'm a free woman now."

"Just a couple questions, and I'll be on my way."

Marilyn Keane sighed. Ben asked her if she knew the name of the man who hung out with Jamison Blake and Melissa Newton.

"I think Clay something. Maybe, Winchell. Or Wilson. Something like that. I didn't know the guy. Like you said, he was just around a lot."

"Did Jamison ever talk about him to you?"

"*Jamison*," she snorted. "The only time Jamie came over was if he was out of beer or money and thought he could charm me out of one or the other. Or both. Jamie was always running his mouth. Didn't take me long to learn to tune him out. That kind of stuff might work on Missy, but not me."

"What about Missy then? She ever say anything?"

Marilyn Keane studied herself in the compact mirror, frowned, and then shifted the liner to her left eye. "Missy was too tranked out most of the time to have anything resembling a conversation. She might have said something once or twice about she thought he was kinda cute. The Clay guy, I mean. Not Jamie."

"This Clay," Ben said, "did he have gray hair?"

"I don't know." She dropped her hand to her hip. "Look, what color do you want it to be? I told you the guy was short and around a lot, and I have a date. You want someone to drop this on, tell me the color of his hair, the style too, and that's what I'll say they were. Then you can leave before you scare the sitter off."

"Think for a minute," Ben said. "What color was his hair?"

Marilyn Keane slipped the eyeliner into the back pocket of her black jeans and then fished around in the front and pulled out a tube of lipstick. Inside the house, the baby continued crying.

"He might have," she said finally. "It was light-colored, I remember that. To tell you the truth, I didn't pay that much attention. I mean, I was going through all this divorce stuff, and besides, he really wasn't my type." She paused and looked over at Ben. "I'm petite. That doesn't mean I like my men to be."

The little girl got up from the couch and returned a moment later with two juice boxes. She put the two boxes back to back and then twisted the plastic straws, entwining them, so that she could drink out of both cartons at the same time and went back to watching television.

Ben tried to tune out the sound of the baby crying. "When was the last time you saw Jamison Blake?"

Marilyn Keane twisted a nub of lipstick above the edge of the tube. The red was about two shades brighter than her hair.

She wet her lips, then said, "I guess probably the day before the fire and him and Missy getting shot. He came over after work. Surprise, surprise, he was out of beer. His arms and neck were sunburned, and he was complaining about that and working outside and the fact Missy had forgotten to buy beer. I gave him two cans just to shut him up, and then he went back over."

"Any place Jamison liked to hang out?"

"That'd be Mac's Shack," Marilyn Keane said without looking at him. "Corner of Third and Sentinel. If he wasn't home, he was there. It was one of the few places around here that would still let him run a tab. He was asshole buddies with the guy that owns it."

"Do you know his name?"

"T. C." She turned and pointed the lipstick tube at him. "No need to ask me. That's all I ever heard him called."

"Ok," Ben said. Something had been quietly bothering him ever since Marilyn Keane opened the door. She looked familiar, but he couldn't place the when or where. The woman, the crying baby, the little girl with the juice boxes. They wouldn't let go of Ben, but he didn't know why.

The harder he tried, the further the details retreated and the more uneasy Ben felt. It took him a moment to understand why.

This is the way Jack Carson must feel all the time, he thought. Slippage. Everything retreating.

"See anything you like?" Marilyn Keane asked. "You sure been taking your time checking out the merchandise." She gave him a freshly lipsticked smile. "Not that I exactly mind you browsing."

Ben snapped back to the porch. In this case, he figured the truth was as good as a lie. "I keep thinking we've met before," he said.

A tilt of the head. Another smile. "Not exactly original, but I've heard worse."

Ben saw the opening and wanted to keep it that way. He wrote down his name and phone number and tore the page from his notebook and handed it to her. "Anything else you think of about Jamison or Missy or the other man, would you give me a call? Like I said, it's important."

She glanced down at the paper, then up again. "Ben, huh? Well, Ben, you just never know when this little old red head of mine might remember something."

"I've been by before," he said. "This is the first time I caught you at home."

"Well, that," Marilyn Keane said. "I took the kids and was staying at my cousin's across town for a while, you know, until all this divorce stuff settled. My ex didn't take the news so good, and she, my cousin, I mean, let me stay with her and her family until it became official."

The baby was still crying.

"Any case, you know where to find me now," Marilyn Keane said. "I got the papers two days ago. I'm a free woman again."

Ben walked back to his car. The last of the afternoon light was breaking up, and sunset had begun flaring along the line of the horizon. He called Anne on his cell, but it went straight to voice-mail. He left a message, saying he was on his way and would see her soon.

The Salt Box was one of a number of old neighborhood restaurants and shoppes that lined the west shore of the inlet in north Magnolia Beach. Most of them had been, or still were, mom-and-pop operations that had been rehabbed to preserve

their retro-charm. The city council had underwritten a series of
low-interest loans for renovations when the tourist boom had first
begun to sound, and the inlet area was thriving and enjoying its
new status.

Ben parked and cut across the lot, bypassing the entrance to
the Salt Box, walking instead to the rear of the building and the
first of three large tiered pine decks that had been built into the
slope and were joined by a wooden Z of railed stairs. Similar sets
of decks and stairs ran from the rear of the other shoppes and
restaurants and ended at a wide unfinished plank walkway that
followed the contours of the inlet's shoreline.

Ben waited for Anne to finish talking to a crew of busboys
and servers gathered at the back of the restaurant. The wind had
picked up, overly warm for the time of day and season, and ruf-
fled the waters in the center of the inlet. A mass of clouds flat on
the bottom but whose top mushroomed in thick folds trapped
what remained of the sunset and burned pink and orange.

Ben watched Anne approach. She was wearing the standard
uniform for the Salt Box—white Oxford shirt, jeans, and athletic
shoes. The wind caught and tossed stray strands of hair across her
cheek, Anne absentmindedly reaching up to tuck them behind
her ear.

She stood next to him at the railing, a little more space than
Ben would have liked between them, but he chalked it up to
workplace etiquette.

"You got your hair cut," he said. "It looks good."

"Thanks for noticing," Anne said. "I had it done four days ago."

She brushed by Ben and moved down the stairs to the Inlet
walkway. Ben followed. The tide was out, and armies of terns and

egrets and gulls and cranes were working the mud-rich flats. Anne stopped and leaned into the railing. Across the inlet, on the northern peninsula, a new condo complex was under construction, its face hung with scaffolding and the small wavering dots of the work lights for the crews putting in overtime.

"Why are you still in uniform?" she asked. "I thought you were working first shift."

Ben gave her a quick run-down of the off-the-clock hours he'd been putting in, starting with the booking photos of Corrine Tedros and her probable connection to Wayne LaVell and giving her a hit-and-run overview of his talk with Vicki Grant and Marilyn Keane and anyone in the Sentinel Avenue neighborhood who resembled anything close to a reliable witness in the shootings of Jamison Blake and Missy Newton.

"Something's there, but right now, I don't know what connects," Ben said, "and what doesn't."

"I could say the same thing about my father," Anne said. "He's disappearing right before my eyes. I don't have the luxury, though, of running around off-shift as a daughter or mother in order to hide from myself and my life."

"Wait a minute," Ben said. "You honestly think that's what I'm doing?"

Anne looked back up the slope toward the restaurant as if someone had called to her.

"I can't carry you anymore, Ben," she said. "I already have two people in my life that need everything I can give them. I'm not ready to turn that into a trio."

"What do you mean *carry*?" Ben asked. "I don't understand."

"I was lonely, not desperate, Ben. There's a difference."

"You sound like you've been rehearsing." Ben saw, in his peripheral vision, a knot of tourists making their noisy way down the stairs to the walkway. They carried drinks in to-go cups and were all laughing and talking at once.

"Someone has to see things for what they are Ben. We rushed into a mistake." The wind caught her hair again, but this time she didn't bother to tuck it behind her ear. "I've packed up your things. I'll drop them by your apartment tomorrow. If you're not there, I'll leave them at the main office."

Ben fought to keep his voice down. "Why? Give me one clear reason for any of this."

Anne looked out over the inlet to the east toward the Atlantic where the clouds had broken and thinned, and a half-moon had risen. "Reason or motive, Ben? Can you even tell the difference anymore? All your talk about dots and connections that aren't quite connections. You ought to hear yourself sometimes."

"You still didn't give me a reason."

"No," Anne said, "I didn't. You don't want that."

"One reason," Ben said.

Anne shook her head and didn't look in Ben's direction, and she spoke quietly, so quietly in fact that Ben wasn't sure he'd heard her start, the words soft and low and torn by the wind. Then he heard what sounded like *I'm not here* or *I'm not her*, and it took him a while to finally understand what she was saying.

"I didn't …," Ben said. "You made a mistake. The names are close."

Anne still didn't look in his direction. "It happened more than once, Ben. It's not like I wasn't there."

"No way. I know the difference," Ben said. "And I didn't."

"Two syllables," Anne said. "Not one."

Ben tried once more to convince Anne that he had not called her Diane, his dead wife's name, when they had been making love.

Below them, a turtle floated in the shallows of low tide, and two gulls picked through an exposed oyster bed. Stands of Spartina grass crackled in the wind, and the half-moon burned through what remained of the clouds.

Ben put his hands on top of the railing fronting the inlet walkway. "Don't do this, Anne. It's not right. Tell me what's really going on here."

"I need to go," she said. "I have to get back to work." Anne waited a moment before adding, "And my life." She stood on tiptoes and gave Ben a quick kiss and then ran up the stairs and back into the restaurant.

Ben watched her go.

He drove back to his apartment, the half-moon following in the upper right corner of his rearview mirror.

He made something approximating a meal.

Ben was initially sure that Anne had been lying to him, but he couldn't figure out why or to protect whom.

The evening sagged, then collapsed around him.

All the old and new certainties began to flee.

Two syllables. Not one.

He had what his old partner, Andy Calucci, had called a Biblical-sized thirst. It was immense and unruly.

Later that evening, when Ben dropped onto the bed, he realized he had forgotten to change out of his uniform.

He looked over at the bedside clock but could not bring the time into focus.

When he closed his eyes and headed for his dreams, Ben was sure he would find Diane or Anne in them.

Neither, however, showed.

FIFTY-THREE

SONNY GRAMM was hollowed out. It didn't take Corrine Tedros long to see that.

The flesh on his face sagged and was creased like a sheet of paper that had been crumpled into a tight ball and then hastily smoothed again. His eyes were watery, and his attempts at shaving had been less than successful. His shirt looked as if it hadn't been changed in a couple days.

He reminded Corrine of men she'd seen in Bradford, Indiana, men who life had used up but not gotten around to tossing away yet. There was little or no vestige—except for the defiant pompadour—of the man she'd known when she'd been waitressing at the supper club, the Sonny Gramm whose earthiness and appetites had been filtered through Old South manners and licensed by a local social standing based on family name, if not quite fortune anymore.

He sat slump-shouldered at his desk in the office at the rear of the Passion Palace, a bottle of rye whiskey like an extra appendage at his elbow. Various combinations of hurt, dismay, and anger played across his features when he looked at Corrine. She'd just delivered Wayne LaVell's offer on Sonny's properties.

"Why?" He asked. "Why you?"

"That's not important." Corrine slid the shot he'd poured her back in the middle of the desk, untouched.

"The offer's low-end and an insult," Gramm said, balling his fist.

"LaVell bought out your debts, Sonny," Corrine said. "He's not going to offer you more. You ought to know that by now."

"He can't do this to Sonny Gramm. I'm not going to lie down and let him walk away with everything that's mine."

The bass-line from the music in the club pounded in the walls. Corrine let Gramm rant a while longer before she interrupted.

"Wayne LaVell will kill you, Sonny," she said. "Believe it."

Gramm lurched from his chair and stood up. He looked around the office. "He can try. LaVell might just find out Sonny Gramm's not as easy to take out as he thinks. I'm not alone in this either. I hired me a new bodyguard, the kind I needed from day one. He's not like the other ones. He does exactly what he's told."

Corrine watched him pour another drink. He saluted the Confederate flag thumbtacked to the wall behind the desk and tossed back the shot. The gesture was hopeless as it was doomed and as doomed as it was ludicrous. For a moment, Corrine almost felt sorry for him.

"It's his final offer, Sonny," Corrine said. "LaVell made that very clear."

The rye had forced some color into Gramm's cheeks. "You delivered the message, Corrine, and you can deliver this one for me.

Tell Wayne LaVell to go fuck himself."

"I'll be going to your funeral before the month is out." Corrine started to get up, but Gramm waved her down.

"I want to know one thing," he said. "You never told me why. What are you getting out of this?"

Corrine sat back and crossed her legs. Another angle presented itself. It had been nudging its way into her thoughts during the course of the meeting.

"Can you pull a trigger, Sonny?"

"What do you mean?"

"It's not a complicated question."

Gramm squinted and scratched at his cheek. A moment later, he let his hand fall. "He's got something on you too, doesn't he?"

Corrine nodded.

"And what you're saying is you and me ...," Gramm began moving back and forth behind the desk.

Corrine nodded again.

"The house would work best," Gramm said, nodding his head. "It's quiet and private. You can tell LaVell that I'll sign the papers, but that I refused to meet anywhere else but there. Tell him too I want you there as a witness when I sign."

"He'll probably bring along Raychard Balen."

"You'll be a good distraction, Corrine. You can wear something sexy, talk things up, move around the room."

"Ok." She'd hoped to push Sonny in the right direction and then step back, stay off the scene of the meeting itself and simply let things unfold, but she realized Sonny was right even if his reasoning was wrong. She needed to be there to monitor his liquor intake if nothing else and to make sure he kept his resolve. There was too much left to chance otherwise.

And that was the one thing Corrine was sure of. They had one chance and only one to finish off Wayne LaVell. He wouldn't give them another.

"What about Raychard Balen?" she said.

Gramm gave a dismissive wave. "Let him scramble back under his rock. With LaVell dead, he has nothing to gain. He won't bother us."

Corrine wasn't so sure about that, but let it pass for now. She'd make sure they got back to Balen.

She waited while Gramm went over the set-up one more time, coaxing the idea of murdering Wayne LaVell into a sequence of actions and then letting the details find and settle into their place in the sequence, Corrine watching Gramm carefully as he paced, waiting for that moment when his expression told her he was ready to carry through.

"It has to be at the house," Gramm said. "It'll only work if he agrees to meet there."

"He will," Corrine said. "He wants the properties."

Gramm stopped pacing. "Why should LaVell believe you've convinced me to sell in the first place?"

"Because he thinks you're weak, Sonny." Corrine paused and stood up, letting him feel the full weight of the insult. "He'll believe because I'll tell him I agreed to fuck you on the side on a semi-regular basis, and you settled for that and his offer."

Gramm cocked his head and looked at Corrine for a long moment. He started to reach for the bottle of rye, but Corrine stepped up and pulled it toward her.

"You never answered my earlier question, Sonny," she said.

"Yes," he said, taking the bottle back. "Hell yes, I can pull a trigger. You'll see."

FIFTY-FOUR

CROY WENDALL was thinking about *shovel* and *radio*. He was digging in the middle of a grove of pecan trees. The ground was hard and dry. The radio was on the cell phone Mr. Balen had given him, and man on the radio was talking about fires. Croy's tooth hurt.

Shovel. Radio.

Croy had tried, but he couldn't find any words to rhyme with either one, so that made the words just what they were and the things he was doing.

He was digging and listening.

There were a lot of fires. The man on the radio told where they were and how big. He said things like "efforts to contain" and "raging" too.

One of the fires was burning near the Two-Bridge River, close to the cabin Croy had stayed at, and he could see the cabin in his head while he dug, and he could see the tree next to the cabin where he had hung the frogs on the limbs, and then he could see the frogs, everything inside them dried out so that their skin was more like little pieces of paper hanging from the limbs than skin, and then he could see the fire on its way to meet them.

The fire was not like *shovel* or *radio*.

It was like the fire had been an idea inside the frogs when Croy caught and put them in the bags and then hung them on the tree, and then inside that idea there had been another one about the frogs' skin turning dry and like little pieces of paper that the fire would one day come and burn up.

Croy quit shoveling for a minute and chewed some aspirin. His tooth was hot. Croy had forgotten to tell Mr. Balen about the tooth when Mr. Balen had called him at the cabin and told him about the crime he needed Croy to do, and Croy had not mentioned it since because he was very busy doing the crime Mr. Balen had told him about.

The sore tooth was like a little fire in Croy's mouth, and when the man on the radio talked about the other fires, it was like he was talking about Croy's tooth too.

Croy picked up the shovel and started digging again.

The man on the radio disappeared.

A woman began talking. She stretched out the vowels inside her words.

The woman was on a radio show called *One Way.* For a while, some people sang God-songs. One of them had a part in it about a fiery sword and lambs and blood.

Then the woman came back on the radio and talked about God some more. She said God was not the name of things in this world. She called him a *Force.*

Croy kept digging. He thought about God the way the woman said on the radio, and he thought about the frogs and the fire that was on its way to meet them, and the day grew very large, and Croy was in the middle of it.

FIFTY-FIVE

BEN DECOVIC LEFT MESSAGES.

He layered the space on Anne Carson's answering machine with them. He called her cell, and when it went straight to voicemail, he filled it with more messages.

He stopped by the Salt Box, but got no further than the front foyer when one of the greeters recognized him and handed over an envelope with his first name inked on it and holding inside a telegraphed message from Anne: *Please. Not at work. I need this job.*

Ben inked one of his own—*where and when then?*—and asked the greeter to pass it on to Anne.

No reply.

Roil and blur. At the end of day or middle of the night, that's what Ben Decovic was looking at. He was afraid things were starting to get away from him again. He resurrected the practice of marking hash lines on the inside of his wrist to monitor his drinking.

He ran his own version of home movies, ransacking his memories with Anne, trying to re-create the moment when everything went bad, when he'd called her by his dead wife's name, and he went from not believing it had happened to not wanting to believe it happened to not sure of anything that had happened except the fact of a dark bedroom, a locked door, and two bodies.

Ben understood exhaustion and what it could blunt or erase. He began volunteering for double shifts. First shift was west Magnolia Beach and Old Market Boulevard with all its attendant commercial clutter. Second shift suited him better. He drew south Magnolia Beach and with it, everything that had begun and ended on Sentinel Avenue.

Ben parked a half block up from where Third Street intersected with Sentinel and radioed in. He walked in the direction of Mac's Shack, which, at least according to Jamison Blake's neighbor, Marilyn Keane, had been Blake's second home.

Ben's visit to the Shack started out as an instant replay of his previous one yesterday afternoon, Ben stepping inside, walking over and unplugging the jukebox, and then asking the not quite rhetorical question about outstanding warrants, the patrons glancing over their shoulders and then down at their drinks, which they quickly emptied before making a mass exodus worthy of any that Moses had been able to muster among the tribes.

Which, once again, left Ben and T.C., the bartender, in a silent standoff.

Maybe a decade and a half ago T.C.'s glower had been genuinely and intractably intimidating, but the years had taken some of the edge off its menace. It had a PG-13 quality to it now, a shopworn malevolence that T.C., with muscle running to fat and ponytailed braid running to silver, could not quite hide.

Ben stood in the middle of Mac's Shack and waited him out.

T.C. picked up a bar rag and then set it back down. He looked over at the jukebox and then back. The muscles in his throat tensed, then relaxed. He was like a chameleon whose protective coloration had temporarily gone south on him.

Ben waited some more.

"Ok, ok," T.C. said finally. "Enough of this shit. I can't afford losing any more business. This is supposed to be Happy Hour. You ask your questions, and I'll conversate."

Ben took a stool at the bar. He waved off T.C.'s offer of a draft.

"About Jamison Blake," he said.

"It was Lester, wasn't it?" T.C. said. "Him or Danny. It just hit me, who it probably was, one or the other who pointed you here."

"It doesn't matter who I talked to," Ben said, pulling out his notebook. "It's you and me now, T.C."

"Those fucking guys." T.C. shook his head and then jammed his hand into the cooler and pulled out a beer. He opened it with a church key chained to his belt and took a long swallow.

Ben tapped his pen against the bar and ran through the preliminaries, establishing that Jamison Blake had qualified as a regular at Mac's and that he'd been living with Missy Newton, who sometimes accompanied him to the bar, and that T.C. had, in fact, been bartending on the day Jamison and Missy had been killed.

"Anything unusual that afternoon?" Ben asked. "Jamison acting differently?"

"No," T.C. said. "Jamie drank some beers, we bullshitted, and he left."

"What'd you talk about?"

T.C. shrugged. "I don't know. This is a bar. In a bar you get a lot of bar talk."

The door to the street opened, and a thin man in a green baseball cap poked his head and part of a shoulder inside. Ben smiled and waved. The man backed out and quietly shut the door.

T.C. sighed. "With Jamie, it was probably about money, ok? He always had money problems. Which I personally can identify with right now on account of what this talk is costing me."

Ben watched T.C. take another long swallow of beer. "How about Sonny Gramm? Jamison ever talk about him or his troubles?"

"Yeah, but so did a lot of other people," T.C. said. "It's not exactly what you call a secret, Sonny Gramm's in trouble. Sonny's been around forever. You hear things. Everybody does."

"What did Jamison have to say about Gramm's troubles?"

T.C. shook his head. "Look, you never met Jamie, right? You don't know what he was like. A nice guy, ok, but Jamie, he liked to act bigger than he was. You know what I mean? No crime in that, but that's what the guy was like. Music, politics, women, anything you got an opinion on, Jamie thought he had the last and best word."

The phone started ringing. T.C. looked from it to Ben and back again.

He sighed and let it ring through. "A couple times," he said, "somebody in here brings up Gramm's Mustang getting messed up, Gramm hiring another bodyguard, you know, like that, and Jamie looks over at me, he winks and got this smile on this face, like he knows something but can't tell. It being Jamie, I didn't think it was anything but business as usual."

"Jamison ever mention Stanley Tedros?"

T.C. frowned. "What? Now you think Jamie killed Stanley Tedros?"

"Do you?" Ben said.

"Nah," T.C. said, shaking his head. "He liked the idea of the reward money. All the regulars in here did. Bar talk, like I said."

"Any sense with Jamison that it was more than talk?"

"Come on," T.C. said. "Remember what I just said about knowing the guy. Jamie was a bullshitter. A couple times he maybe mentioned he could get his hands on what the guy—" T.C. broke off, squinting. "What's the guy's name, the nephew?"

"Buddy Tedros," Ben said.

"Yeah. Jamie claimed he was close to getting what Buddy Tedros was after. Said he had something all worked out, he was going to sidestep the police altogether, just deal with that Buddy Tedros, not give him his name or anything like that. Jamie was going to set all the terms, and Buddy Tedros was going to have to go along with them if he wanted to know who killed his uncle." T.C. paused and hit his beer again.

He leaned closer to Ben. "That was Jamie, ok? He was a bullshit artist. Nothing more complicated than that. He was always hatching something. Once he told me about a plan he had to catch shrimp with magnets. It never stopped with him."

"Was he talking about Buddy Tedros and the reward on the afternoon he was killed?"

T.C. threw up his hands and stepped back. "I don't know. Maybe. Maybe probably. He was in a good mood, I remember that."

Ben looked down at his notes then back up at T.C., who was

standing with his arms crossed on his chest, his namesake tattooed on each bicep, Ben recognizing the old Hanna-Barbera cartoon character, Top Cat. He remembered Top Cat lived in an old galvanized garbage can and wore a straw boater and a vest. What he could not remember, looking at T.C.'s biceps, was an episode in which Top Cat gave someone the finger or held a bloodied knife triumphantly above his head.

The bar lights flickered.

"Old wiring," T.C. said.

"A couple more questions," Ben said.

"Let's get it done." T.C. unfolded his arms. "You've already wrecked Happy Hour. I want you out of here."

"Did Jamison ever talk about any of his friends? One guy in particular, I'm thinking about. Someone named Clay?"

"Croy," T.C. said. "I don't know if that's a first or last name though. Never met him. Jamie was always talking about him not being normal and doing robot things."

Ben set down his pen. "Robot things?"

"Yeah," T.C. said. "I don't know what else to call it. Like counting under his breath all the time. Or buying a bunch of same color shirts. Or eating a certain food over and over for every meal. Things like that." T.C. paused and scratched the bridge of his nose. "Oh yeah. To hear Jamie, this Croy didn't like sex either."

"Where'd Jamison meet him?"

"Beats me," T.C. said.

Ben glanced down at the notes from his interview with Blake's neighbor, Marilyn Keane.

"Maybe at work?" Ben said, leaning back on the stool.

"Jamie didn't work. Neither did Missy."

"I don't think you're being completely forthright with me on this one," Ben said and closed the notebook. "Maybe I'll drop by later and see what you have to say then."

T.C. held up both hands. "That won't be necessary." He paused. "It's just, what you're asking, it involves some personal things of a business nature."

"I'm not interested in your business, T.C. I want to know who Jamison worked for, when he worked, that's all."

T.C. nodded. "Sure you don't want a beer?"

Ben hesitated for a moment, but then said no.

"That's a real first. Never known a cop who turned down a free beer," T.C. said, reaching into the cooler. He levered the cap and tossed it in the direction of a trash can.

"Back to the subject," Ben said.

The lights flickered again, taking a little longer this round to return.

T.C. looked down the length of the bar toward an ancient pinball machine buttressing the east wall. He fingered the end of his ponytail.

"My name doesn't have to come up if you talk to this guy, does it? Like I said, we do some business sometimes. It helps, you know, with the overhead on this place."

Ben waited.

"Russ Sharpe," T.C. said. "He runs a landscaping outfit. Him and me, we go back. Jamie worked for him sometimes."

"Let me guess," Ben said. "Off the books, right?"

"My name, I really don't see why it would have to come up."

Ben took out his notebook again, asked where he could find

Sharpe, and took down the address.

"One last thing," Ben said. "Did this Croy live with Jamison and Missy?"

"I think maybe," T.C. said. "At least Jamie made it sound that way sometimes."

Ben got off the stool and rapped the bartop twice with his knuckles. "I appreciate your cooperation, T.C."

T.C. crossed his arms and resurrected his glower.

By the time Ben made it to his car, a line of regulars had already sidled up to the front door of the bar and started to duck inside. A moment later, the lights flickered, and the jukebox was up and cranked.

FIFTY-SIX

JACK CARSON heard the woman the little girl called Mrs. Wood apologize for having to leave early. The girl said she could take care of things until her mother came home.

"I've given your grandfather his afternoon medication," Mrs. Wood said, "and I put something in the refrigerator you can microwave if you two get hungry."

"Thank you." The girl walked the woman to the front door. "We'll be fine."

The thing was, Jack didn't feel that way. Lately, more and more, he was losing control over his moods. He'd be doing ok, and then with no warning he was angry. He was angry, and then he was crying, and before he could wipe away any tears, he was laughing, and then he was afraid, the moods like competing and shifting weather systems, stretching out indefinitely or suddenly overlapping or colliding, independent of what Jack was doing at the time.

His days had come to feel like a car windshield before the defroster had enough time to clear it.

The girl walked up to where Jack sat in his recliner. She reminded him her name was Paige and asked if he were hungry. She said Mrs. Wood had left a tuna casserole and some green beans and biscuits.

Jack was very hungry, but he heard himself telling Paige he could wait a while before they ate. He wasn't sure why he'd told her that, but it seemed important that he did.

Paige said something about a chat room and went back to the kitchen and her new computer.

Jack watched television with the sound off. There was a show on about icebergs. He closed his eyes and fell asleep for a while.

When he woke, the girl was standing next to his chair. She was wearing white tennis shoes, a new pair of blue jeans, a shimmery top, and two barrettes shaped like palm trees. Jack had forgotten her name.

"Your stomach's been growling," she said.

"I think I feel asleep," Jack said. "Did I miss him?"

The girl furrowed her brow and looked over at the front door. "Who?"

Jack tried to hunt down a name and finally gave up. "The tall man who'd been coming by the house," he said. "Sometimes he would come late at night too." Jack paused. "He was a policeman, I think."

"He went away," the girl said. "You couldn't count on him. He was just another mistake Mother made, like she did with Ray, my father."

Jack tried out a smile. "I didn't leave though, did I?"

The girl looked at him a long time. "No," she said. "You're always around."

Jack's stomach growled again. The girl went to microwave their supper.

He looked around the room. His days had come down to watching television with the sound off, a handful of meds, microwaved meals, a slow parade of faces that he found increasingly difficult to identify, short disjointed naps, and an abiding confusion.

He was sorry to hear the policeman had gone away. Jack had liked him. He was never in a hurry with Jack and talked quietly and smiled and asked Jack questions about the things Jack had built when he'd owned the construction company in Myrtle Beach.

Jack would miss the policeman.

He made good Po' Boys.

FIFTY-SEVEN

AFTER LEAVING MAC'S SHACK, Ben Decovic broke up a chain-reaction assault and battery that started out as a minor-league disturbing the peace on Wilson among four neighbors, then wrote up an early-bird DWI, worked the paper on a new case of vandalism at a convenience store on Camellia, and did the preliminary investigation on a half-hearted break and enter at the Milforde Hotel involving one of its sluggish junkie tenants.

Near dusk, Ben took Pickett and followed it west for four blocks and then cut to Clarke, heading two blocks north. Sharpe's Landscaping and Lawn Service was across from the warehouses for Coastal Trucking, its office housed in a hail-dented white single-wide set on cement blocks and flanked by two long greenhouses and a chain-link fence enclosing two lines of pickups and flatbeds holding lawn equipment and bags of fertilizer. The air was threaded with the smell of gasoline, motor oil, and mulch. Ben called in his location and got out of the car.

Russ Sharpe answered the door after the third round of knocking, mumbled a distracted greeting, and waved Ben Decovic inside. Ben followed him to a small office at the rear of the trailer where Sharpe dropped into a swivel chair and swung away from a desk whose top was lost to piles of invoices, a phone, two Styrofoam take-out boxes, a large silver thermos, and a computer holding a screen-saver of a tree morphing every few seconds into another phase of the seasonal cycles. Ben watched autumn pop up and the leaves dry, brown, and blow away, then sat down across from Sharpe.

Sharpe reached around for the thermos and topped off his coffee. He was a large man in his early forties with thick black hair in a buzz-cut that had outgrown its original lines, his face sun-battered, his skin with the deep pink and texture of a slice of baked ham.

"You're a new one, right?" he said around a sip of coffee. "I don't remember clearing you with Adkin though."

Ben frowned. "You mean Carl Adkin?"

"Who else would I be talking about?" Sharpe asked. "Adkin and the rest of you on Patrol. All the same. Always looking for the free tit."

Sharpe rummaged the desktop until he found a clipboard. "I'll add you to the list," he said, "but we're talking the basic package. Anything else, it comes out of your pocket."

"I don't understand," Ben said.

Sharpe let out a long, tired sigh. "I'm not talking retail, ok? At cost. You want anything extra, a Bradford Pear or a Palmetto, something like that, I'll give it to you at cost, put the bastard in for you, but I'm not throwing it in with the original package."

Ben started to speak, but Sharpe held up a large calloused hand, interrupting him.

"You got a problem with that, take it up with Adkin. And tell him for me he should have called first and cleared this with me. Remind him I got paying clients too. I can't be sending my crews out every time I turn around, to do landscaping and maintenance for all of you." Sharpe paused and shook his head. "Most of the Patrol roster have lawns and gardens that qualify for a spread in *Southern Living* magazine."

"I think you misjudged the situation, Mr. Sharpe," Ben said. "I came here to ask you a few questions."

Sharpe set down the pen and clipboard. "Ok. You're new. Adkin was supposed to talk to you, explain things. No questions, that's the whole point, all the work I do for the Blue."

"Do you have someone named Croy working for you?" Ben said.

Sharpe leaned forward in his chair. "Do you have any idea how hard it is for an independent to compete with all the regional and national landscaping franchises around here? Something comes up, a new subdivision, a new outlet complex, I got to put in a bid like everyone else, except I'm not like everyone else, because most of the other outfits are franchised and can cut overhead through volume, and my bids will be D.O.A. unless I can find ways to stay competitive."

Meaning, Ben thought, keeping a skeleton crew officially on the books and paying the rest of the crews below minimum wage and under the table, no payout for health, unemployment, or workman comp benefits.

"About Croy," Ben said.

"Look, we can work something out," Sharpe said. "I apologize for earlier. We're running behind on two deadlines. And then this drought, it seems like it's never going to end. I get testy, at least that's what my wife calls it, when that happens."

"I need to find Croy," Ben said.

Sharpe rubbed his forehead. "I don't know where he lives. I send a few trucks out in the morning to designated spots around town, and anyone that wants to work is waiting there. We drop them off at the same place that night. Where they go after that, I don't know."

"What's Croy's full name?"

"Wendall," Sharpe said. "Croy Wendall. You mind telling me what this is about?"

"Some follow-up on the murder of Jamison Blake," Ben said. "From what I understand, Croy was a friend of his."

"Jamie Blake. Oh shit. I don't need this," Sharpe said. He went back to rubbing his forehead. "Look, you show up around any of the crews asking questions about Jamie, I'll never meet those deadlines. These are the kind of guys who spook very easy, a cop comes around. The word'll get out, and the next day, none of them will show up."

"You tell me what you know then," Ben said, "and maybe I won't have to bother your crews."

"Adkin was supposed to take care of things like this," Sharpe said.

"Take that up with Adkin," Ben said. "I want to hear about Croy Wendall."

Ben left twenty minutes later, getting back on Pickett and heading toward the low end of Atlantic Avenue. He took his scheduled break at an I-Hop, starting off with the cup of coffee Sharpe had never bothered to offer him and then realizing, after he'd taken a booth, that he'd forgotten to eat today. Ben called the waitress back over and ordered one of the specials.

He took out his notebook.

He needed to find Croy Wendall.

Sharpe confirmed Croy was a friend of Jamie Blake. They usually partnered at the job sites, Jamie pretending to do the work that Croy eventually completed.

Croy was built low to the ground and had a round baby face and prematurely gray hair. He was quiet and a little odd maybe, but the guy was a machine, Sharpe had said, and did twice the work of any of the others on the crews.

The problem, though, was Croy had quit showing up for work. That meant there was a very good chance he'd already left the area.

The waitress brought Ben's meal and refilled his coffee.

He went back to his notebook. Jamison Blake, T.C.'s claim of bar talk to the contrary, was still a strong contender for the one who'd vandalized Sonny Gramm's Mustang with a crowbar. Jamison, ditto the bar talk, had also insinuated he was about to cash in on the reward for Stanley Tedros's murder. And then Jamison ended up dead, killed with the gun that had been taken from Ben at the Passion Palace.

And Jamison's pal, Croy Wendall, had disappeared.

Ben slipped the notebook back in his pocket and watched a car pull up outside. A man and a little girl climbed out. A brown and white dog jumped out too and began running in tight circles. It took a while, but the man got the dog back in the car and then lifted a remote and locked the doors.

Once inside, the father and little girl sat in a booth opposite him. She looked to be around Paige's age. Ben cut through the stack of pancakes in the middle of his plate and listened to the waitress tell the man and girl about the three large wildfires that had broken out on the far northwest and west sides of town. Her husband and brother were part of the firefighting crews. There was talk about extensive property damage and possible emergency evacuations later in the evening.

Ben glanced at his watch, paid for the meal, and walked outside. He took out his cell phone. He wanted to try Sonny Gramm and see if the name Croy Wendall or Jamison Blake meant anything to him, but it was Manny Harrison, not Sonny Gramm, who picked up when Ben called the Passion Palace.

Manny Harrison was Gramm's nephew and new head bouncer and now temporary manager at the Palace because Sonny Gramm had not shown up or checked in all day. Manny told Ben he'd been calling Gramm at home but had gotten no further than the answering machine or a busy signal. He'd also had no luck with Gramm's cell phone. When Ben asked if anyone had been sent out to check on Sonny Gramm, Manny said he'd been too busy to do anything except keep the doors to the Palace open, the drinks flowing, and the dancers working.

"It's called marshalling resources," Manny said. "Lucky for Uncle Sonny I worked at Taco Bell for ten years."

Ben got Sonny Gramm's home phone number from Manny and ended the call. He turned, and out of nowhere, a brown and white blur flew at him.

The dog hit the driver's side window and, teeth bared, immediately started at him again, growling and throwing itself against the glass over and over.

Ben looked back at the I-Hop and the father and girl in the booth. The man said something, and she laughed.

Over Ben's shoulder, the brown and white dog hurled itself against the car window.

Ben walked to the blue and white and called dispatch. He asked permission to leave his patrol sector.

FIFTY-EIGHT

SONNY GRAMM HAD TOLD HER the graves were ready. Two of them. Fresh.

Corrine Tedros sat in the back of the Continental, Raychard Balen at the wheel, Wayne LaVell in the front passenger seat. Outside the window, the sun burned deep orange, and the surrounding clouds were swollen and layered in purple and red. Corrine drummed her fingers on the armrest.

"That's an odd shade of orange." Wayne Lavell gestured toward the west. Even in a Continental, his bulk took up most of the front seat.

"You get that when there's no rain for a while," Raychard Balen said. "That and the new fires. You end up with a lot of sunset."

Balen lifted his hand from the wheel. "Coming up on the left, Wayne." He pointed at the Express Pawn Shop and the 101 Discount Tire Outlet, both of which carried large banners draped across their facades reading "Under New Management."

"What'd I tell you?" Balen said. "Right on schedule. Like a line of dominoes. I doubt the ink's dry yet."

LaVell nodded and then swiveled his head and shoulders so that he was facing Corrine. "You're pretty quiet tonight," he said.

"I just want to get this over with." She could smell LaVell's aftershave. It was blunt and overripe.

Corrine wrapped her fingertips in her palms and squeezed. She worked on summoning up regrets and second thoughts, but in the back seat of the Continental, there was no room for either.

She'd spent her whole life practicing how to empty herself of Betsy Jo Horvath.

For a moment, Corrine wondered, despite herself, if her mother were still alive. Then she emptied herself of that thought too.

Fifteen minutes later, Raychard Balen hit the turn signal and swung the Continental into Sonny Gramm's driveway.

It was covered in oyster shells and dead-ended in a T. Gramm's newly resurrected Mustang was parked at an odd angle, canted on a diagonal, as if behind a display window.

Raychard Balen pulled the Continental into the left wing of the T, then hesitated and glanced over at Wayne LaVell before putting the car in reverse, eventually parking so that the Continental's front end pointed down the driveway toward the road.

Sonny Gramm was waiting for them on the top step under the porch light. He was wearing a snap-button shirt and jeans and battered cowboy boots. He raised a glass tumbler and rattled loose ice cubes at them when Balen, Corrine, and LaVell walked up.

Gramm had turned on all the upstairs and downstairs lights in the house. The night air was dry and smelled faintly of smoke. Waves of moths broke against the downstairs windows.

Inside, small pieces of paper had been taped to various wall hangings and pieces of furniture. The pattern was duplicated in each room they walked through. Under the ceiling fans, the slips of paper trembled and fluttered like leaves about to be wind-torn from a limb.

Raychard Balen paused and pointed with his free hand. After getting out of the car, he'd grabbed his briefcase and then shrugged his way into a brown-checked sports coat with the nap and weave of an old piece of carpet. When he lifted his arm, the sleeve rode halfway up his forearm.

"Hey, Sonny, what gives here?" he asked.

"Everything I had to replace and its price," Gramm said, "after my house got vandalized."

"Insurance, right?" Balen asked, then smiled. "It's what underwrites civilization."

"I'd let mine lapse," Gramm said.

He led them to the dining room, its center dominated by a large oak table and a brightly burning chandelier. There were more pieces of paper. The door to the kitchen was closed. Gramm pointed at two chairs and then walked around the table and sat down across from them.

He handed Corrine his tumbler and said, "Honey, how about making some drinks?"

Wayne LaVell and Raychard Balen sat down. Corrine looked for a place to put her purse and ended up leaving it on the top of the sideboard.

"Rats too," Gramm said. "Dozens of rats. Someone came in here and broke things, and then they let rats loose in my house."

"Well, here's to happier, ratless times," Wayne LaVell said when Corrine had passed out the drinks.

She remained standing just to the left and slightly behind Sonny Gramm and placed her hand lightly on his shoulder. A

small piece of plywood rested on the lower rungs of Gramm's
chair, the butt of the Charter-Arms Pathfinder jutting out, within
easy reach, ready for the moment when Sonny Gramm dropped
his arm.

It was going to be all right, Corrine told herself. Gramm was
following the script.

All those pieces of paper though. They hadn't discussed that.

"Aren't you going to sit down and join us, Corrine?" LaVell
asked.

"She's ok where she is," Gramm said.

LaVell frowned, then shrugged. The room's lighting drew out
the broken capillaries on his cheeks. He folded his hands in front
of him on the table.

"We're businessmen, Sonny," LaVell said. "That's all this is.
Business."

Raychard Balen reached for his briefcase and set it down in
front of him. He flicked its latches.

"I want to hear you say it," Gramm said.

"What?"

"The rats. The vandalism. My car. That you were behind it."
Gramm picked up his glass, finished the drink in one swallow,
then handed the tumbler back over his shoulder to Corrine.

She hesitated. Sonny Gramm kept the glass dangling. Corrine reluctantly took it.

"Come on," Gramm said. "Say it."

Wayne LaVell was smiling. "You wouldn't by any chance be
taping this conversation, Sonny? It won't hold up in court. You
can check that with our esteemed barrister here." He nodded in
Balen's direction.

Gramm glanced back at Corrine. "Not so much ice this time."

Corrine thought she heard movement on the other side of the door leading to the kitchen. She took her time making the drink but didn't hear anything else and finally chalked it up to nerves and impatience.

Corrine couldn't understand why Sonny was dragging things out.

"I'm still waiting," Gramm said to LaVell.

"This is the wrong road," LaVell said.

"We'll see." Gramm took the drink from Corrine. She nudged him twice with her knuckles through the back slats of the chair. He ignored her.

"This afternoon I got out some paper and a pen," Gramm said, "and walked around my house and flagged the damage. Then I found my calculator." He paused, pulling a piece of paper from the breast pocket of his shirt and tossing it across the table.

Wayne LaVell left it lying where it landed.

"I want two things," Gramm said. "First I want you to admit what you did. Second, I want that amount added to the total on the paperwork your esteemed barrister's got in his briefcase."

Wayne LaVell arched his brows and looked at Corrine. "I thought you'd made the terms clear, Corrine. We didn't come to negotiate."

Raychard Balen pulled a sheath of paperwork from the briefcase. "Your Hancock," he said, holding up a pen. "Three places, Sonny, then we're gone. The bank cuts you a check tomorrow morning."

"I knew your mother," Gramm said. "She was a whore."

Balen set down the pen and pretended to dab at his eyes. "Please don't bring up Mom. I always get weepy and nostalgic when that happens. Growing up in a whorehouse leaves one with a virtual trove of precious memories."

Gramm took a long swallow of his drink. "I just thought of something," he said. "I didn't frisk either of you when you got here."

"We're clean," Wayne LaVell said. "No guns. Didn't see the need."

"I forgot. This is business, right?" Gramm said.

Wayne LaVell nodded. "Name one thing that isn't."

Corrine stood behind Gramm, waiting for his hand to drop for the .22 Pathfinder, willing the moment when he lifted it. Her life would begin again on the other side of the shots.

Raychard Balen picked up the pen setting next to the open briefcase. "Hey Sonny, we almost finished here? I think we've all seen this movie."

"Guess you're right, Raychard," Gramm said, getting up from his chair and leaning across the table for the piece of paper holding the figures for the damage. He stuffed it back into his breast pocket and sat down again.

"It's an old movie, and I'm an old man." Gramm dropped his hand and brought up the Pathfinder, resting it on the table next to his drink.

"Whoa there," Raychard Balen said.

"I was really looking forward to shooting Balen and you," Gramm told Wayne LaVell.

Corrine involuntarily lifted her hand from Gramm's shoulder. What Gramm said, she couldn't have heard it right.

Wayne LaVell was looking at Corrine, not Gramm, and smiling.

Gramm picked up the .22 and opened the chamber. He began taking the bullets out one by one and lining them in a row in front of him.

"The car. My house. Hell, my life," Gramm said, taking out another around. "I wanted to hear you say it. Then shooting you would have made a kind of sense."

Corrine couldn't keep the panic out of her voice. "What the fuck are you doing, Sonny?" She took a step forward, then back. Wayne LaVell was still smiling at her.

"A kind of sense then," Gramm repeated, almost to himself. "The way it should have happened." He paused. "Not this way."

Corrine watched him shake out the sixth bullet and line it up with the others. This couldn't be happening, she thought. It couldn't. Her throat had closed up.

"What way is that?" LaVell asked.

"Your way," Gramm said. "Pay someone else to do it. Keep my hands clean. Call it business."

Gramm finished his drink and sat back in his chair. "You can come in now," he said.

Behind him, the door to the kitchen opened.

"I hired me a new bodyguard," Gramm said. "Unlike the others, he does what he's told." He swiveled his head in the direction of the doorway. "Go ahead. Finish both of them."

"Oh Sonny," Corrine said.

Gramm frowned, puzzled, at her tone.

Wayne LaVell kept his hands folded on the table and in front of him.

Corrine watched Croy Wendall walk through the door. He was wearing new blue jeans and a snap-button Western shirt like

Sonny Gramm's. His prematurely gray hair had been dyed a muddy red and was cut close to his scalp.

Three quick steps and Croy was standing behind Sonny Gramm. Wayne LaVell looked at Raychard Balen. Balen nodded to Croy and tapped the table once with his index finger. Croy pulled a .38 from the waistband of his jeans and shot Sonny Gramm in the back of the head.

Gramm's face had barely smacked the table-top before LaVell stood up and buttoned his jacket. Raychard Balen put the paperwork back in the briefcase and pocketed the pen, then stood up too.

"The family," LaVell asked, "you've talked to them?"

Balen nodded. "A son and daughter. From Gramm's first marriage. They weren't close to Sonny. Once the estate clears probate, they'll sign."

"How much?" LaVell asked.

Balen shifted the briefcase to his other hand. "Three clicks above what we offered Gramm."

"Ok," LaVell said. "I can live with that."

They started out of the dining room for the front hallway.

"Wayne, wait," Corrine called out. Croy Wendall had stepped up next to her. He was barely as tall as the neckline of her dress. The upper body, thick and muscled, was out of proportion to narrow hips and thin legs. His face and eyes were absolutely without expression, just as they'd been when Corrine had hired him to kill Stanley Tedros.

"Wait," Corrine called again.

Wayne LaVell stopped on the other side of the next room. He pulled off the slip of paper Gramm had attached to the face of a large mirror with an elaborate gilded frame. He worked the paper into a tight ball and dropped it on the floor.

Then nothing. Not a word to Corrine or a backward glance.

A few moments later, she heard the engine of the Continental kick over.

Croy Wendall cut the phone line running along the baseboard. Then, on tip-toe, he snagged Corrine's purse and took out her cell phone. He put the purse back on the top of the sideboard and then dropped the cell phone to the floor and smashed it with the butt of the .38.

Corrine looked at what was left of the back of Sonny Gramm's head, then away, through the open door and into the kitchen where the white moths hammered soundlessly at the lighted windows.

She hunted down her voice, then put some Phoenix in it, dropped herself back into Valley of the Sun Escorts. She didn't know what else to do.

"Your hair's different," she said. "I like it. It suits you, Croy."

"The box said Summer Strawberry." Croy paused and gently pressed two fingers against his lower jaw. He swallowed and went on.

"You mix it and put it on your hair, and then you wait twenty minutes. You have to be careful not to get it in your eyes."

"Do you like my hair, Croy?"

He frowned, considering.

Corrine took a half step closer. "Would you like to touch it, Croy? I don't mind. In fact, I think I might like that."

Croy cocked his head. "Missy used to say things like that."

"Who's Missy?" Corrine dropped her hands to her hips. "Your girlfriend?" She opened a smile. "Don't worry. I can keep a secret, Croy."

"That's what Jamie said. About secrets, I mean." Croy glanced over at Sonny Gramm.

"Let's not worry about Jamie or Missy. There's nobody here but us, honey." Corrine smiled at Croy. "We can do whatever we want. Whatever *you* want."

She turned so that Croy could help with the zipper on the dress.

"I don't sex," Croy said. Then he stepped over to the table and pulled out the chair next to Sonny Gramm. "You need to sit down now, Miss Corrine."

It took Corrine a moment to understand what Croy was getting at. He needed her to sit because he wasn't tall enough for a clean shot to the back of her head if she remained standing.

The .22 Pathfinder was still in the middle of the table, chamber open, and just to the right of the bullets Sonny Gramm had lined up. No matter how hard she worked at it, Corrine could not come up with one plausible scenario that would let her get even one bullet chambered, let alone fired, before Croy shot her.

She offered Croy money. Despite her best efforts, her voice wavered and broke.

"I already have some," Croy said. "From Mr. Balen paying me to pretend to be Mr. Sonny's bodyguard. Mr. Sonny gave me some too when he didn't know I was pretending to be it."

She was going to die. It was an absolutely simple and absolutely brutal fact that resisted any qualifier. You were alive. Then you were dead. Croy had a gun with bullets. Corrine didn't.

She was going to end face-down on the table next to Sonny Gramm.

She glanced over at the sideboard.

Maybe, she thought.

Croy waited by the chair, patient and polite as an usher.

"When you shoot me," Corrine asked, "does it have to be in the back of the head?"

Croy thought for a while. "I guess not," he said. "There are a lot of other places I could shoot."

"Could I have a drink before you do?" Corrine took a step toward the sideboard. "Just a small one, ok?"

Croy started to say something about the time. Corrine made a half-turn toward the sideboard and the purse she'd left setting on its top.

She threw out her arm, grabbed the dangling strap, levered her hips, and swung.

Corrine realized at the last moment she'd forgotten to compensate for Croy's height.

The purse sailed over his head, missing his face by at least a half foot.

Croy, on the move, grabbed her free arm and forced her into the chair. He put one hand on the back of her neck, keeping her head bowed until he caught his breath.

"Keep still," he said.

He was standing directly behind her. Corrine remembered one of the last things she'd told her mother before she'd dumped Corrine on her grandparents and Bradford, Indiana.

I never asked to be born.

The pressure on the back of her neck began to ease, and a moment later, Croy's fingers were gone.

Without thinking, Corrine threw back her head. She refused to die with it bowed.

The gun suddenly clattered to the floor, and Croy let loose a long howl, animal-like it its intensity.

He was still doubled over when Corrine made it out of the chair and scooped up the .38.

She stepped back. The gun was in her hand, but she had no idea what had happened for it to end up there.

She was still alive. It didn't make any sense.

Croy put his hand on the back of the chair and straightened. His cheeks were wet. He cradled his jaw and began crying harder.

"My *toof.* It my *toof.* It *hurts.*" He bent his head and spit, the saliva thick and tinted pink and red, then lifted his head and wiped at his eyes.

"Aspirin," he said, voice clear again. "My jaw's burning, and the big tooth in back hurts. Just like when I was at the cabin."

Corrine lifted the .38 and shot Croy in the chest.

She went over to Sonny Gramm and pulled his upper torso off the table and back into a sitting position and then had to hunt down a dishtowel for the blood on her hands and forearms after she went through Gramm's pockets for the keys to the Mustang.

Croy was lying in a tight fetal position facing the baseboard. She spotted a black cell phone clipped to his belt and took it, then picked up her purse and dropped the .38 inside.

She stood for a moment, looking around the room. She still had Croy's cell phone in her hand. It was useless, she realized. There was no one to call for help.

Slow down and think, she told herself. There was still a chance she could salvage a future from everything that had gone wrong tonight. It wouldn't be easy, but it was possible. She needed a clear head and a little time.

Wayne LaVell would assume she was dead. That was an edge right there. She'd have surprise on her side. Corrine figured that LaVell, being LaVell, would go out for a meal and drinks after leaving Gramm's so that Balen and he could firm up strategies for dealing with Sonny's heirs.

That gave her enough time to get to LaVell's motel and be waiting for him when Balen dropped him off. If things went her way, she could still close the door on April Rayne and Phoenix.

There would be no need to then go on and kill Raychard Balen. With LaVell dead, Raychard Balen would quickly revert with his customary expediency to acting out of self-interest. Given what she and Balen had on each other now, Balen was too compromised to retaliate or pressure her. He'd have no real leverage. He couldn't implicate Corrine without doing the same thing to himself, and Corrine would make sure it stayed that way by retaining him as her lawyer.

In fact, Corrine decided, Raychard Balen could start by helping her dispose of Sonny Gramm's and Croy Wendall's bodies later tonight.

First though was the matter of killing Wayne LaVell. The rest would follow.

Corrine shouldered her purse and left the carnage of the dining room. The house had an odd feel to it, as if it were full and empty at the same time. She listened to the ceiling fans hum and whir.

Corrine checked the time and detoured to the first-floor bathroom. She was washing up when she heard the footsteps. Then, a second later, the doorbell. Once, twice, three times, the chimes overlapping.

Next came the knocking, steady and expectant.

Corrine slipped out of the bathroom, glanced down the hallway to the foyer, and moved quickly back to the dining room. She'd try to outwait whoever was there. She rested her shoulder against the wall and closed her eyes for a moment, trying to remember if LaVell and Balen had locked the front door as they'd left.

The doorbell again. Then more knocking. Over and over. A muffled voice.

She'd slip out the kitchen door. Hide in the dark of the backyard. Wait. Eventually circle around to the front of the house and the Mustang.

Now, Corrine thought, pushing herself off the wall and turning to cross the dining room. She'd only taken a couple steps when something grabbed at her chest and squeezed.

There was a pink smear on the floor near the baseboard and a couple of matching smears on the wall above it, but nothing else.

Croy Wendall was gone.

So were the .22 Pathfinder and the line of bullets in the middle of the dining room table.

Corrine told herself to move. Something. She had to do something. But it felt like the air in her lungs had solidified.

She forced her fingers to unzip the purse. The .38 lay right inside the opening.

Corrine listened for Croy Wendall.

But what she heard instead was the sound of the front door opening and then Ben Decovic's voice, not muffled anymore, as he called out, identifying himself, and called out again, telling Sonny Gramm he had something important to ask him.

FIFTY-NINE

BEN DECOVIC WENT NO FURTHER than the foyer. The unlocked front door bothered him. The same with the silence that had been the only response each time he called out.

He was sure someone was in the house. He'd heard a muffled thump just after he'd stepped inside, the kind of noise that arose from someone accidently bumping something and quickly righting it before it fell.

The problem was he couldn't tell which part of the house it came from or who might have caused it.

Sonny Gramm himself was part of the problem. Gramm had made it amply clear on each of Ben's visits what he thought of the police, and his paranoia, justified or not, over Wayne LaVell's influence and power had notched that sentiment to dangerous levels, especially if Gramm had been drinking.

Ben had no great desire to die at the hands of the man he was trying to help. Or at the hands of one of the series of revolving-door bodyguards Gramm hired and fired.

Of course, there was also the possibility he was looking at something else altogether. Another break-in. Or worse.

He gave it one more shot, hollering out his name, throwing in his badge number, and asking that Gramm respond. "That's all," Ben added. "Just let me know you're here and all right, Mr. Gramm. I'll leave then. I need to know everything's ok." Ben waited, then went on. "I have some information for you. A good lead. You don't want to talk right now, that's fine. I'll call you later. For now, just let me know you're all right. Then I'm gone. I promise."

Nothing. Just the creak of a ceiling fan from one of the ground-floor rooms.

Ben backed down the foyer and out the front door. He hesitated, then reached back inside and turned off the porch light and stepped outside again, staying close to the wall and taking the radio off his belt.

He was on shaky ground here. The permission to leave his patrol sector had never been officially granted. Ben had left the I-Hop and driven straight to Gramm's farm assuming that permission would come through at any time. It hadn't.

He tried again to play it by the book. He called in to the county but was told, as he had been earlier when he asked for a ride-along to Sonny Gramm's farm, that the sheriff and his deputies were still out with the Fire Department and EMS people trying to deal with the effects of the three wildfires that had yet to be brought under control. Ben then asked the dispatcher to patch in another request to the Magnolia Beach police and one to the state police for backup. The dispatcher said she'd do what she could, but reiterated that the wildfires had everything and everybody jammed up.

From inside the house, a heavy thump, followed a few seconds later by the sound of glass breaking.

Ben unholstered his Glock and stepped inside for a preliminary look.

The foyer opened onto a living room. All the lights were on. Further down the hall, a bathroom off to his left. In the living room, there were pieces of paper attached to a rocking chair, three lamps, one of the windows fronting the porch, and an end table. Nothing, beyond that, looked out of place. Across the room was a partially opened door that looked like it led to a hallway that paralleled the one opening from the front door and foyer.

The house became more cluttered the deeper he went in. More slips of paper taped to furniture. The lighting less bright. A lopsided and unwieldy déjà vu dogged him. Ben glanced at his watch. Still no sign of backup. With his luck, it would turn out to be Carl Adkin. The evening had begun to feel like a rerun of the ambush in the parking lot of the Passion Palace early in March.

Ben forced the thought from his mind. No distractions, he told himself. Stay focused and in the moment.

A pair of French doors opened onto the dining room. A wadded piece of paper lay on the floor below a large antique mirror.

He smelled before he saw that shots had been fired. Ben edged to the wall next to the right panel of the French doors and lifted the semi-automatic, counted to three, and swung the door open, stepping into and then stepping back from the opening.

When he leaned against the wall again, he'd taken the image of Sonny Gramm with him, Gramm sitting upright at the dining room table, the shoulders of his shirt soaked red, the silver-gray pompadour and most of the top portion of his head gone.

The image hung before Ben's eyes until he blinked it away.

He went for his radio with his free hand, his finger already stabbing for the transmit button, Ben glancing at the mirror as he brought the radio up.

A smudge of movement in its lower corner.

Ben dropped the radio, turning, as the door on the other side of the living room was thrown back against its hinges. Then a dark figure in an even darker rectangle of doorway and two shots, both rushed, one slamming into the mirror, the other burying into the wall next to Ben.

He aimed at the center of the rectangle, got off one shot.

He heard the stutter of footsteps, a pause, more footsteps, then nothing.

He scrambled for the radio, ID'd himself, gave the code for emergency assistance, the address, and broke contact without waiting for a reply.

From the rear of the house came the sound of glass breaking.

Ben moved quickly into the dining room, circling the large oak table and coming up behind Sonny Gramm. He stopped next to a sideboard, its top cluttered with bottles. In front of it were the fragments of a smashed cell phone. Ben glanced at the back of Sonny Gramm's head, at the empty glasses on the table, the spray of blood fanning the oak.

The door next to the sideboard was halfway open. On its other side someone was counting in a chant-like rhythm.

Ben glanced at his watch, then moved to the doorway.

A small man was attempting to pull himself upright with the help of the door handle to the refrigerator. The effort had twisted his upper body so that he was facing Ben. The top half of his shirt was wet with blood. On the floor below his dangling right hand was a gun and shards of broken glass.

"I remember you," the man said. "You're the policeman." He let go of the handle and, closing his eyes, slumped against the refrigerator.

Ben stepped over and picked up the gun. There was a slow ragged tear in each of the man's breaths.

"I was looking for some aspirin," he said. "My tooth hurts."

"You're Croy, aren't you?" Ben said. "Croy Wendall."

The man nodded without opening his eyes. "I think I broke a glass," he said. "I tried to put in some water, but I kept falling down."

Ben looked around the kitchen. He grabbed a wad of dishtowels.

"When your tooth hurts," Croy said, "everything gets very orange, and you get thirsty."

"Lie still," Ben said, pressing the wad of dishcloths against Croy's chest. "You've been shot, Croy. Help'll be here soon. Lie still."

Croy looked down at his chest and then pointed behind Ben. "Thirty-six divided by four times three take away five," he said. "That's the number. It's like an echo of itself." He paused for breath. "But it's not the one inside me. It doesn't echo."

Ben glanced over his shoulder.

The feeling, again, of a lopsided déjà vu, of something not quite right.

He took Croy's hands and put them on the dishtowels and asked, "Can you hold them and press? Can you manage that, Croy?"

Croy said, "Every gun has a number, but not every number has a gun. That's why you need to rhyme things."

Ben got up and stepped over to the door and looked into the dining room.

There were three empty glasses on the table. They'd been there all along, but he'd been in a hurry and assumed two because two was what he thought he was looking at.

Behind him, Croy was counting, repeating the same sequence of numbers he'd run through with Ben.

Ben was suddenly nauseous.

A .22 Charter-Arms. That's what he'd taken from Croy.

Ben slipped out the back door. Outside, the air was still dry, but the wind had picked up, a hot steady gusting like someone running full-out. It carried faint traces of smoke from the fires to the west.

Ben worked his way toward the front of the house.

Three empty glasses, not two. He'd missed that. He'd assumed two people, not three.

Just as the adrenaline rush of returning fire had kept him from registering the sound of the two rounds that had been fired at him from across the living room.

He had found Croy in the kitchen and thought he'd been the one who shot Croy. Ben figured he'd caught a lucky break returning fire.

He had not bothered to look beyond that.

But, like a voice, you get to recognize the sound of a caliber.

The two shots in the living room had not come from a .22. Something larger bored instead, probably a .38 or .45.

He slowed as he neared the corner of the front porch. The limbs and leaves on the old trees canopying Sonny Gramm's house were alive with wind, exposing and then hiding an immense bone-white half-moon.

A rattle of keys. A shadow hunched over the driver's side door of Gramm's Mustang.

A moment later, the interior light came on.

A woman tossed her purse inside, pausing in the wedge of light to put her shoes back on. She lifted one leg, her hand reaching back, then froze when she sensed Ben's presence. The hair spilling down her back was silver in the moonlight.

"Easy, Mrs. Tedros," Ben said. "No sudden moves."

"You mean like this?" she asked without turning around and stepped out of the wedge of light, stopping along the side of the Mustang's hood.

"I told you to stay where you were," Ben said.

"Is Croy dead?" She was still standing with her back to Ben, her hands at her sides.

"No, but close to it." Ben paused, then asked Corrine to raise her arms, slowly, and put her hands on top of her head.

She ignored him.

The driver's side door of the Mustang had not been opened all the way, and a strong gust of wind caught it. The door rocked on its hinges and started to close, creating a slow strobe as the interior light cut on and off when the door bounced against the frame.

"Was Croy able to talk?" Corrine asked.

"A little," Ben said. He glanced down at his watch.

She laughed. "I don't suppose there's the chance we could work something between us, Officer Decovic, is there?"

"No," Ben said. He moved a step closer. The wind in the leaves above them was distorting his field of vision. Shadows wavered and swarmed. Moonlight splashed and receded.

"I didn't kill Sonny Gramm," Corrine said.

"You'll probably be ok then," Ben said. "Buddy'll buy you a good lawyer. Now please do what I asked." Ben repeated his request for Corrine to slowly lift and put her hands on top of her head.

She still had her back to him.

Wind. Shadows. Moonlight. Everything roiling.

"Backup will be here any time now," Ben said. "There's no need for this."

She laughed again.

"I think I'm past the point of backup and lawyers," Corrine Tedros said.

The wind hit the car door, and the car door hit the frame and jumped. The interior light went on and off.

"Do you know what happens, Officer Decovic, if you look at anything long enough?"

Ben waited a moment before answering no.

"Oh, I believe you do," she said.

The wind kicking in. A smear of shadows and moonlight.

"I have the gun I took off Croy," Corrine said. "You know that, though, don't you?"

"It'd be better all the way around if you did what I told you," Ben said.

"Nobody asks to be born, Officer Decovic," she said. "No choice there."

"You have one now," Ben said.

Another laugh. "Indeed I do," she said. She slowly lifted her right arm and opened her hand. Something hard bounced on the hood of the Mustang.

"Satisfied?" she asked.

"Steady now, Mrs. Tedros," Ben said. "Turn around slowly."

"Call me Betsy," she said.

Shadows and splashes of moonlight.

Corrine Tedros started to turn.

The leaves shifting.

Ben saw it then.

A shoe, not the .38, on the hood of the car.

Corrine swung and brought up her arm.

Ben stepped to the left and fired.

SIXTY

CROY WENDALL HAD NEVER BEEN in a hospital before. He'd never been shot before either. When he wasn't sleeping, he made lists in his head of other things he had never been. Mostly he slept though and had dreams of very small things.

There were tubes running into and taped to his arms and wires running from his chest and stomach to machines that made sounds like hungry baby birds and flashed bright green numbers.

At first, Croy assumed that when he left the hospital he could take all the tubes and wires and machines with him, and he'd had to hide his disappointment when a nurse explained that wasn't the way it worked. He'd liked the idea that he'd be part-machine and part-Croy and that the machines would read what was going on inside him and turn it into numbers.

The nurse also told him he was in Intensive Care and gave him pills to swallow. Croy kept track of their colors and then swallowed them and watched the machines to see what numbers the colors were.

Mr. Balen came to see him every day. He asked Croy a lot of questions, but sometimes the sleepiness made it hard to remember if Croy had answered them.

Mr. Balen had dark circles under his eyes, and his hands were jumpy.

Today, Mr. Balen stopped the nurse from giving Croy the blue pill and the red pills and told her to bring them back later. The nurse didn't like that, but she did it because Mr. Balen pointed his finger at her and said some lawyer words, and after she left, Mr. Balen had smiled at Croy and asked how he was doing.

Croy said his tooth felt much better.

Mr. Balen tapped one of the tubes running into Croy's arm. "That's because of the antibiotics," he said. "When we get you out of here, I've got a dental appointment set up for you. We'll get the tooth taken care of before you have to appear in court."

The two sides of Mr. Balen's mustache did not quite match, and there were little scratches around his chin where he'd cut himself shaving. He had on a red and blue tie that Croy liked because they were the colors of the pills that the nurse would give him when she came back later.

Mr. Balen leaned closer to the bed. "I need you to listen carefully, Croy. You'll be leaving Intensive Care tomorrow or the day after, and when you do, there will be some policemen who want to talk to you. I've been able to keep them away so far, but that will change very soon. They will be asking you a lot of questions."

Mr. Balen paused and looked at Croy for a while. Then he asked, "Do you remember who you killed, Croy?"

Croy frowned and said, "When?" Croy had done a lot of crimes. Not all of them were killing, but some of them were.

"Since you first met Mrs. Tedros," Mr. Balen said.

"Three," Croy said. "Mr. Stanley, Jamie, and Mr. Sonny." Croy stopped. "Oh, and Missy. I forgot her. That makes four. I don't know about the policewoman I threw into the window of the restaurant."

"Don't worry about her," Mr. Balen said. "Do you remember who shot you?"

Croy told him Mrs. Tedros. Mr. Balen smiled and nodded his head twice.

"I want you to do something for me, Croy," he said. "I want you to forget everything else but those four dead people. Can you do that?"

Croy nodded. Forgetting was easy.

"The police will be asking you questions," Mr. Balen said, "and this is what you need to tell them. You forget everything else, and you tell them what I'm going to tell you. Just that, ok? Nothing else."

Mr. Balen then talked about the crimes Croy had done.

Croy listened hard because even though the four people he was supposed to remember were in what Mr. Balen said, they were not in it like it happened. Some of it was like it happened, but not all, and so Croy was listening as hard as he could because Mr. Balen was watching to see if he was.

This is what Croy was supposed to tell the policemen: Corrine Tedros had been afraid that Stanley Tedros was going to turn her husband Buddy against her. Stanley couldn't stand the idea that Buddy had married a woman who wasn't Greek. He didn't hide that feeling, and Stanley had told Corrine he was going to find a way to break up the marriage before the year was out. Stanley's influence over his nephew was very strong, and Corrine had every reason to believe Stanley would make good on his threat. She went to Sonny Gramm who she used to work for and asked Sonny for help. Sonny introduced her to Croy. Corrine met Croy and offered him money to kill Stanley. Croy did. Then Buddy Tedros put out the reward for information about Stanley's murder. It took a while, but Croy's friend Jamie figured out Croy was the one who killed Stanley, so Croy had to kill Jamie. Missy was in the house with Jamie, so Croy had to kill her too. Then Corrine Tedros called Croy again because she had another problem. Sonny Gramm was trying to blackmail her about hiring Croy to kill Stanley. Corrine Tedros was afraid again and hired Croy to kill Sonny Gramm. On the night Corrine was supposed to pay the blackmail money to Sonny Gramm, Croy went with her. He killed Sonny like Corrine had asked him to. Croy thought she was going to give him some money for shooting Sonny, but Corrine shot Croy instead. She left Croy for dead, and then the policeman shot Corrine when she was leaving Sonny Gramm's place.

Mr. Balen finished the story and looked at Croy.

Croy said that Mr. Balen had forgotten to put Mr. LaVell and himself in what happened.

Mr. Balen nodded. "Mr. LaVell and I are part of what you're supposed to forget, Croy."

Croy said ok and then asked about Jamie and him smashing Mr. Sonny's Mustang and putting the rats in his house.

Mr. Balen said to make that not happen too. "There's no real evidence to tie either of you to the crimes, and with Jamie dead, no one to claim otherwise." Mr. Balen paused and tapped Croy's arm. "Anybody asks, you tell them you weren't there and don't know anything about it."

"That policeman knows though," Croy said.

"But he can't prove it," Mr. Balen said, "and that makes it the same as if it didn't happen."

Mr. Balen got Croy a glass of water with little pieces of ice in it, and then he made Croy tell the story like he had told it to Croy.

"After I leave today," Mr. Balen said, "I want you to tell that story to yourself over and over until you remember it all."

Croy said he could do that. It would be like saying the numbers and rhymes in his head.

Mr. Balen winked and smiled. The two sides of his mustache fought with each other.

Croy asked if the fire had burned up the cabin and the tree with the frogs. He could tell Mr. Balen didn't know what he meant at first, but then he nodded and said that the fire was out now, but it had burned up the cabin.

Mr. Balen looked at him for a long time after that. Then he folded his hands and said, "I remember how much you liked that cabin, and I have a surprise for you. I'm going to build you another cabin, Croy, if you tell the police what I told you to tell them. The new cabin will be yours, nobody else's."

Croy told him he would like a new cabin. He asked if it could be painted orange inside.

Mr. Balen said that would be no problem, and then he was quiet again.

After a while, he said, "There's one other thing, Croy, about telling the story like I told it to you. You killed some people, so you'll have to go to prison for a while. As your lawyer, it'll be my job to make that stay as short as possible, but there's no getting around the fact that you'll be spending some time behind bars."

Mr. Balen went on to talk about mitigating and extenuating circumstances and how the story Croy would tell assigned primary motive to Mrs. Tedros and how if they caught the right judge, Mr. Balen could cook the case so that the sentencing would be bearable.

Croy was thinking about the new cabin and the sound of the frogs in the river at twilight, and he didn't say anything for a while.

Mr. Balen's hands got jumpy again.

"You're worried about prison," Mr. Balen said. "That's perfectly understandable, Croy." He stopped to nod twice. "Mr. LaVell and I have discussed this too. He wants to do something for you, and he wanted to be here to tell you himself, but something came up, and he couldn't make it, so he asked me to tell you for him."

Croy listened to Mr. Balen name some money for each year of his sentencing. Mr. Balen took a little brown book from the inside pocket of his coat and showed it to Croy. Croy's name was in it and an account number next to his name. There were little squares and columns on the pages.

"Each year," Mr. Balen said, tapping the Deposit column. "Just like a payday." He started nodding again. "If you think about it, Croy, prison will be just like having a job except you don't have to get up and go to it every day. You'll already be there."

"And you'll build me a cabin too?" Croy asked.

"Absolutely," Mr. Balen said.

Croy said ok.

Mr. Balen tapped him on the arm again and smiled. The two sides of his mustache weren't fighting anymore. He told Croy he'd be back to see him tomorrow, and if the police showed up in the meantime, Croy should tell them he wanted his lawyer present and then wait for him to get there before Croy started telling the story they'd told today.

After Mr. Balen left, the nurse came in with Croy's pills. She took his temperature and blood pressure and adjusted something on the bag connected to one of the tubes that ran into his arm.

Then the nurse left, and Croy was by himself. He watched the bright green numbers on the machines and thought about the cabin and the river and about prison and about the hospital and about how all the smells inside it were layered, and then he thought about what he was supposed to forget, and did.

SIXTY-ONE

THE TELEVISION IN THE CORNER of the bar at Monroe's was on, but the volume was turned down, and Ben Decovic worked on a cold draft and watched the mayor and chief of police mime their way through the press conference that had been scheduled for late in the day in the lobby of the new City-County Complex. The color on the set needed to be adjusted, the mayor's suit wavering between a watery blue and a bright green and his face shading back and forth from an apoplectic red to a hamburger pink.

Ben lowered his head. He watched himself shoot Corrine Tedros.

Her blood had appeared black in the moonlight.

A disable, that's what he'd wanted to go for, a disable, but Corrine Tedros was forever turning and lifting her arm, and he was forever a second off in reaction time after he'd seen it was her shoe and not the gun she'd dropped on the hood of the Mustang, and in the end, which felt like a forever too, Ben had been reduced to pure reflex and placed the shots without thinking, one at the base of Corrine Tedros's throat and the other in the center of her chest.

Ben heard someone step up behind him.

"Thought I recognized your car out front," Ed Hatch said. He took the stool to Ben's right, lifted two fingers, and signaled the bartender.

"Monroe's used to be a cop bar," he said, "back when the department worked out of East Queensland. Wall to wall blue in here, end of every shift. Now, with headquarters at the Complex, they've shifted base of operations to Schmidt's over on Heritage."

The bartender brought over two beers. Hatch gave him a ten and waved away the change.

They watched the mayor shake hands with the chief of police.

"Heard you were officially cleared," Hatch said.

"The fires," Ben said. An in-house review had determined that his leaving the patrol sector before permission was granted and the subsequent shooting of Corrine Tedros were warranted by the circumstances, the proliferation of wildfires in the region and the danger they'd posed to the residents causing the delays in backup and communication.

"Heard the prosecuting attorney paid you a visit today," Hatch said.

Ben looked over. Hatch wore the same brown off-the-rack suit Ben had seen him in every other time. Add the buzz cut and black-framed glasses, and Hatch looked more like central casting's idea of a middle school science teacher than a homicide detective.

"You," Ben said. "I wondered who'd slipped me a copy of Croy Wendall's confession."

Hatch sipped his beer. When he set it back down and turned his head, the press conference was reflected in miniature on each lens of his glasses.

"The whole confession was cooked," Ben said. "It's one long lie."

Hatch loosened his tie and looked back at the screen.

Croy Wendall's confession had been a simple, uncluttered line of motive. Corrine Tedros, its alpha and omega. Everything had been laid off on her. There'd been no mention of Raychard Balen or Wayne LaVell in the entire transcript.

Everything fit except the truth.

"What did the PA say when he met with you?" Hatch said.

"What do you think? His office is ready to move on an indictment. It didn't bother him that all the other principals," Ben said and ticked them off on his fingers, "Corrine Tedros, Sonny Gramm, Jamison Blake, and Missy Newton, are all dead and can't contest any of the details in Wendall's account."

"Nothing to connect the vandalism at the Palace and Gramm's house?" Hatch said.

Ben shook his head. "Croy Wendall was the one who attacked me in the parking lot. I know it. The PA, though, had the file and kept pointing out that the two men were wearing masks."

Ben picked up his beer and then set it down again. "Even my gun," he said.

According to Croy Wendall, Jamison Blake had bought it on the street. Neither Blake or Wendall had been on or near the premises of the Passion Palace on the night Ben had it taken from him.

Any ties to Raychard Balen and Wayne LaVell squeezing Sonny Gramm had disappeared. Ben had not been able to get the prosecuting attorney to look beyond Croy Wendall's statement.

"An uncontested lay-up," Ben said. "That's what he called the case. Wendall is going to plead out a straight guilty."

Ed Hatch frowned, his mouth set as if he'd taken a bite of something disagreeable. "I was hoping to get another shot at Wendall," he said.

"The guy's lying," Ben said. "He left out Balen and LaVell. They were part of the mix from the beginning. No way they're clean."

"One loose thread," Hatch said. "I thought maybe you'd spot something in the transcript I could use."

Ben scratched his cheek. "I wish there'd been. Believe me, I looked."

"I can't get his voice out of my head," Hatch said. "I hit Wendall hard, came at him from every direction I could think of, but he never tripped up." Hatch paused and shifted his beer on the bartop. "That flat monotone. An answering-machine voice. Wendall giving me the confession back word for word each time. Never deviating on a detail. It spooked me. I mean, I've handled enough suspects who've been coached by their lawyers or who are arrogant enough to believe they're fully alibied-out. They'll usually trip up sooner or later if you keep going at them. They'll give you something to work with. Not Wendall though. He's a whole new species."

Ben looked up at the television. The press conference was ending. The mayor was smiling.

"Time to mow the lawn," Hatch said. He picked up his beer and checked its level.

"Sometimes that's all you can do," he said. "You go home and mow the lawn. Then you eat supper with the wife and kids, maybe watch a little television afterwards. The next day you get up and go back to work."

The bartender walked over. "I'm going to turn it up, ok? Frank wants to hear this." He nodded toward a guy in his late fifties sitting further down the bar. The guy waved a thanks in Ben and Hatch's direction.

An *Inside Look* segment on the Tedros case started.

The anchor's lead had barely begun before Ben turned to Hatch and said, "It appears our honorable mayor decided to selectively leak details from the press conference early to some of his favorite affiliates."

"He knows he has to answer to the tourist bureau," Hatch said. "They're the ones with the behind-the-scenes clout come re-election time."

Ben tipped his beer toward the television screen. "Well, that ought to please them." The take on Stanley Tedros's murder would not threaten tourists or the town's image. There was nothing in it to keep anyone from booking a hotel reservation or buying into a vacation package.

Inside Look had played up and off the ethnicity angle, turning the events behind Croy Wendall's confession into an updated Greek tragedy, Stanley Tedros, the soft-drink king and scion, reigning as a rich and powerful patriarch over a troubled family; Corrine Tedros, the beautiful and scheming woman with the dark past and wife of the heir apparent; Buddy Tedros, the prince of a man blinded by his love for both his wife and uncle; Croy Wendall, the unwitting agent and arm in the murder which eventually opened and emptied the bag of tricks that fate, luck, or the universe held over us all.

In the end, justice was not so much served as served up.

The segment ended and was replaced by a commercial for hand soap and later an update on the three wildfires. They were now contained, but the estimate was still out on property damage. The anchor added that a suspect had been taken into custody.

Hatch cleared his throat.

The guy down the bar said, "Jesus. What kind of parents would do that?" He pointed to the screen. "Hanging a moniker like that on their own kid. Stuff like that's not funny."

Hatch cleared his throat again and rapped the bartop in front of Ben.

Ben looked over at Hatch.

"I admit I was mightily pissed when you went at Corrine Tedros unauthorized," Hatch said. "We were up to our neck in bad tips, and the chief was pushing the drifter angle for the perp, and I didn't need any more complications." He paused and rubbed his jawline. "Your instincts about Corrine Tedros were on the money though. I owe you an apology on that one."

"No," Ben said. He finished off his beer and signaled for another. "After today, it's Corrine Tedros we owe the apology to."

SIXTY-TWO

JACK CARSON LOOKED out the bedroom window. The light was shading to gray. He was late. Normally, he'd be on the job before the sun was up.

His clothes were laid out. He got dressed and walked through the house to the kitchen.

He looked around for his wife, but figured Carol was already in her classroom getting ready for her third-graders.

He ate a bowl of cereal.

He hunted down his work cap.

Carol had left the front door unlocked again.

Jack crossed the landing and walked down the stairs. At the end of the driveway, he paused and looked back at the house.

A girl stood framed in the front living room window. Jack frowned and waved.

She closed the curtains.

Jack looked at the sky and frowned a second time.

Something about the light bothered him.

The wind ran into his face.

Jack started walking to Bob Burnett's house. Bob lived a couple streets over on Tilton and handled a lot of the roofing jobs for Jack. Jack had loaned Bob his truck to pick up a load of shingles for a renovation that Carson Construction was doing on a rundown beach house for a family from Charlotte.

There were street signs on each corner, and he read their names as he walked past, but after a while, the street names were like the ones at the house when he opened a kitchen cabinet, and there were shelves upon shelves of boxes and bottles, and all those names came rushing down at him at once like a swarm of bees.

The light had shaded to a deeper gray. Jack looked toward what he was sure was east, but the light didn't quite match the direction.

He walked some more. Then he didn't.

He remembered his wife was dead. She had died during childbirth.

He tried, but her name would not arrive.

His left knee was stiff.

A horn sounded behind him, and someone said, "Hey, are you all right?"

Jack looked around. He was standing in the middle of the street.

A pickup rolled slowly and stopped next to him. The truck was a bright glossy red and had a long silver antenna sprouting from the hood. A teenage boy in a blue shirt was driving. There were more teenagers in the cab with him and another group riding in the back. There was music playing, and then there wasn't, and the boy leaned partway out the window.

"Man, those dark clothes, this time of evening, you need to be careful," the boy said.

Jack looked down at what he was wearing. They were dark, all right, and on top of that, they looked like old man clothes. He couldn't remember putting any of them on.

He flexed his fingers. He thought he'd been carrying something too.

"Look, you need a lift?" the boy said. "We're headed for Old Mill Beach."

"Party Time," someone said from the back of the truck, and then a girl laughed. Jack liked the sound of the laugh. It was pretty, and it rippled.

"Ok," he said. He walked over to the tailgate, and the ones in back helped him climb in. He sat down across from a young girl. He could see her nipples pressing against her shirt.

Then the truck was moving, and they had the music playing again, and the teenage boys and girls in back were yelling to each other, and sometimes they yelled things to Jack, but he had a hard time following what they said because the wind ripped their words apart as soon as they said them, and the movement of the truck left him a little dizzy and light-headed, like the way he felt when he hadn't eaten for a while.

There were two large coolers in the back and a jumble of rolled sleeping bags and next to them, a pile of logs and some bundled kindling.

The girl's breasts moved under her shirt every time she did.

And then Jack was remembering. No, not quite remembering. Partially developed snapshots. Images that refused to hold long enough to fit in time and become a memory.

Blips on some internal radar screen he couldn't read anymore.

The truck took a corner fast, and before Jack could get his hand up, his cap was ripped from his head. He watched it sail away and then land in the middle of the road.

His knee was stiff.

After a while, there were tall stands of pine trees lining the side of the road and pieces of the sky missing light.

Jack was hungry. He tried, but couldn't find the words to explain that.

His hands were resting in his lap. His ring finger and thumb twitched, and then one of the muscles in his neck did too.

He was hungry, and then he wasn't or didn't think he was, and he couldn't find the words to explain that either, and after a while, feeling hungry and not exactly feeling hungry felt like the same thing.

There were more pine trees and some dogs barking far away, and then the truck stopped, and Jack Carson was looking at the ocean.

When the wind gusted, he could taste the waves.

Two cars and three other trucks were parked on the beach, and there were people moving around a bonfire and voices rising and falling and overlapping and music playing.

Jack heard someone yell, "Hey, you forgot to drop off the old guy. He's still sitting in the back of the truck."

Jack was looking at the ocean. He could smell it too. Everything else was wind.

When he turned his head, a teenager in a blue shirt squatted next to him. Two others stood by the tailgate. One had black hair, and the other had black hair with its tips streaked blonde.

Jack had no idea who they were or what they wanted with him.

The boy in the blue shirt asked Jack his name and where he was supposed to be. He asked Jack that three times.

Jack set his lips and concentrated, but when he spoke, he heard himself asking about a hat.

One of the boys standing by the tailgate said, "He's drunk, man. He's probably one of those homeless guys. Hell, let him hang here. He's too old and blasted to bother anybody."

The boy in the blue shirt shrugged and said, "I guess," and then he helped Jack climb out of the back of the truck.

The boy with the black hair put a can of beer in Jack's hand. "It'll help keep the buzz going, Dad," he said. "Just hang loose now."

The three boys walked back to join the others.

The damp sand around the bonfire steamed. Jack heard gulls crying. His knee was stiff.

He started walking. He had the sense he was supposed to be somewhere. He stayed close to the waterline where the sand was hard-packed.

The sea looked like a crumpled sheet of aluminum foil that someone had tried to smooth out.

He walked through clusters of dead jellyfish. Their skin was clouded as if they'd been given a coat of shellac.

After a while, the water changed and now rushed around his shoes, and Jack was finding it hard to keep his balance, so he moved higher up the beach.

The sand was white there and loose.

Things got slower.

The water made the same sound coming in as it did going out.

Jack stopped a minute to rest.

The sky was cloudless, and the light was leaving it.

He looked back up the beach and saw a fire that seemed to float in the air just above the crest of the waves coming into shore.

He walked some more, and then he was sitting down.

The sound of the waves was mixed with the sound of the wind.

In his right hand was a beer can. Jack wondered where it had come from. He set it in the sand next to him.

The fire floating in the air was orange and yellow and seemed very far away.

His pants were wet to his knees.

He told himself he needed to get up.

He listened to the seagulls crying.

The sea was the same color as the sky.

The waves knocked the beer can over.

Up the beach, a small part of the air was on fire.

Everything was quiet, except for the sound the waves made, and one set of waves sounded the same as the next set, and after a while, Jack wasn't hearing the waves anymore, the sound dropping away and disappearing into the movement of the waves themselves so that it wasn't necessary to listen to them at all, any more than it was necessary for Jack, or anyone else, he thought, to listen to his own heart beating. The sound was the same as its movement.

Jack's pants were wet to the crotch, and he smelled salt.

Everything was very quiet.

Down the beach, a piece of the sky burned.

In front of him was the sea, which was now the same color as the sky, and the sky was the same size as the immense quiet that the movement of the waves left behind, and in that quiet Jack found himself remembering something, not a sliver of memory this time or a snapshot, but a memory that arose before him intact, and Jack's face was wet because he was remembering, and the memory was right there with him, as if it had been waiting here all along for him, and Jack stepped into the memory as one would the sea, and he could feel the pull of both, and then he was sitting on the beach and in the middle of his seventh grade classroom, third seat from the front, Paul Greene on his left, Donny Kennedy on his right, with the month of April pressing against the classroom windows and his notebook open and Mrs. Allen at the board diagramming sentences, Mrs. Allen the new teacher at the school, young and impossibly pretty with shiny brown hair that moved each time she did and dark brown eyes and a flashbulb smile, and Jack sat in the middle row in a body that was outrunning both him and the confines of the desk, and he listened to the *nic, nic, nic* of the chalk on the blackboard and watched Mrs. Allen's dress ride and tighten on the lines of her body as she wrote, and in that moment April forever bloomed in his bones, Mrs. Allen in a bright yellow sundress writing out a sentence and then taking it apart and showing how each part fit, and Jack sensing the power behind that too, of being able to take everything that churned inside him and find the words for it and then to take those words and build a sentence that was true and sturdy as anything in the world, a beauty in that too that seemed as real and desirable as Mrs. Allen herself, subjects and verbs and breasts and hips, all outlined and hidden by the fit of a yellow dress, and only one thing separating them, that would forever separate everything, the gap that Jack sensed even then as he sat at his desk, all hormones and nerve endings and yearnings, the gap that time itself left between everything, the gap between the sight of the curve of a breast beneath a yellow dress from the touch of that breast, the gap between what you felt and the words you used to try and build sentences that fit what you were feeling, time forever separating a boy sitting in a classroom from an impossibly beautiful young woman standing in April light, time forever separating the boy from the man he'd grow up to be, time forever separating an old man from the sentences and everything else he'd built in his life, and as Jack Carson watched Mrs. Allen write on the blackboard, he watched the line where the sea and sky disappeared into each other, and his clothes were heavy and wet, and his face was wet too, because he sensed they were leaving him, all the words he'd ever known and used, all of them leaving and taking the world and him with them, as if they were all being systematically erased from an immense blackboard that was the same color as the sea and the same size as the sky, Jack watching all the words leave until only a handful remained, and he looked out at the sea and the sky which had disappeared into each other like the sound of the waves had disappeared into the movement of the waves, and in the immense quiet, he heard himself speak three words—*Oh My God*—in a voice that, as it broke, could just as easily have belonged to a young boy or an old man, just as, in that moment, Jack Carson could not be sure if the *Oh My God* arose from awe or horror at what lay before him, and he chased those three words until they broke against the sound of the waves and disappeared into the rising wind.

SIXTY-THREE

A CUP OF COFFEE, MAYBE.

Nothing more complicated than that.

Anne Carson's car was in the drive. Ben parked behind it and sat for a moment behind the wheel before getting out. Anne hadn't returned any of his calls, and Ben had quit leaving messages after the shooting at Sonny Gramm's.

A cup of coffee, maybe. See where things went from there.

He climbed the stairs to the landing. Paige Carson answered his knock. She stepped back from the screen door and crossed her arms. In jeans, new athletic shoes, and a white T-shirt, she resembled at first glance a miniature version of Anne.

Except for the eyes. Paige had the eyes of an accountant.

Or a cop, Ben thought.

"I want to talk to your mom," he said, tilting his head to look past her.

"You smell like beer," Paige said.

"Your mom."

"She's not in."

"Come on, Paige. Her car's here."

"Ok, then," she said and unlocked the screen door. Ben followed her inside.

Paige opened the living room curtains and went back to the kitchen table and the textbook and laptop opened on it.

Ben started down the hallway. Anne's bedroom door was open. The bed was unmade, and draped over its lower end was a bright summery dress. Jack's door was locked from the outside. Ben returned to the kitchen.

"Where's Mrs. Wood?" he asked.

"She had to leave early today," Paige said without looking up. She exited the computer and closed its lid. "I told Mother I'd watch Grandfather. He's already had his medication."

Ben glanced around the kitchen and frowned slightly. Something felt different. "Why's he in bed so early?"

"He's not doing well," Paige said. "The doctors keep telling Mother it's time to put him in long-term care. He needs supervision. Grandfather's become even more unpredictable in his moods lately, and he's still finding ways to get out of the house."

"What's your mom going to do?"

"She can't make up her mind," Paige said. "Mother knows what she needs to do, but she's weak."

"Aren't you being a little hard on her?"

"No," Paige said. "I'm not."

Ben suddenly recognized what was different. The kitchen had lost its customary clutter. The countertops had been cleared. All the dishes put away. The linoleum floor had been waxed and polished. The curtains over the sink freshly ironed. The wall hangings taken down except for a calendar and a new clock with a loud steady tick. There was also a new microwave on a new stand in the corner next to the refrigerator. Everything around him was organized and in place. He missed the everyday sprawl and clutter he'd been accustomed to seeing.

Ben stood across the table from Paige. She unwrapped a stick of gum and folded it between her teeth. He noticed she'd had her ears pierced. Embedded in each lobe was a dark garnet the size of a teardrop.

"We saw you on the news," Paige said. "Did you really shoot Mrs. Tedros?"

Ben nodded.

"Mother cried," Paige said.

There was a new coffeemaker on the counter near the sink.

"Where's your mom now?" Ben said.

"You asked that like a policeman," Paige said.

Ben sighed and rubbed his forehead. "You've never liked me much, have you, Paige?"

She shook her head no. Paige picked up a ballpoint pen and began tapping it on the textbook's cover. "You're not right for her."

"What's that supposed to mean?" He rested both hands on the back of the chair in front of him. "I like your mother."

"I'm not talking about how *you* feel," Paige said. "I have to watch out for my mother. I mean, I love her, but she's too emotional, and it clouds her judgment sometimes."

"I can't believe I'm having this conversation," Ben said, dropping his hands. "You're twelve years old, for Christ's sake."

Paige watched him from the chair. "She can do better than you. Anyone can see that. It doesn't matter how old they are." She dropped the pen and added something Ben didn't catch.

"I said none of that matters anyway," Paige said. She looked straight at Ben. "She's happy now. Why can't you leave us alone?"

Next to the textbook was a new hand-sized graphing calculator. A tiny red dot blinked below its screen.

Paige followed his line of sight and picked up the calculator. "I'm doing math three grades above my age level. I went to the guidance counselor's office and took some tests."

"Mr. Deane," Ben said.

Paige smiled.

"Let me guess," Ben said. "All the behavioral problems you were having at school ..."

I'm doing much better now," Paige said. "The conferences with Mr. Deane were very helpful. That's the kind of man Mr. Deane is. He's helpful and understanding." She paused. "*Charming* too. Everybody thinks so."

"Your mother," Ben said and looked around the kitchen again.

Paige reached over and cleared the face of the calculator.

Ben rubbed his forehead. "The microwave and all the other new things around here. Mr. Deane too?"

"No," Paige said. "Mother bought it with the money she got from Mrs. Tedros."

Ben frowned and pulled out the chair and sat down across from Paige. "What exactly are you talking about?"

Paige pursed her lips and sat up straighter. "She came to the house once. They didn't know I was in the kitchen. Before she left, Mrs. Tedros gave Mother some money in a brown envelope. Mother was crying, but she took it."

Ben sat back in the chair. He looked over Paige's head at the new wall clock.

"What was the money for?" he said finally.

"Something about Grandfather and the tape recorder," Paige said. "Are you satisfied now? I only told you because Mrs. Tedros is dead, and you can't prove Mother took anything from her."

Ben's chest felt tight and empty at the same time. He looked down at his hands and then closed his eyes. A moment or a lifetime later, he walked past Paige and down the stairs to his car.

He started back to his apartment. The sky was breaking on full dusk when he pulled off Everest and parked near the center of a strip mall's lot.

Anchoring its north end was a restaurant named Little Athens. Ben went in and ordered one of the take-out specials and borrowed the phone book.

It listed twelve *Deanes* and eight *Deans*. With a little time, he could cull and winnow and eventually come up with the right one. What he'd do after that, though, dead-ended.

Ben stepped back outside while the two brothers who owned and ran Little Athens worked up his order. In the window of the video store next door was a large poster for a rental entitled *Frog Man*, which featured a malevolent cross-wired evolutionary mishap poised above the byline: HE'S LEFT THE SWAMP FOR YOUR NIGHTMARES!

Ben glanced at his watch and walked the length of the strip mall. He was waiting for something to replace the nearly intolerable weight of the clarity that had descended upon him. It was a clarity that denied everything but itself. He felt as if he were moving around a small room under lights that illuminated everything but were too painfully intense and bright to let him find what he was looking for.

Next to the video store was a lingerie shop named Cupid's Arrow. It was followed by a veterinarian's office called Paws Here. Next to that was G&H Accounting, and beyond it was a baby specialty shop named New Arrivals, every other letter in the name alternating pink and blue. It was followed by a liquor store named Spirits. The last store was empty, just a large plate-glass window with Ben's head and shoulders reflected next to a black and white sign reading COMING SOON but nothing else to indicate what.

Ben bought a six-pack of imported beer at Spirits and started back down the strip. On the way, he almost collided with a young woman who'd come rushing out of one of the shops.

One of the brothers at Little Athens held up two white Styrofoam boxes and waved him in. Ben paid and headed back to his car.

He was about to key the ignition when he noticed a young woman a couple of parking slots over walking in tight circles with her head bowed. Just as he was about to pull away, she lifted her head and looked directly at him. Her face was wet.

Ben hesitated, then got out of the car. He called over, asking if she were all right.

The woman raised her arm and let it fall. "No," she said. "I'm locked out of my car." She turned partway and pointed at the driver's side window. "I left the keys in the ignition and my cell phone on the front seat."

Ben took a couple steps closer, and the woman turned and began quickly scanning the lot and storefronts. He stopped and took out his wallet and held up his badge.

"I'm off duty," he said. "Maybe I can help."

The woman slowly nodded and stepped away from the door. She looked to be in her late twenties and was pretty in a way that didn't immediately draw attention to itself. She had trouble maintaining eye contact with Ben for more than a couple seconds at a time.

"I'm supposed to be somewhere," she said. "That's the thing." Her voice trailed off. She wrapped her left hand in her right and looked toward the street.

The car was a dark blue Ford, a basic model, at least a decade and a half older than the woman. Standard locks. No keyless entry.

"Let me check my trunk," Ben said. "See if I have a lockout bar with me."

He walked over to his car, opened the trunk, and found the bar. The woman glanced at her watch, at him, then away.

Ben knelt by the car door. There was a clutch of packages piled at the woman's feet. The top of one of the bags was partially open. Ben saw what looked like a pair of sheer black panties folded in on themselves.

"I guess it's lucky I ran into you." She gave a short, awkward laugh. "Or you into me, I guess it was."

For a moment, Ben could smell her perfume, and when he looked up, he ran into her reflection above his own, their faces caught on the curve of the glass and emptied of color under the nimbus of the mercury lights.

Then the woman's face disappeared, and Ben heard the rustle of plastic as she began to gather her packages.

He lifted the bar and slipped it between the door and glass and worked on jimmying the lock.

The drift of perfume again.

The scent was familiar, but the name eluded him.

Rain Something.

The bar jammed, hanging up until Ben adjusted its angle. He gently lifted, coaxing the bar, and snagged the locking mechanism.

A moment later, he stood up. He waited before he turned to the woman.

"There you go," he said.

She put the packages on the front seat, and Ben caught her perfume again.

The woman turned and ran her hand through her hair. She gave a quick smile and thanked him, then got in and cranked the engine.

Ben watched her drive off, then walked back to his car.

Something Rain, he thought.

He sat behind the wheel until it came to him.

Late.

That was it.

Lynn Kostoff is a professor of English and writer in residence at Francis Marion University in Florence, South Carolina. He's previously written *A Choice of Nightmares* and *The Long Fall*. Visit www.lynkostoff.com for more information.